WELL FED

Also by Keith C. Blackmore

Mountain Man
Mountain Man
Safari
Hellifax
Well Fed
Make Me King
Mindless
Skull Road
Mountain Man Prequel
Mountain Man 2nd Prequel: Them Early Days
The Hospital: A Mountain Man Story
Mountain Man Omnibus: Books 1–3

131 Days
131 Days
House of Pain
Spikes and Edges
About the Blood
To Thunderous Applause
131 Days Omnibus: Books 1–3

Breeds
Breeds
Breeds 2
Breeds 3
Breeds: The Complete Trilogy

Isosceles Moon
Isosceles Moon
Isosceles Moon 2

The Bear That Fell from the Stars
Bones and Needles
Cauldron Gristle
Flight of the Cookie Dough Mansion
The Majestic 311
The Missing Boatman
Private Property
The Troll Hunter
White Sands, Red Steel

MOUNTAIN MAN

BOOK 4

WELL FED

KEITH C. BLACKMORE

Podium

With special thanks to Mark Crouse, Sean Meadows,
SJ Parkinson (mystery writer extraordinaire), and Robert Richter.

Cover design by Podium Publishing

ISBN: 978-1-0394-4987-9

Published in 2023 by Podium Publishing, ULC
www.podiumaudio.com

Podium

WELL FED

1

"Gus."

At the sound of his name, he turned all the way around, ass tight on his chair, baseball bat across his knees, and leather jacket zipped up despite the moist heat of an Indian summer sun. The black motorcycle helmet he wore, a gift from Adam, once comfortably warm on his head only two days before, felt like a very personal pressure cooker.

"Talbert," Gus said quietly, digging at his balls.

Talbert's face screwed up at the display.

"Yeah, that's right," Gus rumbled through his lowered visor as he stood. "I'm scratching my *balls*, Talbert. My goddamn *balls*. Whattaya think about that, huh? Man's gotta right to scratch 'em when he feels like it, right? They itch. I scratch. S'how it works. Fuckin' lost track of how often I scratched them today. Got something to say about that?"

The two men squared off against each other on the lookout mound. The raised pile of dirt gave a decent view of the harvested corn fields, wheat fields, and fruit orchards surrounding the farm, right up to distant tree lines, where the autumn leaves blazed on the ground like papery ash.

"Whatever," Talbert muttered. "Listen. Wanna talk to you about something. Figured I come on out, give you a break here." He smiled thinly and gestured toward the empty fields. "You busy?"

"Yeah, I'm busy. I'm scratching my nuts."

"Lay off your boys for a fuckin' minute, then. Give 'em a rest, why don'tcha?"

Sighing, Gus did just that. "There ya go. All done. Whattaya want, Talbert? And talk fast before I dig in again. Something about you makes them itch something fierce."

As survivors went, Craig Talbert wasn't the most likeable one in the group, which was Gus's way of saying the man was a fucking knob. An axe wound to the genitals had more appeal. Plenty of affable folks lived on the farm, but Talbert was the kind to whisper a joke behind your back, not more than ten feet away, and then crank up the enamel flare in a sickly smile of brotherly love if you turned around—only to roll his eyes the very second you turned your back again. Physically, the man had lost a lot of weight, as they all had. His raspy voice got on Gus's nerves as if he used to smoke four packs a day, and that dapper eyebrow of a moustache was something else. The lip it was attached to just didn't seem to match it, a dainty whisker that Talbert had a habit of slicking with a wet finger or thumb, trying to coax it to greater thickness. In addition, the man always had a perfect part in his thick black hair, a combed-to-the-side eraser line that stitched his scalp and made Gus think of white centipedes for some reason—the long-ass carnivorous kind that entomologists handled with tongs.

Too bad a person couldn't pick whom they shared the apocalypse with.

"Been out and about, y'know," Talbert said with forced nonchalance. "Checkin' out parts of the valley. Seein' the sights. Seein' what's what."

"Adam know you been doin' that?"

"Course he does. Even gave me the thumbs-up. I wouldn't do anything without flyin' it past him."

Gus doubted that, suspecting Talbert and his slicker-than-slug-slime smile could easily ooze on over to the bad side—the *nasty* side, where impulse gripped the reins of reality in hard fists and cracked them often, usually in the worst possible way. If Adam and company hadn't found him first and brought him to the farm, well, Gus had a pretty good idea which direction old Tal might've swung.

A patch of tall standing grass fluttered near the edge of a field, like a trout breaching the evening mirror of a lake, immediately drawing Gus's eye and dividing his attention.

"Yeah, right," he muttered.

"Hey," Talbert barked, offended. "I'm fuckin'—whattaya think I am? A fuckin' *scavenger* or somethin'?"

Gus leveled a *you-really-want-an-answer-to-that?* look.

"What's that for? Hey, *bro*, I got your back. I got *your* back! You got mine, right? Right?"

As sunny Jesus was his witness, Gus hated questions like that, especially from people he considered dicks. Decided silence was the best defense.

"Right?" Talbert persisted.

The break in the grass weaved and bobbed like the world's crankiest Etch A Sketch.

Talbert followed the tilt of Gus's helmet and asked a less challenging question. "Got something here, Gus? I can go out there and stomp on it for you."

"I wouldn't let you scratch my balls."

"Hey, fuck *you*." Talbert snarled right in his face, confrontational and bellowing breath bad enough that it somehow got past the visor. "I'm getting pretty fuckin' tired of you, bro. Pretty fuckin' annoyed. If you got somethin' to say, you just say it. Get that shit off your chest. Hey, never fuckin' *mind* what's over there."

Talbert nailed two hard fingers into Gus's shoulder, forcing him to lock eyes with the dapper douchebag.

"You know what I do out here, right?" Gus asked.

Talbert got right up in Gus's business then. "Gettin' the impression you don't like me, dude."

Gus flipped up his visor, revealing angry pink scars on a brow shiny with sweat.

"Now, where'd you get that idea? Couldn't have been from that big goddamn box of nothin' I gave you on yer birthday. Certainly couldn't be from our daily exchange of pleasantries on the farm here, or does 'fuck off' have a different meaning in your tribe of buddies? Hm? 'Cause if it does, why not, oh, I dunno, *tell* me so there's no side-assed miscommunication next time? How 'bout it, shit flicker?"

Talbert's face set with anger, his black eyes darting up, down, and to the sides in their sockets as he examined Gus's hairless face. Gus had scorched pretty much all the hair follicles around his brow, cheeks, and parts of his chin a year and seven or eight long months before, when he'd unsuccessfully tried to kill himself. His once-mighty beard grew only in patchy clumps.

For a split second, Gus thought Talbert was going to take a swing at him. But then, without warning, the guy backed away and smiled, as quick and easy as that. Gus marveled in disbelief at the man, wondering if he thought a change of tact might defuse the tension.

"Okay, bro—"

"Not yer fuckin' bro."

"Dude—"

"Call me dude one more time, and I'm gonna kick my cowboy boot up your ass."

"*Gus*," Talbert suddenly laughed, smiling as though they were old buddies, which was freaky raised to infinity. "Hey, look, I just came out here to talk, okay? Not fight. Jesus, man."

"Then more *talk* and less pissin' *off*."

Talbert took another step back, hands holding his hips. "Okay. Okay. Found a house farther on down the valley. Just before you get to Digby. Almost missed it, really.

It was off the map and hidin' behind a thicket of trees. Sorta like this place except, well, with a longer road that goes past some apple orchards. Big fuckin' house. A god-damn *mansion*, to tell the truth. Anita Little's from down around there. I talked to her last night. Says that it was owned by a guy named Mortimer, who was the owner of some website for hooking up lonely Christian singles. Sold it for a fortune and became a recluse. Me and my crew are going to head on down there and check it out. Figured you'd want to be in on it."

A puzzled Gus shook his head. "Why the hell you want to go there?"

Talbert's face darkened. "I just said to check it out."

"You mean loot the place."

"Yeah, okay, fuck it, loot the place. You want in or not?"

"I don't understand why you're heading all the way to Digby to loot some mansion. Waste of gas to go down there."

"Not much left in the towns. Not after you took a match to Annapolis."

Gus sighed, loathing the memories of the drunken fire crusade he had carried out upon the city—not because of what he did but because of what he put down. Or *hoped* he put down.

"We got everything we need right here, where it's relatively safe," Gus said. "No need to go to Digby."

"Look," Talbert pointed a finger at the far-off trees. "Me and Sheldon, Mike, and Benny are headin' down there today. Leavin' within the hour. Get there early after-noon. Check it out, camp overnight if we find anything, and come back in the morn-ing. You in or not?"

A dark shape oozed from the edge of the cornfield, filling the bordering ditch like an enormous worm. Gus felt his stomach clench, not from fear but just from annoy-ance. The thing barely moved there, seemingly mystified with the puzzle of the trench. One arm reached up as if it were doing a painful backstroke before dropping out of sight.

Gus took a better grip on his bat.

Talbert looked in the direction of the ditch. A smile slashed across his face upon spotting the gimp.

"Crawler at two o'clock," he said.

Crawler.

Nearly four years after the zombie apocalypse and the resurrected horrors that hungered for living flesh, an end was in sight. The deadheads passed through three stages of unlife in the new world, going from freshly deceased runner to the gimp that staggered about on decomposing feet and limbs to, finally, the crawler, a zombie whose unending shuffling had sanded down the soles of whatever they wore, right to the blue-gray flesh of their feet. It didn't end there as they kept on walking, grating away each layer of flesh, rubbing themselves out right down to the bone and leaving a trail of shredded skin and muscle tissue, until balance failed and gravity sucked the creature down to the earth. Then they pulled themselves along with a wormy locomotion, wearing away their undersides, eroding the chest, belly, arms, and legs.

Right up until nothing remained of its ruined musculature and the gimp stopped in its own streak of fleshy rags and streamers.

These days, the world beyond the farm didn't interest Gus, who had no desire to return to the scorched husk of Annapolis or any of the smaller towns. But he'd heard stories of how Talbert and his boys ventured forth on scouting or supply missions. He heard about what they saw, how bleached and bloated corpses covered streets, sidewalks, parking lots, and front lawns—unmoving until they detected the living, whereupon they writhed in place like sun-baked snakes nailed to the ground, ripping themselves apart at times, starving for a bite of whatever was handy.

Talbert had spoken—boasted, really—about how he danced upon whole skulls, breaking them underneath boot heels. As much as Gus hated the animated dead, however much the sight of them sickened him, there was also an underlying guitar-string twang of pity. They'd been people once—probably had families—and no one deserved the morbid ending of a gimp when assholes like Talbert came along. Talbert *delighted* in killing the undead, had fun doing it. Though Gus couldn't express his exact feelings on the matter, he knew it was morally wrong and psychologically fucked up, which brought him full circle back to his suspicions about Talbert in the first place. If the man got off on killing the dead, could he do the same to the living? What stopped him?

Very little, Gus concluded.

He scanned the fields, already harvested for the oncoming winter, their bounty being prepared and stored away by the other members of the community. Their tiny colony lived off the land like in the old days, in the breadbasket of the Annapolis Valley, subsisting upon grown vegetables, fruits, and berries. Toss in some farm animals that had survived the apocalypse, a little wild-game hunting, and you had the solution to the problem Gus had faced when he lived on the mountain—just how *does* one survive in a world without supermarkets and processed food? Especially when it all expires?

You go back to the very basics.

Seeing nothing else amiss along the farm's borders, Gus ignored Talbert and marched along the road to the outlying ditch. Talbert followed on his tail, yakking, but Gus wasn't listening. He only had eyes for that rotten shell of a once-person, seeing how the depth of the ditch buckled the dead thing's spine backward in a yoga stretch. One arm flapped weakly, festooned with rancid holes that might have been bites. The putrefying gray-black head rocked against the ditch's side, disturbing the dirt. The gimp's mouth opened, displaying wormy gums worn down to the bone.

Gus cringed. The toothless ones bothered him the most. They reminded him of feeble grandparents wanting a kiss.

Gus was thankful the crawler wore clothing: ragged jeans with frayed threads; a filthy film of a T-shirt, chewed through by kilometers of abrasion. The skin of its chest had shredded down to a gray rib cage. Knees missed their protective caps and lay opened to crusty black joints and stretched sinews.

A slug of a tongue stirred inside its mouth.

"Whattaya waitin' for, man?" Talbert said from behind him. "Pop that thing."

Gus sighed.

"Christ," Talbert blurted in exasperation. He stepped around Gus and put his boot through the nose of the trapped gimp, crushing the egg-thin nasal bone. Talbert hooked the skull with his toes, attempting to turn the thing over in the ditch, tearing the head from the shoulders in a fragrant spatter of clumpy ink.

"Shit," he swore before withdrawing his boot and stomping, squishing the head in a burst of bone and brain matter.

"That's how you do it," Talbert declared, freeing his foot from the mess. "The fuck got into you, Gussy? Your tampon in too tight or something? Maybe you should stay back here and guard the farm."

They faced off, and, after several long seconds, Gus broke the stare and sheathed his bat in the leather scabbard draped across his back—yet another gift from Adam. Once that was done, he produced a pair of gardening gloves and pulled them on.

Talbert threw up one hand. "Well, I'm wasting daylight here. I thought you'd be badass for a trip off the farm—badder than *this* anyway—but you ain't. You keep the peace here, and I'll bring you back a teddy bear, okay?"

With that, Talbert turned and walked away, kicking up gravel as he went.

Gus focused on the dead thing cluttering his ditch. One gimp at a time was more his speed these days, keeping the folks on the farm secure. Going the length of the valley to rummage for expired medicine or whatever didn't interest him. Nor did meeting more survivors and puzzling over their true intentions. His lot in life now was keeping the fields clear, protecting the farm, and disposing of the dead.

Little else interested him.

Taking a breath, he grasped the deadhead's arms and grimaced as he pulled the body out of the ditch. A hip bone caught on the edge. Gus tugged, and the torso came free in a dry popping of flesh and bones while the lower part sagged back, leaving him looking dismayed.

"You piece of *shit . . .*"

A hole had been dug nearby for such a catch, and Gus dragged the upper half of the corpse toward the open grave, intending to bury it before lunch.

Talbert walked over to three men waiting near a burgundy minivan. He shook his head to give them advanced notice.

"No?" a surprised Sheldon Smith asked, his sandy hair pulled back in a surfer's beach braid at the nape of his skull. He was the tallest of the four, broad in the shoulders and wearing a set of John Lennon wire-frame glasses.

"No." Talbert flapped a hand. "His balls are milked, dude. If he still *has* balls, that is. Mount up. We're outta here. If traffic's not too heavy, we should be there just over an hour."

He watched the three men climb aboard the van, all eager to break into a mansion and take a look around. Following Sheldon, Matt "Machete" Miller had his namesake strapped to one hip in a leather sheath. Talbert had once witnessed Miller decapitate a pair of zombies with one swing of that wicked blade, something that shocked the shit out of him. Benny Shaw had a hammer hanging off a stripped-down carpenter's tool belt. He wielded that flathead with a speed and power that made Talbert wonder if the man was bionic. All of them were in their physical prime, much younger than the forty-four, forty-five years Gus was hauling.

Gus. Luring that scorched prick wasn't the easiest thing to do, even for a snake charmer like Talbert, and that failure burned in his craw.

Truthfully, exploring and looting was a young man's game.

Talbert wanted Gus along only so he could kill the bastard.

Until the arrival of the old man, he'd been gleefully enjoying the fall of civilization purely for the sheer freedom it allowed. A guy could do whatever the hell he *wanted* in the new world, go anywhere he wanted, with nary a law official around to stop him. Houses, banks, stores, and army bases—all the forbidden places were wide open for business. Talbert's group had already explored the battle-wrecked airbase in Greenwood, having a blast with playing at the controls of the remaining military aircraft, but ultimately disappointed in failing to locate any additional stores of munitions for automatic weapons. The magazines they'd pulled off dead soldiers or found on base had been depleted long before, when the zombies had been more active in their wandering. Recently, any zombie fighting needing to be done was resolved hand-to-hand, unless a house yielded a box or two of regular shotgun shells.

Maggie and Adam made most of the decisions on the farm. Maggie had been designated as the de facto leader since she was a doctor back in the day, possessing invaluable skills that secured her position in the little community. Adam actually owned the property, and Talbert wondered if the old codger wasn't sticking it to Maggie in the wee afterhours. He'd been living at the farm for almost two and a half years, and he still didn't know. Not that he cared. Talbert preferred the younger stuff, but unfortunately, the apocalypse hadn't produced too many young, nubile, ready-to-fuck model types aching to latch onto strong alpha males like himself. The movies screwed up that part. The handful of birds who'd managed to make it to the farm were either married or well past their prime. The distinct lack of fuckable T and A on the farm pissed Talbert off—made him and his boys edgy, restless.

Made them think the farm needed new leadership.

When Adam first hauled Gus's torched ass out of his car way back when, Talbert didn't think anything of it. Adam had even identified Gus as the same guy who'd once fired upon him while he was in town. Maggie got to work and brought the nearly dead man back to health. By that time, people were in more than just a little awe of the burned survivor. Gus possessed a celebrity's aura, which befuddled the hell out of Talbert. When discussing matters important to the farm, all twenty-three of them would gather in the living room of the main house to listen to proposals, and almost *always*, folks waited until Gus mulled an idea over and offered his opinion.

It amazed Talbert how they blindly looked to Gus for guidance for no reason whatsoever, something that Talbert failed to do the entire time he'd lived on the farm. All Gus did was show up, and the toothless cocksmoker became an instant celebrity. Only thing the balding prick didn't have was an entourage.

That kind of confidence, that kind of *weight*, irritated Talbert. If Maggie and Adam came to a violent end, the little colony would gravitate to Gus in an instant.

Gus had to be removed.

The discovered mansion had been an opportunity to rid themselves of the man in a very convenient manner. *There were zombies. Gus was overwhelmed. We got away.* End of story and perhaps a week of long faces.

Except old Gussy didn't *want* to go on safari.

That pissed Talbert off. Leave it to that marinated ass sore to shit the bed. Talbert had to think of another way to kill the man. Perhaps more extreme methods had to be considered. Cracking a few *living* skulls didn't bother Talbert. In retrospect, the last couple of years seemed to be preparing him for that very eventuality.

Gus had to be made gone. Had to be rotor-rooted. Jettisoned.

Another day, Talbert fumed. *After* they checked out the mansion.

His little gang waiting aboard the van, Talbert made a quick inspection. Body armor stripped from the dead soldiers at CFB Greenwood filled the rear compartment, as did a small collection of bats and knives. Tools of the trade.

Talbert took one last look at the main farmhouse, smelling freshly baked bread on the air. Saw the faces of the kids—Becky and Chad—peeking out from an upstairs window. Talbert forced a smile and waved, but the children ducked out of sight. *Goddamn little noisemakers.* He shrugged and turned his attention to the nearby barn. The building had been converted into a small but roomy barracks redolent of dried hay— simple shelter if one wasn't picky.

Perched on a hill and surrounded by apple groves and perhaps more, the mansion appeared to be a leap into luxury. Talbert had a very good feeling about the place, the *potential* of the property.

He yanked open the passenger door of the van and slapped the side. "All right, let's go. Things don't get done on their own."

They drove past Gus, shoveling dirt onto an unseen deadhead. He had his visor up and stopped in midtoss as the van rolled by.

Smiling, Talbert gave him the finger.

2

With the legs of his wooden chair planted firmly into the lookout mound's dirt, Gus leaned back. Visor up, he eyed the outer limits of the farm while taking deep, contemplative breaths. The temperatures felt more seasonal. To the northeast, however, a nearly black bank of clouds spilled toward the valley, closing on the sun. Near the barn, a few people chopped and stacked wood. The background noise of falling axes and low conversation put Gus at ease.

He leaned back a little farther, two wooden legs off the ground, and planted the head of his bat into the dirt. The fields lay empty, but he remained vigilant. The morning before, the zombie, the same piece of trash Talbert had stomped on two days previous, had a visitor—one that both disturbed Gus and lifted his hopes.

A rat.

A dead rat with its dusty snout half buried in the recent gimp's grave. The little rodent wasn't only dead. It was reanimated.

But barely moving.

Gus had nudged the thing with his boot, hard enough to flip the sun-toasted horror over onto its back.

That had been an eyeful.

The rat's underbelly had worn away to nothing, a dried-up shell of madness. It had reminded Gus of a narrow strip of grimy scalp, complete with legs worn down to nubs of bone that twitched. The eyes, resembling tiny raisins, had shriveled up deep inside its skull. He'd nudged the rat a second time, and the snout opened weakly, ready for action.

Little fuck.

Gus had squashed its skull under his boot heel, disliking the eggshell crunch. Burying the abomination had taken only a few minutes, but the memory and significance remained with him. The zombies were burning—no—*wearing* themselves out, their biological bilge finally decomposing to a point at which they almost ceased to be a threat. The same appeared true for the rats. Since their bodies were built low to the ground, the erosion would be much faster than in the regular deadheads.

According to Maggie and Adam, the infected rats never reached the farm—perhaps because they'd never had a putrid trail of bread crumbs to follow, as had the swarm that assaulted Gus's mountain hideaway. In any case, time allied with the living. Soon, very soon, it appeared as if the undead would become immobile. If so, Gus doubted the undead could stand another summer sun. One more hot season would be enough to melt them into foul stains.

And the world could come out of hiding.

There was just one problem . . .

"Gus!"

A rush of déjà vu overcame him. He lowered his chair, turned, and saw Adam approaching, recognizing his short-cropped silver hair, the bulbous nose from a decade of heavy drinking, and the faded gray eyes of a person who'd seen things he'd spend the rest of his days trying to forget. The older man was a little slimmer around the waist but still retained plenty of spring in his coils.

"Howya doing out here?" he asked in his Hants County drawl, stopping beside the chair and studying the lay of the land. "Feel a distinct chill in the air today. Enough to send my boys to high ground."

"If they get too high, you'll have to get Maggie to take a look at them."

"Ah," Adam said dismissively, "she's seen 'em enough, I think. Still. Better to have your boys cupped than not at all. Shit. See any more of them rats out here?"

Adam and Maggie had been the only people he'd shared his discovery with. Gus realized his social skills were still a little wonky from the two years of being isolated on the mountain. Some days, he felt more forthcoming with the others, especially the kids, but some days he kept to the mound and just watched.

"Nah."

Adam squinted at the sun and made note of the clouds. One of the youngsters called out—little Becky Norris—and Adam waved in her direction.

"Chad chasing her again?" Gus asked.

"Yep."

"Nice to see."

"It is. It really is. But . . . who knows. Shit. Right now, I figure those two are pretty much the only children left in the valley. Hard to imagine."

"Yep."

"Unless we find more children out there. Hopefully with their parents alive."

Gus agreed. It was a shitty time to be orphaned.

"They like you, though." A smile accompanied Adam's words.

"Yeah." Gus liked them too. Besides Adam and Maggie, they were the only ones on the farm whom he didn't mind visiting the mound.

"Like they adopted you or something."

"Kinda busy here, Adam."

"Shit, yeah. I see that."

Gus didn't know whether he was being genuine or cleverly disguising a sarcastic dig.

"Anyway, gotta talk to you about something."

Gus sighed, having a fair idea of what *something* was.

"Talbert and the boys haven't come back yet," the older man stated.

"Knew this place smelled better. Quieter too."

Adam rubbed at his head and scuffed his shoe into the dirt. "Yeah, well, I suppose I knew you'd feel that way. Regardless, they went down to Digby and haven't come back. Been a couple of nights now. Maggie's worried. Frankly, I'm worried."

"Don't know why you're worried about Talbert."

"I know you don't care for the guy . . . but he's part of this community. Sheldon, Mike, and Benny are part of this community. And it's four of them. There's only twenty-three of us here, Gus. Twenty-three. I'm sure there are others out there somewhere, but until we make contact, we're it. And missing four from that number hurts, even if they are assholes."

"They're assholes, all right."

"But they're our assholes."

"One's enough for me. It does what I tell it."

"Wait 'til you hit fifty."

"Why fifty?"

"Forget I said that. But think about this. Although we screw up our noses at them, assholes are essential to the body. Important to the whole."

Gus exhaled in sad disbelief. "Assholes are *what*? Jesus Christ, I can't believe we're having this conversation."

"Hey, remember that time when I was drivin' around Annapolis one afternoon and had this guy shoot the hell outta my ride?"

Gus slumped. "That's low, man," he said, the guilt heavy in his chest. "I mean, *low*."

"Still got that car too."

Gus, lips as tight as piano wire, remembered that day all too clearly.

"Loved that car," Adam went on, purposely ignoring his companion's discomfort. "You know I made out with my wife in that thing? More memories in that backseat than I can remember. Still runs too, even though it took enough lead to make the body look like a salt shaker. A shitload of duct tape holds it together now. Plastic instead of a windshield. Damn thing flutters when—"

"*All right*," Gus erupted. "All right. I got it. Stop rubbing it in. I'm sorry, okay? I'm *sorry*. You want me to get you a new car?"

"Nah. Only bringin' that up to illustrate my point on assholes. See, I thought *you* were an asshole, right? One puckered-up, burnt-out, brown-eyed asshole. But I went back, and when I found you in the middle of the road, ripped up like you'd been sucked up by a snow blower and shot screaming into a wood chipper . . . well, shit chute or not, I couldn't leave you there. You understand what I'm saying?"

Gus did but shied away from admitting it.

"I gave you a second chance, man. Shit. I *had* to. You were a *person*, lying facedown in the middle of dead territory. A piece of work who'd broken both arms and pissed and shit himself, no less."

"Please tell me you kept that part to yourself."

"Which part?"

Gus twirled a finger. "The parts about the shitting and the pissing."

"Ah, hell, whattaya think I am? Sure, I kept quiet about that. Sure enough. Even an asshole has some measure of dignity. No need to bring shit like that up. No, sir."

"Thanks."

"Can't say the same for Maggie, though."

Gus lowered his head into a hand.

"Well, she *did* do the majority of the repairs on you," Adam carried on. "Including the cleanup. And I know she talks to Thelma. What can you do? She's the doc around here. Got us by the chicken necks and giblets. Anyway, point is, I thought you were an asshole, but you really weren't. Not at all. Now, look at you. You're the sheriff around here. Wouldn't have happened if I didn't take the chance. You see what I'm sayin'? Talbert. Sure, the man's a dick. Can't say I haven't had my times with him 'cause I have. He's another gut-clenched, rug-burned asshole, but there's another side to him too. He and the others go out there and bring back things we need here. See? They risk their lives to improve ours. What does that tell you? You've seen him go out there. He's not all bad. You just haven't, well, discovered the good side yet."

"Yeah," Gus breathed out, unconvinced but understanding the reasoning.

"Anyway, Maggie and I figured that it might be an idea for you to go look for 'em."

That widened Gus's eyes harder than a finger probing for his prostate. "You're fuckin' kidding me."

But Adam wasn't. Gus saw it on the old guy's face.

"I can't go out *there*! Who'll protect the farm?"

"We've done okay when you weren't here. And the zombies haven't been around like before. Like you said, they're thinning out. Might be, one day, we can go back to the way things were. Minus the creature comforts. We'll do shifts like before . . ."

Gus barely heard the details. Adam's request flickered across his mind like a short-circuiting neon sign. *Go out there and* look *for Talbert? Look for a guy he secretly hoped became a deadhead, just so he could cave in his skull?*

Jesus H. Christ.

"Anything else I could do?" Gus pleaded, very much willing to bargain.

"Nope," Adam chuckled, thinking he was joking. "Just do that. Anita knows how you can get there. She'll give you directions."

"Maybe she should go."

Another giggle. "You're on fire today, ain'tcha? That would be a sight to see. Anita cruising on down the highway, on the prowl."

At sixty-eight, Anita Little was the oldest in the group.

"Adam?" a little voice squeaked, and both men turned to see Becky and Chad standing just a few steps away. Both were seven years old, their cheeks wind kissed and ruddy from running about. Chad's blond hair was buzzed short while Becky's hung down to her waist in a straight cascade of brown. Four brown eyes the size of eggs peeped at Gus, melting any angst.

"Um, could you, um, like, fix our swing?" Becky asked in a raspy squeak.

"What happened to your swing, honey?" the older man asked.

"Well, it happened like this. I was swinging just fine, but when *Chad* took *his* turn, he stood up on the, um, on the seat, and the rope busted on one side, so, like, *nooow* we have no seat for our bums."

"That true, Chad?"

Chad's head hung between his shoulders, caught in embarrassment and probably unaccustomed to standing still. The kid had a wild streak in him, plus an everlasting tank of energy.

"Yessir," the boy muttered, twisting his upper body left and right as if he'd been hooked through the shoulders and couldn't quite wiggle off. "But it wasn't my fault."

"No? How's that?"

"The swing was like, old, see."

Becky had taken on a flat expression of disagreement, but to her credit, she let the boy talk.

"It would've broke *anyway*, so it's best it happened *this* way, before someone got hurt."

"That's true, Becky?" Adam judiciously asked.

"Um, it is, but, like, it's not. If he wasn't, um, hopping on it?" At that point, she took a deep, clarifying breath and focused on a spot past them all—which prompted Gus also to check just to make sure nothing was amiss. "If he wasn't hopping on it, we could still be swinging. But he did, so we aren't."

"You were hopping on it too," Chad accused.

Becky rolled her eyes.

"I'll fix it," Adam declared. "Won't take long. You guys got anything else to do?"

"Noooo," they both chimed, which suggested *that* might need checking on as well.

"All right, you guys better be telling the truth," Adam said. "Say seeya to your uncle Gus."

Gus didn't really like that. He wasn't their uncle. A friend, yes, but not an uncle.

"Gus, are you mad?" Becky asked, charming him.

"Nah, I'm not mad."

"Old Gus just has a lot on his mind," Adam added with a wink. "He might be taking a trip."

Fucking guy. Gus flashed a glare. *Old, my ass.*

"And he never got a hug today either, so go on and give him a hug. That'll make him feel better."

"Aw, they don't—" he got out, just before Becky ran up and threw her arms around his chest and squeezed for all she was worth. The embrace left Gus breathless, the shock as clear and crystallizing as plunging into tropical waters, except it was the cuddle of a little girl. Her hair smelled of unspoiled beaches, her clothes of hand-washed detergent. Gus's frown dissolved under those little arms. A smile surfaced, and he hugged her back, held it for a few seconds, and released. All his fight was sucked out of him.

Then Chad roped him around the neck.

"You're . . . choking . . . me," Gus half croaked, half chuckled. The youngster was strong for his age. Chad eased off, but Gus's arms engulfed the boy and hugged him for a three count before letting go.

"Seeya, Gus." Chad waved as he departed after Adam and Becky.

"See you, Gus." Becky beamed and pulled a few strands of hair out of her eyes.

Gus waved back, feeling a pang of sorrow watching them go. Adam glanced over his shoulder, his smile victorious. Clearly, that had been an orchestrated and outright weaselly move.

They disappeared around a corner of the main house, and Gus's thoughts darkened.

Fucking Talbert.

The next morning, he packed a few supplies into the back of a beige SUV and left as the sun began to brighten a clear night sky.

He didn't say good-bye to anyone.

Not even the children, who slept in warm beds, dreaming good dreams, while November chilled the world beyond their shared room.

3

The sun glared down on the 101, a highway war-painted with skid marks, freckled with craters, and splitting at the seams from hard-punching winters. Gus drove with the SUV's sun visor down. His aluminum bat rested in the foot space of the passenger seat, rattling at times, its handle leaning toward him, ready to be grabbed if needed.

Autumn trees crowded the highway's shoulders, streaking past in a blur of fire.

On road trips such as these, Gus missed the smell of burning leaves. That took him back to his painting days and a dislike of clearing gutters.

Cars, trucks, and long-haul trailers littered the road at times, forcing him to slow down and weave through broken mazes. Gus eyed a few cars lying on their sides in ditches. He'd seen similar collections of traffic before, every time he left his home and drove the trusted route down into the city of Annapolis.

Shadowy, out-of-focus shapes rested behind the steering wheels of some vehicles. Heads gleamed yellow and white, their mouths cracked open in shouts. Some doors hung open, as though the drivers and passengers had abandoned their rides. Ruts and potholes jarred the SUV at times, rudely surprising Gus. Weeds rose through the pavement's crumbling fissures, their lengths stung by the cold and slumped over at wilting angles.

Exits for Middleton, Bridgetown, and Annapolis Royal came into view and flashed by. Anita Little had given him clear directions for this mysterious mansion, a remote home that wouldn't be seen from the highway: "Stay on the 101, and upon your final approach to Digby, about two kilometers beyond an extra passing lane, watch for an ordinary gravel road, one that slinks off into a thick forest, where nothing can be seen beyond."

Mortimer.

Anita, fidgeting in adorable self-consciousness of her gray hair, had told all she knew about the reclusive billionaire, her brown eyes moist and glistening. Once, she'd said, a limo pulled into a gas station just outside of Halifax, and out popped a couple of tanned dishes straight out of a swimwear competition, dressed in micro minis and tight tops—flown up from someplace tropical to Nova Scotia upon the invitation of Warren Mortimer. The driver did his best to corral the women, who might've been snorting something at the time, but one told the cashier they were headed to Digby for a private party.

Word of that episode had gotten to the townspeople of Digby and fueled gossip for a year.

Otherwise, not much was ever heard of that eccentric man living outside town.

Hired servants came into Digby on a regular basis, polite, but every bit as elusive as Mortimer. They lived on the hundred or so acres of land Mortimer had purchased around 2004 to 2005. He flew in architects and work crews to build a home to be the envy of the Hamptons, or so a few of those hired hands drunkenly let slip while letting off steam at a local bar. Carpenters, plumbers, electricians and bricklayers, landscapers and gardeners, all had signed contracts swearing them to secrecy regarding the work they did. No one knew what went on there as a security gate, and guards prevented anyone venturing too far along the dirt road leading to the estate. One story told of a young, overly amorous couple actually parking within twenty feet of the checkpoint without knowing it, and flashlights were shined on them at the worst possible time.

"White ass up and jiggling, I heard," Anita giggled with a charm that prompted Gus to bare his hockey-player smile.

Mortimer couldn't keep out every prying eye in the years following the mansion's enigmatic construction. Deliveries were made, and the drivers would later talk in local bars. Helicopters and small-engine planes would buzz over the property, and stories of a checkered tablecloth of immaculate greenery and glowing buildings flittered through Digby. Tennis courts, raceways, gardens, waterways, and false lagoons were all tastefully arranged within lines of apple trees and cultivated land.

No one had ever laid eyes on the man, and with so much open space at his disposal, was it any wonder? Mortimer lived in a world of his own design.

As time went on, Digby forgot about the man beyond the edge of society.

Anita herself hadn't thought about the man in years, until asked.

Two wrong turnoffs led Gus into deep timberland, which ended in no-man's-land, and simply getting back onto the road became a time-consuming challenge.

By early afternoon, he finally discovered the hidden driveway.

A dirt road branded by fresh tire tracks snaked off into the faded fall brush. Gus eased off the highway, passing through shadows and looking everywhere at once. He drove along one of the roughest stretches he'd ever had the pleasure of meeting. Potholes and shards of rock punished the tires of the all-wheel drive, and Gus wondered if having such a shitty road was part of the grand deterrent as he bounced around in his seat. A web of tree limbs dampened the light, making the woods seem dreary. The rough lane switched back into a curve sharp enough to poke an eye out. Gus eased around the killer bend and spied a white metal gate, opened and pushed aside. It hung off a steel post, opposite a guard station built atop a cement foundation. A dark lick of smooth pavement continued another twenty meters before curving out of sight. Something wide and metallic lay along the road, pushed to either side at the halfway point.

Gus stopped the SUV, turned off the engine, and sat. He contemplated the end of the gravel road and the beginning of the pavement ahead. His fingers played a nervous piano on the steering wheel.

He grabbed his bat, got out of the vehicle, and closed the door to silence the computer voice before it nagged. For a long, considering moment, Gus stood there in regular clothes and boots and just listened, feeling the cold on his scarred face. Hidden birds chirped around the checkpoint. The door to the guard station hung wide open, and forest debris had blown over the floor, but just behind the station stood a house concealed from the road by an impressive hedge. A rosy brick walkway led to the single-story home, built in a Swiss mountain style, set upon a solid cement foundation reminiscent of ancient Japanese castles. Green paint offered some degree of camouflage in the summertime but not the fall. A gabled roof, wide eaves, and thick redwood beams made the house seem cozy and especially solid, ready for a beating if necessary.

And if the smashed windows were any indication, the house had taken its share right on the chin.

Gus glanced around and approached the guard station. He leaned through the doorway. A single desk rested against a sliding window, giving a clear view of anyone stopping at the gate. He rapped his knuckles on the glass and figured it could stop a bullet. A bank of ultrathin monitors rose from the desk's surface while an empty gun rack hung from a nearby wall. Gus prodded the power button on a minicomputer for a few seconds before discarding it as dead. A cracked water cooler lay on the floor. A leather sofa filled the back wall as well as a steel cabinet that had been ransacked. Gus inspected the drawers, noting the top one had been forced open. He slid a finger along the jagged twist of metal around a wrecked lock. Not a viable weapon was to be seen, not a single shell left unshot.

Don't be stupid, a familiar voice cautioned, one he hadn't heard in a very long time. The Swiss house waited.

Leaving the guard station, he walked to the front door, which was also wide open. Twigs and dead branches covered the threshold in a loose mat. He paused there, listening, knowing the dead could be as still as stone. The bat snaked out, and just before he tapped its head against the frame, before he announced his arrival as surely as ringing a Liberty-sized dinner bell, he arrested his swing and considered the silence again.

Then he went inside.

An open main floor reminded him of his own departed home except this one had been redecorated by a drunk tornado. Designer chairs had been smashed, leather sofas gutted, and a kitchen island devastated by a sledgehammer. Most of the windows on the ground level had been shattered, allowing a chilling airflow through the house. Shells, plastic and brass, littered the hardwood floor like hard confetti.

The first body lay at the base of the staircase, its presence halting Gus in his tracks. Black body armor encased a uniformed male corpse. Velcro straps and empty webbing hung off his person. A messy head shot had removed most of the corpse's face above an exposed horseshoe of teeth and a shattered vase of a skull. Gus winced at the golden shine of deep-set molars. The desiccated skin made it difficult to determine whether the guard had been deadhead or human. A dark plume of organic stain plastered the wall above the body, framed in rivulets of matter caked to the wood's surface.

Gus exhaled, remembering to breathe, wishing he had a shotgun right about then.

No weapon on the corpse. No other bodies. Just one guy who might've taken the easy way out, with no hope to continue but courage enough to use perhaps his last shell on himself.

Gus inspected the wreckage of the first floor and deduced the fight overran the gate then the station and stopped at the house. Perhaps a siege then, either long or short, ended with the last man, his back against the wall, tonguing gunmetal before doing the deed.

Of course, that was just one way it might've gone. Gus wiped a hand over his mouth and chin. A wind picked up outside, reminding him of graveyards. That had been the first body he'd seen in months, and he discovered he still wasn't immune to the gut-twisting *wrongness* of the picture. That unfortunate fucker should have grown old with his wife and kids—not planted on his ass with the top of his skull open and unfit for flowers. He took a steadying breath and concentrated on examining the facts, trying to calm his quickening breath, the steady thrumming in his ears and chest.

A fight had happened there, but where were the bodies?

A healthy dose of fear swelled up behind his sternum, forcing its way into his heart and guts. Perspiration moistened his face. The walls felt closer. Stepping out of the house, he fast-walked back to the SUV, immediately seeing dark stains upon the earth before and around the gate. A deep-rooted grease blemish wasn't recent, and the elements had failed to remove it over time. Gus stopped at the rear and studied the ground further, feeling his anxiety levels rise and wishing for the calming burn of a drink—a mouthful of any of his old favorites. He hadn't forgotten about his alcoholic past, although he didn't consider himself an alcoholic by any stretch. Whiskey, rum, beer—but mostly the hard stuff—had all armored him against the horrors of the day, grounding him, granting buoyancy upon an endless sea of walking putrefaction. In the beginning, he believed there wasn't any booze on the farm, but there was, stashed away by the various owners, some whose company he enjoyed, some whose he didn't.

All the while he was on the farm, Gus didn't partake. He never went on scavenging expeditions either as Talbert held the keys to those horror shows. Staying sober didn't bother Gus. The farm and its people had not only healed and sheltered him but had also gradually restored his tattered psyche, which the apocalypse had shredded for two whole years.

The place had rejuvenated him, resurrected him.

There hadn't been a need to numb reality with alcohol.

The world seemed just fine while living on the farm. The farm had been his anchor.

Now, however, he was in harm's way again.

He licked his dry lips and felt the familiar tremble in his fingers. A quick shot of anything forty proof or better would have been magic for his beating heart. Gus went to the driver's side of the SUV and eased himself behind the steering wheel. He set his jaw and tongued the gaps of his missing front teeth, seeing Roxanne's naked form lying right on the hood of the vehicle. The image softened and left him with the road ahead.

Always a road.

Sniffing hard and adjusting his balls for luck, he leaned back in the seat.

Don't be stupid.

"Yeeeah," Gus whispered and got back out of the vehicle. He stopped at the rear and pulled open the hatch. A pile of Nomex gear greeted him—not the original suit he and Scott had taken from the fire station so long before, but a close copy. After he'd been brought to the farm, Adam saw the good sense of wearing the fire gear as body armor and sent Talbert and his minions out to find some. They brought back a load of material, most of which Talbert and his crew dismissed, claiming it was too bulky, among other nit-picking details.

Dumb fucks.

Gus kicked off the cowboy boots Maggie had given him and pulled on his tan overalls, hooking their black straps over his shoulders. The knees had sewn-in padding that would do the job until he could find something better. The steel-toed fire boots went on next, snug and comfortably heavy. Down his right boot went an imitation KA-BAR knife. A firefighter's protective hood covered his head, and he pulled on it until his face popped through. Then came the heavy coat, which he zipped before patting down the Velcro outer flap. Strips of reflective yellow ringed the ankles, wrists, and chest. The old stuff he'd worn while house picking in Annapolis did the job, but looking back, there were too many pieces. This was a little bulkier but only two parts—five if he counted his helmet (nonregulation but what the hell) and his boots and gloves.

The gloves. They were something else.

They resembled combat gloves with their black leather and articulated knuckle plates. Just making fists made Gus want to try punching out a wall. Durable beyond compare, the gloves fit comfortably, and pull tabs sealed up the wrists, reinforcing the cuffs on the jacket. Adam had given the gloves to him, and Gus had asked where he'd found the brutish things, to which Adam only smirked, as though saying, *Don't ask where I got 'em or how I got 'em, just be* glad *I got 'em.*

Gus was. Getting back into the SUV, he most certainly was. He put his motorcycle helmet on, visor up, and kept the bat handy. A familiar building of energy powered up his limbs, and Gus wished again he had something to drink, just to turn his dials down. He was getting too amped up, the expectation of action becoming too powerful.

He started the engine and eased farther down the road, eyeing the hall of dense foliage on either side. His foot hit the brake at the halfway mark.

"Shit," Gus hissed and got out of the SUV, taking the bat with him.

On either side of the road were portable armored barriers, the kind Special Forces hunkered down behind while firing upon an enemy. Steel gray with a slash of red paint across the surface, just below open gun ports, the four walls had been pushed off the road.

Talbert had been there, all right.

A parting in the bush drew Gus's attention, a trail made by four-wheeled quads. Holding the bat at guard, he stalked through the opening and followed the ATV tracks through the forest. Brush snapped and crackled loudly underfoot, making him cringe at times, until he came to an enormous fire pit.

Gus let the bat drop to his waist.

The pit itself might've been made by an excavator, but he figured someone got the shitty end of a deal and had to dig it with a really big shovel. He didn't feel the need to jump down there and measure the depth, but it looked deep enough to stand in with the rim reaching his shoulders or chin. It certainly was deep enough to fry whatever dead things had been piled into it.

And fry someone had.

Ash-flecked bones and teeth filled the crater, dull against the scorched earth. Skulls with their jaws stretched wide sang a hungry dirge while others seemed to howl hysterics at their solitary visitor. Arms and fingers reached for the pit's edges, a necklace of slivers clawing for escape. Gus couldn't remember if he had ever seen so many bones in one place before, and the sight made his knees weak. The woods hiding this horrific barbeque remained still, and from his experience, no gimp would be able to creep up on him, not with the dry brush carpeting the ground.

And he hoped to Christ the rats weren't around.

A drink. Just one to steady his nerves, to take the edge off. S'all he needed—quick and nasty—but the evil part of him, the part that swore he wasn't an alcoholic, murmured sweetly that it didn't *have* to be just one. Seriously. What better way to face the day than by kicking back and tying one on? Or in this case, loading several *in*.

He pulled on his nose, erasing an itch, and backed away from the open pit, just in case the bones did something entirely freaky. If they did, Gus would simply bolt for the SUV and damn Talbert and his boys. *Couldn't find 'em, Adam. Sorry, Maggie.* Matter of fact, that story rang temptingly clear in Gus's head, but he shook his head in slow acceptance of his purpose.

He'd go a little farther.

See the mystery mansion that had tempted Talbert out there.

Find out what happened to that alpha-male shit stain and his butternut bum buddies and return with a full report.

Gus returned to the SUV and started it up. He stared at the edges of the paved road, his peripheral vision seeing the grins of skeletal faces. Sweat covered his face in a sheen that had nothing to do with heat. His fingers tapped on the curve of the steering wheel before he gripped the leather. Fear. Dread. The old, unwanted friends sat astride his shoulders like chortling goblins realizing all his defenses had been lowered and just amazed to have such persuasive seats. Even better . . . they smelled doubt as ripe as putrefying compost.

The road took him down a long spidery tunnel, wondrous in any season, with yellow and orange leaves piled up in stiff drifts. He drove along this late-autumn pipeline, the road straightening out like a neck struggling to swallow a bone . . .

Until it finally opened in eye-popping wonder.

4

Gus knew, from his days as a house painter, that the older houses often presented the most work. They weren't armored against age and the elements like the newer models with their candy-shell vinyl siding. Gables, high-peaked fasciae, and wide soffits could make a housepainter's job tricky at times, and without the safety of a scaffold, the gymnastics performed at the end of a forty-foot ladder to reach those last bare spots rivaled circus acts.

The house before Gus filled the width of the windshield and would've taken him and a professional crew *months* to prep and paint.

Mansion.

Gus tried the word and marveled at the reality. He eased to a stop, brain frozen by the palatial magnificence of Mortimer's superstructure. Overall, the house was white, with a marked Swiss influence of bare wooden beams and brackets lining and crisscrossing the upper levels. The first level appeared coated in a siding of stone while looming balconies dotted a third level plastered in unblemished weatherboarding. The home looked to be three stories tall at a glance, but rising above the center of the home were a fourth and *fifth* level, marked by a gigantic dome perched on top. Spider legs of black girders creased the structure's creamy surface. At a guess, Gus figured the whole construction was easily fifty thousand square feet of living space, perhaps even upward of seventy, all under multiple roofs with eaves wide enough to dance on. Gables, intricate carvings, and moldings of dragons and chimera perched almost everywhere—with one serpentine beast fashioned out of copper and drawing attention to a tall chimney—amazed Gus with their size and the sheer creativity necessary to conceive such a design.

Mortimer *had* to have been a billionaire. This "house" rivaled the size of a shopping mall and would eat up millions in yearly upkeep. Black paneling on sections of the roof glared flatly at him, and he recognized solar paneling but doubted even those few installations could keep up with the power demand. He'd be surprised if the damned monster didn't have elevators in the dome. He'd be even *more* surprised if the place didn't have its own indoor amusement park.

The mansion's monstrous bulk eclipsed the orchards, farmland, and any landscaped or architectural goodies lurking on the other side.

Gus forced himself to stop staring. No wonder Talbert had an Everest-sized chubby for the place. From a survivalist point of view, the man had discovered an emperor's Shangri-la. Hell, he and his posse were probably *still* inside somewhere, exploring the place and its potential treasures—entirely plausible, given the mansion's overwhelming vastness. Searching every cranny would take a week at least.

"Fuck. A frozen duck. Twice," Gus muttered, craning his neck over the steering wheel and taking it all in.

Then he noticed them—on the lower levels and parts of the third, mostly the balconies.

Shutters.

Metallic shutters with the added defense of timbers nailed across them. He'd been so awestruck by the beast of a palace he'd completely missed the obvious.

The place appeared to be tightly secured—tighter than a mosquito's bag stretched over an elephant's ass—all except the double doors comprising the main entrance. Rows of fat, black-veined marble columns partially obscured the doors, supporting an arched overhang that made Gus's jaw drop and stay there. Iron dragons resided there, captured in a regal prance.

"Morty," he whispered, drenched in awe, "You the man."

His foot released the brake, and the SUV crept forward like a dog on its belly sidling up to its master, begging for a crunchy treat. The driveway looped around another opulent example of Mortimer's wealth and taste, a water-green statue of a lion battling a dragon set into and rising above a pool bordering on Olympic size. Perhaps it *was* a pool, but after witnessing the girth of the mansion, Gus suspected it was really a fountain. Mortimer no doubt had a couple of indoor pools just because, since he's spending money, why the hell not? Complete with those bikini-clad, Japanese fuck droids.

"God . . . damn." Dazed, Gus shook his head. "Probably got your own rocket pad out back, don'tcha? You affluent bastard, you."

Parked to the left of the marble columns was Talbert and company's minivan, woefully out of place in such a scene. Damn thing looked like an old tin can resting against a mountain of platinum.

"You are not supposed to be here," Gus muttered, stopping his ride near the minivan. He made sure nothing obstructed the SUV in case he needed to make a quick getaway.

Gus opened the door, and that little click of unlatching metal parts made him pause. Nothing leaped at him from behind the columns. No army of deadheads rose from behind the low fountain wall or burst forth from the doors—only the soft creak of door hinges as he pushed it farther open. He got out with his bat and stood there, poised to jump back into his ride. A deep, steadying breath failed to calm him, and he remembered his nerves were steadier when armored with Uncle Jack.

Nothing moved, and a case of fidgeting overcame him.

His toes itched. His helmet felt too tight. He needed to take a leak. *Christ Almighty*, a voice chided him. *Bring some whiskey along on the next one, willya? Vodka, rum, mouthwash*, something. *You're a wreck.*

Not a wreck, Gus told himself. *Just outta practice, is all.*

The doors beckoned, tall and oaken and lashed with strips of black iron.

The goblins perched on his shoulders felt heavier.

Gus took another deep breath, felt his lungs stretch, and clasped the bat for security. Then he got moving, straight toward the minivan. His attention roved, trying to see everywhere at once. The vehicle's doors were unlocked, so he opened the one behind the driver's side. Nothing. Cleaner than a baby's fresh-wiped ass. Say what he might about Talbert, the prick kept his machine tidy. A quick inspection showed the keys were missing, but that wasn't a big deal. Nothing was in the rear either, which meant the four of them had gone in with whatever they'd brought along and did not come back out.

He straightened and stepped back enough to study the mansion's front doors between the columns. The house towered over him, pondering whether he had the fortitude to venture inside. Gus wondered that himself. The mirrored gleam of the unshuttered windows on the third level made him paranoid.

"Fuck it," he snarled and marched right up to the entrance. The main doors were great slabs of wood that might've been pulled off a German castle and shipped overseas. Nothing seemed wrecked or even damaged. The place reeked of unchecked decadence, money spent on luxuries simply because one had money. It wouldn't surprise Gus if the shitter was made of gold and the toilet paper of silk—maybe even a diamond dispenser.

Silk toilet paper.

That had possibilities.

A doorbell in the guise of a leather cord with a tail of tassels hung from the upper frame. Gus ignored the temptation to pull it, imagining cathedral-sized chimes ringing out deep within the mansion.

He tugged on the wrought-iron handle on the left.

It cracked open.

Gus supposed he shouldn't be surprised at how easily that went. Talbert and his boys had probably come the very same way.

Then the house exhaled in his face.

The breath of a violated tomb assaulted him, a putrid wave of decomposition Gus hadn't smelled in a long time—certainly not on the open farm. The stink flooded his nose and mouth and befouled both, his hand arriving late to cover his face. His shoulders bunched reflexively, and he squinted into the gap, enduring the rotten air.

An elegant inner room with a midnight marbled floor ended in a closed set of lacquered cherrywood doors that simply shone in the meager daylight. A waist-high series of Japanese-style lockers both collected outer footwear and offered slippers. Empty ceramic vases rested on the top in a tasteful décor. A wall-mounted computer screen and ultrathin terminal jutted from the wall on his right. He stepped inside and gravitated toward the machine, tapped its keyboard.

Unresponsive.

Behind him, the door creaked. Gus turned about and took two steps before jamming the bat into the shrinking gap, halting the door's closure. The air smelled a little better now, but a bad vibe remained. The outer door had to stay open. He didn't understand why—it wasn't locked—but a sense of sinister grandeur permeated this first room, a portent of things deeper within.

Gray daylight, a saber of sanity, beamed at him.

Don't, one of those shitbagged goblins whispered sweetly in his ear. *I'm telling you . . . don't . . .*

You're being fuckin' silly, Gus scolded himself. *The door isn't locked. You're just ring rusty, is all.*

Frowning, he let the door swing closed without a squeal of hinges, entombing him. Fear of being trapped gripped his senses, and he lurched forward, found the handle, and yanked.

The door opened with a comforting *Yes? Need something?*

Holding it, Gus leaned out of the mansion and checked on the SUV and minivan. The coast was still clear. All was simply ducky outside. Feeling better with daylight at his back, he grabbed a pair of soft-soled slippers from a locker and packed one underneath the first door, keeping it wide open. Van Helsing wouldn't go into a vampire's lair at night, and having an open avenue of retreat made Gus feel better. He regarded the inner door, amazed at its inlays of threaded gold. The cost and craftsmanship made him shake his head.

Taking one of the inner doors' handles, Gus pulled.

It wouldn't move.

He pushed.

Another mournful gasp of bad gas made him cringe and hold his breath. His shadow stretched over a grand foyer of more polished marble floors. Glittering chandeliers floated overhead like immense jellyfish made of crystal. Dark pillars of bare wood rose up on either side of the entrance, leading into archways and side corridors, black and silence filled. The main foyer ran deeper inside the house, but the light petered out into a nebulous curtain of night . . . which couldn't be right. Even in daytime, some light always squeaked through somewhere, but the path ahead was blackness incarnate. Impenetrable.

Gus kept the door open with his shoulder and wished for a flashlight, swearing at himself for not bringing one along. The feeling of being out of practice rushed over him once again. But the house remained still, silent.

Back in the day, he'd rap on the wall or even shout to announce his presence to the dead, drawing any lurkers into the light where he could conveniently dispatch them.

In this . . . tomb, he hesitated even to clear his throat.

The darkness at the edge of the daylight exuded venom.

The main foyer appeared thirty feet across at least, and Gus had no idea how far into the mansion it went.

Or how many gimps might be hidden just out of sight.

Possibly an army. The place was big enough to hold one. Gus gazed upon the crystals sagging motionlessly above and couldn't see a ceiling. His fist tightened on the remaining slipper.

"Game on," Gus whispered and exhaled.

"Hey!" he shouted, his own voice startling him. "Talbert. You fuckin' in there somewhere? Bark if you're able."

He rapped the bat against the door. "Hear me, shit-for-brains? Huh? Don't make me come in there. Don't . . ."

His voice left him.

Along the right wall, just at the edge of daylight, lay a boot sole. Gus almost missed its dirt-caked grooves—toes down, which meant it was still on the lower leg of the owner.

"Fuck around . . ." he finished as if waking from a deep sleep.

Then he heard it.

Somewhere, deep in the mysteries of the house, was the barest tinkle of something glasslike being nudged.

It distracted him.

Footsteps. Two stealthy barefoot slaps rushed behind him. Gus had half turned when a pair of hands shoved him *inside* the foyer. Gus yelled and fell, helmed forehead cracking off the marble, kicking and flipping himself over to find whoever the hell had pushed him into the deep end.

A figure stood at the second set of doors, arm raised as if touching something farther up on the frame.

The inner doors closed with all the finality of a death trap being sprung.

"Hey!" Gus yelled, scrambled to his knees, heart pounding, propelling himself at the portal just as it clicked shut. His gloved hands and bat crashed against the hardwood surface before fumbling in the sudden dark.

"Hey!" He yanked on the door, relieved for a split second that they opened from the inside . . .

To reveal only a sepulchral blackness.

5

Gus felt for a handle on this new barrier, finding nothing.

"Oh, shit," he panted over and over like a breathless mantra. "Oh shitohshit—"

Something heavy hit him from behind.

Gus mangled a scream and twisted around, confused at the lack of space before realizing his attacker was the hardwood door, which he had previously yanked open, closing on him. Taking a breath and glaring, he stomped a heel into the door's base, keeping it away from him while he turned his back and felt this new wall preventing him from leaving the mansion. The notion that some nimble cocksucker had snuck up and pushed him inside motivated him to find a quick escape. He'd seen enough old "Technicolor by Deluxe" movies in his day to know a human sacrifice when he saw one. Anger fueled him. He clawed at the barrier's surface. He slammed his bat against it and realized it wasn't wood at all but metal—steel perhaps, like a protective seal to prevent harmful fallout from seeping inside.

Or keeping scavengers from leaving.

Gus found no purchase in the precise seams of the barrier's edges. This new wall had dropped or slid across without a sound, sealing him in. He couldn't remember hearing anything, not even a metallic whine of gears except that quick padding of bare feet before the push. The force of the shove would've left him choking on his dentures, if he had any.

Gus searched the doorframe from one end to the other, finding nothing except the slipper he'd dropped.

Sealed in. Snared. He placed his back against the new wall and let the inner door close upon him like a nutcracker, struggling to hear anything over his own frantic breathing.

Nothing. Not yet.

But it was coming.

Gus slipped away from the doorway, allowing the inner door to close. He stared into the dark, visor up, swearing at the lack of light. Blackness—a haunted meat freezer of night that scared him almost to the point of immobility. His breathing intensified, the shock of his predicament finally hitting home. He didn't want to be there, wanted to play it all over again as one would in a console game after dying in a totally unacceptable fashion. Then he threw his head back and cracked his helmet off the wooden door behind, the impact shocking, sobering.

In the aftershock of that blow, a sound reached his ears.

A soft shuffling, at times squeaking.

Gus recognized it immediately.

Feet. On bare marble. *Many* feet, hobbling along like slippered grannies without their walkers. He knew this scenario. He'd played it many times before, heavy handed and with no apologies.

You were drunk then, his mind pointed out.

"Fuck off, brain," Gus growled, staring wide-eyed into the deep darkness. He arched his head to the sides, his peripheral vision adapting and discerning flickers of inky movement lumbering toward him, the whisper of their soft-soled stampede frightening him more than his last stand at the house. An overpowering stench of decomposing flesh accosted him, as if he'd been blindfolded and had a rancid slab of ripe and wormy steak rubbed under his nose. It woke him up faster than a shot of smelling salts from a corner man. The moans and low, poisonous hisses followed, like a parking lot of cars all losing air pressure in their tires, closing in on him.

"All right." Gus bent over, hands tightening around his bat as the nearing ghosts became chilling traceries in the dark.

"You pushed me in here," he said, "but I fucking *guarantee* you'll be kicking me out."

His eyes flickered everywhere, barely seeing anything. The memory of a wide-open foyer, straight into the heart of this multistoried beast of a residence, sprang into his mind like a lonely strand of life-granting rope.

Stay in the open.

Don't get boxed in.

Take no chances.

The first gimp appeared almost right in front of him, just a ripple in the dark. A spider's flutter of fingers grazed his left shoulder, hunting for a grip. A ghoulish face, skeletal below the nose, materialized, and Gus jerked back and slammed against the wall. He ducked and barreled forward. His shoulder caught a pillowy midsection and ripped a chunk from it, immediately releasing an explosive whiff of pent-up gastro delight. The gimp didn't crash to the floor but rather *sloughed*, like a huge sock of skin being shed and dropped from a height.

Gus charged, bent over at the hips, feeling a millipede's patter of fingers over his back. The zombies were just as blind as he and walked with their arms straight out. These he ducked under, smashing into sides or hips, spinning the dead around on twisting ankles. He swung his bat low, connecting with a knee cap, and the attached body collapsed like a dropped suitcase. More crowded into him, but he plowed through dozens attempting to grab his Nomex hide. His helmet became a rounded bullet. The zombies caroled evilly in that pitch-black soup, but Gus stormed through, fear morphing into a spite-fueled desire to do as much damage as possible.

He plowed through a defensive line, holding his bat before him like a horizontal length of pipe, connecting with bodies in devastating fashion. Nearly blind as he was, he had no means to verify any kills, but killing wasn't in his mind right then.

Fucking up as many as possible was.

Adrenaline made his pistons glow with heat. A body hit his lowered bat dead on and actually *split*, the torso spilling over his back and the legs tripping him. Gus stumbled, landing on all fours in a clatter. Zombies clutched at his back, his shoulders, his head. One bit into a shoulder, to no avail. Gus scooted between legs, knocking several gimps off balance and feeling them fall. The space cleared, and he got to his feet, charging low once more. A zombie hit his shoulder and twirled away. A wall of flesh crashed into him dead on, a fragrant mashup of septic foulness and rotten tissue. Gus shoved it aside with some effort. He picked up lost speed. A ghoulish glimpse of naked deadhead loomed, its hips moving like a rusty ice auger while the head seemed to churn in the opposing direction.

Gus stopped and swung, removing its skull in a burst of bone and filth.

He stumbled on, past silhouettes closing in from the edges, a veritable mass of dead things converging on the main foyer, zeroing in on the one piece of still breathing—still *running*—chunk of meat.

Then there were no zombies about him, and he thought about finding a corridor and maybe getting above the ravenous crowd when both of his knees clattered into something stone-like and unyielding, and he flipped over in the dark, ass over tits, and landed hard on his back.

The impact knocked the wind from his lungs.

Struggling to make sense of it all, Gus floundered weakly. He heard a train coming, distant but heavy on the rails, making the very earth thrum. His fingers flexed and worked, but his knees felt hyperextended within a hairline of breaking. They moved but were none too happy about it and made it known.

The goblins hitched on his shoulders shrieked in evil delight, their howls resonating from ear to ear.

Gus turned his head, seeing nothing but a vat of tar. Then a face slunk out of it, less than a foot from his eyes. A grandfatherly gimp, with a gauze of clingy hair spattered to his forehead. A single, off-kilter eyeball stared through those greasy curls. Its lips eroded into a wicked gleam of golden teeth. As Gus's mind attempted to contact his unresponsive limbs, that evil face inchwormed forward until its chin slid over his shoulder. The face shuddered as if the corpse had been gut shot. Then it bunched up, like a worm about to gnaw its way into an apple. Those yellow teeth sank into the Nomex, not five fingers away from Gus's face, with all the patience of a doctor attempting to inject a patient. The thing's jawline flexed. Its single bulbous eye, white and unseeing but ogling the ceiling, showed no change in emotion as its teeth slowly *shifted* at its disintegrating gumline. Spear-like roots of enamel leaned forward, puncturing their black moorings of flesh like the heads of maggots while a dreadful wail rose in Gus's ears, reminding him of approaching trains.

He realized it was *him* screaming. Violently.

His legs came online, and he jerked away from that head, yanking out several golden teeth entirely. Gus kicked out with heavy boots, pulping the melon-sized bauble of skull and skin against something solid.

A wall.

The thigh-high wall of a fountain.

And he stood inside its dry cavity.

Shoulders and chest heaving, Gus climbed to his feet in time to make out a terrifying mob of hands and faces reaching for him. He lurched away from the stony rim of the fountain, bumping into a shadowy figure perched on a bone-dry dais. Zombies pressed against the fountain's low barrier and spilled over like drunken birds attempting a sip. The front of the hunting party stalled.

Getting his bearings and feeling the curve of the fountain, Gus slid around as fingers grazed his outer arm, shoulder, and the side of his helmet. A hand pawed at his face, swiping his visor down and blinding him completely.

Gus screamed.

And the interior of the mansion erupted in an explosion of light.

As luck would have it, the frightful cadaver had lowered Gus's visor at the best time. The burst of light from multiple suns overhead illuminated the entire floor, which would have surely fried Gus's dilated eyes and rendered him near helpless, flailing at a mass of dead creatures. The tinted screen of his helmet shielded his vision, though he still shied away from the brightest overhead fixtures. For seconds, he pressed against the fountain's figurehead with his head lowered before chancing a peek.

He gasped.

An army of undead flooded the main foyer. They converged on his position, their stained, filthy heads in stark contrast to stylish pop art images and elaborate landscape oil paintings affixed high on the walls. Gus spotted a wide hall at the rear and scissored his legs over the fountain wall. Gimps crowded him as his boots hit the floor. Lowering his head, he barged through five feet of soft, rancid flesh until the sheer *volume* of the dead forced him to his knees. There, he took the low road and crawled between legs to freedom. His shoulders plowed through knees, and they fell against each other.

Even on top of him.

Feeling the growing weight on his back, Gus pressed himself to his feet, shrugging off hands clawing his back. He shoved and pushed back grinning heads, nearly spent from his exertions and yet distantly marveling over the extravagance of the mansion's interior, all fully revealed under searing spotlights that robbed the walls of color. Gus screamed back at the moaning faces and pressed forward.

Then he was free and stumbled into a run.

Archways and closed doors of mahogany flashed by at a delirious rush. More figures shambled into the light, hissing, moaning, moving, and clawing. The hall split at a junction, marked by a displaced brick wall that bent Gus's senses and stopped him in his tracks. The center of the wall crumbled inward, trailing bricks and sandy ribbons, revealing a huge hole into deep space. Bright stars surrounded an orbiting starship while the glowing face of the sun hung far and away in the background.

Only when Gus placed a hand against the mural did the illusion break.

Deadheads crept in from his flanks.

A uniformed woman with half her head shorn away reached for him with one arm; the other had been ripped entirely from its shoulder.

Gus took a batter's stance and smashed the remaining chunk of her ruined skull.

He spun and balked at a leather-covered fright. Glossy black clothed the gimp in snug fashion, its shoulders a needlework of spikes. An eyeless mask, revealing a torn zipper for a mouth, shambled forward, stunning Gus with morbid fascination. When the thing reached for him, he swung and squashed the leatherhead's brainpan to one side, gray matter squirting out from improper stitches.

Gus ran down a corridor, sidestepping zombies when he could, feeling the weight of his arms. A chef's kitchen nearly blazing with light flashed by then an archway to a library complete with sliding ladders.

In a sunken movie theater, about a dozen decomposing torsos turned his way as he ran past.

In an office filled with designer furniture and overturned desks, the undead staff pointed at him.

A wide stairway beckoned, and he raced to the second floor, feeling a savage burn in his calves and hamstrings, forcing them to work. He got halfway up the stairs before crashing into a solid wall. He stepped back, blinking at the wondrous illusion of an ascending staircase before the pursuing mob urged him to back up and stagger off in a different direction.

An oak door caught his attention. He raced through it, stopping inside yet another library. He whirled and closed the door with effort. Gus saw no lock, so he dropped his bat and pushed a luxurious sofa against the wood, straining hard enough to believe something arterial was about to burst. He shoved the piece of furniture tight against the door just as something heavy slammed against it.

Nearly exhausted, Gus sucked in air as he slid his visor up. The light was softer in the reading room. He backed away from the door, relieved to see it holding. Hands hammered the wood from beyond, but the door barely budged.

Nothing but the best for Mortimer.

Gus retreated and plopped down on another posh sofa. He looked around the place in breathless wonder. The library was smaller, cozier, filled with bookshelves and comfortable furniture. A monstrous stone fireplace befitting a ski lodge in the French alps dominated one wall. Every tall window in the room had been smashed and replaced with metallic shutters. Arcs of glass glittered on the carpet.

Gus sagged into the sofa. With the sudden burst of running, crawling, and bat swinging, he felt he'd just completed a goddamn triathlon in less than a minute. His heart felt ready to explode. Sweat coated him in a fine sheen. He sucked down great lungfuls of air as more hands slapped the oaken door.

Gus kept his eye on it, but for the moment, he felt secure.

The mansion, however, was a nest.

"A nest," he wheezed. "Jesus Christ. A fuckin' grade-A *hive* packed with lips and assholes."

His breathing smoothed out, and he became aware of his sweat-saturated clothing underneath the Nomex. Needing to feel fresh air on his face, he pulled off the helmet and dropped it onto a cushion. The flailing of hands and limbs on the thick door outside didn't bother him.

The urge to find the bastard who'd pushed him inside this pit sprang up in Gus's chest and head. He also wanted to know where the controls for the overhead lights were located. And what was the purpose of those exquisite 3D renderings that challenged the mind and fooled the senses right up until impact?

Right then, he felt as if he were inside an enormous mousetrap.

And he sure as hell could use a sip from a silver flask of goodness.

No sooner did he think it than the lights winked out, as if for punishment for even considering it.

But the drumming of fleshy limbs against the door continued.

Hidden in the dark, Gus lay on the sofa, boots high, recuperating while sifting through his thoughts. People were in the house—maybe not the original owners but someone. How many was unknown, but at least one had access to the outside. The house had a power source. It surprised him to a degree, but he didn't freak out over it. Mortimer possessed more than enough acreage to put up a row or two of wind turbines or even a few reefs of solar panels—perhaps even something more advanced, like the floor generators of New York, which harnessed the energy in every foot-on-sidewalk impact and converted it into a whopping fifteen percent of the city's power needs. Mortimer also liked flicking the lights on and off in his house, which summoned an image of an old guy hunched over a grand desk, cackling while playing evil overlord with a switch.

Gus sat and stewed on the mysteries of the mansion while the thumping against the door lessened. When he was ready, he stood and felt his way around the nearly pitch-black room. Secret passages popped into his head, wiring him awake and granting him a break from his growing thirst. He hadn't brought anything with him on the trip—not one crumb or drop. It was only supposed to be a day trip, a quick in and out. Listening to a ravenous pack just beyond three inches of wood informed him as to how shortsighted he'd been.

Zombies. A slew of them. Walking and chewing. Perhaps the smooth floors kept them upright longer than if they'd been outside dragging their feet on asphalt. The army cornering him here was the largest single group of deadheads he'd encountered since torching half of Annapolis.

He wished he had his hands on his old Benelli shotgun. That thunder duster would punch holes through the entire gang at the doors. As it was, all he had was the bat and a knife. Gus felt his way to the fireplace and stuck his head in, seeing what he could up and beyond. Through a plate-sized opening far above, clouds darkened.

The day was getting older.

Gus returned to the sofa. With a bouncy plop, he settled in. He had a feeling he was in for a long wait, remembering his times stuffed away in attics.

Time crawled by, punctuated by the irregular pounding of fists upon wood.

Heat seeped into the room, low but there, and he wondered if old Morty had invested in a floor heating system. Probably had. Nothing seemed too good for the man. The sofa worked its magic, taking some of the edge off and allowing his body to recharge.

Slowly, against his will, sleep took him.

6

A scream woke him, yanking him into a sitting position. Gus fumbled with his bat, his attention locked on the library's door. The room seemed darker than before, and his internal clock sensed the sun had set recently. Getting off the sofa, he whipped the bat in searching arcs, just in case something might have crept inside without him knowing.

All clear.

He found the door, still holding, and listened.

Another piercing note, deep in the marble guts of the mansion, long and lingering as if someone were being tortured at leisure. That made Gus screw up his face. What the hell passed for *leisure* in this place? His mind fluttered for a moment, realizing his unloving pursuers were no longer pounding on the door, and a thread of light outlined the doorframe.

The lights were back on outside.

Gus hauled the end of the sofa back, gathered his helmet, and pulled it on. His hand located the door handle, and he took a breath before pulling it open a crack.

Well, holy shit.

Blue light from the ceiling cast an icebox hue across the hall and floor. Gus realized the interior of the house had cooled considerably. Gimps stood in the hall, directionless, waiting for another scream and no longer interested in the morsel trapped inside the reading room.

They didn't wait long.

Another skin-tightening wail hooked the attention of the zombies and lured them away.

Not interested in following, Gus crept away from the undead flow, along a corridor three times the width of a regular one. The ceiling lights glowed overhead, spaced out along the corridor like a segmented spine. Collapsed tables lined the baseboards. Decorative art pieces lay on broken legs. White dust from shattered vases and small statuettes coated the floor. Over time, the dead had shattered the various pieces of furniture and kicked everything against the wall. Gus slunk past two separate washrooms, their heated thrones intact, and he fought down the impulse to check for toilet paper.

The scream rang out again, farther away now, marking almost a minute.

Gus stopped and put his back against a wall. *A minute? Was someone prodding a person on a clock?*

A handful of zombies came around the corner, five castoffs from an S&M party dressed in their finest leather and zipper masks. In the blue hue of the lights, they shambled toward him at best speed. Gus gawked at them, seeing for the first time how the floor in their path wasn't a floor at all but a huge pit the width of the corridor, not twenty feet from where he stood.

Gus didn't move. His helmet hid his smirk.

"That's right, you freaks. Come to papa."

The first deadhead, dressed in a slick getup that spoke of wild sex parties, walked over the pit.

The illusion of the floor art threw Gus for a moment before he retreated from the advancing pack as they waltzed across, sneering as if they'd known all along.

When they got into range, he dispatched the five with relative ease, bashing open their brainpans and scattering them across the floor. He walked to the center of the floor art, impressed with the detail, disbelieving that such a level of trickery could be achieved. A short note of pain echoed again through the corridor, almost a grunt that time, urging him to hurry. Gus didn't *want* to hurry, scared of what he might discover.

He moved to the end of the corridor, which branched right and left. Alternatively, he could check out what was behind a door just ahead. Gus looked for undead and, seeing the coast clear, went to the door and tried the knob. A rewarding *click* followed.

A sudden, frightening hiss split the air, and something punched Gus hard in the center of his back, squashing him against the wood. The force stunned and startled him. He fell and rolled over just as a second hiss bounced his helmeted head off the marble. Gus groaned and pushed himself into a sitting position, looking around as he did so.

Jesus Christ.

Walking toward the floor pit and dressed like a predator from the apocalypse was . . . an archer. The archer wore a Korean mask depicting an old man grinning hugely, his right eye looking down an arrow nocked to an archaic but still effective bow. Snow-white fatigues, camouflage for winter hunting, took on a blue tone under the lights.

Gus's face contorted in horrified wonder.

Just as the archer released.

The missile hissed through the corridor like a black bolt of lightning and nailed Gus's sternum, bucking him against the wall—a perfect shot any other time, ruined by the heavy folds of his Nomex gear. It wasn't bulletproof—hell, as far as Gus knew, it couldn't stop a hunting arrow either.

But it had. Cold.

However, Gus's sternum felt as if it had just been stomped on by a sumo. He winced, holding a hand to his chest. It wouldn't surprise him if the impact had fractured bone.

The Korean Mask peeked up from the bow, enormous grin blazing in the blue light. He smoothly extracted another arrow, notched the bow, and drew back until his fingers touched a wooden cheek.

Gus lurched into motion, feet finding traction and propelling him forward just as a shrieking arrow *twanged* off his left thigh, dropping him to a knee with a yelp. The meat of his leg felt as if it had just been tenderized by a sledgehammer.

"You *fucker*!"

The archer stoically walked forward, nocking a new arrow. Gus could see the white plumage of several more missiles over the man's shoulder, deadly to any other guest, but thank the Lord above for quality-made fire gear. Gus stumbled out of the way just as another arrow split the air and imbedded itself with a *whuk* into the doorframe, splintering it and missing Gus's ass cheek by a few fingers.

Shaking off the effects of the arrows, Gus hobbled at best possible speed down the trashed hallway, weaving from side to side to present the hardest target possible.

SsssssssTT!

An arrow slugged him in his left shoulder, twisting him off his feet and sending him crashing through a doorless entry. The clatter of the missile falling to the floor echoed through the hall, and Gus caught that mournful scream again as he stumbled toward a sofa set. He flipped over it, bouncing off soft cushions and onto a plush rug. Metallic shutters blanketed and protected a glass wall spanning the width of the room. Light reflected in its surface. Judging by the rugs, sofas, and the pair of massive white brick fireplaces adorning the north and south walls, Gus figured he was in a living room as he slammed himself against the edge of the opening.

"Who are you, huh?" he yelled, bringing up his right hand, frankly amazed he still had a hold of his bat.

No reply.

He glanced up, seeing the handrails and a walkway of the second floor, jutting out twelve feet above him and leading back into the area above the hall he'd just come from. Hope flared, but how could he get up there? With the overhang, there was no way he could climb over the fireplaces. Grunting in discomfort and still feeling the numbing effects of being struck by arrows, Gus lumbered back to the entrance and discovered the door actually slid across on rollers. Grabbing the handles, he pushed with everything he had, intending to seal the living room off like a bright vault.

The Korean Mask filled the closing crack, appearing in the last second just as it shut with a clap of wood. Gus straightened with a grunt. There was a simple eye hook on the frame, and he flipped it into place, locking the door just as the man on the other side attempted to open it.

Gus smirked in false sympathy at the attempt. He turned around, taking in the far wall of glass, and one feature grabbed his attention.

A set of double doors marked each end of the glass, leading nowhere as the metal shutters beyond forbade any escape outside.

Gus chugged toward a pair, anxious and not believing for a second he'd escaped the snow-camo archer. Crossing the living room floor, he saw the doors opened *inside* and immediately craned his neck up to the overhang and walkway above. He opened both doors and threw the closest one wide open, as far as possible, and stopped it below the edge of the overhang. Gus eyed the doorknob.

A foothold if he ever saw one.

He sheathed his bat and staggered toward a heavy-looking sofa chair. A second later, he manhandled the furniture piece into position against the door. He climbed onto the chair, got one boot on the nearby doorknob, and swung his other boot to the knob on the other side, straddling it like a pogo stick. It worked for all of a split second before Gus fell back, unable to keep his hands gripped to the doorframe. He eyed the glass for a moment before punching the pane, shattering the glass with a combat-gloved fist. Then he stepped back onto the knobs and looped an arm through the wrecked frame of the door.

Gus reached up . . .

And his fingertips touched the closest wooden post. Close but no cigar.

Never easy. He bent his knees, prepping himself for—

He jumped four inches, clasping onto the post for dear life. His bruised shoulder quivered with pain, cranky as a rusty winch, but he held on and slowly hauled himself up, wishing he'd done more chin-ups in his life. He wheezed. Squealed. His boots scrabbled against the door. He snaked an arm between two posts above and swung his left leg—wincing at the charley horse still in his thigh. Taking a quick breath, he opted for his right leg, feeling it drag against the door below.

"*Fuck*," Gus gasped, spittle spurting from his lips. Leave it to him to do it the hard way.

Panic gave him precious strength, and he pulled his head up to where he could rest his chin on the second level if there was room. But then he burned through whatever strength he had, straining, sucking down huge gulps of air while gravity dug in and pulled him back down.

A set of hands latched onto his forearms.

Shock dropped Gus's mouth wide open.

"Fuckin' *work*, willya!" Talbert grated, covered in body armor and grimacing as he struggled to pull Gus up. He grabbed the Nomex by the loose folds covering Gus's thigh and flipped him over the railing like a heavy sack of fertilizer.

Both men collapsed on the walkway, staring at each other.

"The fuck you come from?" a dazed Gus puffed at the missing man.

"The fuck *you* come from?" Talbert shot back, stooping low behind the railing.

"The fuck you mean 'you'? Adam sent me to look for your missing ass."

"Yeah, well, y'took your goddamn time."

"I just fuckin' *got* here!"

"I heard you come in a couple of fuckin' hours ago! The fuck you doin' down there? Makin' a sandwich? Tourin' the goddamn grounds?"

"Hey, dicksmack! There's a fuckin' army of shitbags down there, in case you haven't noticed. And a Snow White bitch shootin' *arrows* into my fireproofed ass."

"Yeah, I know all about that afterbirth," Talbert said, becoming serious. He wore no helmet. The black plates and scales of his armor looked intact, but the creepy part in his hair had been tussled.

"You know him?" Gus barked.

"Jesus Christ, I've been holed up here for fuckin' half a *week*—course I know about him."

Something puzzled Gus. "Where's the rest of your knob gobblers?"

"Hey, they're *assholes* to you. They're dead."

That one word took the wind out of Gus.

Talbert shook his head and was about to speak when he looked to the first floor. His eyes narrowed. "Holy fuckin' *shit*."

The Korean mask archer stepped through the door beneath, bow held at the ready.

"It's him."

"Who's 'him'?" Gus wanted to know, pressing himself against the wall.

"Fuckin' Donald."

The sudden mundaneness of the name befuddled Gus's bullet train of thought.

"Who?"

"Gus, shut that shit trap you call a mouth for a second, willya?"

The archer sidestepped toward the fireplace on the living room's far side, grinning mask upturned in their direction, studying them merrily. He retrieved a fistful of arrows from his back, nocking one and managing the others between his fingers of his string hand.

"Well, shit," Talbert grated. "You better be able to run."

"Yeah, why?"

"Good, 'cause he's gonna machine-gun us, and I'm not fuckin' carryin' your saggy ass."

"Wha—"

"*C'mon!*"

Talbert bolted for the far end of the carpeted walkway, toward a doorway. Gus froze for a second before rising and following, running, sneaking quick peeks at the ghostly figure of Donald below. The archer wasn't moving at all.

But he *was* aiming.

Then the arrows flew.

A section of the railing splintered from the impact of the first barbed head.

Another arrow ricocheted off Gus's helmet, bouncing him off the wall. He crashed to the floor.

A third snake sizzled between two posts and struck him like a pickaxe.

"C'mon!" Talbert yelled at him.

Gus pulled himself up, feeling like a fly ripping its own wings off, and staggered forward to the doorway, where a crouched Talbert waved him home.

"Run, y'chickenshit, *run! Everything you got! C'mon!*"

Three more arrows sizzled through the railing, pummeling Gus's frame and hindering him like a wounded elephant. The shafts bounced off and hit the wall, raining onto the carpet. Bent over, on hands and feet with his ass up, Gus staggered to the door.

The last foot, Talbert reached out and grabbed him by the shoulders, hauling him out of harm's way.

Gus fell onto a queen-sized bed while Talbert slammed the door behind and propped a chair up under the knob. Gus groaned, feeling as if he'd just been pulled out from under a stampede. Every movement hurt.

"All right," Talbert said. "If that cocksucker decides to climb up after your ass, he's gotta come through that door. And if he does, I'll split his fuckin' head open and giggle all the while."

Gus saw Talbert brandished Matt Miller's machete. The bedroom, rustic with ergonomically matching furniture and eye-pleasing earth colors, spun for a second.

"You okay?"

The question coming from Talbert surprised him, but his helmet hid it. "Feel like corn kernels . . . in a flattened piece of shit."

Talbert chuckled darkly. "You're a poet, bro."

Gus let that one go, seeing how the dickhead had saved his ass and all.

"That coat," Talbert nodded, indicating Gus's. "Must be puncture proof. Same shit as Kevlar vests."

"Yeah? So why do parts of me feel like I've been run over by a truck?"

"Said it was puncture proof. The arrows probably still leave a bruise or two."

Great. Gus's head fell between his shoulders.

"All right," Talbert went on. "You just lie there for a bit and listen. Okay? I'll fill you in on what happened these last couple of days."

"We safe here?"

"Yeah, we're safe. They don't let the zombies onto the second floor."

"Huh?"

Talbert smiled, a crooked ribbon of snow. "You heard me right. Congrats. You made it out of the arena in one piece. Minus your balls, of course. Not like you had a set anyway."

At that crack, Gus pulled his annoyed self to a sitting position.

"All right, listen to this," Talbert cautioned. "You'll need to know."

And he started talking.

Talbert and his lads had pulled up in front of the mansion, wide-eyed, weaponized, and eager to explore. The front door was wide open and not a gimp in sight, so they immediately went to work going through rooms. The place was just as they imagined, luxurious to the point of near disbelief. Almost right away, they picked up a few killer-slick military-grade weapons straight out of a sci-fi movie, sick instruments of wrath none of them had ever seen before. Plenty of guns . . . but no ammunition. In the end, they left the arms where they'd found them.

"That is a problem," Gus stated.

"You gonna listen?"

"Go on."

Talbert scratched at his head and continued.

After he and his boys had gone back out into the main hall, the door was closed. Worse, a steel plate had slid across and finalized their trapped asses. They were actually working on digging through the wood and seeing if some rewiring might open that bunker-sized slab of steel when the gimps attacked in force—a whole township, it seemed.

"And the lights were on?" Gus interrupted.

"The lights were on, but it gets better."

They fought a running battle though cathedral-like halls and were holding their own when voices started coming out of speakers built into the walls. Giggling voices. Also, the halls had tiny cameras fixed in nooks and crannies, little black snowdomes turned bottom up and stuck to the ceiling, watching every move. Talbert and his men stuck to the side rooms, running through doorways, securing the ones with locks. They managed to evade the zombies in the beginning until they turned a few corners and wound up on an indoor bowling alley. Busloads of dead men, women, and children trailed after them, pinning them in the alley, which had no windows and no other door besides the one they came through . . .

A door that had mysteriously *unlocked* itself after Talbert himself had locked it.

"That's what's up with this place," he said. "About half the rooms on the bottom floor are safe. They can be locked. The others got dick-all, and some . . . can be locked and unlocked *remotely*. You have to pay attention to where you are."

Talbert cleared his throat before continuing.

They fought through the mass of zombies. Matt "The Machete" Miller was in his element, hacking and cutting like an electrified dervish. Benny swung his hammer while Talbert and Sheldon used their bats, and after a while, they actually thinned out the dead, enough to leave the alley. Back in the hall, however, Donald introduced himself from the third floor by sinking one of his arrows into the back of Sheldon's neck.

The memory of the attack left Talbert speechless for a moment, and Gus didn't press him.

Talbert started again, recounting how they tried to get upstairs to Donald. The voice on the speaker system started speaking. They were trespassers, the voice said, and as such had no rights to anything except a slow death. Sheldon had died slowly, painfully, kicking and twitching in his own blood. The point of the arrow had cut through his Adam's apple, and no doctor was needed to tell he was a goner. Sheldon slipped and staggered about like a wounded buck, the others too damn stunned to do anything, listening to that horrible rasping of air being forced through bleeding airways. Sheldon actually started clawing at his throat in the end, and that was the last image before the lights flickered off. Benny and Matt started freaking out while Talbert gave up trying to compose them and flailed his way through the dark as a fresh wave of undead piled into the corridors. Though he couldn't see it, behind him, in that suddenly suffocating darkness, he heard Matt Miller swinging his machete and calling out for his companions. Talbert heard the harsh connections of the machete, heard Miller straining against that black pitch tide of limbs and mouths. Heard the curses become shrieks then muffled gargling before that horrible, nerve-slicing sound of . . . *feeding* . . . filled the hallway. Talbert wanted to help him, but that writhing midnight soup of limbs and mouths stopped him cold. His own panicked screams drowned out the dying Miller.

"Matt went down swinging. Give him that. Right in the center of a mob. Didn't know what happened to Benny until a day later. Sheldon bled out. At least I *hope* he bled out. Matt cut up more 'n a dozen of the things. I found the heads the next morning, and this"—Talbert held up the machete—"right in the middle. No Matt, though. No Benny either. Lights were still off, but there was some lit farther in the house, not that I was in any mood to explore then, so I barricaded myself in a neat little bathroom I'd managed to crawl into the day before. Plenty of running water. Raised sinks. Tub with a TV screen and even a silver minibar—empty, though, but I mean, *Christ.* Best thing? The toilet flushed. I mean, the place was nicer than my fuckin' *bedroom.* I stayed in that shitter for a day and a half until I saw the light shining in from under the door. It stayed on, and a couple hours later, after I couldn't hear anyone out there, I stepped out."

Stepping out into that dreadful quiet, catching a whiff of air ripe with offal and viscera, and seeing what was left of a buddy left Talbert shaken. A zombie had wrenched his bat away, so he used the machete and went from room to room, deeper into the house, retreating into bathrooms upon seeing any walking corpses and hiding out like a mouse in the walls. Sometimes, he had to fight, and he killed them straight out. The lights always went off just as a pack of zombies came into sight, and Talbert quickly learned that whoever was being cheap with the power was playing a game. Light to lure him out of hiding. Dark just before the gimps tried to eat him. Sometimes, Donald stalked about with his bow. In a short time, Talbert learned where the rotundas were and sections where a person could stand on the second and third floors and gaze down into the first. His armor had saved his ass from Donald's arrows three times already.

"Donald usually stayed up here, and I couldn't find a way up. The staircases were all shut off. Only reason I got up to the second floor was by getting a fancy cord cut from a length of curtain, tying it off around the hilt of the machete, and spearing that through the posts of the railing and hauling my ass up and over. Only way. Up here, there's pretty much nothing, and the stairways to the third level are boarded up as well. Tried going through one of them barricades, but the racket brought the dead on my ass, and in the end, I couldn't break through—not with what I have here. Tried to find another way out, but . . ."

Talbert shrugged.

"We can't get out?" Gus clarified.

"I haven't found it. This place is ratproof, bro. We're safe up here, but for how long I don't know. And . . ."

He trailed off, smiling weakly. "I don't think I've ever been more hungry in all my life. You didn't happen to bring anything to eat, did you?"

For all his dislike of the man, Gus felt a moment's pity when he shook his head and saw the hope drain from Talbert's features.

"Sorry," Gus said. "Wasn't prepared for this. Didn't even think there'd be any gimps still walking by this point."

"Must be the floors or something. Not as rough as scuffing along pavement."

"Maybe."

"Searched the kitchen and pantry down below. Nothing. The cupboards were bare."

"And we can't get up to the third?"

"Not yet. Maybe with you here, we can figure something out."

Gus nodded. "Maybe."

"Don't know how much good I'll be to you. I'm pretty much spent. Must be the tension or something, burning up calories. Surprised myself when I pulled your ass up from below."

"Who's doing the screaming?"

Talbert cocked an eye at him. "Below? Hate to say it—I think it's Benny."

"Benny?"

"Donald caught him or something. Didn't let the gimps have him. Anyway, I think it's Benny. Been listening to that for the last day or so. Deeper in the house, in a part I'm staying away from because they seem to migrate there when the screaming starts. It's like . . . you know how hunters will use duck and deer calls? To lure critters in?"

"Yeah?"

"I think that's Benny. Think Donald's keeping him alive long enough to use him as a fuckin' morbid duck call."

"To draw the gimps away from the door?"

Talbert nodded. "And to sucker us into going after Benny."

That straightened Gus up on the bed. "Jesus."

"Yeah. It's like that."

Benny wasn't one of Gus's favorite people simply from association with Talbert, but knowing the man might be being used as bait soured his sensibilities.

"So then," Talbert said. "You're all caught up. We're stuck here until we can figure a way out or we both starve. Wouldn't hold out on the starving, though. Donald knows we're up here, so I expect he'll be along shortly."

"Then it's two against one."

"Maybe," Talbert acknowledged, but his expression wasn't so confident.

"You don't seem so sure."

"Well," he said after a bit, "thing is—"

"*I trust you gentlemen are resting up?*" a gravelly voice inquired eerily through the walls, causing both Gus and Talbert to jump as if icy hands had cupped their testicles.

7

The disembodied voice paused for a moment, allowing Gus and Talbert to creep to the main door of the bedroom.

"Step out into the hallway where I can see you," the voice continued with crisp, cultured enunciation. The speaker volume lessened.

"Fuck that," Gus muttered. Talbert nodded agreement.

"I applaud your resilience, gentlemen. Most succumb to the zombies of the house. Otherwise, Donald cleans up. One of you, the one wearing the military-grade armor, has actually broken the record for longest period of survival on the first floor. That's quite an achievement, considering the history. You've been duly noted in my journal—an honorable mention, if you will."

Gus cracked open the door to the dimmed hallway and scanned the ceiling, feeling the moody oppression of the place.

"Who are you?" he yelled.

"Ah," the voice sighed. "I'm the owner."

"Mortimer?"

"Ahhh, you know of me."

"Heard a few stories." Though the voice sounded clearer, Gus couldn't locate a camera.

"Are you from Digby?"

"Annapolis."

"I see. I actually visited that small city once, unannounced. Incognito. One benefit of electing a recluse's existence—the common folk fail to recognize you upon making appearances. Annapolis. What a miserable, self-indulgent mash of second-tier industry and misplaced elitism, sprouting from soil drenched in weekend alcoholic binging, academic malaise, and an eroding military presence—an unlikely economic synergy that refused to perish. Astonishing, really. Even more so when all those quaint little towns amalgamated. Town pride and all that."

Talbert's *what the fuck?* expression said it all.

"Well, in any case . . . gentlemen, you've forced me to play my hand."

"Why?" Gus demanded, scanning the hallway.

"What do you mean 'why?'"

"Why are you doing this?"

"*Why?*" the voice repeated, incredulous. "Why *not?* In the absence of a police body, one must defend one's property. To be perfectly blunt, you're trespassing. And neither you nor your surviving companion have been the first to violate my home. If being besieged by the undead wasn't deplorable enough, you can't possibly imagine how . . . displeased I felt to discover that the remnants of humanity had, in effect, taken some self-deluded high moral ground and believed anything was up for the taking—especially a self-contained, self-sufficient dwelling such as my manor and the lands surrounding it. This piece of honeyed real estate drew clouds of human flies, who weren't at all responsive to my attempts of dissuasion. In fact, like petulant children, they couldn't fathom *why* I refused them entry into my domicile. Can you believe it? I never associated with any of them during the preceding, lethargic juncture reached by civilization, so what would propel me to do so in the apocalypse, at the very height of barbarism? Humanity? Oh, they pleaded that point until it bled. And when I still refused, well, the subsequent acts of vandalism and violence only confirmed my suspicions of their uncivil and barbarous nature. Their myopic crabbiness served only to strengthen my resolve to forever distance myself from the surviving, warring populace.

"There was one problem, however. More and more of these desperate refugees, armed to the teeth in some cases, became the law unto themselves. Self-proclaimed pillars of the community, braying righteousness, willing to do whatever was necessary to protect their children, courteous one moment, infuriated and frothing at the jowls the very next. Every group that stopped on my doorstep seemed more willing than the last to resort to violence in order to gain entry into the kingdom. It actually started to amuse me to see how a simple refusal could not be processed—how a blunt 'Go away' let slip the dogs of war. Scenes I never thought probable manifested themselves right on my very doorstep, all because I *had* and they didn't, thus, they would *take*. And take by force. Humanity."

The word bubbled with loathing.

"In the first year of the apocalypse, sheer *spectacles* of depravity and violence played themselves out on my doorstep. People had reverted to their baser instincts, their covetous nature. Entirely id, you see, labeled by the rather ambiguous term of *survival*. I eventually recognized that the solution to dissuading these packs of roving Huns was right before my eyes."

At the abrupt space of silence, neither Gus nor Talbert had the capacity to say a word.

"The *dead*, you see," Mortimer purred. "For is not the enemy of my enemy my friend? Dealing with the dead was far more preferable and, dare I say, palatable to denying the living. The remnants of the Digby populace only had to be persuaded to relocate to the estate, an undertaking my employees took upon themselves."

Employees? Gus mouthed to Talbert, who made an incredulous face and shrugged.

"Trusted men and women with years of service," Mortimer continued. "Of course, I allowed their families to exist underneath my roof. But these raiding, unaccepting, ill-tempered . . . *fuckers* waged war on my people. Just couldn't take no for an answer. In the absence of a cohesive body of law and order, they reverted to their base urges. Cursed us, cursed *me* when they forced me to dire measures, whereupon I summoned a festering and famished flood of undead to cleanse my property of the hateful living. And that was only the first year. A *year*, you must understand. To witness firsthand how quickly civil order dissolved was more horrifying than anything you might have witnessed or experienced in your years out there, among the unliving. In time, after modifications to the house had been completed, I permitted my defenders entry inside my walls, provided them with shelter under my roof. It's been an admirable, dare I say, mutually beneficial relationship, you see. They protect us, and we provide them with . . . sustenance."

On that cue, a pitiful scream drifted from deep within the haunted corridors.

"Over the years, fewer people came here," the voice continued, "but their proclivity for violence increased. Monstrous battles were fought inside these walls as it became apparent the best solution to dealing with any scavenger coveting the property was simply to . . . open the front door. Allow them to waltz inside and be dealt with in a manner you've already experienced firsthand."

"Just let us go," Gus pleaded. "We won't come back."

Talbert's back noticeably stiffened at the words.

The voice cut in. "Heard that one before. You must realize, I've heard *every* promise there is, when in truth, the only one ever kept has been my own. I was never this coldhearted, please understand. In the beginning, some parties left the grounds, but they returned almost always in force, sometimes under different leadership, seeking to enter these premises with deadly force. How often must I grant leniency until I recognize the futility? Before I'm perceived as a gullible fool? The answer? Not often at all. Human nature isn't that unpredictable under duress. No. I am what I am because those who've come before you *made* me this way."

The gnashing of teeth around that word was unmistakable.

"What about Donald then?"

"What about him?"

"What's up with the hunting gear?"

"Ahhh." A smile accompanied the sound. "After the harvests and during the winters, the creature comforts here that we so fervently protect are all that we have, you see. Boredom *will* find you, eventually, and sink its dreary fangs deep into your throat. What my boys do to amuse themselves is entirely up to them. One paints, well enough to bamboozle our captive guests, much to our mutual amusement. Otherwise, I have no influence on their impulses, as they have none upon mine. Donald ascertained, rather correctly I might add, that stragglers such as yourselves could survive quite a while upon the first floor, even dangerously exhausting our supply of corpses. Thus, he took it upon himself to root out any of the more stubborn guests. In time, how he did this duty evolved, as you've already seen, to a more . . . *sporting* event. Simply put, the boy's just having *fun*."

"That's fucked up," Gus whispered.

"My sentiments exactly," Mortimer agreed eagerly. "But I must insist, my staff and I are *not* the villains in this story. We never were. We are the *defenders* of our castle, whereas you and the ilk before you are the invaders. Usually, our uninvited guests perish upon the hunting grounds of the first floor. Can you imagine my dismay at discovering rats had managed to climb into the *belfry*? I applaud you both on your resourcefulness. Those before you succumbed to fear, weakness, madness, or all three in the end. I can guarantee measures will be taken to ensure no one will find refuge upon the second floor ever again. In one way, I must thank you for revealing the flaws in our designs. You've forced us to consider recourses we've never needed to consider in the past."

"Well, fuck me," Gus muttered.

"Oh, he's a winner, all right," Talbert said.

"No, I mean . . ." Gus stared him in the eye. "I mean I understand *exactly* where the old bastard's coming from."

Talbert appeared shocked as if slapped. His face darkened. "You fuckin' *agree* with this piece of shit?"

"Not agreeing—just understanding, is all."

"There's a difference?"

"Course there's a difference, y'goddamn moron."

Talbert cautioned Gus with an unfriendly look.

Then the unmistakable buzz of a chainsaw cut in.

8

That vicious whine rendered both men speechless. A second later, the angry drone spiked in pitch as the chainsaw's teeth met resistance.

"Sweet fucking monkey balls," Talbert swore.

Gus agreed.

"We'll kill anyone you send up here, man," Talbert shouted over the chainsaw's fury.

But Mortimer was gone. Or at least no longer responding.

"What's he cutting?" Gus asked Talbert.

"Something nearby, by the sounds of it."

"Where's the stairs?"

"The closest?"

"Yeah, the closest."

"All right."

Pushing past Gus, Talbert threw the bedroom door open and walked out into the white-carpeted hall, the barest light frosting the fabric like a polar bear's scruff. Ornate tables displayed vases of black woods and small wooden chests. Alabaster nymphs spilling milk from buckets occupied shallow niches. Grand paintings of sweeping landscapes lined the walls between. All were intact, untouched.

The chainsaw paused, the echo lingering through the house.

Then it bit again.

They speed-walked down the corridor before turning left, passing doorways, glimpsing sensuous, bare-timber-beam bedrooms. The sound of the chainsaw grew. Talbert stopped at the head of a wide staircase descending to the first floor. A solid-looking wall of heavy planks barricaded the stairs halfway down, measured and boarded up to near perfection, keeping the undead at bay.

Gus knew he'd seen this before but from the other side.

The chainsaw's head cut through that wall separating the first and second floors in a projectile spray of wood chips. The chainsaw pushed inward, working with saw-dust fury, before being pulled out of sight, and Gus realized light was tracing around a huge door-sized cut in the barricade.

A heavy boot dislodged the lower part of the cut slab with a loud *whump*, tilting it inward. Work-gloved fingers clasped the upper end and pulled it down with a squeal. More sawdust billowed. The section came free in a clatter.

A large man, bare chested and heavily muscled, stepped into the opening, wearing a skirt of leather that might have been a butcher's apron, a chainsaw held at his waist. Empty bandoliers crisscrossed his chest while shoulder pads of spikes covered his shoulders. Sweat shone upon his muscular frame, glazed with dust, but the thing that disturbed both Gus and Talbert the most wasn't the outfit. It was the shining Japanese Noh mask hiding his face.

One subtle alteration marred the mask. Battlements of crooked teeth filled its open mouth, the corners hinting at an evil smile. Half-moon eyes, wide and brimming with perverse blackness, stared unblinking at the two men.

Then, at some unheard cue, the imposing figure stepped out of sight.

"Holy *shit*," Talbert whispered, already backing away.

Gus held on a little longer until he saw the dead shuffling into view. First, it was a single set of feet, then lower legs, then a viscous, tidal seepage of bodies, some hunkered over, some tall, and none of them crawling. The sound of all those feet, dragging across a fortune of marble seconds ahead of the gut-turning stink of flesh soon to follow, rode the air currents like a colorless, debilitating membrane. The mass converged on the hole in the wall, and the sight of them made Gus back up two steps, wishing he was back on the farm, smelling brewing tea instead, underneath a night sky all aglitter.

"Let's boot," Talbert yelled, slapping his companion's back.

"We could fight here," Gus said, pointing to the hole. "That's a bottleneck."

"Too wide, bro."

"Where'd that—"

"I'm going!" Talbert shouted and jogged away. Gus divided his attention between the breech in the wall below and Talbert's fleeing back. The gimps ascended the stairs, worming through the hole three abreast as if under pressure. One stumbled, and three followed in a domino effect. The dead behind the fallen struggled over them.

Gus hefted his bat, struck the pose, hesitated, and then rushed after Talbert.

He chased the man down another wide corridor, rounded a grand archway of fitted stone, and saw Talbert standing at a rail, gazing out over an open space. Sofa chairs lay arranged around a fine-looking glass table while towering potted greenery, which had to be imitation, adorned the whole area, creating the illusion of a piece of captured jungle.

Talbert regarded Gus and pointed with his machete.

Checking on their pursuers, Gus stopped beside his only companion and balked at what lay below.

An underground cavern draped in earth tones stretched out before them, an enormous indoor grotto dominated by an Olympic-sized swimming pool in its center. Moody shores of fabricated sands ringed the entire scene, with cone-shaped stalagmites rising around it and stalactites hanging from above, a few of which even connected, creating emaciated pillars. Drooping greenery filled the corners, bestowing unnecessary shade upon daybeds, single chairs, and boat-drink, patio-size tables.

That was all peripheral.

What lay *inside* that fabricated vision shocked the two men into near paralysis.

Zombies.

Zombies choked the pool's depths, like an ill-kept flower bed of rotten animation. The undead swayed against each other like undersea flora caught in deep-sea tides, wailing, mesmerized by the fact they couldn't escape the pool's depths. One end, the shallow part near Gus and Talbert, had a wooden barrier that clashed with the cavern's ambience but effectively kept the zombies trapped there. Only the heads and hands were visible. The pool sloped into a deep end, and the height of the dead slanted with it to a point where the black and gray-headed figures near the bottom couldn't reach the sandy edges.

But that was only half the horror.

Suspended by a system of ropes and metal poles, just beyond the edge of a diving board, hung Benny by his hands. They had stripped him of all clothing, and his bare white ass faced the two men. His bare feet dangled not six feet above the deep end, where a ghastly array of pasty white arms, bare hands, and fingers weakly clawed for his out-of-reach toes like a ravenous carpet.

"Oh, Jesus Christ," Gus whispered, stunned by the scene. He'd thought he'd seen all manner of zombie collections over the years, but perhaps he'd simply told himself that to prepare himself for the sights yet undiscovered. Whoever had captured Benny had strung him up like a prisoner about to be made to talk, but instead of sharks, a more sinister fate awaited.

Something mechanical crackled to life, and Benny was lowered toward the pool, much to the delight of the trapped zombies. The pool became a nest of clutching and upturned faces. Benny's descent was torturously slow, long enough for him to awaken and whine in mindless terror, a sound a trapped animal might make.

Both Gus and Talbert recognized Benny's petrified vocals. Gus cursed his leaving the farm, thinking he should never have given in to Adam and Maggie. It was far better to live being perceived as an ungrateful prick than to witness Benny's execution.

"Those fucking sonsabitches," Talbert swore, practically vibrating with his inability to save his friend. "What can we do?"

That flummoxed Gus. What could they do? He studied the sandy poolside below, where the ropes and winch were moored.

"I want you to see this," Mortimer's voice spoke around them, the eagerness in his voice unmistakable. "You *need* to see this."

"You shit-lubed sonofabitch," Talbert swore, looking toward the ceiling. "You realize what you're doing?"

"Of *course* I do." Mortimer chuckled. "We've conducted this exact execution at least a dozen times before. I must confess it is true what they say, you never quite forget your first time. Now, while there is a sublime stirring of excitement, I do find myself becoming rather . . . detached from the spectacle. Like a person who's seen the ending to the same movie repeatedly. I've become desensitized to the pleadings, the . . . the feedings. The horror has been reduced to, say, the equivalent of a child tearing the legs off a grasshopper."

"Talbert!" Benny screeched, twisting, peeking over his shoulder. "*Talbert!* Oh Christ, man, *do* something!"

"He *is* doing something," Mortimer pointed out, sounding puzzled with the man's request. "He's watching. Watching what the Hollywood establishment might label 'torture porn,' I believe."

"I'll fuckin' torture porn your ass," Talbert swore. "I'll pile-drive a red-hot poker up your shit chute. And when your ring hole's fuckin' fused around that piece of iron, I'll yank it out and do it again."

Mortimer's growing laughter boomed across the cavern's pool, a phlegmy rattle that agitated the zombies even more.

Then, at the distant end of the grotto, a familiar figure appeared with bow in hand. The Korean Mask stared up at the human onlookers.

"Ah, Donald's arrived," Mortimer choked out, attempting to control his laughter. "Just to ensure nothing happens on your end."

Talbert brandished the machete, looking to hack a head.

Benny wailed hysterically, thrashing against his bonds and swinging, his wavering feet not a meter above the teeming pool.

"C'mon," Gus said and turned away.

"You will *not*," Mortimer warned, his voice cold. "You will *watch*, else . . ."

With that, the rope spun out in a lick of sinewy heat, and Benny plummeted to within a foot of the nearest set of hooked fingers. The man freaked, lifting his knees to his stomach.

"*Don't!*" Talbert screamed.

"Move anywhere, and I will finger the controls to drop him. Straight down."

"You're going to fuckin' kill him anyway!" Gus shouted over the ravenous chorus and Benny's screeching.

"Yes. I am. I am. But in the moments *prior* to his death, before that mind-freezing instance where the first finger grazes a bare toe, then the bottom of the foot, the ankle—grabbing it in a graveyard death clench. Pulling the rest of him down into that festering morass where others can touch, can . . . *grip*. And then, that first exquisite *bite*—every bit as electric and brain blowing as, say, slamming a car door on your finger. The head being thrown back, the sounds as one's flesh is devoured. In slow, gnawing mouthfuls. *That's* what I want you to behold. To experience. As fucking *penance* for ever driving up my lane and believing you could trespass on my property."

With another lurch of the rope, Benny shrieked as he plummeted, his toes dipping into that wiggling surface of fingers. The contact made him jerk his limbs back up to his belly, as if he were performing a midair crunch.

"*TALLLLLLBERRRRRT!*"

Hearing his name, the man slumped to his knees, eyes bulging helplessly. He pulled back his machete arm to throw it, but Gus stopped him.

"No," he said to Talbert's broken face. "That's not going to do a damn thing."

"*TALLLLLLBERRRRRT!*"

And then a new sound, a chainsaw starting up once again, chewing into the evil hide of the house, caused both men to look over their shoulders.

"Yessss," Mortimer purred. "Life goes on. And walls must fall. Stephanie has been instructed to continue releasing the hounds. Flood the second floor. Part of why I wish you to see your friend's demise. The upper floors had never been breached until you little shit stains came along. You see—you see I mean to catch *you* as well. Catch you and sling you up, cock swinging and bare assed like your squealing little piggy friend there, maybe even headfirst this time, or one will be headfirst while the other one hangs by his fingers, feeling every bone snap as your own body weight pulls the joints apart."

"*Apart!*" Mortimer screamed into the microphone. "*While the other one has his fucking eyes chewed out!*"

Gus gripped Talbert's shoulder but got pushed away. He stumbled back a step and saw the approaching shadows emerging from the corridor, creeping along like intrepid explorers of an undiscovered country, lipless grins blazing.

Never should have left the farm. Gus swore, taking up his bat.

Overhead, Mortimer babbled on with his hateful rant, leaving no doubt in Gus's mind the man's brain had long since short fused. Crazy bastard could be shitting in his own hand and writing on the walls, for all Gus knew.

"*Talbert! Oh, Jesus! NONONONOOOOOOAHHHHH!*"

Gus swung at an undead workman dressed in a blood-caked T-shirt and jeans. The bat crumpled the workman's skull and spattered moldy jelly against the far wall. As it dropped to its knees, Gus hammered another brainpan, mashing it into its shoulders and skewing its fleshless jaws into a weird V. Arms reached for him, and he swatted them away with a series of swings, angling himself toward the unobstructed corridor on the other side of the lounge area. Benny howled in the background, pausing only long enough to reload his lungs. Unimaginable agony turned his words into a blaring siren.

Mortimer continued insisting that Talbert and Gus watch, *watch* how trespassers were punished in this part of the world, actually swearing at them to look, vowing even more disturbing punishment once they were caught.

"Talbert!" Gus roared, roundhousing a gimp and removing its jaw in a burst of rubbery flesh. "*Talbert!*"

Talbert retreated from the railing, offering a glimpse of Benny being lowered into that chilling vat of death, head thrashing on his shoulders while his vocal cords frayed. Gus didn't want to imagine what happened first—Benny's legs tired, and he had to lower them into that nest of mouths and claws, or he just kept being lowered until the zombies took him whole.

Mortimer screamed, all civility gone from his voice, cursing the two men as they smashed and chopped their way through attacking deadheads. Talbert sided with Gus, and together they retreated from the oncoming front of undead. The foremost of the zombies tripped and fell over their headless brethren, revealing the corridor behind them choked wall-to-wall with shadows.

The lights went out.

And Mortimer *screeched* into the microphone like the singer in a death-metal band stuck in a rage, a madman's squawking, oddly in sync with the furious song of the chainsaw. The corridor walls shook with the aural warfare, unnerving Gus.

"I'm gonna rip that old fucker's nutsack off," Talbert swore in the dark.

"I'll hold him down," Gus vowed, flipping up his visor so he might see a little better in the decadent tomb. They fumbled along, passing open doors, and scampered up a short flight of steps before heading through another stone archway into a midnight-black living room. Talbert ran around outlines of plush recliners and crystal coffee tables, toward an archway on the far wall.

Then he halted. Gus drew up beside him.

The chainsaw had stopped.

Mortimer had ceased his caterwauling.

Poor Benny, however, did not stop. His death cries sounded fainter in the distance, delirious, almost completely dunked into that tank of dead limbs, open mouths fastening onto Benny's naked flesh.

Gus shook himself free of the image.

"They're coming," Talbert said, looking back. Gus glanced one way and then the other, trying to hear.

"You sure on that?"

Talbert's dark features faced him. "Oh shit, yeah. That bastard with the chainsaw opened up another stairway."

"You can hear them?"

Talbert's shadowy head nodded. The man was holding it together better than expected, and for that Gus was grateful.

"Oh shit, *run*," Talbert barked, leaping through the archway and bolting to the right. "Follow me," he called out.

Gus intended to do just that, but the house interior was nearly black. He crashed into a table, kicked a fallen vase, and hit a low-hanging arch with his shoulder. Talbert turned a corner, and when Gus followed, he saw another railing of squat columns, another set of stairs, and a teeming black gush of bodies pulling themselves through a new hole, staining the dull glow of dreamy white.

"Flooding the upstairs, all right," Gus observed.

"Yeah, but I know something," Talbert said and half smiled. "I know where another set of stairs are. This way."

As they hurried along, barely navigating the hallways, Talbert explained. "While I was here, I did get some exploring done. Fuckhead Morty can't completely board up the rotunda, and that's where the staircase rings the walls right up to the third level."

"So?"

"So? Chainsaw Steffy is on his way there now And I'm betting he'll be delayed by whatever dead fucker's still below hunting for us."

They passed through halls, dens, and even kitchenettes until they raced through a dim gallery lined with landscape paintings. The far wall opened into the majestic space of the rotunda, a design of metal and glass stolen straight out of a fairy-tale ballroom. Above, night sparkled, seen through vast panes of glass somehow molded into the cavernous dome Gus had seen from outside the mansion. No shutters barred the heavens from above. An eerie marble staircase with elegant pillars coiled upward along the walls, seemingly glowing in the low light, to end at the topmost level. Narrow archways were evenly spaced apart on the first level, branching into halls that led to mystery.

"Wait," Talbert said, reaching in behind the chest plates of his armor. He pulled out a fancy rope. "I cut this off a window. Used it to haul myself up to the second level here."

He tied one end off around his waist and offered the other to Gus. "Take this."

"And what?"

"What are you doing?" Mortimer's suspicious voice clicked overhead.

The two men ignored him. Talbert glanced back the way they'd come. "Get down there and stop that masked fuck from sawing open those barriers and letting more zombies up here."

"How many are in this place?"

Talbert shook his head. "I'm figuring we all must've put down a hundred so far, and more keep showing up. He must have a goddamn reserve stashed away."

"Stephanie, they're at the rotunda," Mortimer's voice barked. "It looks as if they're going to leap back down."

"Noisy bastard," Gus growled and looped the cord around his waist. "Don't you cut that rope," he warned as he slung himself over the railing.

"Fuck you gonna do about it? *Sayonara*, fat ass."

With that, Talbert stepped forward and shoved Gus, dislodging him from the rails and sending him swinging into space.

9

Gus yelped as his body maxed out the short drop and swung inward, the cord tightening around his midsection, tipping his upper body back as if he were Tarzaning it.

And in that arc, he glimpsed the leather-skirted bulk of the man called Stephanie . . .

Just before his feet crashed into the man's chest.

"*He's here!*" Gus blurted and immediately got dropped to the floor.

Talbert had cut the cord.

Stephanie, in all his ferocious leather attire, limped to his feet just as Gus stood and one-armed his bat, lashing the aluminum across the Noh mask with a satisfying *crack*. Mortimer's stunned henchman stumbled backward against a wall, his mask hanging askew. Stephanie tried to correct his ghostly face while thumbing the electric start button of the chainsaw.

Gus got another hand on his bat and clocked it across his adversary's head a second time, staggering him visibly. The chainsaw clattered onto the marble.

"Donald! To the Rotunda! *Run!*" Mortimer blared across the dome's expanse. "They have Steph! *Run!*"

Taking a deep breath, Gus smashed ol' *Steph* clean across the face again, sending the mask scuttling across the floor. The fourth blow landed flush on the big man's temple, and he collapsed in his leather duds.

Gus reared back for another strike and paused for all of two seconds.

It had been almost two years since he last killed another living person.

And gazing at the freak at his feet, he didn't feel a lick of guilt.

Gus swung the bat over his shoulder and down, breaking Stephanie's skull. The brute collapsed, twitching in a widening pool of maroon.

Undisguised grief and rage cut through the loudspeakers, intense enough to threaten blowing the wiring. Gus flinched at the sound.

"*I'll kill you,*" Mortimer frothed in a rattling voice. "*I'll kill you. I'll nail your bleeding ass to a table and keep you like a pet! I'll make your death as slow and painful as—*"

Gus tuned out the rest and glanced around the empty rotunda. A pair of legs appeared from the second floor, and Talbert lowered himself with a grunt.

"The fuck you do?" he asked as he got his feet under himself.

"Killed a bitch."

Talbert straightened and inspected Stephanie's bulk. "One fucked-up bitch."

"And the way Mort's screaming, you'd think it was his son."

"Maybe it was."

"If it was," Gus said, gathering up the chainsaw with his free hand, "maybe he'll rupture something while screaming his nuts off."

Talbert's features scrunched in disdain.

"I'll give him a couple of things to scream about," Gus vowed, brandishing the chainsaw in one hand and pointing at the dead man nearby. "That's one."

"That's one," Talbert agreed.

"Feel like gettin' the others?"

"Oh, fuck, yeah."

"Watch my back, then," Gus ordered and went to the wide stairs and the first barrier there.

He placed his bat to one side and powered up the chainsaw, thumbing the start button.

"Startin' to think," Gus said as he braced his legs on the stairs, "that cutting through these barriers is a good thing. Why should we have all the fun?"

Talbert's face lightened with comprehension, but before the buzzing saw snarled into wood, he pointed to the second level and a crowd gathering around the railing. A knot of zombies descended the steps, only to be stopped by the wooden barricade.

Gus saw them all and powered down the chainsaw.

"Well, shit."

Zombies pushed against the upstairs rail. Several toppled over and fell to the marble floor with a sludgy *clap*, like sacks of wet cement bursting at rotten seams. All manner of organic muck squirted from the corpses upon impact, a viscous soup reeking of spoiled meat. A pool slowly formed, spreading outward with every new diver splattering upon the fine marble. Some crashed upon the ones actually rising from the expanding mess.

They continued piling against the rails, leaning over until gravity sucked them down.

Gus prodded Talbert in the shoulder, pushing him to the lower steps.

"Get into the open," he said, "let 'em see you."

"What?"

"Just a few seconds, anyway. They're thinning themselves out."

Upon the rotunda's floor, bodies pushed through that foul stew like half-frozen tadpoles. Some of the dead sat up straight in the deepening pond of bodies, ignoring broken bones, only to have new corpses flatten them from above. Talbert descended and split the skull of one uniformed serviceman, halting its creeping progress. He placed his boot heel against its shoulder and wrenched the machete free. A hand reached out from the sloppy pileup of corpses, trying for an ankle. Talbert hacked the hand off, blade ringing off the floor.

The dead wailed at the living. Their voices carried to the upper dome, making it known through the house that fresh meat had been found.

Gus dropped the chainsaw, took up his bat, and joined Talbert. He bashed limbs and heads as if he were flattening wheat beside a pond of industrial filth. One zombie, a white-dressed maid with the front saturated in gore, actually climbed to her feet and walked toward them both, lipless jaws chattering. Gus smoked her across the face, and her remaining features disintegrated in a chunky burst.

But she didn't drop. Despite having her entire sinus cavity laid bare and displaying squashed organic tissue Gus had no clue of, she walked on, arms raised, dainty hands ending in peeled fingers.

Gus hesitated at the fright.

Then Talbert's machete split the deadhead's noggin to the eyes. "Recognize someone, didja?"

He kicked the corpse off his blade. Gus composed himself as the rain of bodies slowed. At a glance, it appeared most of the dead had fallen in crippled heaps.

He realized then that Mortimer had ceased screaming.

Zombies spilled out of the archways on the ground floor.

"All right," Gus barked and bounded up the stairs. "Keep them back."

He left Talbert and switched out his bat for the battery-powered chainsaw. The tool came to life with one jab of its electric start button, and Gus cut wide across the top of the wooden barricade. Chips and dust flew into his face, making him pause to slap his visor into place. Talbert chopped and hacked, slowing the mansion's residents.

Gus completed the first cut in less than fifteen seconds, pulled the saw free of the thick wood, and finished a pair of downward strokes in an equal amount of time. The chainsaw had surprising power, and Gus wondered how much juice remained in the rig after gnawing through those sturdy planks. At the end of his final stroke, he pulled the blade out and laid a boot to the wood, kicking the slab free of its remaining fibers.

"Talbert!" Gus shouted and buzzed into the head of a straggler gimp just on the other side of the wall.

Talbert stood not three steps behind him, up to his knees in a growing wall of corpses. Pale faces gleamed under the dome, the only flickers of light in a haunting mob of outlines.

"You made the hole big enough!" Talbert yelled, clipping his shoulder on his way through.

"It's called a fuckin' *bottleneck*, y'moron! Hold them there while I cut through the next one."

With that, Gus retrieved his bat and sprinted up the curving stairs, the thick layers of his suit steaming him. A few zombies crossed his path on the second-floor landing, forcing him to choose between his two weapons.

He dropped the bat.

There was a feral glee in applying the chainsaw's whirling teeth to decomposing flesh, but the ferocious back spatter quickly blinded his visor, and he realized it wasn't the weapon of choice. He tossed the chainsaw, spent precious seconds wiping his visor clean, and slapped it up.

He picked up his bat at the edge of the stairs and cracked two remaining gimps.

Then he hoofed it toward the third landing and the wooden wall barring passage halfway up the stairs.

The lights came back on, illuminating everything.

Farther behind, Talbert cringed at the blinding light, still chopping at anything piling through the opening in the first barrier. More dead things shambled into the killing floor of the rotunda, fully revealed, enough to send a chill of worry through the man. He chopped the head off another handyman-type deadhead. An arm reached for him. He hacked it off with one cut, flash-exposing a black cross-section of the forearm. Another zombie squirmed through, its torso slick with slime. It slipped on the stairs and fell.

Talbert crushed the head under a boot heel.

The chainsaw buzzed above, chewing into a wall and distracting him. A zombie hit his chest, driving him back, and he fell hard against the stairs. His unprotected head bounced against an edge. Another gimp slicked through the breach, its face grimy and skeletal, reaching for him.

Talbert tried to move and discovered, with a doped rush of fear, his limbs were responding with a hypothermic sluggishness. A hand wreathed in tatters of skin and musculature pawed at his thigh, nails clawing into armor plating, discovering sections covered only in denim. Fingers sloughed over straps and buckles, digging into jeans . . .

Grunting, Talbert held the machete across his chest and pushed the blade forward, scalping the gimp's soft skull as if shaving a sliver of cheese off a stubborn block. Each cut lifted the zombie's head. He kept cutting, his senses slowly leveling out, feeling fingers clutching at his upper thighs. More zombies squeezed through the glut at the opening in a horrid bloom. Some fell onto his lower legs, squashing the deadhead's fingers for valuable seconds Talbert needed to push the head back and stab the machete underneath the chin, up into the brain.

The creature's death-grinning face flopped into his crotch, and Talbert had never felt more grateful for a protective cup than at that exact moment.

Grimacing, he kicked free of the oozing bodies, flipped onto his hands and knees, and crawled away from the stalled bottleneck.

Then something kicked him in his side, plastering him against the wall.

Pain robbed him of his breath, and for several seconds, he fixated on an arrow sticking out just above his hip, where the plates of his body armor were kept in place by straps.

Blood seeped from the wound, dark and precious.

Grimacing, Talbert looked toward the second floor and saw no one, hearing only the buzzing of Gus's chainsaw somewhere above. The zombies still crawled through the hole in the barrier, reaching for him on the stairs.

Clenching teeth, Talbert tried getting to his feet, feeling how the arrow moved inside, and blinked against the flashing black motes before his eyes. He glanced toward the rotunda floor.

There, seen through the posts of the staircase, stood Donald.

The archer had taken up position inside an archway, his Korean mask smiling pleasantly.

Aiming another arrow.

Donald released, and Talbert twisted to escape—not fast enough, however, as the arrow spiked his left thigh, grazing bone and jacking nerves as if zapped by a live wire. Talbert gripped his leg. A missile sizzled toward his face, and he ducked while reflexively lifting his left hand to protect his head. The shaft perforated his palm with a shocking *whump*, the impact twisting him off balance. Talbert cried out and dropped onto his belly, seeing the barbless point of the arrow sticking clean through the meat of his palm. Whimpering, he gripped the shaft and pulled five inches free with a grunt and a spurt of gore.

Something grabbed his foot.

"*Fuck off,*" Talbert said and instinctively tried to kick with his wounded leg—a shot of hot agony lanced through his entire side, paralyzing him for seconds.

Enough time for a deadhead's hands to grasp his knees.

Gasping, Talbert flipped onto his back and booted the zombie's face with his good leg, squashing the dead thing's features. He kicked twice more, removing the head from the zombie's shoulders. The victory was short-lived as a stream of gimps oozed through the opening in the barrier, slipping over each other like buttered worms.

They crawled toward Talbert.

Grimacing, Talbert pushed himself up the stairs, dragging the boneless rubber of his leg and leaving thick blots of blood on the staircase. He glanced toward Donald and grunted a laugh at seeing the archer fighting off a handful of attackers.

A zombie stood up from the scrimmage of undead creeping after Talbert. Another gimp rolled over and hit the standing deadhead's leg, jostling it against the wall. The zombie righted itself and walked up the stairs. The thing had no eyes, and a long ribbon of skin, from its bottom lip to its Adam's apple, had been ripped away. It floundered after Talbert. Unseeing eye cavities fixed on him, picking up his location by either smell or hearing or some unknown sense bestowed upon the undead. The monster stepped on another zombie, pinning it to the steps.

The blind gimp reared its head up as if hearing something and reached for Talbert's retreating ankle.

Talbert peeked over his shoulder at the thing, hearing a pneumonic wheeze escaping its chest.

Then in a flash, the zombie's head burst apart with a grisly pop.

"C'mon," Gus shouted, aluminum bat in hand. He hooked Talbert's armpits and got him to his feet.

"He got me," Talbert winced.

"In the side, right?"

"And the leg. Hand."

"Goddamn shooting gallery here," Gus grumped, looking in Donald's direction as he lugged the bleeding man up the stairs. Talbert stumbled and almost pulled his rescuer off his feet.

An arrow screamed into the wall behind them, embedding its head deep.

Another one punched Gus square in the shoulder, dropping him to his knees and causing him to spill Talbert.

"Christ," Gus gasped, feeling as if he'd been jabbed with a prong.

"He's getting another one ready," Talbert said and flattened on the stairs. Gus placed his body between the wounded man and the archer, set his jaw, and hauled him along by his armpits, past the landing. Talbert cringed as he threw his arm around Gus's neck. Together, they stood and staggered up the staircase until they made it through the hole cut into the third barrier.

No arrows came from Donald.

Gus ignored the stairway continuing to the fourth floor and instead dragged Talbert down a polished corridor basking in warm, angelic light. They ducked inside a bedroom where night could be seen through unshuttered windows. Gus carried his bleeding companion to the bed and dumped him on a rosy-red duvet, eyeing the adjoining en suite.

Talbert broke into giggles as Gus returned to the bedroom's entrance.

"Fuck's wrong with you?" Gus demanded, closing the door and finding the light switch. Red light illuminated the room, stopping him in his tracks.

Talbert hoisted himself a little farther onto the bed before plopping his head onto a plush, tube-shaped pillow. He lay there, staring at the ceiling for a moment, then smiled and chuckled again.

"You, bro," he gasped between peals of mirth. "You see what you did?"

Gus didn't see. He pulled a recliner toward the door to barricade it.

Talbert's form rattled with another belly laugh, lasting puzzling seconds, before he sighed and stared at the ceiling. "You saved . . . my ass."

Shoving the chair into place but questioning whether it would do much good, Gus regarded the man on the bed.

"Yeah, well, don't get used to it," he said and went to the bathroom. He found some thick white towels and facecloths hanging off metal racks and brought them all back to the wounded man.

"I'm no expert," Gus muttered as he applied a towel to Talbert's leg and side, "but I bet you're wishin' you wore your fuckin' fireman's suit now, eh?"

"Only if . . . I was on a stage . . . wigglin' my ass at the ladies."

"Yeah, right."

Gus drew away the towel and saw the dark bruise soaking it. His innards went cold at the sight of so much blood. He clawed buckles open on the armor plates covering the top of Talbert's leg and flipped them back. He immediately took a long towel and looped it around the thigh, creating a tourniquet.

"Y'know . . . what's funny," Talbert said, his voice becoming slurred. "I . . . I actually wanted to off you. Out here. Make up any story I wanted then."

"Yeah?" Gus said, knotting the towel and drawing a deflated hiss.

"Fuck, man, take it . . . take it easy," Talbert whispered and turned his head toward the windows. "Nice. Nice place."

"Yeah." Gus grabbed another towel and applied it to Talbert's wound above his hip, balking at whether he should remove it or leave it in. He left it in, pressed the cloth around the arrow tightly, and held it there, watching the material slowly bleed dark.

Silence from Talbert, deep and reflective. Then, "Sorry, bro."

Despite his dislike for the man, Gus's throat constricted, which surprised him. He'd gotten used to thinking of Talbert as a piece of shit for so long that . . . that simple, exhausted apology touched a chord within him while the towel around Talbert's wound darkened.

"Nah," Gus rumbled and sniffed, clearing his filling sinuses. "Don't worry about it. Can't say there wasn't a day or two I thought the same thing."

That surprised Talbert enough to lift his head off the pillow. "You wanted to kill me? You treacherous fuck, you."

Gus chuckled then, and Talbert joined him. And for a moment, they shared perhaps the only enjoyable moment they'd ever shared since meeting each other.

"Thanks for pulling me up," Gus muttered. "When you did. You saved me back there."

"Yeah, I did. I saved you first, didn't I?"

"You did. Don't make a thing out of it."

"Gus," Talbert said sleepily, his eyes closing. "You . . . you make them fuckers pay."

Gus didn't have to ask which fuckers.

"Hear. Me . . . ?"

Gus removed his hands and regarded the towel, blinking at the steady seepage of blood.

Time braked then.

A thump came from beyond the bedroom door, but Gus ignored it. Talbert lifted his good hand off the bed. It rose slowly, like a toll bridge being drawn up. Gus clasped the hand and held it tightly, sniffling a little more than he should be. Talbert looked back at the window, blinked once as if terribly sleepy, and closed his eyes.

"Goddamnit," Gus whispered, shaking his head. He couldn't fucking believe he was getting emotional over *him*. "Talbert. Talbert. *Bro.* Don't be . . . don't be a prick here."

But Talbert didn't respond.

When Gus realized the strength had gone from Talbert's hand, he lowered it over the man's belly and gave it a solemn pat.

Another thump demanded attention from outside the door.

Gus rose from the bed, his face a shadow of loss, and regarded the dead man on the duvet. Then he considered his bat.

The anger welled up.

10

Soft mood lighting illuminated the spacious corridor, making the dark baseboard wood and white walls glow with festive warmth. Crystal lamps, worth a fortune to certain collectors, perched on delicate tables and glittered. Paintings of abstract landscapes tastefully covered the walls and begged to be interpreted. A strip of beige carpeting stretched out from the rotunda's archway and traveled the length of this particular wing of the mansion. An ominous trail of blood dappled its cushiony surface, some blotches larger than others, marring the plush highway all the way to a closed door.

A dozen deadheads ambled down this corridor, spaced out in an unintentional hunting pattern, led by sight and, in some of them, smell. Every step they took fouled the pristine carpeting. One zombie nudged a table, and the lamp tumbled to the floor with a startled, glass equivalent of *oh* before shattering in a burst of fine slivers. Another deadhead stumbled into a wall, dragged its shoulder across an out-of-focus cliffside painting, and left a nihilistic barcode of grime. The dead did not care what they fouled with their presence.

They didn't care about much, really.

But when a bedroom door opened not ten strides ahead and a piece of living meat stepped into view, confronting them with a short club, which quickly elongated into a dented bat . . .

The dead cared very much.

They ambled toward this challenger with surprising vigor.

Gus stepped to the middle of the carpet, the overhead glow giving the cathedral-like hall an almost joyful feel. Christmassy. It truly was a beautiful home—fit for a king, an emperor. Talbert had been right about that.

Gus slapped his visor into place and brought up his bat, scowling at the approaching dead.

A real shame to fuck it all up.

The closest deadhead had its entire head slugged from its shoulders. The bony bauble bounced off a resplendent oil painting, rattling the frame. The body of the zombie fell as if the very floor had given out underneath it.

Gus took the legs out from the next gimp, a butler with its uniform in a shameful array of tatters. He crushed the skull under his boot, stomping it twice into the beige carpeting.

Then he tore into the rest.

Perhaps it was perfect spacing or the pace of the attacking deadheads. Maybe it was the lack of numbers or just the familiar grace he'd acquired over the years in combating the undead.

Probably a combination of everything.

Whatever the reason, Gus ripped through the remaining zombies, killing each with devastating accuracy and oftentimes spectacular blows. Skulls exploded in sprays of chalky fragments and spoiled brain matter. Some heads flew from shoulders or simply caved in with a black spatter. Gus marched through the corridor of dead fuckers like a two-legged wrecking ball, destroying each corpse as it entered his range. He never tired, never uttered a single curse, his focus as keen as a surgeon's scalpel. He lined up each decomposing face as it came toward him and smashed it into the next week.

A part of him dearly hoped that Mortimer was watching on his closed-circuit surveillance cameras . . .

And shitting his goddamn diapers.

When the last gimp fell in a dusty tumble, only one figure remained, framed in the archway, wearing what looked like a jumpsuit of white.

Gus's visor muted the glare, but there was no mistaking the grinning face of the Korean mask. Worse, Donald had his bow up, an arrow readied and aimed. A dark eye lined up the visor of Gus's helmet, freezing him in his tracks.

But Donald did not release that steel-tipped shaft.

Instead, he eased off on the draw and lowered the bow. With infinite care, he placed the weapon on the carpet before straightening, his gloved palms facing out in a gesture of *See? I'm unarmed.*

"You must fuckin' think I'm all for fair play or something," Gus seethed and immediately stepped forward, gearing up with the bat.

Donald snapped his right leg up and out, front-kicking Gus in the solar plexus hard enough to propel him back onto his ass, into that nasty carpet broth of spilled headcheese and rancid blood. Gus released the bat and rolled onto his stomach, audibly attempting to draw air into a paralyzed diaphragm. The corridor became a blurred plane, shifting and distorting before reforming. He gasped, wheezed, dragging in air that seemed to cling to his remaining teeth, refusing to go where it was most needed. The bashed head of a gimp resting on its squashed side smiled with inhuman mirth. The whole scene wavered as if Gus had plummeted into deep water. The impulse to get to his feet and defend himself was there, but his body refused to obey, refused to refill on air, panicking him. Donald came into view, fitting metal to his hands, taking his time in adjusting the nightmarish upgrades.

Finally, Gus's lungs allowed a sip of oxygen. It rushed to his brain. He got up and regarded his foe, standing in a martial-art pose, fists held low to his body, his legs spaced apart just a little more than his shoulders. His knuckles shone like chrome nightmares, and it took Gus a moment to realize that old Donald had put on brass knuckles—or at least the equivalent . . .

Complete with spikes.

Grunting, pissed off, Gus stood.

Donald blurred into a spin and slammed his boot heel into the side of Gus's helmet, sending him into the wall. The world went lopsided, spilling him off a flat edge. When he opened his eyes, he was on his back once more. Helmet saved him that time. Puffing and groaning, Gus sat up with the help of an elbow, considered Donald's wide-footed stance, sighed, and shook his head.

"My fuckin' luck. A goddamn ninja."

The smiling mask didn't answer.

Gus climbed to his feet and got his guard up, his head clearing with every second. He stepped toward his adversary, jabbed and missed. Jabbed twice more before swinging a roundhouse for that grinning face. Donald dodged them all and countered with a pulverizing combination of strikes, knuckles machine-gunning Gus's body and head with deadly force.

Gus's visor flew off.

His head got jacked to the right and left.

Each punch tenderized his torso and stuttered him back into the wall—the only thing keeping him up.

Seeing his prey falter, Donald spun and torpedoed his heel into the lower abdomen of his opponent.

Gus dodged it at the last split second, and Donald's foot hammered through the wall, halfway up the shin.

Seizing the opportunity, Gus barreled into the off-balance man, shoving him backward and hearing a yelp of pain from the grinning mask. He punched that smiling face twice, the wooden facade splitting under hard knuckle plates. The third punch torqued Donald's head into the wall. The mask fell, revealing a black ski mask and stunned eyes.

Gus kicked the foot Donald stood upon, and the snow-camouflaged killer dropped awkwardly, his other foot still trapped. Remorseless and remembering every arrow bounced off his ass, Gus stomped on the ski-masked head, repeatedly striking his target until he placed both arms against the wall and didn't bother looking.

When Gus couldn't make Donald any more dead, he backed off, chest heaving, and ignored the mess at the base of the corridor. His chest sore and heaving, Gus looked left and right, saw no other threat, and wearily retrieved his bat from where he'd dropped it. Something drew his attention to the ceiling, where the dark snow cone of a surveillance camera gleamed at him.

"That's two," Gus muttered and walked unhindered to the landing. He peeked around the corner and saw a heap of zombies blocking the opening he'd made in the first barricade. Gimps shuffled along the edges of the rotunda's ground level, but none tried climbing the stairs. He reckoned the corpses he'd just killed were the last few crawling through after Talbert.

The chainsaw lay on the landing, and Gus picked it up, not knowing why but catching a whiff of grand destruction on the air. Tool in hand, he walked away from the rotunda, over the unmoving bodies in the corridor, and followed the carpet to wherever it took him.

<h1 style="text-align:center">11</h1>

The kitchen lay at the end of the hall, just before a set of double doors that opened into a games room. The area reminded him of a few favorite bars back in the days of his youth, when he roamed Annapolis on Friday nights, frequenting two-for-one happy-hour sessions and guzzling his share, making moves on the cutoff-jeans honeys and their tanned legs.

Happier times.

Unlike the vengeful shit he was about to wreak.

Why the hell Mortimer had a fully stocked kitchen on the third floor *before* the zombie apocalypse simply befuddled Gus's commoner's sensibilities. If the old man had foreseen the end of the world, well, that was different. But to build a mansion the size of a Hyatt Hotel and then decide it was too much effort to walk all the way downstairs for a midnight snack didn't justify the decadence.

He dropped the chainsaw and bat on a flat countertop and stopped in front of a shiny sink, realizing how parched he was. The cupboards above held coffee mugs. He pulled one down and filled it with water from the faucet. The mug filled slowly, revealing the water pressure at that level wasn't the strongest.

Once finished, he removed his helmet and downed his drink, leaving the mug on a tidy dish rack.

Gus studied the ceiling and saw a water distributor hung almost over the stove and its four burners . . .

For a sprinkler system.

Sniffing, Gus grabbed his bat and test swung it twice. The nearest camera was outside the kitchen, so he pulled a chair out from the island and used it to climb up onto the granite countertop. Once there, he studied the sprinkler before bashing it free of the ceiling. Water trickled from the remaining metal stub.

Satisfied, Gus dropped to the floor and inspected the cupboards once more, finding stores of freeze-dried food and a bottle of cooking oil. He palmed the cooking oil and hefted it thoughtfully. Fire was an old friend of his—he knew it quite intimately—and he wondered . . .

The oven drew his attention.

"You seein' this, Mort?" Gus asked as he flicked on the oven and hiked the temperature to its limit. He opened the metal door and squeeze-sprayed oil over the exterior and interior, drenching it in canola gold. Some dish towels hung off a rack, as well as a roll of paper towels, and all that got heaved inside. A round wooden table and chairs filled one corner of the kitchen, and Gus shook his head at the convenience of having such combustibles nearby.

The furniture quickly fell to the chainsaw's teeth, and Gus relished the smell of sawdust and smoke. A *whoomp* made him turn around just as the fire alarm went off. The oil had reached its flashpoint, and a great orange lick of fire filled the oven's metal mouth. Smoke spiraled from its depths. Gus approved. He gathered up his bat and sheathed it.

Fuel. The word got him moving.

He tossed a chunk of table wood into the oven and jogged around a corner to the nearest bathroom. The facecloths and hand towels came off in hard yanks and got fed to the flames.

All except two.

Gus gathered up a chair leg and tied one end off with a towel. The other got stuffed as far as it would go into a pouch on his Nomex jacket. He didn't care if it caught fire eventually. The Nomex had saved his life more times than he could remember, and he trusted its protection completely.

"What are you doing?" Mortimer asked from beyond the kitchen, yelling to make himself heard over the high-pitched droning of the alarms.

The old guy sounded fearful.

Gus returned to the oven and held his makeshift torch inside the blaze. The towel caught and burned brightly in the overhead lights, which Mortimer seemed content enough to leave on.

"You're burning my kitchen!"

Quick. For an asshole. But no one ever said assholes were universally stupid. They weren't. They were just assholes.

A frenzied whine erupted from the speakers then, as if Mortimer were searching for something lost among a pile of rubbish. Gus didn't care. Hefting his torch, he left the kitchen and decided to take a walk—to explore this magnificent castle.

As he walked, he applied the torch to anything that would burn: curtains, oil paintings, even the clothing of unmoving zombies. The bedrooms on either side of the hall contained a rich source of combustibles, and Gus applied flame to thick duvets and wall-length curtains. Some of the towels in the en suites he used to replenish his torch, but once done, he left the bathrooms in flames and smoke. He ignited fine-smelling linen closets filled with summer sheets of silk and winter cotton blankets. One door hid a walk-in station used for storing chemical household cleaners, all wonderfully flammable. Shelves contained cleaning utensils, rags, and roll upon roll of toilet paper. It all went into a clothes hamper of flame, doused with whatever fluids the servants had stored there. He left the area before the acrid smoke from the cauldron of burning chemicals could cause him harm.

"You're insane." Mortimer's voice grated through his microphone, sounding close enough to swallow it whole. "Simply insane. How can you—how can you live here if you burn it all? How? The destruction . . . You'll never be able to repair it. Listen. *Listen to me*. If you want me, I'll tell you how to find me. Just stop burning everything. Here, I'm in a safe room on the top floor, just come on up and you can kill me easily. I'm just an old man."

That was something to consider, but Gus had no interest in ever seeing the face of the owner. Mortimer was smart. No telling what manner of booby traps or pitfalls he protected his inner sanctum with, and listening to the old bastard's voice, dripping with ill-hidden desire, only prompted Gus to continue on his current course of action. He much preferred listening to the panic in Mortimer's tone, which was as fine a tune as any. Feeling surprisingly serene, Gus walked from bedroom to bedroom, burning as he went. He kept ahead of the growing blaze, however, and *tsked* upon discovering a substantial fire hazard in the third-floor library. Not even a sprinkler in the ceiling, but then, with the low water pressure on the upper level, having one wouldn't have made a difference. He emptied shelves of paperbacks and textbooks onto the floor, some appearing notably old and probably worth a considerable amount of money. The flames devoured it all.

"You can't *do* this!" Mortimer droned on. "My books, oh sweet Jesus, my books! You have no idea of what you've done. I've collected them since . . . oh *stop*! At once! Stop! What do you want? I'll give you whatever you want! You want food? Medical supplies? Cars? Anything. Wait! What are you . . . that painting cost *thousands*. In the name of Christ, what is it that you *want*? Name it, and I'll direct you to where you can find it. Wait! *Wait! You're destroying private property!*"

Plush chairs, rugs, even thin pieces of ornamental wood, all felt the lick of the torch, all fed a different kind of beast. The halls became smoky tunnels, which started making Gus cough, the gauzy haze choking his airways. He had no worry about burning himself, but he knew most house-fire deaths occurred from smoke inhalation. The thought that he hadn't planned out his attack thoroughly enough occurred to him.

The hallway he followed took him into forbidden areas of the house, the smoke billowing. When he finally turned around, the sight made him stop and stare, blinking his unprotected, watering eyes.

He'd unleashed an inferno.

Flames waved merrily from open doorways as if well-wishing his departure, glowing eerily in the rising clouds of smoke. Like any good fire, getting it started was the difficult part, but once it got going, feeding it was your only concern. The rows of bedrooms, libraries, living spaces, linen closets, and everything between possessed plenty of fuel.

"What is it you want?" Mortimer wailed over the loudspeakers. "What? Just *tell* me."

Fuck you, Mort.

Gus stepped through another door and entered yet another bedroom. As antisocial as old Mort was, it was difficult to believe he needed so many. A king-size island dominated the center of the room, covered in delicate sheets of what appeared to be mosquito netting—or perhaps some fairy-tale décor beyond Gus's everyman sensibilities. An adjoining en suite had been sculpted from blinding porcelain, glittering gold light and sink fixtures, and more marble. A glass doorway led to a shutter-free deck outside. Mortimer had the bucks to burn, and that made Gus chuckle. The short laugh got him coughing harder, squinting against the smoke clinging to his ass, and he decided it was time to leave.

He tossed his torch into the en suite, closed the door, and went about stripping off bed sheets. These he quickly cut into strips with his boot knife and tied together, coughing the whole time. Once done, he carried his makeshift rope back to the balcony door, splitting smoke into twirls. Gus stepped outside into the night, gasping at the pure air.

The blaze rumbled against the walls like a low-grade earthquake.

The damn thing caught a whiff of air as well and *liked* it. Couldn't tell him fires weren't living creatures.

Gus tied off one end of his makeshift rope to a stumpy granite post and heaved the other over the balcony.

Under a night sky bristling with stars, he clumsily rappelled to the ground, three stories below. He crunch-landed in a wiry hedge of some sort. Once free of it, he realized he stood at the back of the house. Coughing out the smoke in his lungs and feeling positively polluted by the bitter fumes, he took a moment to stop and watch flashes and flickers behind dark windows.

Mortimer's voice was noticeably absent.

The night twinkled, at times clouded by cottony wisps.

Gus walked away, aware of his aches.

Any moment, he expected an arrow in the back or his face, exposed by the missing visor. Perhaps even a zombie might shamble out from the darkness, or even better, one on fire. Nothing of the sort happened, however, and in a few long minutes of following the wall of the house, he circled back to the paved driveway and spied Talbert's minivan and his beige SUV.

Gus sagged into the driver's seat, utterly exhausted and relieved to be inside. The higher windows of the mansion flashed fire every so often, catching his attention. Mortimer's immense home would take hours to burn, and as much as Gus wanted to sit and watch, he decided against it. He'd destroyed a man's castle that night, and an odd sense of déjà vu haunted the darker corners of his mind. If Mortimer was in a panic room of sorts, he'd have to leave it before the fire trapped him, and trap him it would, eventually. If he was being truthful, and Gus suspected Morty incapable of lying, the reclusive billionaire was probably well on in years.

Perhaps even ancient.

In time, the floors would fall into the lower ones, and if left unchecked, Mortimer would be homeless by the morning.

If he survived the barbeque.

Fingers on the steering wheel, Gus found the keys left in the ignition and started the machine.

The dashboard clock displayed 4:56.

Five in the morning. The sky was as black as if the sun had burned itself dry and left the world spinning.

Gus put the SUV into gear and drove away from the burning mansion, not the least interested in watching an old man's final bastion perish in the dawn's light. He hit the 101 in short time and drove perhaps twenty kilometers before his body demanded he stop and rest.

He parked the vehicle at the top of a low incline, his muscles aching. The rearview mirror revealed the glow from the massive conflagration, large enough to be seen kilometers away.

Gus watched it as his eyelids grew heavy.

He dreamed of fire.

12

The sun blazed through the fogged-up windshield like a prison spotlight, waking Gus. The dashboard clock stated the time as 10:42 a.m. He eased himself out of the SUV with a moan, knowing Donald had gotten in his share of punishing licks. For the next fifteen minutes, Gus extracted himself from the Nomex and threw it into the back of the vehicle. The farm was too far away to drive home wearing the heavy gear, too uncomfortable. Once it was off, he pulled on a light windbreaker. The black sweater and jeans he'd worn underneath the Nomex stank of sweat.

In the distance, black rolling clouds marred the morning sky as if evil incarnate stirred a huge cauldron just beyond the hills.

He tuned out for a short time, listening to the twittering of hidden birds. Weeds sprouted through cracks in the pavement. A few derelict cars littered the highway.

Empty.

Gus got into the SUV.

The drive back home relaxed him despite his hurts, and twice he pulled over to nap, the solemn landscape lulling him to sleep. Upon waking, he made the mental note to have Maggie take a look at him. Gus resumed driving. Thoughts of Talbert and his frat crew lingered as he rolled down the final strip of highway to the farm— even old Mortimer and his boys. Also, the loss of what had been a very valuable piece of property in the mansion recalled his own house a long time before. His mountain fortress took his mind off the driving, and he went a good ways before noticing black curls of smoke rising up on the right, over a wall of trees, vile and polluting the deep blue of the otherwise empty sky.

They twisted and coiled, blotting the air currents, worrying him. Gus sped up, watching the sky and road while a growing dread urged him on. Every bump in the highway traveled up the steering column and rattled him a little bit more. In seconds, he spotted the farm's dirt road and turned onto it at just after two thirty in the afternoon. Dirt sprayed from his tires. Unfilled potholes made his back teeth clatter.

A flock of crows took to the sky, swearing at having to do so. The farm loomed into view, and Gus's innards crystallized at the sight. He braked, hearing the crackle of cold gravel underneath steel-belted rubber.

The four corners of the main house stood charred and blackened like greased spits over a low-burning fire. The blaze had consumed the house right down to its bones, where the interior was a smoking pile of unrecognizable debris. Part of the second floor sloped down to the ground level like a charcoal slide. Chrome gleamed from what remained of the kitchen, along with the singed hide of a once-yellow refrigerator.

Gus's breath sped up as if he'd burst into a sprint even though he hadn't even put his ride into park. He did so a moment later, adrenaline flooding his system as he fumbled for the stick and swore when he finally got it right.

Then he saw the bodies.

He stumbled from the SUV and walked across the bloodstained ground as if gut shot, whimpering in terror. Smoke drifted across the corpses, but Gus knew them. The sight of all those people he'd known switched him off in complete shock, like the sound of a two-ton weight crashing down on an elegant set of piano keys right at his back. About thirteen bodies sprawled on the ground, and he felt as if Donald had put one last arrow through the frontal jelly portion of his brain. Gus's knees buckled, and he plopped down on the gravel, staring at the corpses, seeing how the crows had violated them.

He covered his mouth and stared until his eyes blazed red.

"Oh *shit*," he squeaked, grief rendering him breathless. "Oh shit. Oh, oh *shit*. Oh . . ."

Crows shrieked somewhere in the distance, their harsh cries sawing at reality. If he had a shotgun, he'd silence the whole goddamn works. But that swell of murderous intent receded, leaving him sitting and gawking at the rows of the dead, peeping out throat-constricted grunts of disbelief.

They'd been executed; that much was clear.

He wondered who had done it. *Mortimer?* Gus couldn't believe that. He'd left the old man to roast. Not even his ghost would know the location of the farm.

Then another shot of fear, pure and mind-splitting, widened his red-rimmed eyes.

"Oh my *shit*," Gus whispered with emotion. He got up, staggered to the bodies, and tried to clarify what exactly he was seeing.

Adam lay facedown with a gaping hole in the back of his skull, blood caking and forever tarnishing the silvery gloss of his hair. Gus didn't turn him over for fear of seeing what the blast had done to his face. Anita Little lay two bodies over, her one eye as brown as the dirt she so closely studied in death. Her gray hair splayed around her shoulders in muddy strands, and memories assaulted Gus of how she'd fidgeted with her locks like a little girl. The others he recognized by hair or body shape or face partially blotted by the ground. Cory, Emma, Louise, Art, Mike, Clara, Elmo . . .

Gus stopped, palm-wiping his eyes and nose. A rueful growl ripped from his chest, and he inspected the bodies again, forcing himself to continue.

He had to make sure.

No Maggie.

No Roger.

No Thelma.

And *no kids*. Becky and Chad weren't among the dead, and that little burst of relief gave him strength. The thought came to him right then, as he stood as still as a tombstone, that if anyone was lurking, he'd have known already. They could have picked him off. As it was, he'd only been gone overnight, not even two days, and the farm had been ravaged.

He stepped back from the dead, noting how they'd been either shot or brutally bludgeoned to death. Mike Julian, a New Minas native Gus used to talk shop with, lay facedown with his right hand hacked off. Tortured, perhaps.

Gus walked around the dying fire pit of the house, spotting the dirt mound where his chair had toppled. A pair of boots jutted into the air, out of place against the far-off tree line. Roger lay on his back, staring at the sun with a bloody hole through his chest. The crows had been picking at his ruddy cheeks, plucking the eyes, displaying what hooked beaks could do to an unmoving knob of meaty flesh.

Gus almost collapsed right there.

But he didn't. He pushed on and confirmed four people were indeed unaccounted for among the deceased.

So where were they?

The question flared in his mind. *Where were they?*

Gus frantically searched for signs of *anything*—behind the house, around the equally torched barn, the storage sheds, and the immediate fields. The little storehouse full of harvested foods preserved for the winter had been razed to the ground. The root cellar remained intact but emptied of its treasures. The few cars parked around the property had been cooked to husks, dashboards melted into grimaces. Most of the livestock—cows and goats—had been released to the fields where they grazed peacefully, unconcerned with the deaths. The chickens were gone.

And then he came to Adam's old beater of a sedan—roasted on the spot.

A buzzing grew in his ears as Gus headed to his SUV. He jumped aboard the vehicle, started it, and was about to slam it into drive when the farm stopped him.

The sad, shocking picture of it all.

The smoking remains of his home and of the people with whom he'd shared it for almost two years slammed into his chest and robbed him of his voice.

Have to bury them, he thought. *Have to bury them.*

And he would. He swore he would—swore to whatever ghosts were lurking nearby he'd return. The urge to leave grew almost irresistible, but then he composed himself with a mighty breath and got the machine rolling.

I'll be back, he vowed.

Tires spun dirt as he whipped the SUV around and rumbled to the main drag. Trees flashed by. Potholes made him bounce in his seat, his head nearly connecting with the ceiling.

Questions raced through his mind. *Who did this? Where were the missing people? Were they nearby?*

Dirt merged with pavement up ahead, and Gus still had enough presence of mind to spot a clue he'd missed. He slammed on the brakes and leaned over the steering wheel, barely hearing the idling of the motor.

In the dirt lay the jagged parallel curves of tire tracks, tearing off the back road and peeling off on asphalt. A spray of gravel marked the speed and power the fleeing vehicle used. Gus could almost hear the *yeehaw*ing as the driver gunned the pedal, shooting over pavement in a squeal of scalding rubber. Black scars marked the road, heading north on the 101.

Toward Annapolis.

Smoke. He'd been staring at smoke when he turned off the road, completely missing the obvious.

Someone had come upon the farm—someone willing to kill, to loot.

But why had they taken only four?

The answer hit him between the eyes. He couldn't be sure about Becky and Chad, but Maggie was priceless. She was a doctor in the old world. She was also training Thelma as her nurse. In the *new* world, anyone would be hard-pressed to find such a valuable pair.

They'd been kidnapped. Perhaps the kids were taken to be used as leverage, to press Maggie into performing without argument.

Gus looked ahead, measuring the curves in the road until trees on either side forbade his sight. The gas tank indicated half-empty.

Gripping the wheel, Gus stepped on the pedal and hauled ass up the highway, knowing he couldn't be any more than a day behind the killers.

With the sun dipping, he stuck to the main highway and weaved around deserted cars, heading toward the city limits of Annapolis. He scanned the shoulders for clues, anything to let him know he was still on course. Despair took up residence in his mind, as he knew searching the city could take weeks, something that he wasn't sure Maggie or Thelma or the kids had.

The SUV crested a hill, and the decimated plate that was Annapolis lay before him. Even though he'd been higher than a Chinese satellite, purging the city by fire had seemed like a good idea at the time, but sober, Gus found it hard to gaze upon his handiwork. It had been his home at one time, after all, a city filled with memories, most good, some bad. Currently, it resembled a blackened tablecloth of steel and concrete, split wood and broken glass. Some of the taller buildings remained intact, casting tombstone shadows across an otherwise scorched landscape.

The whole of the city seemed to stare back at him. Hateful. Remembering.

Gus drove into the urban crater, determined to find Maggie, Thelma, and the kids. He became a steel-and-fiberglass missile, aimed at the dead city's heart, rumbling with determination, revving willpower. The SUV coasted through the city's outer limits, Gus's face becoming a vengeful glower. Annapolis exuded waves of raw animosity, like an unchecked radioactive core. Nothing walked. Debris littered the road and quickly imposed a slower speed. He saw the ruptured streets, burst from beneath by powerful explosions of gas, all his handiwork.

The city hated him.

He knew it—didn't give a damn.

"Yeah, that's right," he muttered, taking a firmer grip on the wheel. "Your boy's back, bitch. Roll over and take it, and I'll leave quietly."

A collection of cars littered the road, sparkling in the setting sun. Gus drove up on a sidewalk before steering back onto the main drag.

"But make a move, and I swear to sunny Jesus I'll twist your tits so hard your ass'll squirt butter."

A deadhead crawled right on the dotted line of the road. Its head was down, as if searching for its glasses at ground level. Gus didn't blink as he lined up a front tire and rolled right over the undead, feeling his tire *pop* the skull like an aerosol can tossed into an open fire.

That was the only one. Nothing else crossed his path. *As well it shouldn't,* Gus thought and scratched his balls.

Like a great beige shark, the SUV prowled through the sun-dried wounds and fissures of the streets, avoiding the arterial clogs of vehicles and taking the easier routes. The sun slipped from the sky, leaving a deepening evening blue. That worried Gus, agitating his misery over the missing people. Annapolis was the *last* place where he wanted to camp overnight. The thought of returning to his old house came to him, quickly dismissed with a snort that said, *Return to what?* He was too sentimental to go back, anyway, knowing he'd bawl his eyes out if he ever laid eyes on the old homestead. Such distractions weren't needed—not right then.

An hour later, the sign for the 101 appeared in the glare of his headlights, and he drove for the highway.

Annapolis, as far as one frantic pass could confirm, was empty of life.

The open road beckoned.

13

Morning found Gus stopped just outside Windsor on a divided highway with a rusty-looking set of railroad tracks on his right. The Bay of Fundy tidal flats and saltwater marshes lay on his left. Tall yellow grass fluttered over mud banks singed with a collar of twinkling frost. The sun stared in through the driver's window like a police officer's flashlight, waking Gus none too gently. He'd slept in the SUV, seat lowered way back, with his baseball bat at the ready on the passenger side. The Nomex gear was a warm but bulky substitute for blankets. He'd cracked two windows, and while it wasn't home, it certainly could have been worse. Sleeping outside a couple of years before would've attracted a whole lot of flesh-eating attention.

The morning faced him, and a pensive Gus stared back. He was in a hole, and the depth of that shit chute slowly dawned on him. Maggie and the rest could be *anywhere* in the province if they were still alive, and while there were only so many highways he could follow, the search would take time and burn gas, and every wrong turn meant lost ground.

Fuck me, Gus mulled in frustration and eyed the unmoving traffic on the highway. Gone.

They were gone—plucked from the farm while he was off searching for Talbert and his merry men. He cursed Talbert for going off to loot Mortimer's shack in the first place. If Talbert had stayed back, five men would've been defending the farm from the cold-blooded sonsabitches who'd gutted the place.

The thought of never seeing Maggie, Thelma, and the kids ever again left him miserable. He got out and took a shivering piss on the side of the highway, gazing across a small body of water he wasn't sure was freshwater or salt, and saw a smattering of houses situated on the opposite hillside.

Supplies. He'd need supplies.

Whatever had been of value on the farm had been either stolen or burned to the ground, and Gus wasn't in the right frame of mind to root around ashes and memories to ferret out anything useful.

He tapped himself off and zipped, flabbergasted he didn't even have so much as a single fucking roll of toilet paper to his name.

But Windsor, the town gleaming in the distance, potentially did.

Seconds later, the SUV rushed toward the sign designating the exit for the downtown section. Gus drove up a low hill and made the necessary turns before coasting into the outskirts of a commercial area. A few Victorian-styled houses, battered and flaking paint badly, stood on his left. A dusty Tim Hortons beamed at him from down a side street. Small businesses dotted the road on either side, occupying either single-story or taller buildings. Many of those were made of brick and metal and had only a few broken windows. A few doors lay open or ripped from their frames entirely.

Gus eased his foot onto the brake. More cars and trucks stank up the road. A motorcycle appeared at one point, lying right on the solid line, chrome bright in the sunlight. Ripped saddlebags lay nearby, the contents long since scattered or stolen. Gus killed the engine and lowered his window. A light breeze breathed on him, cold but not uncomfortably so, and the sound of it struck a melancholy chord.

It was Wednesday. Or Thursday, and a bright morning in November. Pensions might have been deposited into bank accounts today, generating a brief shopping frenzy. The Tim Hortons would be bustling, and though he didn't really care for the coffee, one whiff of those percolating beans would have made him break down right there. Kids would be in school, maybe even testing before their Christmas break, so they'd be off the street. Bright morning chatter, casual sidewalk conversations, queries about last night's hockey scores or when Martock might be opening the ski slopes.

Gus rubbed his chin and felt a sadness he'd thought had long since passed.

The place was desolate. Lifeless. A ghost town. Even the lack of gimps did nothing to alleviate the sense of emptiness. More than ever before, he felt he was about to violate a mass open grave. He couldn't remember ever being that way when he lived alone. Perhaps, in the time spent on the farm, he'd become too accustomed to having people around, and that precious human contact had made him more sensitive to its absence.

Gus sat up and bit on the inside of his cheek. His entire world had been shitbagged overnight. He had to revert back to how he'd been, living alone on the mountain when the undead walked instead of crawled.

He laid on the horn and blasted that dreadful silence. Three times he sounded the horn, his eyes darting to the left, right, and rear in case someone tried sneaking up on him.

No one did, however. Not even after he waited five minutes.

"All right, then." Gus fired up his ride.

The tires crackled over thin ice as it pulled alongside what looked to be a locally owned coffee shop, just a parking lot over from a sign announcing the Windsor Mall. Gus eyed the businesses listed on a roadside directory and stopped on one in particular, one that very much caught his attention.

The Leather Shop.

He studied his coat. Underneath, he wore jeans, a black sweater, and matching motorcycle boots. *Christ.* He was never one for fashion, so why change now?

The air chilled him as he exited the vehicle, still wary of the streets. He took his bat and pulled on his helmet, wanting to find another with a visor, wondering if the mall might have something his size.

The glass door to the coffee place opened with a squeak, and he paused on the threshold. Gus entered a small sitting area filled with undisturbed tables and chairs. Bare beams crossed the ceiling, and decorative wreaths hung around the walls, nearly in season once again. Gus wondered about that. The apocalypse had broken out around late summer. He'd put down many a gimp in bathing suits. Perhaps the wreaths were up all year, but they struck him as being totally Christmas.

Bracing himself, he rapped the bat's head three times off the nearest table.

"Hear that?" he asked the coffee shop, eyeing a small counter. Wire bins with torn sheets of wax paper lay behind the shattered glass displays.

"Anyone in here, you godforsaken fucks?"

No response.

He crept forward, feeling nostalgic for house picking. Back in the days of living off the mountain, he'd actually had a perverse feeling of discovery when scouring for supplies in other people's property, a treasure hunter's rush of finding something useful. Handy goods could be anywhere.

A quick search underneath the counter revealed nothing. The space underneath the barren cash register contained cupboards. Gus stopped at the swinging doors leading into the kitchen. Darkness ruled beyond, and he wasn't feeling particularly brave.

"Hey," he barked and slapped a door with the bat. It swung inward with a long squeal. Nothing moved.

Gus went inside.

He fumbled about until he discovered a washroom and three fresh rolls of toilet paper. A bottle of chemical cleaner was perhaps three quarters full, as well as a pump bottle of soap that flowed like glue. Gus gathered up the toilet paper rolls and returned to daylight, stacking them on the counter. He found a few heavy sacks of flour mixture—clearly labeled for making muffins—in the back of the kitchen. He knew three bakers in the new world. Anita Little was one of them. A man named Larry had also lived on the farm, as well as Scott—whose whereabouts were utterly unknown. Two of them were dead. Gus supposed he could have travelled into Halifax and searched for Scott, but truthfully, he didn't want to see if the rat plague had reached the capital city—not after what he'd witnessed at his mountain fortress.

Gus left the coffee shop with the toilet paper and one sack of muffin mixture and loaded up the SUV. The crap wrap went into the back seat as he kidded himself that he had enough for a month if he stayed off the booze.

The mall was next.

The metal grate of the entrance protecting the glass doors had been smashed aside and left hanging like a drooping blind, as if someone had rammed a truck through it all. Gus parked and got out, grimacing at the mess. Dull glass glittered and crackled underfoot. Shriveled bodies carpeted the floor and walls as if the whole town had sought shelter at the mall. Some had their skulls smashed in or removed entirely from their neck. A breeze, full of regret, sighed through the shadowy cavern of steel and concrete and glass.

One carcass, a mall cop by his uniform, sat with his back against the wall just inside the entrance. He stirred and lifted his chin slowly. Gus watched the dead thing's attempt to will its limbs into motion. The face resembled a melted mask, blackened and frightening. Gus crushed the head with a boot heel, grunted at having to stretch a leg up so high, and awkwardly regained his balance.

A clump of scalp matter clung to his boot.

Gus made a face at the clinging flesh and stomped, which didn't dislodge the rag of skin. Huffing in disgust, he dragged his foot over the twinkling glass then wiped it on another body wearing a shirt and pants and yet another body with a denim jacket. At first, his efforts were slow and deliberate, but as he repeatedly failed to clean his boot, he put more exasperated energy into the swipes.

"*Goddamnit*," he swore and tried to ignore it. The trouble was he could *feel* the scalp dragging along with each step. Gus grunted in annoyance, placed a hand against a wall for support, and used his other boot to vigorously pin the scalp to the floor and rip it away.

He freed himself in a few seconds, test-walked, and found his stride returned to normal.

"Worse 'n dog shit," Gus muttered, making a note never to stomp in a head ever again.

Movement then. Even in the dim, cavernous halls of that retail crypt, he picked up on crawlers and drew back a few steps. At the absolute edges of the dark, fingers slinked into view and clawed at the floor.

Gus waited, but nothing came out of the dark.

Realizing the zombies couldn't move, Gus still retreated a few more steps, toward daylight. Something about those fingers, moving like stunned crabs, repulsed him, creeped him out.

He needed a flashlight. No way was he going to go someplace dark without one. Not after what had happened at Mortimer's. He got aboard the SUV and drove off, cruising the downtown area for a hardware shop. The minutes dragged on, and he realized he was wasting time, so he decided to go back to the basics and stopped at the first house on his right. He didn't mind little houses like this gray-painted, two-story Victorian. A sunroom faced a front lawn that might have been the envy of the town back when people still lived. The grass had grown unchecked to knee height and presently bent over with frost.

Gus got to work.

By midmorning, he'd picked his way through four such homes, encountering not one gimp in his search, and locating a heavy, rubber-grip flashlight that took four D-cells. Gus thumbed the switch, but the beam was too weak to be of any use. Pocketing the flashlight, he went on the hunt for better batteries. He didn't find any, but he did pick up two cloth grocery bags, the environmentally friendly kind, and stuffed in a kettle, along with five boxes of dried, cheese-flavored Kraft Dinner. He grabbed a set of Tupperware from a kitchen, including a set of spoons, forks, and knives. A can opener also went into a bag. On the second trip, he snatched a midsize pot and a no-stick frying pan.

Gus paused and listened each time he returned to the SUV in the street. Bodies, like wisps of cloth and skin, ravaged by the elements over the years, lay facedown or on their sides. Nothing moved, and Gus remembered what Talbert and his boys had reported to the folks on the farm.

The dead weren't a problem anymore. Not in the least.

The rear of the SUV quickly filled with supplies, and Gus took stock of everything before getting inside and driving a little farther down to the next collection of houses. He could've walked but didn't feel like leaving his ride too far behind him. That tempted fate.

And Gus needed her on his side.

He parked ass-first in a paved driveway, driver's side lined up with the front door. This house gave up some duvets, which he heaped into the back seat, four plastic liter water jugs, and another two rolls of toilet paper. A rifle was also present in the living room, held in the papery hand of the individual who'd last used it to exit the world via gunshot. The top half of the skull appeared like a broken flower pot—and Gus wondered why the hell the long-gone wore smiles in the afterlife. Those eerie grins spoke to him, last messages to the living.

The guy had a family gathered around, two children with weedy hair clinging to their heads. They sat on a sofa with blown-apart pillowcases over their heads while the wife relaxed in a stretched-out recliner, sporting a hunting rifle hairdo—one more family who had decided that the easiest way out was suicide.

Gus moved on, trying not to dwell on it.

Unable to find any ammunition, he left the firearm. Also, prying the item free from the guy's fingers seemed like bad mojo.

A basement door opened without a problem, and Gus peered down carpeted steps to a landing, a discarded slipper, and blackness beyond. He didn't like going into basements, and that one felt spooky. He took two steps down, hating the squeal of old wood, and thought, *Fuck it* before returning to the kitchen. Cans of food lay stacked in cupboards, but he left those, wary of long-expired dates. One cabinet hid a heavy-duty spotlight flashlight with a weak beam, the lithium battery near the end of its existence but still serviceable.

After finding little in the kitchen, he wandered back to the basement stairs, took a none- too-pleased breath, and went down.

The slipper on the landing wasn't a slipper at all. It was a crushed rat. The discovery froze Gus on the steps. He swung the flashlight beam throughout the rest of the basement, sweeping it one way and then the other, seeing other squashed invaders.

"Little shit stains better not be down here," Gus warned. "Y'hear me? You better not."

He toe-flicked the unmoving fur stains of the rats, screwing up his face, glad he wore boots. The wavering beam illuminated a good section of the basement and revealed a laundry area and a washroom (another four rolls of crap wrap). A short hall led to a stylish arch with a rec room beyond, containing a modest gym, a pool table, and a comfy-looking sofa set arranged around a wide-screen TV and a fireplace. A discarded duffel bag lay crumpled in one corner, and Gus prodded it repeatedly before opening and examining its folds. Ancient hockey gear filled it, which he emptied onto the floor. He wasn't that much of a pack rat just yet.

He clacked the cue ball off a knot of multicolored cousins and listened to the resulting soft chatter. Poking around revealed a stack of *National Geographics* but nothing else of interest. The rats appeared to originate from a displaced drainpipe, which Gus believed was the only entry point in the whole basement.

No shells for the rifle. The toilet paper came with him, and already his asshole felt that much more loved. Gus stashed everything in the duffel bag and returned to the surface.

The larger flashlight would have to do until he found something better.

He saddled up and drove back to the Windsor Mall.

14

The lack of noise seemed to hum in his ears.

Gus stood at the dark mouth of the mall's entrance. Geared up and carrying his flashlight, he paused before thumbing the power switch. The beam flared to life, making the search seem official, and he cautiously walked inside.

"Hey!" he yelled after walking ten feet into the retail cave. "Just takin' a look around, is all. Doin' a little shoppin' on credit. That's all. So stay the fuck back."

He waited, fidgeting on the crinkling glass. The bodies carpeting the floor didn't move. The police officer lay toppled on his side.

"Fuck it," Gus muttered and moved deeper, getting a better grip on his bat. The beam revealed withered heaps of cloth and flesh, which he navigated past, feeling more than a little nervous. He passed a huge, smashed bulb containing a crane and claw and plush toys; furry little limbs stuck out from the scruffy-looking mass. Gum and candy dispensers stood in a two-tiered wall, cracked open, their booty scooped out. More ravaged bodies. He flashed the beam toward a CLEARANCE SALE sign outside an Eager Andy's chain store. A mound of corpses blocked the glass doors from closing. One of the bodies, a ghoul dressed in a white T-shirt and cargo shorts, slid off the top with all the grace of a crocodile taking to water. Its blackened skin appeared leathery in the light. Gus speared its skull with one quick jab.

Two more crawlers attempted to pull themselves out of the flesh heap before Eager Andy's discount shop, but the weight of the dead piled atop their lower spines prevented them from reaching freedom. Stick-like arms fluttered weakly in the flashlight's beam as if searching for car keys.

Gus dispatched those as well.

Tables came into view farther along the corridor, filled with waxy smokestacks of candles, some tall, some reduced to puddles. The residents had turned the place into a refuge of sorts until it was finally breached. Gus found a box of long-necked bar-beque lighters on one table, which he stuffed into the duffel bag. He then regarded Eager Andy's, wondering what the hell Andy had been so damn eager about, and climbed over the clump of carcasses blocking the entrance to the shop. The dead cluttered the wide aisles. Gus waded through, having to go around heaps of unmoving flesh at times. The shelves still contained some household knickknacks but nothing that grabbed his attention.

Hurry, his mind urged.

Five minutes later, he gave up and hunted for the Leather Shop.

The glass doors to the hole-in-the-wall outlet lay wide open. He ignored the fancy bags, wallets, and shoes, and homed in on the pants. A quick search brought up two pairs his size and another two pairs of a size a little bigger, so he could double bag himself. A biker jacket hung off a rack, a little too large for him but with an under-layer of a sweater or something, it would be perfect. These he grabbed, as well as a pair of belts.

With his booty, he made his exit.

A head or two lifted weakly, as if pulled up by their scalps, but Gus didn't bother engaging them, focused on the glowing entrance and the parked SUV.

He walked, hairs on his neck standing on end, waiting for unseen deadheads to pounce.

But nothing did.

Once more, Gus loaded and arranged his booty in the rear of his vehicle. Sweat soaked his clothes underneath the Nomex. He gazed back at the depths of the mall and mulled over his next move. The sun beamed overhead, marking noon.

It was time to leave and get searching.

Gus just wasn't sure of where to go.

He left Windsor, driving back to the 101. As the town disappeared in his rearview mirror, dreadful doubts uncoiled in Gus's mind. Too much time had passed. He'd taken too long with his modest outfitting.

The trail might've gone cold.

The idea that the killers hadn't holed up in Annapolis seemed solid, but it only made him wary about following the highway down into Halifax.

If any time remained at all, Maggie and the others didn't have much.

The kilometers whispered past in the barely heard hum of tire rubber. An abandoned collection of metal and glass periodically tangled the highway, forcing him to drive slowly. Gus's stomach informed him it was about to tear a rib off if he didn't eat soon. He couldn't remember when he'd eaten last. *Has a day passed? When did I eat last?* There were five boxes of KD in the back, and he had the means of cooking the noodles— all he needed was water. Rolling timberland rose up on both sides of the highway. A dirt road passed by on his right, snaking through the brush to parts unknown. A blue sign stood on the shoulder, informing him that Exit 3 was approaching, but that didn't interest him at all.

The next sight did.

Gus stopped on top of an overpass with a lonely squeal of brake pads and got out. Feeling like the last man on the planet, he eyed a small body of water to the right of the lanes running underneath. A large eighteen-wheeler was nose down in the ditch on the opposite side of the highway. The long container had stayed upright but jack-knifed across two lanes, with the hood of a car lodged between a set of trailer tires. Four smaller cars were scattered around it.

Gus gazed up and down the divided highway, seeing no movement and hearing nothing. He shook his head in wonder at the spectacle below the overpass. The road had seen some excitement. He could make out the head of the truck driver, facedown on his steering wheel as if bashing his forehead in frustration.

Gus returned to his vehicle, backed up, and drove down Exit 3. He stopped along the cement wall bordering the pond, got out, hopped the barrier, and made his way down to the water's edge. He sampled it, swishing a mouthful around before swallowing, and hoped it didn't give him cramps or worse. More went down the hatch, and when he'd drunk his fill, he got to work.

Gus warily filled the three jugs and a cooking pot. It took a couple of trips, but he carried the water back to the SUV, as well as some brushwood he'd picked up along the highway. A short time later, he started a small campfire with the butane lighters. There was nothing to hang the pot from, so he held its handle with his gloved hand until the water boiled, wishing he'd had the foresight to grab a grill.

The trailer kept drawing his attention.

The Kraft Dinner cooked in a short time, the powdered cheese plopping into the mixture like an orange nugget. There was no milk or butter, and he could taste the age of the macaroni, but it went down fine. A small amount of leftovers went into a Tupperware dish.

Once fed, Gus let the fire burn itself out while he studied the tractor trailer across the quiet lanes. He pulled out his bat and regarded the vehicle. That lengthy, white storage box called to him.

His boot heels clicked on cracked pavement as he crossed the highway, checking both ways, making a mental note to inspect the cars for fuel. Though the cars of the day had security measures to prevent the siphoning of tanks, there was no safeguard in place to prevent him from cutting into the gas tanks. Fuel stabilizers and other additive mixtures still kept octane levels high well after the apocalypse. With the millions of combustion engines abandoned and cluttering roadways, housed within stylish fiberglass and carbon fiber shells, finding a fuel source wasn't difficult. It was only a matter of drilling into a tank and having a receptacle in place or drop cloths to soak up the gas. Gus didn't have a drill, but he did have a hammer and spike, which would get him into most plastic tanks. The metal ones ran the risk of sparking when he punctured the tank, but after four years, he was still popping.

But all that would happen after he checked out the trailer.

He crossed a sloping median of yellow grass. A few shriveled bodies decorated the asphalt like fallen scarecrows. The door to the truck's cab lay open, the seat buckle keeping it from closing properly. Gus pulled it open, ready to be jumped, but when nothing happened, he hauled himself inside, pushing the dead driver aside, and took a look around. A neat bunk with barely a sheet out of place tempted him to stop for the night. He searched a set of panel wood drawers and left the canned food therein. A notepad PC had swung out on a platform attached to the bed, and when Gus pushed it, he discovered suction cups keeping it in place. Overhead compartments spilled clothing when opened. The rig was an automatic stick shift, but the dash was a mystery of dials and gauges that he left alone.

The sound of his heels slamming the pavement carried, enough for him to stop and listen. Feeling overly paranoid, Gus went to the rear of the trailer, sensing a prize within. He ducked under an open door of the trailer and spotted a ring of rocks marking a fire pit on the pavement. He pondered that for a second before looking into a spacious cavern on wheels—stocked with a living room set. Gus pulled himself into the interior and inspected a deep-earth-brown sofa that had its protective covering torn away, its cushions stained. The corners of a wooden coffee table were scuffed bare. Dusty boot prints tracked across the flooring, at least four different treads. A posh queen-size bed lay at the back. The mattress's plastic covering had been torn off, and boot prints stained the cloth surface, as if someone had worn their footwear while sleeping.

Someone had used the trailer as a very comfortable campsite, right across from a nearby water supply. Gus turned to leave when he spotted—sticking out behind a black sedan—a pair of very small feet, wearing slippers with scuffed bottoms, toes down in the dirt.

Getting bad vibes, Gus hopped out of the trailer and cautiously approached the body.

He edged around the car and stopped with a chill. The gaping hole in the back of the woman's head momentarily distracted him from recognizing her gray hair. When he realized he'd found Thelma, the air left his lungs, and he slumped against the car. Sweat coated him in a cold, miserable dew. After a moment, he rolled her over to confirm it was her. Wide eyes stared back, flat and lifeless and caked with dirt. In death, she appeared utterly shocked, her little mouth open, as if she hadn't expected the trigger to be pulled.

"Well, Jesus."

Feeling weepy and sick to his stomach, Gus lifted her and transported her to the back seat of the black sedan. With infinite care, he tucked in her legs, tried unsuccessfully to close her eyes, and covered her with a blanket from the trunk. Her limbs weren't stiff just yet, and the skies were without crows, so she hadn't been dead for very long. He closed all the doors and windows and gazed in at her, feeling like a cold shit for leaving her that way.

"I'm sorry, Thelm," his voice rasped. "I'm sorry. At least the birds won't get you. Or anything else. And . . . it's not a bad car. Good stereo system." He meant every word.

He smiled weakly. "Anyway, you just sleep now. Thanks for the sign. I'll see if I can find Maggie and the kids. They're still out there somewhere, and it's a mighty big province. God willing, I'll find them, and I'll bring them back."

To where?

"Haven't gotten to that part just yet," he sighed, shoulders heaving, "but I'll work on it."

Emotionally drained, Gus ran a hand over the car roof and gave it a final pat. He returned to his vehicle and strapped himself in, frowning at the road ahead.

Halifax called.

It was absolutely the last place he wanted to go—a hellish maze of urban planning gone bad—but he had to travel there for the sake of Maggie and the kids.

The sun slipped behind a dark cloud as he fired up the engine.

The road thickened with abandoned vehicles the closer Gus got to Halifax. He slowed to a crawl, threading his way through bottlenecks that nearly strangled the roads of Lower Sackville. Cars had become above-ground coffins for their occupants, the highway transformed into a collage of dull metallic roofs and open doors.

"Jeeezus," Gus hissed in awe.

The main drag in Annapolis had been bad, but the highway to Halifax was horrific. The scary thing was that he wasn't even in the city yet, let alone downtown. The magnitude of his quest suddenly threatened to overwhelm him.

Anywhere. They could be any-fucking-*where.*

Gus forced the despair down. He was going to find them.

Wrecked gas stations, rows of houses, and a line of ubiquitous chain restaurants rolled by, reminding him he still had a little leftover Kraft Dinner. An exit turned off toward what appeared to be a collection of stores like Walmart and Mark's Work Wearhouse. A sign advertised indoor-track go-kart racing in front of an enormous three-story box of a building. Downed power lines draped a pickup truck, a black husk of an arm hanging out of its open window, an attached head thrown back in a maniacal chortle.

The deeper Gus drove down that highway of haunts, the more uneasy he became. Any time he went down into Annapolis, he'd made good and certain he drank a certain armoring amount of Grandpa's special sauce. On the farm, he'd fought down those urges that periodically gripped him. He wasn't an alcoholic—not in the least.

But the memory of how he *used to* deal with the horrors of the days gone by tempted him.

Made him . . . want. Wish.

He kept his speed down, driving like the only float in a stalled parade. Daylight waned, and the dash clock said it was a little after four. No way was he driving around that graveyard at night.

The SUV swung onto an off-ramp for Lower Sackville's residential area and rolled down a road crowded with houses on either side. Front lawns grew wild, some high enough to tickle the bottoms of sills. A few cars filled driveways. A pickup had parked itself uncomfortably over a fallen power transformer. A sign displaying Hallmark Avenue strolled by, and Gus absently thought about birthday cards. Dark bodies in the road brought him back, and his tires rolled over the dead already flattened into the asphalt.

He wanted a house for the night—one as easy to defend as possible.

All he saw were split-level designs. Split-levels and *more* split-levels. *Jesus Christ.* The developer must've had a split-level hard-on. Gus snaked his way through the streets until he stopped in a cul-de-sac directly in front of a two-story house with a double garage. It wasn't his first choice, but then, with the common theme of houses on the street, he probably wasn't going to find anything better.

He backed into the driveway and stopped before the garage door. Gus still wore his bulky Nomex and left his ride's nose pointed toward the highway for a quick getaway. A plump propane tank stood at the side of the house and gave him fiery flashbacks to another time.

Bat in hand, he walked to the front door and tried the knob. Locked. Gus stood back and knocked, just in case. While waiting, he sized up the other houses nearby and thought about checking them later.

No one answered, but that didn't always mean anything.

Gus walked around the back, ignoring the patio stones and the grass fringing each square. He stepped onto a stained deck, studied the glasswork of a sliding door, and smashed the section near the lock. In a second, he entered the home and closed the door behind.

"Anyone home?" he asked, sniffing at the end of the question and adjusting his helmet.

No answer.

Gus strode into a modern kitchen, circled the marble island, and peeked inside the fridge and nearby cupboards. Finding nothing, he wondered if the owners had left in a hurry. He left the kitchen and wandered through a comfortable living room with a gas fireplace and a thick rug that might have cost hundreds of dollars. A small plastic castle lay in one corner. A little dollhouse lay on its side and stared brightly at the ceiling. *Young kids*, Gus figured.

Memories of the hospital and crazy bitch Alice entered his mind.

His balls *still* ached from that encounter. He tapped the castle with a toe and regarded the staircases with a melancholy air. Jesus, he hoped the family reached someplace safe. For some reason, the castle and the toy house upset him more than he thought possible. Perhaps it was the thought that little Becky would enjoy herself there. Or it might be that, after having been around children for the past couple of years, when they were gone—when *anyone's* children were gone—the space they'd once filled seemed all the more empty and just a little more drab.

Leaving a few toys on the floor might entice the rightful owners to come back.

Gus grunted and stood behind a thin veil of drapes over the picture window. This he liked, a clear view of anyone coming into the cul-de-sac. He climbed the stairs to the second floor and meandered through, searching for deadheads and relieved to find it empty—not even a rat. A chest of drawers in a little girl's room had been cleaned out, as if someone had left in an awful hurry. The same went for the little boy's room, mom and dad's, and the closets.

The garage was also bare.

He wondered where the family had gone.

Wondered how far they got.

Gus retraced his steps to the living room and plopped down on the sofa with a direct line of vision of the cul-de-sac.

Listened.

Heard not a thing, except that drone deep in the ear canal that manifests in the absence of noise.

Gus waited, watched. After his break, he opened the garage and parked the SUV inside, out of sight. The garage had a few gardening tools that he thought about taking, some duct tape, and a peg wall full of useful tools and items, but then he thought of the children's castle.

No. He wasn't going to take anything from this place. Breaking the window had already tainted this seemingly content little home. Even though the owners were gone, even though Gus had never hesitated cleaning out a house before, a spirit lingered in that place. Taking something would feel like swiping something from a church.

But, if it was all right—and he hoped it would be—he would stay the night and leave in the morning.

He ate the leftover KD at the kitchen table, his working flashlight sitting nearby if it got too dark. Five packets of dried noodles, the ones with the granulated flavor packs, had been left in a cupboard. Gus took them, hoping whoever owned the place wouldn't mind that either. Once he'd finished with supper, he explored the other cupboards, finding dishes and boxes of long-dried-out cereal.

The cupboard above a blue bread box held a surprise, however.

Gus opened it and stared slack-jawed at a bottle of Captain Morgan's amber rum.

The decorative logo was changed somewhat, from the usual figure to an enlarged face of the moustachioed sailor, one corner of his wide-brimmed hat drooping quite dashingly over an eye. The welcoming smile on the old naval officer damn near glowed in the dark of the cupboard, as if Gus was the very person he'd been waiting for.

Well, shit. Gus's mind balked.

The pirate's shrunken head stared right at him.

That wasn't an entirely bad thing, not in the least. In fact, in that hour of need, he welcomed the officer's familiar presence.

"Hello, my buddy," Gus whispered, just standing and staring at the bottle. "Been a long time."

The Captain didn't answer.

"That's okay. That's fine. Hell, I'd be more worried if'n you *did* start talkin' back."

Gus gently extracted the plastic container, studying the label, reading the alcohol content, where it was distilled. All good information to know, and dammit if he wasn't just a bit tempted to have a chug. The bottle was full, the seal unbroken, and the liquid gold sloshed against the plastic.

Gus wasn't an alkie. He'd proved that over the time spent on the farm.

Not on the farm anymore, a voice whispered.

"No," he said, eyeing the Captain's merry features. "No, I'm certainly not. Oh my, oh my."

Gus walked with the seafaring officer to the sofa, sat down heavily, and scratched two of his dearest buddies. He stared at the face in the darkening room. The bottle was only a small quart—three hundred and seventy-five milliliters—or as the Newfoundlanders would say, a flask, but the appearance of the Captain calmed Gus in a way he'd never thought possible. The last time he'd felt so pleasantly surprised was perhaps a Christmas morning with Tammy, discovering Santa had deposited a similar bottle in his red stocking.

Gus sat and stared at the Captain's grinning features. He ran a thumb over the surface of the bottle, and the liquid trembled ever so slightly.

"What to do?" he whispered, smiling at the question. "What to do . . ."

15

"I heard something out there, man."

Sherman Wayward regarded the starless night before leveling his gaze to the road. A light breeze whisked past his ears, frigging his hearing for a moment, and he was about to say as much to his guard-post companion, Raymond Cole, who was almost shapeless in the dark, when he *did* catch the barest rumble of noise—long and huffing at times, mechanical.

"You hear that?" Raymond asked.

"Yeah," Sherman said.

"That's a motor."

Sherman didn't respond right away. He kept on listening, leaning over the hood of his car and staring off into the blackness. The rumbling became louder, deepened.

"That's not one motor," he muttered as it dawned on him. "Those are motors."

"Who the hell is it then?"

"Fuck if I know."

"Should I get Pat?"

Patrick Riley was the de facto leader of the little community of forty-four people living just off the 105 in New Brunswick. Over the past few years, they'd been surviving the zombie apocalypse by avoiding the death traps of Saint John, Moncton, and Fredericton and keeping to the outskirts of the smaller communities, hiding at the ends of back roads and becoming seminomadic. At the peak of the zombie plague, they'd driven in trailers from park to park, creating defensive zones with the people and equipment they had and conducting sorties into nearby towns for food and essential goods. Riley had traveled the province over in his scarred Winnebago, keeping to the less-traveled roads, and gathered his little troop of survivors as he drove along.

The sound of his home-on-wheels had attracted the remnants of humanity like an ice cream truck.

Eventually, they settled temporarily on a deserted farm just off the 105, situated in the Saint John River Valley—and there they'd stayed for two years, situated on a low plateau, facing the wide Saint John River, which would twinkle like diamonds under full moons. A single dirt lane sloped down from the house and parked trailers to the guard post deemed necessary day and night. A chest-high wooden fence faced the main road, another feature the inhabitants of the farm appreciated.

There had been a few situations with outlaws but nothing the little community couldn't handle. But tonight . . . tonight was different. Somber flashes of metal could occasionally be seen through the inky dark, moving along the 105 with the slow-moving grace of a train. As it was November, the night air promised to bite if offered bare skin. Sherman sniffed at times, clearing his sinus cavity of running mucus.

"The fuck is that?" he asked, every bit as perplexed as Raymond beside him. If things got bad, the practiced drill was to reach in through the open window of the parked Accord and sound the horn. Sherman moved to that very station, shaking his head in wonder.

"Maybe it's someone coming in?" Raymond asked.

"Who the hell's coming here this time of night?"

"Blow the horn?"

Sherman nodded and reached for the steering wheel, sending a surge of relief through his companion. Sherman was keeping his eyes on whatever was coming up the 105 when he heard a short, indignant gurgle from Raymond, as if a dentist's drill had slipped and speared the back of his throat. It evaporated into a squeaky puff of breath.

Confusion gripped Sherman, and he glanced over his shoulder to see Raymond slump to the ground. A shadow blurred forward, and Sherman had just enough time to gasp before a length of knife stabbed deep into his right eye, delivering a split second of pain not unlike being zapped with a few thousand volts. He flopped to his knees and got held for a moment before being gently lowered.

Sherman was dead before he touched dirt, his brain scrambled by six inches of razor-sharp steel.

A wraith stood and wistfully regarded the little community on the hill. His companions called him Sick, and his name—as well as his reputation—was rightly earned. Sick could discern no sign of alarm, primarily because of the growing motorized drone in the background. He furtively wiped off the knife on his victim's clothes and stepped up to the open window of the Accord. Sick looked around, confirming his task had been completed, before laying on the horn: three quick, startling toots.

In answer, the 105 became a tower of headlights and overhead spotlights. The beams blazed through the dark like lasers fired from the face of a monstrous spider. And if Sherman or Raymond had still been alive to see the show, they would have been struck speechless once again.

For the wall of lights seemingly rose up from the ground to the height of a three-story building.

The ground-level beams fluttered as figures passed before them, crouched over like commandos.

The fight was over before it began.

No one fired any shots until people started coming out of their trailers and motor homes, and when they did, seeing the monstrous lightshow at the bottom of the hill rendered them speechless. Then the first chatter of gunfire rang out, and voices commanded everyone to drop to their knees. Three of Reilly's people had responded with semiautomatic pistol fire, peppering the night with the hurried pop of firecrackers. One person raced toward the barn near the rear of the property, only to be cut down by a curt *sonavabitch* burst from an assault rifle. The remaining defenders died after a brief gun battle.

The rest of Reilly's group surrendered without incident.

Camouflaged soldiers quickly rounded up the remaining people. They forced the captured souls to lay flat on the ground, facedown, their limbs spread out nice and wide under baleful spotlights. A handful of children lay on their bellies as well, mewling and sniveling and hitching in eyes-shut terror. Every now and again, a gunshot punctuated the night air, and the kids screamed.

"Shut those little shits up," Shovel commanded in a sonorous voice, appearing almost magically from the flood of light. Times like that one were the worst, and understandably so. Those folks had been sleeping only minutes earlier, and now they were wrangled together and planted facedown in the dirt without a clue as to what was going on. Some of them might've even been getting around to fucking. The children sure as hell didn't know what was happening—only that their parents, real or adopted, had burst into their rooms and hurried them out the door into a night that was positively shocking after the warmth of their beds.

Shovel had to admit it was harsh.

But then again, it was a harsh world.

A soldier moved to the wailing youngsters and made an example of a little girl, swatting her upside the head.

She shrieked.

The mother shrieked.

The father bellowed, "Leave her alone!" and got to his knees.

One of Shovel's men stitched a killing line up the Dad's back, smacking him face-down in the dirt. The mother truly freaked then and jumped up surprisingly fast. In another burst of light, she jigged backward while chunks punched out of her back. Cordite lingered in the air.

The kid wailed on until a woman hugged the little one close, muffling her nearly feral crying.

Shovel didn't chastise the slayings. His men had orders to start popping anyone who sang above acceptable decibels. Once unleashed, they wouldn't ease up until deeds were done and the law laid down.

Shovel's job was to lay down that law.

He brooded, decked out in a winter coat and ski mask, much like the others in his little army. A compact but ugly submachine gun hung from a shoulder strap across his midsection, an old Heckler and Koch automatic. Some of his followers had full-blown soldier uniforms taken from overrun depots since people seemed to think the army was a good thing. It worked quite effectively as a ruse until—*surprise*—folks realized they weren't soldiers at all.

In another life, the core of Shovel's pack had been rig pigs. Roughnecks. Oil and gas workers situated in the far north, where only desolate tundra and stunted wilderness kept the apocalypse at bay.

And Shovel?

He'd lorded over them all.

His bulked-up shadow spread across the flattened prisoners like a monolithic stone threatening to topple over.

"Listen now," Shovel began in that deep, liquid-gold voice that belonged way in the back of a cathedral choir. "Listen, because for some of you, your very lives depend on it. Listen."

They listened.

Twenty men fenced in the prisoners lying on their bellies. They were armed with an assortment of high-tech, military-grade weapons, all trained upon the people at their feet. Balaclavas—black ski masks worn by counterterrorism operators—hid their features, dehumanizing them.

The smell of fecal matter perfumed the air. Shovel made a face. It happened every fucking time.

"The world as you know it has ended," he continued, screwing up his face at the stink. "There are no more credit ratings. No more mortgages. No more public systems and no more online shopping. But there's still debt. A fuckload to pay. To settle. In a new currency. Neighbor turned against neighbor. Old empires fell, and new ones struggled to rise. And the dead ate the living, as fucked up as that sounds. Listen to me. Listen. The *dead*. Ate. The *living*. And in some cases, the living . . ."

He let that hang for a moment.

"*Ate* the living. As fucked up as *that* sounds."

He paused then, allowing that sentiment to sink in and percolate.

"Because of our isolated location," Shovel went on, his voice hypnotic, "me and the group around you missed out on most of what happened. *Lucky you*, you might think. Well, we had our own troubles. Our own desperate times. But we overcame them. And once we overcame them, we rallied together and descended upon the warmer lands, riding hard from our northern hell. We descended upon the insane and the refuse and the warlords and the petty men of might, and we struck them down. It was a bloody time. A chaotic time. But we prevailed. By the way, did you know that the prime minister even attempted to reestablish order in his kingdom? He did—if you can believe it. Hiding away in a bunker, he actually sent out teams of soldiers—*special* soldiers, mind you—to help the surviving populace. To tell them to group together for safety until matters settled down. How do I know this?"

Shovel paused, hearing the muffled sniveling of the children. Some of his followers flexed trigger fingers. None of it was lost upon Shovel. He made it his business not to miss a single detail. Details could kill a person.

"We *found* these special soldiers," Shovel stated with a trace of smugness, "or rather, what was left of them. Holed up in a courthouse, of all places, surrounded by an undead army that might have been the entire population. The dead had been piled up around that stone-and-brick bastion like an ocean of bodies and limbs and teeth. Whatever weapons those soldiers brought with them, whatever tactics and strategies, they used them. They *unleashed* with a wrath I daresay was spectacular. But to no avail. In the end, they exhausted their ammunition and killed the undead with broken-off broomsticks, chair and table legs. Eventually, bare hands and combat boots. It was the Battle of Thermopylae all over. If it wasn't for us, well, they would've certainly perished. As it was, we rescued the sole survivor of a team of twelve. He had a choice, as you do. He could join us in the greater purpose of ridding the country of the scourge that devoured it whole. And once that was done, he could help us establish law and order.

Our kind of law. Of order. His choice? Well, he refused. In reality, he talked like politicians when asked a straight yes-or-no question."

Shovel smiled grimly at the memory of the battle, which had turned into a savage shouting match. Sick stepped across one of the beams of light, interrupting Shovel's train of thought, and stopped inside the dark, more at ease there.

"That same choice I'll offer to you," Shovel resumed. "We need people. We need your skills. We *especially* . . . need your children. Come with us as we search the country for like-minded souls. I'm not offering a return to the old ways, the old systems. I'm offering citizenship in a new world."

Shovel paused for effect. "But first. The kids. They come with us. Don't say a word and don't resist. If you do, not only will you be shot, but the two people on either side of you will be executed as well."

Soldiers moved among the captives and took six children away from the carpet of prisoners. The kids exchanged frightened expressions with their parents but nothing more.

Shovel was impressed.

The soldiers herded the youngsters away and out of sight. The boys and girls ranged from five to ten. A tall boy was pushed back down. Shovel had deemed teenagers would be treated as adults.

"Now," Shovel continued. "Any miners among, you? Hm? Any doctors?"

Nothing.

"You're sure of that?"

Again, none of the prisoners moved. It didn't really surprise him, but he had to ask. Skilled professionals and tradespeople were like two-legged slabs of gold in the new world.

"All right. Now, then, know that the children'll be well taken care of, and that in time, this night will be forgotten. *You* will be forgotten. Unless you join us."

One of the men facedown in the dirt held a hand in the air. A soldier walked over and placed the squared-off barrel of a compact machine gun behind the man's ear, nuzzling it.

"Speak," Shovel commanded.

"Are you *crazy*? After—after all of *this*?"

"This?" Shovel answered with a slow, disdainful shake of his head. "This is nothing. You were all dead, really. Dead. You just didn't know it. This place. This farm. If it wasn't us, it would've been a clan far, far worse. You know we actually discovered you a week and a half ago? You had no idea we were watching you. None. We had this whole place under surveillance. Watched your patterns. Your routines. We know who goes to the row of shithouses out back at what time of the day. What time your lookouts changed shifts. Regular, just like clockwork. We have a pretty good idea of who's cheating on who behind the barn over there. For *days*, we observed you, and you had no fucking idea despite all your precautions, all your . . . defenses. Oh, they're fine against the dead, but the dead are all gone. What's left are scavengers. The gangs. Raiders. Tribes of road savages who roam the land looking only to butcher, rape, and consume. Highway killers bent on drinking down whatever's left in the world, preying on the weak."

Shovel paused again.

"That's you," he clarified.

"From your viewpoint, we're the same. In some ways we are, I'll admit. But we're stronger. Better organized. We have a greater goal in mind rather than just day-to-day survival. In this day and age, only the strong's going to get by. And you? Obviously, you just weren't strong enough. Sooner or later, someone was going to find you and slaughter you like little piggies."

"You could have asked," said the man.

"Asked?" Shovel chuckled. "And if you said no, would you expect us to just leave you? Just like that? Leave you—more specifically the skill sets you might possess for someone *else* to come along and take? To utilize? To use your numbers against our own?"

"What the hell are you talking about?"

"Ah"—Shovel shook his head—"like I said. You're all dead. Just didn't know it. Still thinking in old-world ways."

"So we just join up?" the man asked.

Shovel smiled wryly. "Whoa, partner. Slow down. We'll see after a test. We don't just take *anyone*. Like I said, the world as you know it is over. Only a special breed is going to make it, and I suppose it's time to see who's got balls and who doesn't. No disrespect to the ladies. Half the people with guns on you now are ladies. All the padding and body armor kinda makes us all look the same. I'm told it's a . . . psychological thing."

Sick, wearing his own menacing ski mask and standing a little taller than Shovel's five-foot-eleven frame, stopped beside his leader and held out a toolbox.

Shovel nodded in approval. "So, who wants to become part of the solution?"

"This is *bullshit*. You'll kill whoever doesn't sign up," said the man eating dirt.

"Well, you're partially right. People *are* going to die here."

"Then we all join."

Shovel sincerely doubted that but decided he had to start somewhere. "What's your name?"

"Reilly."

"Reilly, you speak on behalf of your people?"

"Yeah."

"Then, I thank you for joining first. Stand up. Just you."

The soldier with the gun at Reilly's ear backed off. A cautious Reilly got to his feet. Filth dusted his jeans and red flannel shirt. A thick beard hung off his face, and Shovel didn't appreciate the murderous glower. He recognized trouble right away. Always the way with the leaders.

"Stay right there and pick. Screwdriver or hammer?" Shovel asked as Sick set the toolbox on the ground and pulled out the pair of tools.

"Huh?"

"Screwdriver or hammer. Pick one."

"What for?"

"*Pick one, goddamnit,*" Shovel barked.

Reilly jumped. The fire in the bearded man's eyes diminished with uncertainty, which was more to Shovel's liking.

"Hammer," Reilly muttered.

Sick tossed him the tool.

"Now," Shovel said, "who else wants to join?"

A show of hands.

"That one." Shovel pointed to a short but stocky individual, another beard grower. It was the style of the times. "You get the screwdriver."

It landed at the man's feet.

"Now, as I've said," Shovel explained, "only the strong survive. And we only want the strong. But also, we want a special breed of survivor. A *survivor's* survivor, you see. You two—step over there, away from the crowd. And don't run. Don't you dare run. Not if you value the lives of your friends still on the ground. Either of you run, we light up the works."

A glaring but understanding Reilly and his companion meandered over to the indicated spot. Shovel saw the leader sensed trouble. The farm boy wasn't stupid.

"Now," Shovel declared when the pair was clear of the others. "Time for the hardcore. You got your weapons. Now you fight. Right there. To the death. We'll take the one who kills the other."

Reilly appeared utterly stunned. "You sick, twisted fucker."

"If you don't fight, we shoot you both. If you think about rushing us, we'll blow your knees out first. We'll arbitrarily do the same to whoever is handy, and then you all get to see the next matchup from where you bleed out on the ground. And I guarantee if that happens, the person shot will curse you and your family like you've never heard before."

"You're a fucking lunatic," Reilly said in disbelief, his words vapor in the nearby headlights.

The stocky one, however, was considering it. He actually brought the screwdriver up to his waist in an underhanded grip, ready to stab, weighing his chances. That was his downfall: too *much* thinking.

Reilly noticed that and immediately tossed his hammer into the dirt. "You can go fuck yourself," he directed at his captor.

The stocky man squaring off against Reilly eyed the discarded tool before looking down in shame, regretting his thoughts. Without a word, he dropped the screwdriver. A triumphant Reilly focused on Shovel, and, for a moment, the tension grew and threatened to erupt any second.

Shovel regarded the leader's smug expression of superiority, as if he thought he'd really *won* something by not playing along. Shovel frowned, truly despising self-righteous pricks like Reilly.

"Shoot 'em."

Three soldiers fired, the night flashing and snapping. Bullets chewed into the two men while fragments sputtered and spurted from the front and rear. The impacts launched them into the air about a foot before they crashed to earth in bloody lumps. Some people screamed. One woman bolted. She made it nearly ten feet before a black-garbed killer took aim and damn near cut her in half with an extended burst of gunfire.

Everything died down after a few seconds. Steam issued from the executed. The people still on the ground sobbed and squirmed, replaying in their heads what had just happened.

Shovel inhaled and appraised the situation, feeling the tension return and build once more. Fearful eyes looked up from the ground.

"Who's next?" he repeated.

16

The morning was a dark shade of eggshell white.

Gus rubbed at his eyes and stared at the ceiling, slowly coming to his senses after a deep sleep. Blankets from a linen closet covered him from neck to toe, completing a bunk he'd made on the comfy sofa. He felt guilty for resting—guilty for not being out there, searching for Maggie and the kids. However, crawling forth into the night of Lower Sackville and Halifax wasn't a plan to him. That would've been more like asking for trouble.

The Captain stood at attention on the coffee table. Gus had placed him there the night before, but the sailor's smile got on his nerves after a while, so he turned him around to face the road.

"Give a shout if anyone drives up here," Gus had told him.

He hadn't drunk a drop the night before, proving to himself and the Captain that he didn't depend on his wares anymore, that he could function without them, regardless of how tempting they were.

It was just after nine in the morning, sunny but feeling of winter.

Gus threw off the blankets and sat up, rubbed at his eyes and face once again, and took a deep, sobering stare out at the cul-de-sac.

"Whattaya think?" he asked the officer and allowed the silence to grow. "Yeah. Let me get something to eat, and we'll get moving."

Knee-high grass almost hid the firepit in the backyard. Gus borrowed a handsaw from the garage and cut a few pieces of wood off a nearby elm tree, not so concerned about the noise. He put a lighter flame to some leaves, grass, and twigs filling the firepit. Within an hour, he was eating noodles, feasting on two packs of the aged delicacy. He wished he had some of the cured deer meat or beef that Adam and the boys had prepared for the winter, but that was gone with the storage shed if it wasn't stolen.

"Probably shit a nugget," Gus muttered after finishing his breakfast. He made his way to a downstairs bathroom and was delighted to find toilet paper still hanging from a wall dispenser. After a meditative moment that lasted close to ten minutes, he hoisted his jeans and went to the living room. He gathered up the Nomex gear and stowed it in the SUV. The leather duds he'd taken from the Leather Shop went on over his regular clothing.

Having done that, he went to the garage door and worked the crank, allowing the day inside.

A man stood not thirty feet away, dressed in a black, knee-length winter duster. A pirate's stocking cap descended and snaked a couple of times around his neck. A trimmed tumbleweed of a beard graced his chin, and that, along with a wide pair of sunglasses, hid his face damn near perfectly. On any day before the apocalypse, Gus would've pegged him as a street busker.

"Mornin'," the stranger said jovially and gave a ratty smile, his hands deep in his pockets.

"Mornin'," Gus replied warily, glancing around.

"Sleep good last night?"

Gus fought down his first response to tell the stranger to go fuck himself. "Yeah. I did."

"It's a nice house. Nice street."

"Yep." Gus realized his bat was in the SUV and his knife was in his fireman's boots.

"You're probably wondering why I'm here," Stocking Cap said.

"I am."

"Saw you drive up yesterday. Didn't feel like barging in then. Figured to hold off until the morning."

"Good idea."

"Yeah, I thought so."

"You live around here?"

"Me? Hell no, I'm from Bridgewater."

"Come up here to look around?"

"You got it. For food mostly. Supplies. Anything useful."

"Just you?"

Stocking Cap nodded. "Yep. Just me. But don't worry. I'm not interested in fightin' or killin' or anything. Just fair tradin', if you're into that sorta thing."

"What if I'm not?"

Stocking Cap shrugged. "We part ways."

"Yeah? Nothing else? You won't try to kill me?"

"Why would I wanna do that?"

Gus stood right in front of the SUV's grill and couldn't decide what to do with his arms. He finally decided to hold on to his hips and hoped it didn't seem too confrontational. The coast still looked clear. "Lotta bad people out here. Folks who aren't too worried about chopping a person up and leaving them for dead."

"Yeah?"

Gus nodded that it was fact.

"Yeah, well, I'm not one of them," Stocking Cap established while glancing at the sky, straightening his back as if it bothered him. "Ain't that many people left, anyway."

"No. There's not."

"You know, you're the first person I've talked to in about three weeks."

"Three weeks, eh? 'Sa long time."

"It is."

"Well, I gotta get movin' here," Gus said. "What was it you wanted?"

"Trade mostly. Won't take long."

"Okay. Let's trade."

"Got any ammunition?"

"Nope."

"Whiskey?"

"Nope."

"Nudie books?"

"Nudie books?" Gus repeated.

"Yeah. Just the regular kind. None of the weird stuff."

"Who the hell trades nudie books?"

"You'd be surprised."

"Y'mean more than I am now?"

"Well, okay. Toilet paper?"

"None that I want to trade. You running low?"

"Not really," the stranger admitted, "but I try to keep stocked. You can never have enough of that stuff."

They agreed on that.

"Just to be clear," Stocking Cap said, "you don't have any nudie books."

Gus winced. "No nudie books."

"All right then. Anything to eat?"

"When was the last time you ate?"

"A day ago."

That didn't sit well with Gus at all. "Well, I . . . fuck it. I got some noodles and Kraft Dinner. If that's okay."

Stocking Cap brightened. "That sounds like a banquet right now. Need any nudie books?"

Gus shook his head . . . but then actually considered it. "Nah, you keep those. The food's free. You got anything to drink?"

"No," the stranger replied with a shake of his head. "Nothing. But water's easy to come by. Actually came by some powdered Gatorade about three or four months back. Life was good. Anyway, like I said, plenty of water around."

"More than some things. Well, here," Gus stopped and regarded the stranger cautiously. "I'm going to get it out of the back."

"Jesus, thanks, man."

"Just don't cook it up here, in this house, is all," he called out from the rear of the garage.

"Something special about this place?"

Gus returned from the back with a pair of KD boxes in hand and a pack of noodles. "Yeah, something like that. Listen, I don't want to sound all paranoid and shit, but how about I just toss this to you?"

"Ah," Stocking Cap said. "How about this. You place it on the lawn there, and I'll get it later?"

That suited Gus fine. He walked over to the high grass and placed it on the ground. "How's that?"

"Great. Appreciate it, man."

"It's not quite half of what I got, but," he shrugged, "should keep you going for a couple of days."

"It will. Thanks." The beard smiled.

"Well," Gus threw out and felt at a loss as to what to say next. "Good luck."

"Hey, you don't need anything?" the stranger asked.

"Not really. The only thing would be food, and I think we just covered that. Unless you got some guns stashed around?"

"Sorry, man. No guns."

Gus rubbed at the back of his head, felt the hair growing there, and realized he wasn't wearing his helmet. "Well, that's it then, I guess."

"You sure you don't want any nudie books?"

That brought on a chuckle. "No, man. I'm okay."

"I got information," Stocking Cap offered.

That was something. "What kind?"

"Where you going?"

"No offense, but I'd just as soon keep that private."

"Okay, okay. Forgot myself. Haven't talked to many and all, y'know. Well, anyway, you should know Halifax has become a bit of a nest lately."

"A nest?"

"Yeah," Stocking Cap said. "Road savages floating in. They don't wanna talk unless they have you tied down. Looking for guns and whatnot. Vicious. Almost got my ass shot off one afternoon down on Barrington. They chased me for four blocks before I finally lost them."

"You been down there?"

"Yeah. City's a morgue. Bodies . . . well, let's just say it's a mess."

Gus digested that. "You see anyone with kids?"

"Kids?"

"Yeah, kids. A little girl and boy. This high"—he marked space with a hand—"and a woman in her sixties."

Stocking Cap thought about it. "No, sorry."

"Yeah," Gus nodded, feeling his stomach unclench. He'd put too much hope into that one question.

"I did see a pair of pickups shoot up the 102 yesterday morning, however. Seemed like they were in a hurry."

That stopped Gus, and he considered the stocking-cap man. "Pickups?"

"Help any?"

"Maybe."

"Well, let me tell you this. I passed through Truro a few weeks back and actually went into New Brunswick before turning back. It's Wild West out there. Whoever's left over is gravitating into groups of survivors. Coming here. Road savages. And they're not friendly."

"Yeah." Gus knew from his own experience. "Thanks."

"Hey. Thank you." Stocking Cap nodded at the packaged food. "Where you from, anyway?"

Gus didn't think there was any harm in giving up that information. "Annapolis."

"The Valley? The hell you doing down here—oh wait—looking for those youngsters?"

"And the lady."

"Something happen?"

Gus regarded Stocking Cap. *What the hell.* "Two days ago, the people I'd been livin' with for a couple of years got executed on the front lawn. All except four. I found one of them yesterday, dumped on the side of the road like so much garbage. I'm gonna find the others."

Birdsong drifted from beyond the cul-de-sac, filling dead air.

"Listen," Stocking Cap said. "Sorry to hear about your people. I keep out of sight a lot. Take risks as I see 'em, like here and now. But I'll tell you this. It doesn't really surprise me to hear about your troubles. In the last year alone, I've heard more gunfights than I can remember. Run into a lot of gangs. Folks who are militant. And they're more than happy to put a bullet in you. Or worse."

Gus nodded. "Thanks for that."

Stocking Cap waved dismissively. "The Valley had a lot of farms up there. Still do?"

"Still do. Most of it grows wild, but it was feeding us for a couple of years. Would've kept on, too—until this all happened."

"Still got apple orchards?"

"It's all there," Gus said with a squint. "Apples, melons. Blueberries. Corn. Hard work, but it's there."

"Hard work doesn't bother me," Stocking Cap said. "These days, it's back to the basics or nothing."

"Heard that. I suggest you head on up there. Check things out. Bypass the city and head for the smaller communities past Greenwood. Berwick. Those places. You'll find the farms. Livestock too. If you can catch 'em."

This pleased Stocking Cap greatly. His beard moved when he smiled, and that time, he showed teeth—or what remained of them. Gus kept a neutral face. He wore his own scars.

"Good luck to you then," Stocking Cap said.

"Good luck to you too . . . stranger." Gus smiled at having tagged that on. It felt good. He got behind the wheel of the SUV. Stocking Cap offered a lazy salute and backed off, making way.

A part of Gus, the paranoid part, warned him to exercise caution. Perhaps Stocking Cap had a companion with a gun sighted on him. Gus sighed. If he did, Gus couldn't do a damn thing about it until after the shot. That feeling of having just gotten off the farm made him uneasy. The world had changed, and he'd existed in a bubble during the most important parts.

He eased out of the garage and drove past Stocking Cap, who stood aside good-naturedly and actually waved, causing Gus to let slip his prize-winning grin. A third of the way out of the cul-de-sac, he felt better about the encounter and glanced into his rearview mirror.

Stocking Cap was already picking up the food.

Gus stayed on the road and, after a minute, realized he was still alive.

The gray lick of cracked pavement stretched out before the SUV like a dead man's tongue. All manner of vehicles haunted the road, some with sun-scorched corpses nearby, others just empty, as if their drivers had pulled over to stretch their legs and never came back. Black minivans, red sedans, a few sporty coupes, and others scrolled by. A few had left the road entirely and crashed into trees or run up sloping hillsides covered in yellow grass, their doors hanging open and drivers missing. Power lines drooped from steel frameworks along one side of the highway, their cement bases concealed behind trees. Roadside attractions and pit stops called to Gus at times, tugging loose memories of his younger days when he and his girlfriend or buddies would rip out of town, seeking the lure of the open road and a quick meal at KFC or some other food joint. Those moments seeped into his mind like bright poison, and Gus relived every one until his heart ached. The SUV stayed steady as he rolled northeast, up the 102. Tall transports cast long shadows, giving him pause—he mistrusted their corners until he snuck past them. A comfortable heat flooded the interior, and the plastic reincarnation of Captain Morgan sat on its back in the passenger side, gazing up in bright merriment. The Captain hadn't said a word, maintaining that gallant smile, and for that, Gus thought himself fortunate.

The days when the old sailor *did* talk to him had to have been the darkest.

Wide rivers and open fields swept past his windows. Green signs counted down the distance to each approaching town. A heavy truck had stopped under an underpass, its flatbed of cut logs still stacked high, and he shot past the shiny red beast without stopping. When his fuel ran low, he stopped and spiked gas tanks, losing more than he could catch in one of the Tupperware dishes, but eventually gathering enough to satisfy the SUV.

During one long stretch of highway, Gus glanced into his rearview mirror and thought he detected movement. It bothered him enough that he slowed atop a crest and finally stopped and got out to peer back. He stood there, waiting a solid minute, and saw nothing. Being in such an open area, alone, was strangely disconcerting even though his old house had been a respectable drive outside the city limits. It hit him that he'd driven into Annapolis pretty much blasted out of his gourd, unlike the present moment, when all his senses were humming. After about ten minutes, Gus rubbed his bald head and got back behind the wheel. As an afterthought, he watched his side mirror in case anything was creeping up on him.

Nothing did, however.

The Captain's smile seemed to widen.

Gus stopped for brunch in the parking lot of a dilapidated building near the word BINGO painted on a billboard facing the highway. He studied the word as he ate, repeating it in his mind, sensing a greater meaning he failed to grasp.

The once-bustling town of Truro came into view much more quickly than he'd remembered, and he stopped on a hilltop to gaze over it, eyeing large structures stamped with logos and brand names. He shielded his eyes with a hand, seeing the horizon rise up in a ring of frosty hills. A nearby sign pointed the way to lower Truro and Bible Hill, but nothing drew Gus in that direction.

Eventually, he drove off.

Clouds filled the afternoon sky, and around three thirty, Gus started thinking about getting off the road and camping for the night. The highway, with all its deserted cars, reeked of melancholy that he didn't want to experience after dark. If he'd taken the right chemicals, he believed the shoulders of the road would be thick with the ghosts of motorists long gone.

The land opened on either side of him, the pale grass sometimes divided by fences of trees. The roads split more often into ramps leading to overpasses, but he didn't take any of those just yet, knowing the 102 would eventually loop around into the 104, which crossed—like a T—the northerly road he currently drove on. A concrete wall began on his left, crumbled in places by crashed cars, but one lane remained open enough for him to proceed. In the distance, another overpass loomed. Several trailers rested on the bridgework crossing overhead, and something at the back of Gus's skull sounded an alarm.

His foot eased onto the brake pedal, slowing his vehicle.

On the driver's side, several cars had mashed their noses into the concrete barrier.

One minivan had two webby eyes perforating its windshield.

Bullet holes.

The sight drew Gus's attention, distracting him.

A startling *crack* interrupted the hum of the SUV's engine. The windshield splintered inward, and shards screamed past his right ear fast and hot enough for him to feel its heat. He stomped on the gas, jerking the wheel to the right in a screech of tire rubber and a twisting lurch of his guts. Cars and pavement blurred, becoming landscape. The front wheels bounced over an embankment much higher than he expected. A pond rushed toward him, only barely glimpsed through the blinding tracery of the bullet holes.

Then the dashboard exploded, and the world died.

17

Something hammered into Gus's stomach, forcing a gasp to explode from his diaphragm. Another blow made his darkness pirouette from the impact. A rumble of thunder reached him then, echoing off distant hills, sounding suspiciously like whale song.

"—hit him again and put—"

That string of words came to Gus in a tangle of consciousness just before he drifted off once more. More strikes to his body felt as if they were happening perhaps twenty fathoms down in a very deep sea. He rocked, trying to swim, but couldn't summon his arms or his legs. The sensation of reaching for something occurred to him, which puzzled that one little, still-functioning part of his brain. Then a sharp pain stabbed him, as if a ship had gone hard to starboard in his lower abdomen before the hull crunched into unforgiving ice.

"—dead I'm fuckin' tellin' ya—"

"He ain't dead. Look."

Another blow rang him like a bony gong.

"I think he's wakin'. He look like he's wakin' to you?"

"Fuck I look like? The goddamn surgeon general? I'm outta my element here. *This* is what I do best."

Laughter, distant yet resounding directly in his skull, ended with another solid crunch to Gus's ribs, pulling him out of that midnight stew of blackness by his arms.

"You do that very well," a voice said, middle-of-the-road in terms of timbre.

"Think I broke my fuckin' hand that time," someone winced.

"I did that shit once. My right hand too. Had to wipe my ass with my left."

"Think I remember that. You smelled of shit for a month."

More laughter—good old boys just hangin' out and shootin' their mouths off. Gus almost smiled then, nearly surfacing right there.

"Look!" another voice said, charged with discovery. "Fuckin' meathead damn just *smiled* that time."

"Wha?"

"Edgar's right. That not-dead fucker smiled. He's comin' around."

"Fuckin' about time. Only been tenderizin' his hangin' ass for the last hour."

"You fuckin' hit like a goddamn girl anyway, Murray."

"Yeah, your mother said the same thing."

"Don't you be saying shit about my mother. Don't you even fuckin' *dare*. That shit's disrespectin'."

"Sorry. Meant to say *fuck you*."

"No, fuck *you*."

"All right, lay off, both of ya. Jesus Christ."

"Murray's only pissed off cuz fireboy wasn't a woman."

"I *am* pissed. I was hoping for a prime slab of meat. Not *this*."

"Fuck, bro, you think you're the only guy here hurtin' for a piece of pink?"

"Yeah, but you got Ryan there."

Harsh laughter was drowned out by a low and menacing, "The fuck you say to me, cocksucker?"

"I said . . ."—a throat cleared in earnest at that point—"on the good nights, when you need that little extra-sweet lovin', Ryan even takes his teeth out."

"You little—"

"Look, he's wakin'," another voice said, cutting off the discussion.

In his private darkness, Gus realized he *was* waking.

"He should be. Lazy fucker been sleeping long enough. Goddamn sonavabitch truly is a hunk of hangin' meat. Goddamn tired of this fuckin' bullshit nonsense. Lemme cut his balls off. That'll make him holler."

Laughter—someone moved closer to him. Gus tried to move his arms, but they weren't working. His chin rested on his chest, and his eyes opened, revealing his bare feet lashed together with a dirty piece of rope and anchored to a rusty tire rim. His shoulders ached in their sockets, and his ankles felt as if they suffered from extreme carpet burn. Cold prickled his skin.

A mixture of bad body odor and motor oil enveloped him.

"Good mornin', sunshine," a phlegmy voice said, greased in false cheer. A tall, lean individual appeared, dressed in a woodsman jacket that had seen better days. Gus raised his chin and balked at a black-bearded brute with sparkling gray eyes—the eyes of a killer no longer fearful of exhibiting once-suppressed urges. Those smoky marbles glistened, taking Gus in, seizing him, and the beard hitched back into a sweet smile, revealing not the salmon pink of a healthy set of gums but rather a viral lime *green* that might have taken root all the way to the man's brain. A pair of eroding incisors dotted the horrible mouth. If Gus didn't know any better, he would have sworn a mad trapper had come down out of the hills.

That frightening visage raised a knife—a big, gleaming sword of a blade, with a curved tip as tapered as a candle's flame. Gus lifted his chin further and pulled on his bonds, quivering in place like a crudely twanged bowstring.

"Shhh, now, shhhh . . . *shhhhh*," Gray Eyes said, pouting dramatically. His round eyes blazed with a feral craziness so bright it was difficult to tell if the man had eyelids.

For the first time in his life, Gus felt genuinely fearful of what was about to happen.

"Been waitin' all mornin' for you, sunshine," Gray Eyes whispered and smiled that maniacal grin. Indistinct shapes crowded in behind him. "Been waitin' for you to open them pretty eyes of yours."

The knife's cold tip touched the fleshy bag under Gus's right eye, and he suddenly held his breath. He realized with horror he'd been stripped down to just his blue Fruit of the Looms.

Gray Eyes kept his berserker smile in place and drew closer, his eyes growing bigger, impossibly wilder, to the point where Gus didn't think he was a man at all but some feral missing link somehow mistaken for a man. Gray Eyes zoomed in closer while evil chuckles sounded around the edges of reality, issuing from the watchers. Gus never had a chance to compose himself. He was trussed up good and damn-near-bowel-looseningly fearful. Gray Eye's face started to tremble, as if a thousand volts suddenly ripped through his frame, his eyes as maddeningly bright as headlights. The knife dug into the baggy sac below Gus's eye, and Gus released a whimper of terror. A shiny rivulet of scarlet streaked over his cheek.

"Do it, Boll," someone hissed anxiously in the background. "Hook that eye out."

"One flick of the wrist, bro. All that's to it."

"Fuck yeah—I'm *hungry* here."

"I wonder," another speculated, "if an eye is on the cheek—just hangin' there but, like, still attached to whatever, y'know?—like, can it still see? Or is it all swively and shit?"

Insane Boll and his train wreck of a smile still didn't blink. He moved closer until his left eye stared into Gus's, not an inch away.

"Go on," Boll chuckled in that tainted, gravelly voice of his, which reeked of graveyard meat. "Go on. Do somethin' . . . *heroic.* Like head butt me. Y'know, somethin' *crazy.* Go on."

But Gus didn't. Instead, he squeezed his eyes shut and braced himself for that terrible hot or cold—or both—sensation that would come with being stabbed in the face.

"Well, Jesus H . . ." Boll grumped, the eagerness in his voice suddenly tepid.

Then a chortle of hyena laughter rose from the audience.

"Scorched shit flicker *pissed* himself!"

Gus realized it was true. His terror had grown to such proportions, he hadn't even realized his bladder had had enough and just cut loose, saturating his Fruit of the Looms.

Boll backed away in obvious disgust, his smile disappearing behind that monstrous duster of a beard. Those hell-bright gray peepers dimmed as he glanced down—and Gus saw that the man did indeed have lids—but then they flicked back up and beheld his captive with a disgust so raw Gus thought his time on this depopulated planet had finally come to an end.

"You fuckin' almost pizzled on me," Boll grumbled like a Kodiak coming out of hibernation. "You dirty bird, you."

Boll stepped forward, slashing downward in an overhand chop, his knife parting the skin covering Gus's ribs and grazing five of them before the razor edge leaped off the last rung and missed the fluttering snare drum of his exposed stomach.

The sound of pattering reached his stunned brain, and Gus wasn't sure whether it was from his bladder emptying itself or his blood. He glanced down and saw Boll's cut, one that would definitely need stitches, issuing a red river that positively gleamed against his pallid flesh.

Gus panted, nearly passing out.

The butt of the knife bounced off his nose, stunning him in a flash of black light and keeping him in agonizing reality.

"Y'get to keep your eye. This day," Boll warned and ambled off toward a huge motor home.

Gus winced and shifted, noting he was in a chuck-wagon ring comprised of big RVs, some white, some tiger striped, and he was hung from the hook-and-boom winch system of an old tow truck. A cluster of men surrounded him, five total, sitting in leather recliners or on lawn chairs. Each resembled something milked out of the ass end of some inbred clan of mountain folk. Heavy beards hung off unseen chins. Gold teeth glimmered. They laughed and shook their heads. Boll's little show of terror had greatly amused them all.

"Well, then," one of the hillbillies announced and stood up. Unlike the others, his was the only head shaven to the quick. A leather coat hung off gaunt shoulders.

The coat flapped open, revealing a thick sweater as well as a sheathed knife hanging off a belt. "Murray, get on up to the overpass. Time's a wastin'."

Murray stood, a short wall of a man layered in winter clothing and topped off with a purple stocking cap. A set of black bike goggles regarded Gus with a sullen jiggle then switched to the leather-clad speaker and back to Gus once more. Murray nodded and scuffed at the frozen dirt like a petulant school kid. A machete in a crude sheath slapped against his hip. Gus saw most of the men wore edged steel in such fashion, along with their tribal beards.

"Boll, hang around here for a bit. You listenin' to me, son?"

Gus focused on the man who had sent Murray on his way. Boll had parked himself in a recliner and leaned forward until his elbows rested on his knees.

"What'd we find in that SUV?"

"Nothin'," Boll answered.

"Nothin'?" the leader asked and regarded a silver-bearded bruiser sitting in a recliner.

"The man had dick all," Silver Beard replied. "KA-BAR knife in a boot. Aluminum bat. Firefighter gear, which I can see as being as practical as strapping a blast mat to your hide. Some magazines, water, noodles, small bottle of rum, and a sack of flour for whatever reason I can*not* fathom. Of all the things layin' around to pick up, a fuckin' sack of muffin mix isn't that high on my grocery list."

"Huh," the leader said in an *is-that-so* tone. He played with the rounded hilt of his knife. "Damn strange."

"Oh, and toilet paper," Silver Beard announced.

"Can find a use for that," one man said, thumbing the hammer of a large revolver.

"You might, but not old Murray," said another. "I think Murray wipes his ass with the entire roll like he's whipping up cotton candy or something. Just jams his finger into the roll there and—"

The speaker went through the motions, stirring up some groans and chuckles.

The leader studied Gus. "Y'know something, fireboy? We've been collecting tolls here on this strip of highway for a long, long time. And I think you are in fact the first person to come along and *not* be carrying anything of interest. Except the toilet paper. Sure, there were some folks that wheeled through that were too big for us to handle, but for the most part, everyone else we've stopped has had . . . *something.* Makes me wonder if you're not hiding anything . . ."

"Not hidin'," Gus grunted, feeling the cut's angry sting down his ribs, the blood outlining his exposed contours. "I'm . . . lookin' for someone."

"I'd say you fucking *found* someone."

Gus suffered through a few more breaths as the cold punished his nearly naked form.

A thoughtful expression covered the leader's face as he meandered over to where his prisoner hung.

"Who you looking for?" he asked.

Gus hesitated, and a fist hammered into his exposed gut, ejecting all air from his lungs.

"That," the leader stated while observing Gus gasping for breath, "is for makin' me wait. It's as good as you're gonna get in this situation, and I'm not tellin' any lies here. You ain't pussy, and you ain't got nothin' of value other than that knife and that tiny quart of rum. We waited all last night for you to come to, and we ain't waitin' any longer. Really, you're just here now because of a dangerous combination of curiosity, boredom, and amusement. None of those feelings are your friends right now. You best answer when I question you, and maybe I won't take it into my head to do something cruel. Understand?"

"Yeah."

That put a smile on the other man's face. "Better. Now, who you lookin' for?"

"A woman and two kids."

"Really?"

"Yeah."

"That's all. An old bag and two mouths? Boy and a girl?"

Gus squinted in pained curiosity.

"A few people traveled through here matching that description. The men with them paid the toll, so we let them through. We operate a fair business practice here."

Dark chuckles erupted all around. Boll scratched hard at his beard.

"You failed to see the signs on the road, which is why we shot your ass off the highway. Anyway, tell you what. You're going to be our guest for the next while. If we get along, who knows? We might even let you go. Maybe even recruit you. Always looking for new talent."

Then he leaned in, his eyes narrowing. "If we don't get along, well . . . at best, we'll kill you. At worst, crazy man Boll over there will kill you. Then skull-fuck you. Balls deep."

Gus panted, heart kicking, positively terrified and not trying to hide it.

"So relax," the speaker said and smiled warmly. He reached out and thumbed drying blood off Gus's face, not so very sweetly.

"Hang in there . . ."

18

And hang Gus did . . .

Like a chunk of hairy meat under a cold sun.

His arms burned to the point where he suspected circulation had been restricted. He stood on the tire rim, the steel gouging its cold brand into the bare soles of his feet. Every breath of early winter, however brief or soft, felt as scalding as a whip. *Blood*, his mind confided in him. *Keep the blood moving.*

Gus had to smile at that.

He realized he hung from the tow truck only if he bent his knees. If he stood straight, he could lift his arms above his head a half inch and enjoy some slack—a finger of wiggle room—and he made the most of it. He twisted his hands, touching the coarsely woven fiber with nearly bloodless fingertips. The men ignored his struggling, confident that the bonds would keep their prisoner in place.

Gus had to admit they'd done a fine job.

Even if he could somehow claw his way free of the rope, his arms would probably fall to his sides like a pair of beef hindquarters. Then there was Boll's cut, dried but stinging like a foot-long needle pounded into his skin and running a couple of hundred volts. His feet ached on the rim and had no relief there. Gus alternated between standing straight and hanging from his arms. Muscles he'd never known existed screeched with each movement. He tried separating his mind from his body, studying the area he was in. The overpass gang had parked their motor homes on a dirt-and-grass clearing. He craned his head around. The raised slope of the highway loomed just behind, with guardrails reinforced by wood and sheets of metal. Gun ports dotted their length. One lane led into the assembled ring of trailers, with a fire pit and an outdoor grill marking the center. Skimpy lawn chairs and more luxurious recliners rested near their owners' homes. A small flatbed trailer housed a crude wooden shed, enough to protect its treasure from the elements. The low purr of a gas generator emanated from within. Power cables ran to the RVs. All in all, it wasn't a bad setup in the least, as long as the gas lasted. Even Gus wondered how much longer the additives would prolong the life of the fuel.

Time slowed, so each shivering breeze seemed like a day. Hollers from the gang occasionally blotted out the creaking of the rope. Boll appeared, scratched his crotch—something which Gus could relate to—and retired to one of the wheeled homes, slapping the door closed behind him. Some of the windows were tinted and dark, but others weren't, and Gus could see Boll glancing his way every now and again, just checking in.

Around noon, the other gang members retired to their Winnebagos for what Gus believed to be lunch. Harsh laughter penetrated the white and striped walls at times while his feet truly began to hurt while standing on the tire rim. He rested his head against one arm, shivering and enduring the knife-like pain in his shoulders, trying hard not to think of what provisions the gang members might have inside their luxurious walls.

By midafternoon, Gus started identifying the men other than Murray and Boll, through shouts and heated, out-of-sight conversations. Some walked past him wearing scabbards filled with knives, the edged weapons hanging off their hips like badges of terror. Sidearms were slung into leg or chest holsters.

R. J. Comeau was unquestionably the leader, and he wandered along the walls and gaps like a sidewinder with no rattle. He strutted, his head bobbing left and right with every step, leather jacket flung open and swinging, conjuring images of old gunslingers marking their territory—a manner Gus would have found amusing if he wasn't strung up like a plucked chicken. When Comeau barked, however, the others obeyed, suggesting a history where someone might have been made a bloody example as warning.

Boll, however, reminded Gus of old episodes of *The Muppet Show* and the character of Animal.

Nate Boone was a stick of an individual, resembling a walking cadaver who'd look more stylish in a mortuary sheet rather than the dusty denim tuxedo he wore. Gus couldn't tell if his hair was naturally brown or just filthy from the perpetual dust cloud hanging about him. Boone had a steely six-shooter hand cannon strapped to his left thigh.

Whenever Boone came into sight, Gus's attention fixed on that weapon.

Edgar made Gus nervous the moment he stepped into view. The man was another black-eyed hillbilly type wearing a blue bandanna with a screaming eagle in a tight tourniquet around his forehead. A bulbous mole protruded from the man's right cheek, large enough that, at one time, Gus thought it was a healing gunshot hole. The only time he appeared, he did so with menace as he leaned up against one corner of the tiger-striped Winnebago and leaned back, folding his arms. He stood there and studied Gus, unnerving him—the way a diver caught in a cloud of blood might feel with a great white swimming around. That session ticked off the seconds until Gus lowered his head and closed his eyes, hoping the monster would be gone when he peeked.

The last was a midsized man called Prout, who might've been an overweight doughboy in a previous life. Prout wore the stupidest mohawk Gus had ever seen. None of the others made light of the gauche hairstyle, however. The guy seemed to be constantly picking his nose and flicking the results into the dirt. At lunch, he'd gone into his home, eaten, and emerged with a streak of yellow glop clinging to his sizeable beard.

Around late afternoon, with the shadows growing on the ground, Prout came down from the overhead pass and dropped into a recliner not ten steps away from the tow truck. He grunted loudly upon sitting, enough to get Gus's attention. Prout leaned the chair back and pulled out a *National Geographic* that looked vaguely familiar.

Prout made a scene licking his thumb and started turning pages. His expressions morphed at irregular intervals, flowing from mild boredom to genuine interest. At one point, a look of pure *what the fuck?* covered his face, quickly followed by head shaking and more page turning.

In the end, he left his prisoner alone.

Sleep eventually took Gus.

"I said, *hey*."

Gus lifted his chin and squinted miserably at Prout, who stewed in the recliner and regarded him like a schoolboy caught doing something he shouldn't be.

"You asleep over there?"

His shoulders ached, and he couldn't feel anything in his arms. "No."

"Good. Y'know something?"

Gus exhaled, and that little movement caused agony around his shoulders. His urine-soaked undershorts burned his skin.

"I never much liked *National Geographic*," Prout lectured. "Liked the pictures, y'understand, but if I had a choice, I'd go with something that showed a little more skin. A little more *bounce*. But, after all that's happened through the years, and maybe it's just boredom talking, but now I'm starting to *like* reading the articles. Never did that before. People change."

People change. True words. Gus laid his chin back down and shifted the minutest degree, wincing as he did, trying to get comfortable or just to alleviate the stress in his shoulders or even his feet. He knew it wasn't going to happen, though.

"You a firefighter?" Prout asked.

"Huh?"

"A firefighter?"

Where that question had come from perplexed Gus, and he wasn't in the mood for a Q&A to begin with. "No."

"You had that firefighter gear in your ride."

"What?"

"I said, you had that firefighter gear in your ride. Great idea, in my opinion. I expect nothing could get through that hide. You know the same company makes Kevlar. The older suits weren't as tough as yours, though. Yours is puncture proof—to a point, anyway. Bet nothing could bite its way through those layers when you had it on."

Gus didn't comment.

"You hear me?"

Gus did, but it was a single voice being heard over the twin loudspeakers of his shoulders. All he wanted was to be cut down or, if that wasn't possible, just left alone. That was all he wanted at that point—to be left to his suffering in peace.

Prout's face became drawn. He stood with a loud groan, making the recliner work. "Y'know, I'm gettin' tired of your attitude. Try to be civil here, and you don't have the time of day for me. I can take a hint."

Footsteps approached Gus. Though his head felt like a fifty-pound bowling ball, Gus managed to raise it in time to see Prout's fist connect with his stomach. All the wind left him, and he hung there, spiraling to the right, eyes squeezed shut and unable to breathe. Prout spoke then, but the words washed over Gus's senses like rain speckling glass.

That earned him another punch to the gut.

Another followed.

Breathing hard, Prout stood back after teeing off and belting a salvo into his captive's bruising midsection.

"What'cha doin', dicky?" black-eyed Edgar rumbled, coming into the ring. "Havin' some fun with the prisoner?"

Slit-eyed and nasty looking, Prout eased off and regarded the bandanna-wearing woodsman. "Cocksucker doesn't want to be conversational, so I figured a few fists would get him talking."

"Work any?" Edgar stopped alongside him and inspected Gus like a trophy kill.

"Can't tell just yet."

"Havin' too much fun tenderizin', huh?"

Prout nodded.

"You want him to talk, there are better ways than punching. Cracking him any-wheres might do more harm than good. For example, slug him one in the nuts, and well, he won't be chattin' for an hour. Too sensitive."

"Yeah, I thought so," Prout agreed. "Why I hit him in the gut."

"That's not bad," Edgar noted in a clinical tone. "But even then, you'll have to wait a bit before his diaphragm unlocks. Gotta have breath to say anything, right?"

"Yeah, you're right." A light of understanding went off in Prout's eyes. "So, where do you suggest?"

"Well, if it was information we were tryin' to get out of him, I'd say lower him and put his head into a washtub of water. Or cover his face and pour water over it."

"Drown him?"

"No, no, not that. What does the CIA call it? Waterboarding? Has a powerful effect on folks. Gets them all kinds of social. But I'm old-fashioned. If I want information or just a conversation, I say bend things until they break. Or twist. Cutting is fine too. Nothing like being helpless like fireboy here and feeling a knife coast on down your ribs or whatever. The threat alone is enough to get most folks talking, even if it's just shit."

Gus studied Edgar with narrowed eyes, disbelief rendering him speechless.

"Course, that way's messy as all hell too. And you run the risk of bleeding him out. So stick with the other two. Bend or twist."

Prout nodded understanding. "So no punching?"

Edgar took a contemplative breath, completely at ease with the conversation. "Oh hell, punch him if you want. Whale on him. I mean, whatever floats your boat, bro. Just that you have to wait for him to recover, right?"

As if to prove a point, Edgar reached up with fingers that might've been made of iron and pinched Gus's upraised triceps, hard enough to get a gasp of pain from the man. Edgar twisted it, as if attempting to rip it from the bone. A short whine erupted from Gus's bearded face, baring his incisors.

"See," Edgar said. "Like that."

"I don't really get off on that torture shit," Prout said.

Edgar cocked a brow. "Y'don't?"

"Nah. I mean, I'll hit the guy just to straighten him out, but I'm not into hurtin' just for the sake of hurtin'."

"Didn't know that about you, Ryan."

Prout shrugged.

"Well, if the urge takes you . . . that's how I'd do it." Edgar sized up Gus's hanging form, studying his bonds and then his body, looking for God only knew what.

"Stomp on them feet too," he eventually muttered and pointed. "Ain't nothing more painful than a good old-fashioned foot stomp. Target the toes. Small bones. Easy to break. Painful as all fuck."

"Jesus, Corey," Prout said. "Where'd you learn this?"

Edgar's dark, disturbing eyes regarded Gus with no more emotion than a knob of rock. That monstrous mole dotting his right cheek resembled a mark left by a lit cigarette or a blowtorch. "You go around the block a few times," the man drawled, "you pick up on things. Pavlov would ring a bell to get his dogs to salivate. Pain'll condition a subject in a similar manner, except faster. Some would argue, anyway."

Edgar smirked then, his mouth a furry line under that jungle of a beard. He reached forth and gripped the back of Gus's head, grabbed the fringe of hair growing there.

"Be a good dog, hear me?"

"Yeah," Gus answered.

That pleased Edgar, and he released him.

"You still got some of that dried beef that last bunch traded?" Edgar asked Prout.

"I do. Planning on doing up a cooked supper, actually. Still got some of that powdered gravy too. That shit doesn't go old."

"Gravy," Edgar smiled, his mole making him wicked. "Gravy sounds like a feast, doesn't it?"

"It does, it does."

The two men meandered off to a white Winnebago. An exhausted but relieved Gus watched them go, shivering from both the pain and the cold. His plunked his forehead against an arm and closed his eyes, locking himself away in darkness.

In the evening, as the dark crept in and around the site like the Atlantic tide, four of the gang members gathered in Prout's Winnebago. The wind picked up, complaining in Gus's ear. Every so often, a burst of laughter spiked the walls of the home on wheels, and shadows moved past lit windows. The cold tightened its grip on Gus's bare skin, making him wish for heat of any kind and freezing the long, ugly cut Boll had made earlier in the day. His feet transformed into numb blocks of ice, and his shoulders barely spoke at all. He shifted and straightened at times, his body screaming. That was fine with Gus. Pain was a good thing in that case. He wiggled his fingers and toes, stood and moved his legs. Everything felt sluggish, nearly frozen but functioning. He wondered when the suffering would end.

The men departed for their individual homes well after night had fallen, their shadows staggering between the RVs as if they'd drunk too much.

A *drink*.

A sip of anything would've hit the spot right then, would've thawed him from the inside out.

A door slammed, and a dark outline appeared beyond the flatbed with the generator shack. Another joined it, and they huddled out of sight before one retired, exclaiming, "Fuckin' cold out here tonight!"

Yes, it fucking is *cold out here tonight.*

Only a snow flurry or two was needed to garnish the scene.

The other figure came around the corner of the shack and approached Gus, boots scuffling along the frozen ground. It stopped four paces from him and stood there, studying.

"Comfy?" Comeau asked.

Gus barely had the juice left to raise his face.

"Hm," the leader grunted and walked past. Metal tinkled, and a motor flared to life. Gus felt himself crumple to the ground, smashing a knee off the torturous edge of the tire rim he'd balanced himself on for most of the day. The knee split and bled immediately, as if it were a mouth spitting out bad wine. The ground shredded his skin like broken glass. Gus cried out, took the pain and drew up his knees. His arms responded but barely, still attached to the lowered boom.

A door opened and closed. An engine started up, grabbing Gus's attention seconds before the tow truck pulled ahead, stretching him out on the harsh earth. Then the red lights flared like demonic eyes as it backed up a foot, giving him that much slack in his rope.

Not that he could do anything about it.

A ghost appeared over Gus. It pulled on his rope bonds, testing them. Then it stepped back and tossed something over his naked form, blinding him.

"Here y'are," Murray spoke.

"Got that tarp down?" Comeau asked, getting out of the truck.

"Right here."

"Yeah, that should be enough. Not like he's going anywhere."

"You're too kind, R. J.," Murray said.

"I know, right? Fuck it. He's still a man. That'll keep the snow off him until we decide what to do with him. Y'hear that, fireboy? We're debating your fate. You be good now, and maybe, just maybe, we'll cut you loose in the morning."

Murray chuckled, and Gus agreed with him. There was no fucking chance of being cut loose. Gus squirmed under the tarp, the heavy plastic crinkling as he moved.

"In case you're wondering, it's about four or five degrees out right now," Comeau said. "Might dip below zero—might—course, I'm no weather man. The weather's made a liar of me before. Hell, you might be buried under a foot of snow come morning."

A boot stepped on the tarp. "Best curl that up around you if you can. Tuck yourself in, in case the wind picks up. Seeya in the morning."

"Seeya, fireboy."

Gus set his jaw in an effort to stop its chattering. He listened for a moment, hearing the voices drift away. His wrists were crossed over each over, and just moving them wrung a gasp from him. His feet were a different matter entirely. They'd tied that rope tight enough to forever leave its print in the skin there, provided he ever got the rope off.

After hanging from his wrists for most of the day, Gus pulled his arms into his body, wiggled upon the coarse turf, and took one deep breath as comfort—comfort that he wouldn't get from that night's bed. Though shivering, bleeding, and lying in his own filth, he was still alive.

And tomorrow was another day.

19

The night was torture.

Gus dozed at times but only until he woke from violent bouts of shivering or sharp pain. His crotch burned from his urine, feeling like a tea bag that had partially frozen. During the night, the wind had picked up, making the edges of the tarp crackle with movement. Gus didn't have the strength to lift his legs, as they were still tied to the tire rim, so every now and again, a cold draft lifted his only sheet and rudely tickled his legs. His sinus cavity oozed mucus that he snorted down his throat and swallowed, his only meal of the day. The pebbled ground only punished him more.

At some point, Gus lost track of time.

Then morning found him, cold and bitter and trembling. Voices surrounded him, but none approached, giving him hope that maybe they had forgotten about him.

Or maybe they were just getting ready for an execution.

"So, R. J., what are we gonna do with this shithead?" Murray asked, sounding tired of having Gus in the camp.

"What's wrong with just keepin' him here?" Comeau wanted to know.

"He's starting to stink up the campground here."

"You can't smell that?" Prout asked.

A pause in the conversation.

"Yeah, he is smellin' a bit ripe," Comeau admitted. "Suggestions?"

"I say we drive him out to the lights and keep an eye on him." Prout again. "Do some fishing. See what's biting."

"Not a bad idea."

"We could do one of them Mexican piñatas," Murray offered. "That'd be fun."

"You're sinking to Boll's level now."

"Well, fuck it, I don't know," a frustrated Murray exclaimed. "Let me shoot him then if you want to be all humane and shit. Hell, if it's up to me, I'd just as soon stick a knife in his ear and rotor-root it."

"And you worked at a bank in a previous life?" Comeau asked with mocking disbelief.

"Yeah, what bank was that again?" Prout asked. "A branch of Fuck You, Incorporated?"

"Fine, you guys do what you like then," Murray muttered. "I'm keeping out of it."

The wind fluttered the tarp blanketing Gus, then someone yanked it off. Though it had provided little heat, its removal set off a bout of violent shivering. He instinctively tried to pull his knees in, but the rope around his feet stopped him.

"Man, oh man," Comeau snarled in distaste. "You shit yourself last night? Jesus."

"Gotta feeling any fudge he might be holding on to is frozen," Prout said with a cruel grin.

"Any frostbite?" Murray asked, and Gus squinted at the goggles-wearing man.

"Wasn't cold enough for that," Comeau said and screwed up his face. "Maybe only zero last night, if that. Give it a day or two, though. The cold'll come back. Gotta be below zero for a bit before anything freezes. Or below minus ten for a few minutes—and by 'a few,' I mean like twenty or so."

"He's chilled," Prout observed. "But not stirred. Right, fireboy?"

His boot nudged Gus in the ribs like a knob of grit-crusted ice.

"Fuck me, he *does* stink," Murray said. "Christ, R. J. He sure as hell ain't no god-damn air freshener."

"That fresh pine scent left him long ago," Prout sneered.

"All right, all right," Comeau cut in. "You guys wheel him on down to the lights and then drive on back."

Comeau studied Gus, a sympathetic smile covering his face. "Well, this is where our paths part. As you figured out, we talked it over and came to the conclusion that it's just too damn much of a risk to keep you around. You might get feeling vengeful or something like that later on. Can't have that. And you *do* smell like shit. Not sure if that's fear or just plain old BO, but you stink. Anyway, bullets are a little scarce these days, so you'll understand if we don't shoot you outright."

He moved in closer, until his boots were a foot away from Gus's head.

"Just so you don't think we're total bastards, you're going to sleep for the next bit."

Comeau soccer-kicked Gus in the side of the face.

*

In the dark, a place Gus was growing fonder of every time he visited, pain didn't exist. There was a sense of stretching at times, of pulling, but never anything that lingered. Once he believed he was floating, or attempting to, but his feet prevented him, keeping him close to earth. That was a bit disappointing. When the world was real, he enjoyed flying, though he'd only done it twice. Both times, he flirted successfully with the female flight attendants. Those memories he kept tucked away, for days when he wasn't feeling very good about himself.

Someone spoke in an alien language, and others chuckled, the sounds reaching him like an old record playing at the slowest possible speed.

Then he realized he was back, facedown and hanging from the tow truck once again. The wind grazed his skin, and he lifted his chin and looked around.

Comeau was walking around to the cab of a pickup.

Murray and Cam Boll were up in the back. Murray had his goggles on and was grinning nastily. Boll wore a disappointed frown.

Sorry, Boll, old man . . . but go butt-fuck yourself anyway.

Murray held up his sidearm and fired three quick shots into the air while shrieking a high-pitched yodel. Boll reached up and pulled the man's gun arm down, speaking words that were lost in a squeal of tires on pavement. The pickup's engine sang, strong and willing, bearing its passengers away.

Gus watched them shrink, down a length of highway, toward the overpass in the distance, perhaps three or four hundred meters out. Yellow grassland surrounded him, swaying hypnotically. At its heart was a crossroads of pavement. A single set of traffic lights dangled just overheard.

They had parked the tow truck right in the center of the intersection.

Gus pulled at his bonds and saw that they'd been tied with a fresh length of rope. The tire rim pulled his feet to the ground. He still had a little bit of wiggle room, just not enough to do anything helpful. He inspected himself, still pretty much naked, with only a soiled pair of drawers covering his naughty bits. He still hurt, but just being out of that wagon circle of motor homes lifted his spirits considerably. The notion withered almost as soon as he realized what the gang of highway bandits had done to him. They'd brought him out to this crossroads for a reason—most certainly a bad one.

Gasping at the pain flaring in his shoulders, Gus swung himself to the right and left, seeing only long strips of gray highway and the unmoving metallic husks of cars decorating it. Sunshine made their rooftops twinkle.

He raised his feet off the rim—only an inch—and felt his body weight pull on the overhead boom. There he hung, shoulders screaming, until he squeaked defeat and stood once more. He yanked on his overhead bonds, weakly at first but with growing fury, all to no avail. Gus panted, his eyes watering, and looked around again. There had to be a way to free himself. He couldn't go out this way.

The pickup had reached the campground and disappeared around a trailer.

"You fuckers," Gus hissed with frustrated venom. "You goddamn, evil-hearted sonsabitches."

The wind blew tenderly across his face, ironic for such a day.

The part of the boom where his hands were tied drew his attention. A tight-looking knot lay to one side of his left hand, like a filthy bow on a grubby present. His fingers twiddled with the knot, twanging the cut ends. Gus tried twisting his wrist to get a better grip but felt the fibers cut into his skin, refusing him. A gasp left his lips, and he growled, shaking in rage enough to make everything hurt.

Then he screamed.

Gus howled in the morning air. He rattled about, thrashing against his bonds. His mouth felt like a dried washrag, but water still leaked from his red-rimmed eyes. He pulled again on his wrists, fiddled in growing frustration with the knots, unable to grip them and furious because of it. He bellowed in angst again before he relaxed and stared with raw hate at the distant overpass.

"Sonsa . . . *bitches.* You rat-fuck cocksuckers. You diseased fuck twats! I hope you fucking *roast* in hell, you bunch of evil shitstains! *You hear me?* Huh? *Hear me, you goddamn preying pack of sick, depraved* FUCKS!"

Gus screamed again, long and hard, tapering off into a series of angry whimpers. Part of him wanted someone to put a bullet in him and just end the game. Maybe that's what Comeau had in mind. They had the firepower to do so. The same rifles that had forced him off the road would let the air out of him like a pellet gun round through a water balloon.

Then he went berserk.

He shook and raved, calling them every dirty, offensive name in his vocabulary, insulting their mothers and fathers, their wives and girlfriends . . . their *boy*friends. He called them back, challenging them to a *real* fight. He dared them to stop holding each other's dicks and come back. They could even use knives if they liked, and he his bare hands. He screeched and twisted and pulled with an energy that took him along like a monstrous wave about to crash down on a rocky shore.

Then it did.

Gus let his chin drop and felt the anger slowly ebbing away into despair. Why the fuck had they done this to him? There weren't any deadheads around anymore—not like there used to be, anyway. So why? *Target practice.* He was going to be the recipient of some full-metal-jacket tickles in a few minutes, guaranteed to thrill and eventually kill.

"Do it!" Gus panted, shaking in disbelief, feeling infectious heat in his body for the first time since they shot him off the road. He glared at the overpass, too far to see any movement on the heights. They could be dancing jigs up there, for all he knew . . . or drinking coffee.

"*Do it*!"

The scene didn't change. Nothing showed that anyone or anything had heard him, and that disappointed him almost to the verge of breaking.

"Do it," he whispered miserably. Anything to be free of this life. He'd given it his best shot. Done what he could with what he had. He apologized to Maggie and Becky and Chad and hoped that, wherever they were, they'd get by as best they could. His thoughts drifted to leaving the farm in search of Talbert, recalling how he hadn't wanted to, not for that guy. Adam had convinced him to go, and that set into motion the chain that killed him and torched the farm. The farm . . . the best little place he'd come to know since the zombies had arrived.

Gone.

His thoughts flowed in a circular current, right back to where he was—hanging like a slab of donair meat out in the middle of nowhere, waiting for someone to slice a strip off his hide.

Gus arched his head back, sniffled at the cold sun . . .

And just waited.

A scream jerked him awake.

He gasped as if breaking the surface of a deep swimming hole, blinking like a man who'd been underground for a month. A long, piercing cry of sheer, thrill-seeking delight spiked the stillness, coming from the direction of the overpass. The sun was past its zenith, and Gus squinted, trying to make sense of the single, startling note. He glanced around and saw nothing.

However, a tingling settled into the base of his neck, turning his head back to the right. He still heard nothing, but that little buzzing wouldn't stop. He strained against the ropes, twisting his body and neck as far as they could go, the ache in his joints growing.

Hearing the faint *clip-clop* of boots, a drunken tap dance of doom approaching from behind him, Gus held his breath. The sound paused for a moment but then continued in a dragging scuffle, as if that one stop had rusted the joints of the walker.

Gus's eyes widened. He cranked his head around, expecting the crack of vertebrae.

Then he spotted it.

He realized with sinking horror why the watcher from the overpass was screaming his head off. Gus chuckled darkly, perhaps even a touch insanely.

Moseying into the very outer rim of his peripheral vision, a shadow swayed. Gus closed his left eye to better focus his right as fear crashed over him in a freezing wave. Dark forest camouflage clothes covered the figure. It came on very slowly, as if each step was upon shattered ankles and sparking the utmost agony, and when Gus heard its low moan, his breath crystalized in his throat, and his scrotum tightened.

A deadhead.

One deadhead, but Gus figured it would eat like a family.

"Well . . . shit."

Another cry of delight flared from the overpass. Gus cowered from the undead creature and the yells from whoever was watching. That realization struck him cold, and he stared in that direction. They were *watching.*

"You sick bastards," Gus muttered, flabbergasted at their depravity. He'd met a few assholes in his time during the apocalypse, but this sank them all. "Sick, twisted fuckheads."

He strained to see over his right shoulder, muscles protesting. The gimp took its time traversing a line that would cross the highway. It ignored the traffic lights. Gus's flesh broke out in a sweat he didn't believe possible. Like some evil, diseased scavenger creeping out of its hole, the corpse shambled toward him. Gus no longer felt like shouting. He silenced himself, suddenly hoping the underworld fright might miss him and just wander on by, oblivious to the sacrificial snack.

He closed his eyes and waited.

Then he opened them.

The gimp was still on course for the tow truck.

"Fuck." Gus gnashed and looked at his wrists. He pulled back on them with whatever strength he possessed, feeling the rope cut into his skin. Any moment, he expected blood to dribble over the bonds. He bared what teeth he had remaining, shook his arms as if that might help, and lifted his legs up from the bald rim, hoping the extra weight might bring results.

Nothing.

Gus wheezed and glanced over his shoulder. The gimp waltzed across the highway as if gut shot, boots scuffing raw asphalt. It wore a soldier's kit, but what really chilled Gus's guts, what really made his balls go cold, was the vest protecting the chest and the helmet covering the head. A military-issue pot helmet rested upon its skull, with a visor slapped down over its upper face, masking its nose and eyes.

He could see the mouth, could see it hanging open.

"Sweet Jesus," Gus whispered in panic.

He freaked out.

He exploded in a bout of frenetic thrashing, twisting his body in every direction, hoping to work himself free or break the ropes. The skin around his wrists finally broke, and bright blood beaded over, some drops lining his arms all the way to his shoulders. He pulled, joints *screaming* at him to stop, until his last reservoir of strength drained empty and left him spent, panting, and still hanging. A few drops of blood fell from his triceps to the ground.

Gus checked on the whereabouts of the gimp.

His breath caught in his throat.

The undead stood at the corner of the tow truck, leaning against the metal as if having a smoke, its dusty visor gleaming in the overhead sun. A grimace of green-black teeth appeared waxen until the thing moved its jaw. Something dark and sluggish shifted within the shallow cave of its mouth. Then Gus smelled it, a pungent cloud of spores that bypassed the combat uniform clothing the zombie, and simply breathing that filthy air made him feel infected.

The softest of moans seeped from his throat.

The undead gimp rolled itself around the corner of the truck and almost stumbled, giving Gus a fleeting flare of hope where there wasn't any.

Then the creature coolly righted itself and staggered toward Gus.

"Jeeee*zus*," Murray said from where he stood with his binoculars, his mouth morphing between a twisted smirk and a grimace. "After all this time and them fuckers still creep me out."

"What's it doing now?" asked Prout, leaning in and holding out a hand for Murray to relinquish his set.

"Just standing there."

"Huh?"

"He's just standing there," Comeau said, holding the only other pair of binoculars to his eyes. "Just sizing him up. Like he's inspecting a fuckin' buffet or something."

That rendered the other men speechless. The entire pack of them stood behind the makeshift gun ports of the overpass, nestled between a scattering of derelict cars and spike strips, casting their attention at the not-so-horrific ending of their most recent prisoner.

"They do that?" Cam Boll rumbled at his leader. "I mean, can they do that?"

"This one is," Comeau reported, adjusting his focus.

"Maybe it's just tickled with having a last meal or something," Edgar proposed and was ignored. No one really paid him any real attention at the best of times. Comeau secretly debated shooting the man outright, just to spare the rest of them from his annoying attempts at humor. He still might, and he wondered if Edgar's buddy Prout would come to his defense. Those days, numbers meant strength, and Comeau realized killing his own wasn't effective management of human resources.

But, goddamn, he was tempted at times . . .

"*Now* what the fuck is it doing?" Murray asked. His goggles were pushed back on his head, ogling the sun. Prout lost patience and snatched the pair of binoculars from the man, who merely scowled at the lack of manners.

No one tried to take Comeau's. "Looks like fireboy is talking to the thing."

That drew stares of surprise from the others.

"The man's a fucking dead whisperer," Boone chortled.

"People do that?" Cam Boll asked. "Seriously?"

"No, they can't fuckin' do that," Comeau snarled. "Jesus Christ, Boll."

"That zombie's got headgear on," Prout said as he focused on the situation. "Maybe it can't bite for some reason?"

"Helmet only covers the upper part," Comeau answered. "The mouth is free."

"So what's he sayin' to it?"

Comeau shrugged. "Maybe it's a man."

That quieted the pack and made the others gaze intently in the direction of the tow truck.

"Can't be a man," Prout said. "I can see the hands. Look like they've been dipped in a full shit pot."

"I don't think it's a man either," Comeau agreed. "But fireboy is sure as hell conversing with the thing."

"I could fire off a couple of rounds," Boone offered. "See if the dead fuck can dance."

"Nah. What will be will be. That's a zombie, and it could be the only one around for kilometers."

"Maybe it's just enjoying the sight before it digs in," Edgar said, but no one took him up on his theory.

Regardless, in the middle of nowhere, the helpless living and undying dead were facing off.

"What the hell is fireboy saying?" Prout demanded. "Who can read lips?"

Grunts of derision answered that question.

"I know what he's saying," Edgar offered, a smile coating his words. "Oh fuck. Oh shit. Oh fuck-fuckiddy-fuck-*fuck*."

"Y'know," Murray said, rubbing at his nose, "once heard that actors who fill up the background of a scene, say if it's in a coffee place or restaurant, all they say is 'watermelon' over and over, to make it seem like they're having a conversation."

"I heard that too," Cam Boll said.

"'Watermelon'?" Boone asked. "Why fuckin' 'watermelon'? Why not have a real conversation but just whisper it? Or just mouth the words?"

"Sounds fuckin' retarded to me," Prout threw in.

"Only saying I heard, is all. Hell if I know if it's true or not."

"Watermelon, watermelon," Comeau muttered, standing tall and not dropping his gaze.

"I call bullshit," Boone scoffed. "Stupid. *Watermelon*."

"It's because that one word works the mouth in all sorts of directions or something to that effect."

"Once knew a woman who could do that," Murray said.

"She was your sister," Boone snapped.

"Ah," Comeau smiled under the binoculars before any further shots could be fired between his two companions. "There we are."

The zombie moved in and raised a hand to an exposed shoulder. Fireboy dangled and twisted and screamed at the touch, suddenly very much alive and very vocal. His lingering screams drifted across the open space of the grass fields, sounding very far away.

The dead thing leaned in close to the twisting, turning prisoner, smothering the weakened man with an arm. Fireboy wailed as the zombie dipped its hard-shelled head to his wildly moving one. They struggled, like an old couple waltzing on an uneven dance floor, one partner visibly tiring while the other slowly closed in, intent on delivering a very messy hickey.

Then the blood sprayed, and fireboy's wails of terror became squeals.

"Mmmm, good," Prout exclaimed and held up his binoculars for anyone interested.

A genuine smile slid across Comeau's face.

20

"You okay?"

The question left Gus slack-jawed stupid. He had to blink twice, and even then he wasn't sure of what was happening. He stared at the gimp before him and couldn't summon his voice, so instead, he just hung there with his mouth open, stunned as if someone had hooked booster cables to his toes and frazzled his system.

"Huh?" he finally got out.

The zombie placed himself before Gus's dangling frame, and instead of coming forward and chomping into him, it merely stood and inspected. Or at least Gus *believed* it was inspecting. He couldn't see the eyes.

"Said, you okay?" The mouth worked stiffly, as if the cold affected it. "You look like shit."

Gus balked. "You're not . . ."

The gimp waited.

"You're not . . . gonna . . ."

"Eat you?" the zombie asked. "No. Just the opposite. Gonna get you out of here if anything. Think you can move?"

"I'm dreamin'."

"You're not dreaming."

"You're a figment of my imagination."

"Listen," the gimp said with deliberate clarity. "I'm not here to kill you, okay? I'm going to cut you down from there. But we have to hold on for a minute or so."

"A minute."

"Yeah, just a minute."

"Who the fuck are you?"

The creature's pallid lips drew back, exposing those terrible black teeth cemented in place by a green, receding gum line. That horrid smile caught Gus off guard.

"Clay Wallace. You?"

"Gus. Berry."

"Well, Mr. Berry. Offhand, I'd say you're lucky I happened along here."

Gus snorted in disbelief. "You don't fuckin' say."

That caused Wallace to smirk with all the grace of a snake. "I do. The gunshots drew our attention."

"*Our?*"

"My partner and I."

"There's *two* of you?"

"Yeah."

"Where is he?"

"Don't worry about that. Right now, eyes are on us, and we have to put on a show."

"What?"

"Can you scream?"

Gus didn't like the sound of that. "What do you mean?" he asked warily.

"I need you to scream. Just until I tell you to stop, okay? Scream like a dying man might. Someone who's being devoured by zombies."

The distrustful expression on Gus's face said it all. Wallace reached up and carefully undid the first three buttons of his combat shirt above his drooping vest. His hands were as filthy and bleached as those belonging to a fresh corpse. Every so often, bones crackled, but his fingers manipulated the buttons until a gap hung open. He reached inside and pulled forth a bottom of what appeared to be a squeeze bottle of ketchup.

"Now," Wallace whispered, stepping closer, "don't freak out. Jesus, you stink."

Gus couldn't answer, still unable to discern if this speaking ghoul was real or not, and he didn't appreciate the thing getting closer. A memory of a dentist leaning in much too close with a poised drill came to mind.

"You ready?" Wallace asked, the visor considering.

"Yeah," Gus said with unmasked dread, squirming to the right just as Wallace lifted a hand to his shoulder and made cold contact. Gus's innards twisted, revolted, as if being invaded by a knot of maggots, and any remaining mental fortitude burned away as that diseased maw drew closer.

He screamed without prompting and yanked away as much as possible from the zombie's grip.

"Good." Wallace's voice sounded soothing. "That's good. But stay still."

Gus shrieked again, freaking out—the zombie's shocking mouth was far too much for him.

"You're a natural," the monster said.

Gus lost it entirely.

But Wallace moved closer and hooked an arm around the man's neck, pulled his weakened form in close. The corpse leaned in, absorbing the frantic thrashings. He aimed the ketchup bottle at Gus's bare chest.

The last thing Gus remembered before passing out were the helmet closing with his neck, those horrible teeth, and jets of red spritzing the air before his eyes.

Comeau lowered his binoculars and mulled over what he'd just witnessed. The zombie had latched onto fireboy's neck and opened it up, covering the hanging man in a mess of blood. In seconds, the screaming died away, and the man hanging from the tow truck went limp.

However, something bothered the gang leader.

That zombie wasn't right to him.

It wasn't gorging itself on its human lunch as others would've. If Comeau didn't know better, the thing appeared to be simply nuzzling fireboy's neck. The binoculars were at their limits and didn't allow greater scrutiny, which meant he'd keep an eye on the feeding for a little longer—just to make sure.

"What's wrong?" Boone asked.

Comeau didn't answer him right away. "You got eyes on that corpse, Jack?"

Murray had snatched the binoculars back from Prout and resumed watching the action. "Yep."

"What's it look to you?"

"Honestly? Looks like the two of them down there are necking."

Comeau shook his head. "That dead bastard hasn't really made any progress, has he?"

"Nope."

"Something's wrong?" Edgar asked, scratching at the screaming-eagle bandanna cutting off his scalp's circulation.

"Something is," Comeau muttered. "Just can't figure—"

A suppressed burp flung Boone's stick-like figure over the gun ports. Edgar's head exploded in a messy plume of hair and skull fragments, the screaming eagle spurting free and flying like a bloody lasso falling to earth. Prout only half spun around when his chest burst open in a smoking spurt of red, a fine spray erupting from his other side. He grunted in surprise, and as he sank to his knees, Murray's cry of "Hey!" was silenced by three more of those soft coughs as his torso slammed into the metal railing. The bodies slumped to the ground. Comeau dropped his binoculars and spun about to face a figure dressed in light green-brown camouflage and wearing a ski mask.

A suppressed pistol was in the masked attacker's hand.

"Wait—" Comeau got out as Cam Boll rolled to the side, pulling his knife free of its sheath.

The man in black shot Comeau twice in the chest, backing him up against a nearby car door, before smoothly altering aim and firing twice more, tearing a chunk out of Boll's midsection and buckling him over. A third shot blew out the back of Boll's head in grisly streamers.

Comeau lay against the car, holding a hand to one of his chest wounds and gasping as his blood flooded a lung and his heart bleated a code his brain recognized as dire. No more than four seconds . . . four seconds before, they'd all still been alive, shooting the shit while watching the circus on the crossroads from afar. Now, Comeau's darkening vision took in the slain forms of his companions as their killer walked toward them, pistol trained.

Careful, Comeau realized, close to blacking out. *Quiet.*

Stealthy, his mind corrected . . . before shutting down.

Gus moaned and rolled his head to one side, repelled by the potent smell of vinegar. He rubbed his scruff of a beard before his arm flopped back to the pavement. A shadow passed over him, and he opened his eyes, grimacing at the bright flash of the sun. A moment later, he realized he was lying on his back, no longer bound to the tow truck. His arms buzzed with renewed circulation and moved haltingly, as if thawing after a long winter. Something moved just beyond his head, and he turned with some discomfort to see a man disappearing around the corner of the truck.

Gus tried to sit up. Cramps seized his legs, and he winced at the biting pain rippling through his thighs and calves. His arms ached, but he could move them . . . slowly.

Dream. Had to be a dream. A delirious dream. But who had cut him down?

"Hey," he called out. "Who's there?"

Silence. Then a metallic clatter of something bouncing.

"Hey! What's happening?"

He rolled onto his belly, wondering why the hell he was coated in spoiled ketchup, and saw boots underneath the truck on the driver's side. Whoever wore them stood on the balls of his feet, leaning into the vehicle. Pebbles stuck to Gus's belly and chest, and lying down as he was, he felt the clingy saturation and burn of his undershorts. That wrenched a sigh from his tortured form.

Boot heels came down and moved back around the truck, distracting Gus from his aches. Whoever the guy was, he took his time coming around the truck, but he wasn't walking like a deadhead, and for that, Gus was grateful.

The figure stepped into sight and towered over Gus, forcing him to look up, his face slackening into an expression of horror.

That fish-belly-colored jaw and the face only half revealed by a lowered visor . . . the skeletal smirk and horrible teeth . . . A stiff hand rose and adjusted the helmet.

"How you doing?" the gimp asked.

Gus couldn't reply. And when he finally did, it was a heartfelt "Holy shit."

Silence stretched out after that sincere answer.

The zombie ended it. "That a good *holy shit* or a bad one?"

"It wasn't a dream," Gus whispered, keeping the dead fucker in sight.

"No. It wasn't. You're free to go. If you can walk, that is."

"I can walk."

"Well, that's a good thing."

"Who are you?"

"Mr. Berry, we've covered introductions."

"I mean," Gus's voice grated, "who the hell *are* you? And why did you . . . ?"

He couldn't say anymore, overwhelmed by Wallace's presence.

"I was a professional soldier, Mr. Berry," Wallace stated, lips working as if fresh out of a dentist's chair. "Now, I suppose I'm freelancing. Lucky for you we came along when we did."

"You're fucked up." That didn't merit a reply, so Gus tried again. "I mean, you look like a zombie."

"Well, you know what they say about looks, Mr. Berry."

Gus knew.

He placed his hands flat to the pavement. With a growl and a surge of pain as if his guts were about to drop, he attempted to push himself off the ground, gave up, and struggled into a sitting position. His legs felt too stiff to support him just yet, so he sat and shook them out as if recovering from a far-too-lengthy stretch.

"You take your time," Wallace said and glanced in the direction of the overpass. "We're good here now."

"What does that mean?"

"It means we're safe. Relatively speaking. How many of those men were there? The ones that did this to you?"

"Six."

"I see."

"*Are* you a zombie?" Gus blurted, fixing his rescuer with a harsh look.

Wallace surveyed the land, and for a moment, Gus wondered if he'd heard the question. The man's head bobbed oddly, as if he were concentrating on listening.

"Yes and no," he finally answered.

"Yes and no? Well, what is it?"

But Wallace turned around and left him. "I'm heading over to that campsite. Climb onto the back if you want, and I'll drive you over."

"The back? Why not the front?"

"Because you stink."

The driver's door opened. That got Gus moving. He pulled himself up to the tailgate, his arms and legs on the verge of being torn apart. He stood on shaky legs and regarded the boom-and-winch system taking up the rear of the vehicle. Gus couldn't see a place to climb onto, so he waddled around to the passenger side, walking as if he wore plaster casts on both legs.

The truck started up.

Gus opened the passenger side door, sweating precious water he couldn't afford to lose, and hauled himself onto the seat. Wallace waited but didn't offer a hand or turn his head to watch. Groaning, grunting, Gus got himself tucked away and closed the door.

He glanced at Wallace's intimidating profile before rolling down the window.

Gus wasn't the only one who stank.

The soldier put the truck into drive and rolled away from the crossroads, back toward the overpass. He drove slowly, his head again weaving in that erratic, odd fashion that reminded Gus of Ray Charles. But Wallace wasn't blind. Far from it.

Gus rested his head against the doorframe and watched the plains roll by. "Taking your time, aren'tcha?"

Some trace of civil politeness forbade him from further questioning his rescuer about his condition, which was totally fucked up in Gus's humble opinion. It felt like asking a terminal cancer patient, "How you feeling?"

Wallace focused on driving. His pale hands gripped the steering wheel, the skin tight and white around the knuckles.

Gus directed his attention back to the road.

21

The tow truck pulled into the center of the ring of motor homes, brakes squealing as it slowed to a stop. The leather recliners remained situated in front of the white and tiger-striped blocks, waiting for cutthroats nowhere in sight. Wallace placed the gear stick into park and got out without a word, letting Gus stare after him in unchecked horror.

What is this guy? He's infected, but how can he function?

The fact that he didn't *eat* Gus while he was strung up proved the soldier didn't have the killer appetite of other zombies, but his appearance suggested otherwise.

Wallace ambled around the front of the truck, allowing Gus to inspect him at length. He didn't move well, as if every joint was afflicted with arthritis—or he'd been shot in the ass and couldn't be bothered to dig the bullet out.

"Get him?" a woman called out, breaking Gus's study of Wallace. He leaned forward, looking into the side mirror.

There, between two RVs, sauntered a figure clothed in camouflage gear, complete with ragged body armor, tactical webbing, and assorted pouches. A sidearm rested in a hip holster. A black ski mask completely covered the face.

"He's in the truck?" the woman asked, and Gus took a moment to realize the approaching soldier had spoken.

"Yep," Wallace answered. "How many you get?"

"Six."

"That checks out. Anything useful on them?"

She stopped and shook her head. "A bunch of knives. Some Glocks. A couple of high-powered hunting rifles up top but nothing special. Debating even taking them along."

"You know the answer to that."

"Aye that," she said and looked into the mirror, causing Gus to flinch a bit. "The bad people are all dead and gone now. You getting out or staying in?" Her voice was harsh and gruff, as if she'd been screaming for a very long time.

Gus had to prompt himself to answer. "Still a little stiff here."

"And more than a little ripe," Wallace commented.

The ski mask regarded the motor homes. "Stay there, then. I'll check out the showers. See if we can't get you cleaned up. These fuckheads had a pretty sweet setup here. I'd be surprised if the showers aboard these beasts don't work. You could even get one if you like," she told Wallace.

"I'll stick to deodorant."

Whether she smiled or not, Gus couldn't tell, but Ski Mask nodded before walking off toward the tiger-striped motorhome with the barest of feminine swaggers. She placed her back next to the RV's side door and gripped her sidearm. Though all the gang members had been killed, she still practiced caution.

In a flash she threw it open, scanned the interior from one angle then the other, and went inside.

Though he didn't feel up for it, Gus opened the door and slid out of the truck, grimacing at every movement. The mobile home trembled at times, shivering at Ski Mask's probing.

"Anything else you want to tell us?" Wallace asked.

"Huh?" Gus blurted, taking his attention off the one-woman sweep-and-clear in process.

"Anything else . . . you want . . . to tell us?"

"Uh, no. I . . . I didn't really see anything else. Too fucked up. Far as I know, there were only six of them."

"So you said. That's going to leave a scar."

Gus glanced at the crusted-over cut gracing his ribs. "Yeah. Guess so."

"All clear," Ski Mask informed them as she emerged from the doorway. "Go get that shower, buddy. Unless you prefer to stand around in your undershorts."

"You best check him out, Collie," Wallace said, sizing up the encampment. "Mr. Berry has a nasty laceration on his ribs there."

"Don't hafta call me Mr. Berry all the time." Gus muttered. "First name will do."

But Wallace showed no indication of hearing him.

"That does looks nasty," Collie said as she walked over to Gus. "Looks clean enough. Just nasty. Unfortunately, I'm out of all the cool, quick-healing stuff, so it'll be plain old catgut for you."

She stopped before the bearded man and briefly met his gaze. Though her mask hid her face, her blue eyes stunned him like a jolt of adrenaline. It wasn't as though Gus had never seen blue eyes before—he never really cared for them—but never had he seen a pair of blinkers so damn bright, so *frightening* in their marble brilliance. He wondered if she hadn't had them laser polished at some point, before the apocalypse. A sprinkling of crow's lines, a tattoo perhaps, encircled the skin around her right eye socket and stretched back, disappearing beneath the edge of the mask.

If Collie noticed his inspection, she didn't show it. She scrutinized his cut. "Bet that stings. Not much I can do now. Gonna leave a mark, though. Good news is they didn't cut any arteries, else we wouldn't be having this conversation. Head on in there and get yourself cleaned up. Wash around the cut but don't disturb the scab, and I'll do the rest. Find some fresh clothes. Whoever owned that rig also had a washer in there. I swear. If that thing is any indication, they were living in luxury out here. Big TV. Holo-set. King-size bed. Washer dryer. The fucking thing even has a goddamn *bar*. I'm thinking we should seriously consider driving it off into the sunset."

Wallace kept his thoughts on the matter to himself.

"I'm Collie, by the way," she said, not offering her hand.

"Gus."

"Hiya, Gus. Glad to see you're still alive. Why don't you head on in for that shower now?"

"Yeah. Yeah, sounds like a good idea."

Collie's startling eyes flashed back with the glaring intensity of spotlights but only for a second before she started speaking to Wallace, going on about the motor home's upscale interior. Their conversation dimmed as Gus staggered on stiff legs toward the open doorway. He almost passed out as he climbed the steps into the rig, and he floundered on a length of sofa fixed to a wall. When his senses stabilized, he rolled onto his side and stared like a druggie coming down off a high. It was nice inside the trailer. A kitchen area with seating for two was right at his head. Lacquered wooden panels lent a cozy ambience to it all. The door to a small bathroom and, Gus assumed, the shower lay straight ahead, and he stared at it longingly.

Still alive.

Almost two years of pretty much nothing had led up to a few days of hellish close calls. He pulled himself to a sitting position and used whatever knobs, tables, or chairs were handy to get himself into the shower. The RV's door remained open, and Gus cursed it for being so. His shorts dropped to his ankles and nearly tripped him as he entered the bathroom. It was tiny, but since it actually had a clean-looking shower, he didn't complain. The showerhead dripped, so the plastic floor squeaked just a bit when he stepped in, eyeing the wall slot where a worn bar of soap rested. He had to stoop a bit to fit inside the stall, but that didn't bother him. A shower would make it all better.

A blast of cold water made him gasp. He fumbled at a knob, and the flow got warmer, flattening whatever scruff ringed his bald head and chin. He didn't know how long he had before the tanks ran dry, but he wasn't too worried about that either. The wall came to his shoulder, and he leaned against it, sinking his head to his chest in quiet thanks and feeling the hot water blast his back, working its curative magic on both flesh and mind.

Still breathing. Still kicking.

Since he'd survived this latest episode, Maggie and the kids had to be alive as well. Had to be. His ass hadn't been pulled from the fire for anything else.

With a weary sigh, Gus reached for the soap . . .

And dropped it.

He began to weep.

Ten minutes later, he shut off the water just as it turned cold, and he stepped out of the shower, clean and composed. He toweled off with the one handy in the bathroom, taking care with the slash down his chest, and then shuffled into the bedroom, where a king-size bed dominated a very comfortable-looking area. Blankets neatly covered the mattresses, as if whoever slept there made the bed habitually. A sliding door at its foot was ajar, and Gus peeked in to see a washer-and-dryer combo taking up the closet space.

"Christ," he muttered, taking it all in. He shuffled to a chest of drawers and opened each in turn. As much as he hated the idea of using another man's clothing, especially anything belonging to a member of the toll-highway gang, he needed something until replacements could be found. Luckily enough, the sizes weren't off by too much, and everything smelled surprisingly fresh. He pulled on a blue-striped button shirt that was a little too big but not annoyingly so, and the black jeans he settled on could be adjusted with a leather belt. A plain brown sweater went on over his head, and he groaned as he bent to pull on thick socks. Once he finished dressing, he searched the remaining cupboards and drawers and located extra winter clothing and T-shirts for the summer. A separate closet contained an impressive hoard of skin magazines, which perked his interest for all of a second. Paperbacks and a few of his *National Geographics* were stacked on a night table. Gus didn't feel like any heavy lifting just now, so he left everything.

He hobbled back out into the main area of the motor home, his attention focused on a closet just off the kitchenette. The door opened at a soft tug, and a rack of rifles stared back at Gus's pleasantly surprised face—hunting rifles mostly, with an ample supply of ammunition stacked away on an overhead shelf. A pair of stainless-steel handguns was stashed away at the base of the closet, and Gus pulled the twins out to marvel at their lines. "Sig Sauer" stamped the barrel, along with "P441." He felt nostalgic for the old Ruger and Benelli once in his possession. Gus recognized the Sauer brand, but the version of the pistol meant nothing to him. What did interest him were the stacks of loaded magazines held upright in a block of foam padding—eight in all, of unknown capacity, with a Tupperware box containing a veritable bounty in loose shells. He lifted the plastic box and saw three cardboard boxes holding even more shells—an additional fifty shells all neatly tucked away and separated by molded plastic dividers.

"Baby, baby," Gus whispered, the aches and pain of the last couple of days suddenly overridden by the shiny hand cannons. He pulled them out and held them up to the light, admiring their workmanship and lethal promise.

"I knew your cousins," Gus said quietly, inspecting the old-fashioned iron sights.

"All cleaned up?"

The voice made Gus jump, and he almost aimed the Sauers. Wallace leaned into the open doorway, his lower face no longer smiling, the visor dull in the shade of the interior.

"I said, 'All cleaned up?'"

"Ah, yeah."

The visor didn't retreat. "Found some pop-guns, did you?"

"Yeah," Gus said with a toothless smile. "How about that, eh?"

"Seems these guys had a small arsenal lying around." Wallace didn't appear the least bit concerned with Gus having the weapons.

"Fuckin' A, they had a small arsenal. One of them blew me off the goddamn highway. Cheap-ass sniping sonsabitches."

The soldier didn't have anything to say to that, so Gus carried on. "You found more guns?"

"Calm down there, blinky," the soldier said in that even tone of voice, oozing Zen. "I think the general idea in situations like this is 'finders keepers.' Unless you absolutely need something. Like shoes, for example."

"They took my boots. And whatever else I had in my SUV."

"Well, we're still poking around. Maybe they'll turn up. In the meantime, maybe there's something here for you to wear on your feet. Until we can find better. And something to holster those pistols in. Take a look where you found those puppies. Maybe there's a tac vest or webbing around."

Gus glanced from the closet to the floor and spotted a cupboard underneath the sofa.

"You're going to let me have these?"

"Don't see why not."

"Geez, I could be anyone," Gus started. "You don't know. I mean, I could—"

The visor seemed to zoom in on him, and the toothy mouth below it hardened, as the temperature seemed to immediately drop ten degrees.

"You could do what . . . civvie?" Wallace asked in a suddenly lethal tone that suggested Gus best not finish the sentence. Instead, he cleared his throat and studied his feet.

"Nothing."

Wallace kept staring, making Gus more than a little uncomfortable.

"Well, I didn't mean anything . . . y'know, bad or anything, uh . . ." Gus trailed off, but when he glanced back to the doorway, it was empty.

Wallace was gone.

Feeling the need for a fresh pair of undershorts, Gus limped to the door and watched the soldier amble toward another RV, the one Comeau probably owned. Wallace took his time walking away, not a care in the world, and Gus shook his head in disbelief at the strut.

"Oh, no, I'm not just cool," he muttered, emphasizing the word and directing it all at Wallace's back. "Heaven forbid. I'm the 'I' in *ice.*"

Gus retreated inside.

The cupboard gave up a new pair of sneakers. They were two sizes too big, but Gus wasn't picky at that point, and after a few strolls around the living area, he decided he wasn't about to fall over with them on. A second search of the gun closet revealed brown worn-leather shoulder straps with a pair of holsters and pockets for extra magazines. There weren't any suppressors like the ones he'd had before, but he was glad to find the accessories. One couldn't have everything.

Gathering his things, he studied the leather straps and figured out they went across his back somehow. He fiddled with pulling them on and eventually got it right.

"Oh yeah," he breathed, impressed with himself, sticking his chest out and immediately regretting it as the cut over his ribs asked him none too kindly what the hell he thought he was doing. The two stabs of pain felt like an indignant *Hey, HEY.*

"I hear ya," Gus grimaced and placed a hand over his wound. The sensation of bleeding reached his palm, and he lifted the sweater and shirt for a quick check yet found nothing but the ugliest crusted-over line. Hissing in discomfort, he stiffly walked out of the Winnebago and made his way over to the one across the way, where Wallace and the still-masked Collie stood in a doorway, paused in their conversation.

"Alive and well, I see," Collie observed, fixing Gus with those intense blue eyes.

"Well, alive anyway."

"Ollie here says you're in need of footwear," Collie said.

Gus stopped about four paces away from the pair and fixed Wallace with a look that asked, *Ollie?*, not bothering to contain his smile.

The visor and the bared teeth underneath seemed to frost over. "She gets to call me Ollie. You call me Wallace."

Gus nodded complete understanding before facing Collie. "Yeah. A size eleven. If you got it."

"You're in luck," Collie said and stepped out of the doorway. "Go on in. Got some new guns there, I see."

"Uh, yeah," Gus carefully lifted one arm to better show off the holster on that side. "Feel like a cop with it."

"Looks good."

"There's more over there."

"More guns?"

"Rifles, mostly. I—" he shrugged with one shoulder. "I took the good ones."

To his surprise, Collie chuckled. "We'll check it out. A little later."

"Ah, just want to say"—Gus shrugged—"thanks for saving my ass. Really. Appreciate it."

"You're welcome," Collie said while Wallace's visor only stared at him.

Having gotten that out of the way, Gus stepped into the Winnebago . . . and gasped.

Dry foods and other assorted goods crammed the interior: racks of clothing, boxes of canned food, plastic jugs of water, winter outdoor wear, board games—Gus couldn't help but smile at seeing Monopoly. More boxes were labeled "IMP" and further divided into breakfast, lunch, and supper. There were even Mason jars of preserved jams and meats, which Gus recognized from the farm. Then he spotted the boxes of Arctic Blue Chilled Vodka stowed away in a corner, and a familiar tightening of his throat returned.

"Holy shit."

"Something, eh?" Collie said and rubbed at the corner of an eye. "These boys have been at this for a very long time. And they haven't been too nice about it either. Along with stringing you up, that white motor home over yonder there had handcuffs hooked into the bed's baseboard, so I'd hazard a guess these pricks have had quite a few guests in the past."

Gus looked her in the eye. "Any sign of kids? Or . . . bodies?"

The dread in his voice wasn't lost on Collie. "No. Nothing like that. Course, they could've done anything with regards to bodies. Dumped them somewhere."

"Oh."

"But Wallace did a short walkabout while you were getting a shower. Found nothing of the sort."

"Unless they made it a habit to drag them off and leave them hanging," Wallace added.

"Yeah," Collie said, fixing on Gus once more. "You looking for someone out here?"

"Yeah. A woman and two kids."

"Wife?"

Gus shook his head. "No. She's a friend. A doctor. Saved my life once. The kids are orphans. A couple of days ago, I lived on a farm outside of Annapolis. Long story short, I left it to do a job, and when I got back, the place had been torched, and most of the people I lived with were killed. Four of them were missing. I found one left on the side of a highway. I'm looking for the others."

The soldiers quieted at that information. Then Collie sniffed and moved in close.

"Lift up the sweater and shirt. I wanna take a look at that cut again."

Gus didn't debate and complied.

"Yeah," she stretched the word out as she prodded the grisly cut. "I can do something with it. Good news is it doesn't seem to be infected."

"That is good."

"Listen. I want you to shave your chest. At least the area around the edges of the slash. I've got some cloth bandages and a wad of duct tape. Not the best, but beggars can't be choosers. You get that shaved, and I'll slap something on it to keep it clean for a while. But no heavy lifting for you. How's your hands and fingers?"

Gus held them out. "They hurt."

"Yeah," Collie said. "That's just circulation restoring itself. How long they have you hangin'?"

"A day. Overnight. Outside."

"It wasn't the warmest last night either, but it wasn't below zero. I don't see anything bad here. No frostbite or nip. You can move your hands and fingers okay?"

"Yeah. With some pain."

"Well, keep an eye on it. My guess is you'll be fine in a couple of hours."

"What are you going to do between now and then?" Gus asked.

Collie drew back and studied him with her unsettling eyes. "Well, I think we'll take a look around for brunch first. Those IMPs are good for five years, and I saw a couple of boxes with curry written on the side. I don't know about you, but I'm fuckin' hungry."

With that, she finally took off her ski mask.

Gus couldn't help but stare.

22

Shovel sat and brooded, dividing his attention between the map of Ontario on his desk and the picture window at the end of the command trailer. The window offered a respectable view of the nearby mountain and the dismal digging efforts underway there. He sighed, filling his lungs with damp air, and glared at the slab of wilderness outside, feeling a wave of hopelessness rising inside. Distant shouts pierced the trailer's hide, piping above the constant grind of a working engine. Hard hats bobbed in front of the window, growing into workers carrying pickaxes and shovels and pushing wheelbarrows, heading toward the mouth of a cave, herded by armed guards wearing balaclavas.

Shovel glanced at his watch and saw it was nearly four o'clock.

Second shift was going in.

He shook his head. It had taken almost six months to find Whitecap, the secret bunker where the Canadian government had hunkered down to wait out the apocalypse, located north of the town of Cochrane, roughly three hours along Highway 574. *Look for a crown of mountains,* the dying and delirious spec-op spook, a JTF-2 man, had revealed to him, *a crown consisting of five peaks. Then watch the left side of the road for a sign that reads Private Property, hanging from a chain. Then another two-hour drive over a dirt road that becomes asphalt.*

And straight on until dawn.

Or so the fairy tale went.

That sounded easy enough, but in reality, it was a goddamn puzzle as elusive and mysterious as King Solomon's mines. Finding Highway 574 among the maze of back roads had been bad enough, and it wasn't made any easier by the fact that the road was a god-awful *long* one. Once they'd located the private property checkpoint, the special forces operative failed to tell them that the old road split into forks and split again. In fact, the roads branched off and ran all over the place, often nowhere, and several times the motorized convoy consisting of Shovel's little army found itself at a dead end, staring at rivers or blinded by thick forest. Upon making that first mistake of leading his people into a dead end, Shovel sent scouts ahead to check out all the other side roads—more time wasted.

Even worse were the maddening glimpses of the five mountains between the treetops or just over the next hill, but several roads believed to lead to the bunker abruptly switched back and went in the opposite direction. Signs popped up at regular intervals, reminding them that they were trespassing upon government property and chanced being arrested.

In the end, though, they found it, concrete checkpoints and all—right up to the promised land.

However, the promised land wasn't in very good shape.

That fact was another little gem of information the operator had neglected to divulge, just before Shovel shot him between the eyes—another mistake, but there was no way he was going to bring along a special forces operative, just waiting to raise hell. Whitecap, the country's last bastion of civilization, wasn't the paradise they'd hoped it to be.

Far from it.

Shovel stood up and walked around his spartan desk, clasping his hands behind his back. He carried himself well, despite being bulked up by bare hockey pads over his orange workman's uniform. His hair had thinned out considerably, but that was more from genetics than stress. The beard coating his chin grew unchecked, and he even entertained thoughts of twisting the ends into war braids, as the Norse savages did. Scars covered his face as if he might've been whipped by barbed wire at one time, while half of his left ear was missing entirely. His brown eyes bordered on black.

Shovel stared through the glass at the Whitecap's imposing mountainside, an enormous, forested pyramid set in the middle of nowhere. He stooped just a little so he could see its top superimposed against heavenly blue. The scale of the installation was huge, according to the JTF-2 man—a veritable hotel built half a klick underground, started around the end of World War II and completed around the same time the Korean War concluded. It possessed everything a surviving populace needed and was accessible to parliamentary members, their families, close friends, logistics and communication staff, and medical and scientific research teams—not forgetting, of course, a formidable military presence consisting of both regular and ultra-special forces.

JTF-2, or Joint Task Force 2, was the Canadian counterterrorism branch of the armed forces, arguably on par with the world's best. JTF-2 had run covert operations alone—or in support of or in collaboration with US Delta Force or England's SAS. Civilians had never heard of their missions. Shovel didn't know much about the secretive branch. Government officials were quite guarded about the activities of JTF-2, whose official motto was "Facta Non Verba"—Deeds, Not Words.

Thank the Lord for the ramblings of one trooper on his way out, who was more than compliant when asked questions about where he'd come from and if there were more.

Whitecap.

Food, water, geothermal electricity, medical professionals, soldiers, and most important of all, munitions. All there. Enough to supply an army—or hold one off if necessary. Since the bunker was supposed to house the government through times of extreme crisis for years if necessary, the storage capacity of the installation equaled the living and work areas of Whitecap. The entire complex sounded like an apocalyptic Shangri-la, a remote, well-protected oasis in the middle of nowhere, everything anyone could ask for in these dark days.

Shovel had gone there looking to barter with the prime minister or whoever was in charge in that hole. He'd been prepared to fight.

What he found was rubble.

Something had happened to Whitecap, for the tunnel mouth leading, presumably, to the bunker's entrance had been collapsed by explosive measures. For whatever reason, someone had destroyed the tunnel access, bringing the roof down as tons of rock and debris fell and sealing the bunker, rendering it a pain in the ass for Shovel.

But not impossible to access.

His people had brought up a backhoe from the nearest town and moved the camper and RV units that'd been parked in a wide ring around the base of the mountain, where the landscape had been leveled and paved in an area of about four football fields, all surrounded by deep ditches, razor wire, and heavy-duty chain-link fences. The place even had an empty helicopter pad and an accompanying hangar. The motor homes and trailers lent the area a shantytown look of sorts, but Shovel didn't give a shit about looks. It was livable until they could dig through the garbage blocking the way into the bunker.

Miners. He'd give a shaven testicle for a couple of people who knew what they were doing. Skilled tradespeople were in short supply. Training a few heads to operate the backhoe wasn't a problem as Shovel's own background lay in heavy equipment, but clearing a collapsed tunnel made him and everyone working inside the mountain quite nervous. He knew enough about digging to know he needed professionals. Trouble was, he didn't *have* professionals. He had programmers, bank tellers, legal secretaries, janitors, lawyers, soda-pop-truck drivers, convenience store clerks, gas pumpers, car salespeople, and line assemblers—even a woman who actually worked on and conceived new artificial flavors.

That was the gene pool Shovel had to work with: factory workers, paper pushers, and chemical freaks; wingnuts and dingbats; lugnuts and assholes. For three shifts a day, around the clock, they were all put to work after joining up, with the more solid ones being granted tenure within Shovel's clan and the privilege of becoming an armed soldier.

Shovel gazed out at the mountain base, taking in the dark maw that had already been cleared. It reminded him of a mouth with its teeth kicked in. A good two hundred and ten meters all told, it was a straight tunnel just a little bit wider than the backhoe itself. They had found the intact cement wall on the east side and kept to it as a guide, but Shovel worried: if an entrance might be on the west side somewhere, it was entirely plausible that they might dig right by it.

Miners.

He needed miners—or even a geologist with a rudimentary understanding of the earth-clearing process. Even more equipment—bulldozers or hydraulic roof supports would make life easier. What he had was best intentions. Giovanni, his right-hand man, had even suggested a bunker of this size had to have air ducts or possibly even a back door of some kind, just in case the people inside had to evacuate for whatever reason.

Shovel liked that thinking. Trouble was, the bunker was situated underneath a fucking mountain, slam bang in the middle of goddamn nowhere, with ample vegetation growing up to effectively conceal any such hidden entrances. He actually sent people to search for those alternate entry points, but the ghosts of Whitecap had left a rude surprise for such search parties.

Land mines.

They weren't just little antipersonnel mud bangers either, but the honest-to-God hammers of destruction, powerful enough to blow the unlucky bastard and anyone else in a twenty-foot radius to pieces. Mines had been banned from warfare decades before, but Whitecap had apparently deemed them necessary in holding off the undead and had authorized liberal sprinkling of the devices throughout the grounds beyond the wire fence. Shovel didn't know if the weapons had been broken out of some ancient crate somewhere or if a line of professionals had sat down and line-assembled homemade improvised explosive devices.

In any case, discovery of the weapons cost Shovel two search parties.

But at least they had a greater sense of security, knowing the mines were out there.

A knock at his door broke his spiraling thoughts.

"Enter," Shovel called.

Giovanni walked in, tight-lipped and nodding at him. Gio was thought of as a company "yes man" from way back, back when they had all been marooned up north on a drill site, when the food finally ran out and tar-sand beetles eventually became a treat. When the world slid into ruin, Gio was one of the few who kept his head and maintained order even when things got hairy among the rig pigs and the inevitable violent purge of the malcontents commenced. Tall, lanky, but with a bush of a beard wired with silver, Giovanni had shed his rig-pig profession and family-man history and evolved into a ruthless enforcer with a preference for regular hammers if he could spare the bullets.

Sick followed Gio inside. If Gio was ruthless, then Sick was goddamn unsettling. He was Shovel's height, give or take a half inch, and as well built as any of the soldiers. Shovel believed the man still had a face—he faintly remembered having seen it once or twice two years or so before—but Sick rarely took off the black balaclava covering his head. The arresting green eyes staring out from that black slit were as flat and dull as beach rock—eyes that had seen horrific acts, probably performed by Sick's own hands, and had discovered both a talent and a peace therein. Shovel's clan had found the man in Brandon, Manitoba, back when they numbered in the fifties, running and fighting a pack of crystal-meth-baked crazies calling themselves the Norse. Sick didn't speak much, if at all, but that wasn't a problem for Shovel. Sick did as he was told, especially when the job necessitated killing. Whenever Shovel gave Sick the order to put someone down, he felt as if he'd unleashed the grim reaper. If they scouted out a group of survivors, Sick was the ghost sent in to eye matters up close. A pair of Glocks hung in holsters under his arms, but it was the prominent Bowie knife at his waist that demanded attention. Sick had a habit of squeezing the hilt as if it was a rubber tension ball. Shovel suspected it was damn near the only way the man kept his shit under control.

The next few people to step inside the trailer were a surprise.

In came a woman and a pair of kids, a girl and a boy, wide-eyed and obviously frightened. The lady, gray haired and stiff backed, carried herself well despite her guards. Shovel thought she was in the "plain but attractive" zone. Once inside, she turned her blue eyes upon him and curled an upper lip in contempt. That surprised Shovel even more. A person didn't often hate his guts from the get-go. That usually took a few minutes.

"Something interesting, Gio?" Shovel asked as the hulking form of Nolan closed the door and guarded the front step.

"Something, all right," Giovanni answered and indicated the three newcomers. "This young lady right here is a doctor."

Shovel allowed the surprise to register on his face. He blinked at his henchman then at the woman. "No fucking way."

"Way," Giovanni said simply. "Boys you sent over to New Brunswick, well, they spotted one respectable holdout along the water there, up in Chaleur Bay. Too big for them to handle, so they took note and decided to head on down to Nova Scotia. Drove around for a few days, scouting things out as per usual, and came across a few little pockets of civilization. Some were larger than others. One was a farm. Nice little setup. There were a few root cellars filled with potatoes, carrots, bottled jams, and the like, all ready for the winter. They even brought back a bottled deer and chickens for roasting."

"Holy shit," Shovel hissed, becoming even more interested in the woman and her youngsters.

"There were others, but old. Slick Pick put them down and left them in the dirt. Says there was a nurse to go with the good doctor here, but they ended up shooting her on a highway somewhere. Got mouthy or something or other. Guess she figured she was too valuable."

"Stupid," Shovel hissed and centered his attention on the doctor. "Don't get me wrong. Some of my finest, most capable people are women. There's no sexism in my camp. But there is an intolerance for stupid people."

She didn't answer, and the silence stretched out long enough that both Giovanni and Sick turned their heads in her direction. The boy and the girl didn't notice Giovanni, but they certainly took stock of Sick. Most people did, regardless if they wanted to or not. He had that effect.

"What's your name?" Shovel asked her, thinking it was best to be nice in the beginning.

But she didn't answer.

Shovel released his breath in a long, drawn-out sigh and fixed her with a death stare. "I asked you a goddamn question."

Her thin lips quivered, but she got out, "Maggie."

The death stare softened. "That's better. I'm Shovel. You've met Giovanni and Pick. The boogeyman to your left there is called Sick. You're a doctor. What kind? General practitioner?"

"No."

Shovel eyed her from underneath his bushy eyebrows.

"Emergency," Maggie explained. "I worked emergency. Mostly."

"Emergency." Shovel tasted the wondrous word, studying her face and the crow's feet about her eyes. "Well, you'll be a welcomed addition to the camp. We don't have a doctor, you see. Matter of fact, these days we're reading books on home remedies if we have a problem, so you're quite the catch. Don't suppose you can do any dental work?"

Maggie frowned with exasperated disdain. "No, I don't."

"Care to learn?"

"Not really, no."

"Let me try that one again," Shovel said, his deep voice rumbling as if he were speaking directly into a microphone. "You *will* learn. There's a few folks around here that need the attention of a dentist. If anything, you'll have a better idea of how to administer anesthesia than the rest of us. If we can find some, that is. And if you can't handle the pliers or the pulling, you sure as hell know how to stitch. That extra skill set will only increase your value around here. Might even get you the right to vote one day. Hell, to lessen the load, I'll even give you some support staff. How does that sound?"

Maggie didn't reply right away. "Your men shot and killed my . . . my friends."

Shovel didn't flinch from her suddenly red-eyed gaze. "You not over that yet? Then do so. They're gone. You're not. Your kids aren't either if you get my drift."

With that, he turned his attention to the girl and the boy standing at Maggie's sides, clenching her hands. "And what're your names?"

They didn't answer.

"Come on now, we're going to be seeing a lot of each other. I'm Shovel, and that's all you need to call me. So who are you?"

Still no answer.

He flicked a warning glance at Maggie, who understood the message right away.

"Answer the man," she said, giving their little hands a shake.

"Chad."

"Becky."

Shovel allowed a little smile at the introductions and nodded at the good doctor. He reached out and caressed the cheek of the boy then the girl. Both earned marks for not flinching at the contact.

"We have other little girls and boys in camp here," Shovel told them. "Even have a place for you guys to play around in. Until you get a little older. Then, well, you'll have to work like everyone else."

"What do you mean by that?" Maggie asked him.

"Just what I said," he replied squarely, arching a brow. "I don't know what you were teaching them on your farm there, but here, things are a little different. When they hit thirteen, they're big enough to pull their own weight and will be expected to. The boy in particular will be useful. Even the girl if she takes to weapons training."

Maggie's mouth dropped open.

"Don't give me that look," Shovel said stoically. "This isn't a nursery. This is civilization with all-too-real dangers. Ain't no police out there to solve our problems. No court of law. There's just the basic law of the land, and I think you know what that is. Anyone who thinks otherwise is just fooling themselves. The dead are gone—or almost, anyway—but the living are still around. Some in little groups, some in bigger ones. And some of them, well, they aren't nice at all."

"These are just children," Maggie said. "You can't expect them to—"

"Children are the future," Shovel cut her off. "I know that just as much as anyone. But there's only a limited number of hands around here. When it comes to harvesting or mending or any little job that the kids can handle, well, they'll do it. They'll work for their supper, and they'll have earned it."

Maggie kept quiet, and Shovel saw suspicion on her face. "No, don't worry about that. No perverts around here. We're not total assholes. And if it happens, Mr. Sick here doles out the punishment. Now then, there's a little shack here in camp, which has been designated as the hospital—not much, but we try. I'm sure you'll help fill in the blanks of what else we need, and when that happens, I'll assign a few folks to head out to the nearest clinic or hospital and see what's available, but let me be clear about something. We're in the middle of back country out here, neighbor to the middle of butt-fuck nowhere. This place used to be a secret bunker for the government, which is why we're here. Bunkers are protected. There's a chain-link fence around this area, with galvanized-steel razor wire on top and at the base. You know why it's called razor wire? Take a wild fucking guess. Even if you had tools to snip through that shit, it's all under tension and designed to lash out when cut, like a neat little butterfly knife. Or a scalpel, since you worked an ER. Now, say if someone did make it through that, well, then there's the terrain itself to deal with. Land mines dot the surrounding forest like pimples on a freshly shaven ass. If you're lucky enough to bypass that, I'd say a good three-day hike to whatever shitsville you might stumble upon. Populated by, well, nobody. If you're lucky. Even if you drive, you'd have to get by the armed checkpoint in and out of this place, and you aren't going to drive."

Shovel smiled sympathetically.

"Who knows what else is out there. I don't. But if the government was willing to put up chain-link fences and razor wire, well, I imagine there's all sorts of unpleasant shit out there. The country's crawling with more 'n a few fucked-up meth heads and crazies—some with cannibalistic tendencies. But the main reason you won't run, the one I want to stress, is because *if* you do attempt it, we'll find out. And when we find out, we'll make it a game of finding you. One with a very nasty ending for you and anyone else going along. Fingers. Toes. Ears. Something will come off—and that's the first warning. Try escaping a second time and, well . . ."

Shovel shrugged nonchalantly.

"I'll kill you. Slow, if I'm really pissed off. Now, if I haven't scared you yet, I'll leave you with this nugget. Think of the kids."

A visibly shaken Maggie swallowed.

"You understand me?"

Silence.

Shovel smiled wetly. "Don't make me repeat myself."

"Understood."

"Excellent." He brightened. "Then welcome aboard. Get comfortable. As a doctor, you're entitled to your own private room and latrine. We'll get a nice blue porta-potty hauled in behind the hospital, and someone will empty it twice a week. I said 'hospital,' but it's really a clinic. You'll see. Well. I think that's all. Nice meeting you."

He didn't bother offering his hand. "And Becky? Chad?"

Their gazes lifted and centered on his face.

"Be good," he warned them with a finger. Feeling he'd made his point, Shovel looked at Sick. "Show the good doctor her new home, and then take the kids over to theirs."

"They're not staying with me?" Maggie blurted. "I'm the only one they have left."

"No, they'll stay with the other kids. It's better that way. Security, you see. Making sure you won't try running or something stupid. Don't worry, you'll get to see them." He shrugged one shoulder. "If you're good."

"I won't do anything if they don't stay with me," Maggie said.

Shovel regarded her curiously. "Didn't you just hear my little speech?"

Maggie didn't answer. He became clearly annoyed until she nodded.

"Well, read between the lines," Shovel said, his deep, deep voice enough to rattle the windows. He hooked his head toward the door, and Sick pulled it open and waited for the three new additions to the army. After considering for a second, Maggie pulled the kids outside while Shovel and Giovanni watched them go.

The door closed, and the two men were alone.

"Thoughts?" Shovel asked his henchman.

Giovanni shrugged and finger-combed his impressive clump of beard. "I think she'll get along. She'll be too worried about them young ones."

"Hm. I hope so. First fucking doctor we've come across in a dog's age. Hate to have to mutilate a kid to get my point across. I'll do it if I have to, but I'm not a complete bastard."

"Aw, she won't try nothing. We'll keep an eye on her for the first few months. She'll make friends then forget her old life. In a year, she'll be one of us."

Shovel walked around his desk and sat down heavily, mulling things over. "Yeah. Maybe. Anything else from Pick?"

"He came across a small place in New Brunswick. Some hard cases running the place—got folks working the fields and such. Set themselves up. You know the type."

I'm the type, Shovel mused. "All right. We'll mount up in a day or two and head that way. Liberate the good people and bring them over to the light. Wouldn't it be something if we came across another doctor?"

"Or a dentist."

"I'm with that," Shovel agreed. "How many bad guys?"

"Maybe a few dozen or so. Pick didn't spend too much time on it. He wanted to bring the doctor over right away. He hadn't come in immediately as he'd killed Maggie's nurse on the trip to make a point. Figured you be somewhat pissed."

Shovel stewed on that and shrugged. "Only a nurse. And point was made, I figure."

"Yep. Point was made."

Giovanni sat down across from Shovel without asking. He was the only man in camp who could get away with that indiscretion. They went way back, to when they were just roughnecks starting out—not *toughnecks,* as Shovel never had liked that moniker. The noise of activity permeated the shell of the trailer, and both men listened to it for a while.

"How long do you think before we break through?" Giovanni asked, which surprised Shovel. Usually Gio was the one who had the attitude of "It happens when it happens."

"Who knows. Could be any day."

"We're spread really thin out here."

"I know."

"With the crews hunting up food and water and the scouts out east, I'm feeling a little exposed."

"Good thing we got the big gun."

"Good thing is right," Giovanni agreed. "We're running low on gas. And diesel."

Shovel considered those reports. The fuel powering their thirsty machines was dwindling, and some of the new fuel harvested from derelict vehicles wouldn't actually burn, the additives that preserved octane levels finally showing their limitations.

"How long you think we have?"

Giovanni shrugged. "Depends. Best case, months. Worst case, weeks. But it's coming. The fuel will be worthless. Maybe if we had the facilities and the know-how, we could do something, but we don't. Just the power demands needed for a functioning plant kills the very notion. Besides that, the exact process is beyond our crew. We never refined or enhanced, only drilled."

"We'll be riding horses by this time next year."

"If we can find them," Gio commented stoically. "Any animals we find will have to be caught and domesticated all over. Too bad we didn't lasso a few heads from that herd we saw out in Alberta two years back."

"Too bad."

"In any case," the right-hand man continued, "bicycles will make do until we can come up with something better or find someone with a chemical background in processing and refining hydrocarbons."

"We'll be okay," Shovel assured them both. "One thing at a time. We could punch through to the bunker any time now. They're in there deep enough. All manner of goodies await. I guarantee it."

"You still think there's undead in there?"

"Course there's undead in there." Shovel kept his voice soft so as not to offend his friend. "That spook fella didn't know this place had been blown. He didn't know. That means the tunnel was blown for a reason, and with the way everything above ground was still in shape, that reason—or threat—came from within. Someone got infected, and there was an outbreak. Maybe a zombie got in there somehow. Or pissed in the water supply. Who knows? But someone blew that tunnel, and you can bet your nutsack it was because something dire went down. Over twelve hundred personnel here. I figure if there was a firefight, probably six or seven hundred of them got wiped out. Zombies, I mean. That leaves the rest unaccounted for, but I'm not worried. The crews going in have their guards, and they all have orders to run back to the cave mouth and get clear. Anything following will get mowed down by the mini. I'm not worried about any of that."

Shovel let that sink in.

"Once that threat's been removed, we'll move on in and see what treasures the vault holds."

"I'm hoping it's a good haul," Giovanni said.

"I *know* it'll be a good haul, especially seeing how good those JTF-2 guys were outfitted. If they were any indication, then I figure there's a veritable gold mine of weapons down there. And the ammo to go with it. The only challenge then is figuring out how the shit works. And if the place still has the generators going, well, we could be looking at our new home. Wouldn't that be nice? Power. Plumbing. Showers. Running hot water. Heat controlled by a touch pad or dial."

"Does sound good."

"And out here," Shovel reminded him, "no one will have an easy time finding us, and if they do, with existing defenses, they won't live to tell."

"You're in a good mood," Giovanni observed.

"I should be. Today, we just got ourselves a fucking ER doc—not a foot doctor but an honest-to-God frontline medical professional. Old Maggie is a godsend. I'm even thinking she can train midwives once we get to that point. You said Pick brought in some chickens? I say we have ourselves a barbeque tonight."

Giovanni's expression lightened considerably.

A barbeque sounded like a plan.

23

The storage RV contained some of Gus's old gear. He found his gloves with the hard plates fixed about the knuckles, his leather jacket, and his cowboy and steel-toed fireman's boots—even a boot knife, but it wasn't his. There wasn't anything else, and he figured the rest had stayed with the SUV. Collie convinced him to join her for something to eat, easy to do as he was feeling peckish, and they took a few of the IMPs and a little of the bottled deer meat taken from the farm.

They dined in the kitchen area of a motor home.

Wallace did not join them.

The presence of the deer told Gus that whoever had kidnapped Maggie and the kids had come this way, but he hadn't a clue as to which direction to go. He took his time with his meal, finding the IMP—Individual Meal Packet—to be good and not at all nearing the end of its five-year shelf life. It was a real surprise to find that Comeau and his boys had secured several boxes of the Canadian version of MREs. He discovered, much to his delight, each meal packet contained not only the main course but also side portions of food or juice mixes, packed in individual wrapping: chocolate chip cookies, cheese spread, peanut butter, bread, rice and soup mixes, and even . . . butterscotch pudding.

All of these tasted fine when prepared in a functioning kitchenette.

"The older versions were only good for three years, but *these* are new and improved," Collie said. "Sometimes, the forces would buy shitloads of MREs from the Americans, and there'd be jawing about which tasted better."

"Which one did?" Gus asked.

"Big surprise. A good many of them were produced in the States, anyway. Don't ask how many or for how long because I don't know. Anyway, I've tried both, and there's not that big a difference, other than the IMPs seem to have a few more goodies when it comes to the dessert menu. And they all contain about thirty-five hundred calories—enough to keep a soldier going in the field."

Gus ate soup with a few pieces of bottled deer. Collie shovelled in beef curry, and while that smelled tempting, he kept to the simpler fare. A meal of curry in his current shaky condition would turn his asshole into the Pacific Ring of Fire, as much as he hated to think about it.

He tried not to look too hard at Collie's dark complexion. She'd shocked him when she'd pulled off the ski mask, and her sympathetic smile at his reaction said it all. He didn't know when, where, or how, but she'd obviously been in a fight—probably a few fights, maybe one or two she'd even lost.

The tip of her nose was missing, as if someone had actually bitten it off. Skin grafts had made the remaining nub slightly presentable, but tearing one's eyes off that battle scar—and the two gaping holes leading to her nasal cavity—was difficult. The crow's lines at the corners of her eyes, only partially visible because of her mask, were actually black tattoos of thorny vines. The tat on her right side was inked over a sizeable section of burnt flesh there, which didn't reach her cheek but did slink down her neck. Her left ear was missing, and a spider's web of scar tissue covered that side of her head. Her ferocious eyes floated on a gathered tar of fleshy lines. Her top lip was thin but the bottom one full. Her hair—what little grew—was brown and buzzed short, sprouting out on the scalp and devastated sides.

"Insurgent grabbed my ponytail once, so it was snip-snip," Collie had revealed, the only history she'd disclosed at the time. Recalling the episode, Gus figured any more explanation would have taken an hour, and she'd already stated she was hungry.

Though her attitude suggested otherwise, Collie was a walking horror of battle wounds.

And, Lord above as his witness, Gus struggled with her appearance—as much as he hated to admit it—despite his own collection of scars.

"I'll clean up," Collie announced in her gruff voice after they'd finished eating, and threw the packaging into a nearby waste flap underneath the sink. "Get that rug on your chest shaved. When you're ready, just holler."

She left him sitting at the table. The door slowly swung shut as she went outside.

Gus stared after her, wondering but unable to ask how she'd gotten so fucked up—*afraid* to ask.

The food made him weary, so he polished off the last of his butterscotch pudding and went to the bedroom, where he collapsed on a wonderfully soft ocean-blue duvet.

Sleep took him almost immediately.

*

He woke up at the end of a loud snore and for a split second thought his arms had been chopped off. Then he felt his beard and almost freaked out, thinking a dead squirrel had been superglued to his chin. He collapsed back on the bed when he realized both thoughts were way off the mark.

"Sweet Christ," Gus muttered and sat up. His arms had returned to normal. A quick inspection showed the red marks around his wrists had almost faded, and his chest and belly had been cleanly shaved, the knife cut padded with gauze bandages and stuck in place with strips and X's of duct tape.

The fuck? He ran a finger over his bald man-breasts, feeling how weirdly smooth the whole shorn area was.

"How the hell did this happen?" he asked the empty room, getting to his feet—his legs even feeling stronger—and gazing at his white skin.

A shot of horror stopped him in his tracks, and he tentatively checked his junk, pulling away the waistband of his jeans and peeking almost fearfully. Nope—all was well south of the leather, which was heartening At least she hadn't shaven him down there. At least, he *hoped* she'd done it and not Wallace. The thought of his grinning mug doing the job wasn't calming in the least.

Gus noted his shirt and sweater lying on a chair near the foot of the bed. He got dressed and stumbled to the toilet. After finishing his business there, he hauled on his ill-fitting sneakers and stepped outside.

The day was overcast.

"Afternoon, sunshine," Collie called from the other side of a white F150 pickup, parked within the wagon circle of motor homes. "Sleep good?"

Gus regarded her smiling wreck of a face. "Guess I did since I didn't feel a thing while bein' fuckin' shaved. And what time is it?"

"Ornery, ain'tcha? It's nearing two in the afternoon. You've been out all morning."

"All morning?"

"Yeah."

"How the hell did I sleep all yesterday and last night and get my tits shaved without waking up?"

Collie leaned over the lip of the pickup's box and gazed at him pleasantly. "I'd guess it was the stress that did it, from your ordeal. That and not being properly rested. Your body just went into repair mode. But that's just a guess. I'd put more faith in the diphenhydramine I slipped into your soup."

Gus stopped cold and fixed her with a look of disbelief. "You what?"

"I drugged you."

"Oh."

"You angry with me?"

Wallace shuffled through the doorway of an RV, his helmet visor leveled in Gus's direction.

Angry with her? "No, no, nothing like that," Gus confessed. "Just feel weird, is all."

"That's probably a side effect of the antihistamine."

"The what?"

"Diphenhydramine is an antihistamine."

"It does that? Make a person feel weird?"

"Not really. I just said it to make you feel better. Just so you could get over your feelings of being violated. Nice tits, by the way."

A mortified Gus kept his mouth shut.

"Don't worry," Collie soothed. "It was the best way to clean up those cuts."

For the first time since getting up, Gus felt the patch under his right eye, where Cam Boll had almost threatened to hook it out.

"As for your chest," Collie nodded, "well . . . couldn't very well shave around it. And once I started, I couldn't exactly stop. That'd look fucked up. And I only did the chest and the belly. Nothing else. Left the beard. Didn't touch your back. Or your balls."

"Well, thanks."

"Don't mention it. But if you do need your thingy mowed—"

"I don't need my thingy mowed."

"But if you do . . ."

"Give you a shout?"

Collie drew back. "Not me. Ask Clay over there. He'll do you up."

Framed in the doorway, Wallace shook his head in derisive doubt at the suggestion.

"Yeah, well," Gus said slowly, regaining composure, "I think I'll be fine. Thanks."

"Anytime. Feel better now?"

"Yeah. What're you guys up to?"

Collie gestured to the box on the pickup. "This? Just loading up shit that won't perish in the weather or anything. Scavenging, some would say."

"Ah." Gus had no problem with that. "You come across an SUV?"

"Wallace did in fact find an SUV drawn up on the shoulder of the road over there, on the south side and down a ways. Front's all crunched up, though. And it had a couple bullet holes decorating the windshield. Deployed air bag. That your ride?"

"Well, yeah, it was."

"There were some things scattered around the rig." Wallace joined in the conversation, his head tilted to one side.

"Well," Gus said, "anyway, I think I'll head on down there. Get the rest of my shit. Sorta attached to it all."

He made to turn away.

"Hey, Gus," Collie called.

"Yeah?"

"You still gonna look for your doctor and those kids?"

Gus didn't even think of that as a question. "Yeah. Matter of fact. After I check out the SUV, if it's okay with you, I might take one of these motor homes."

"They got shitty mileage."

"Only until I can find another ride."

"Huh. Well, listen, Wallace and I have been talking. We'll help you find the doctor. If you want."

Gus regarded her battle-scarred features and took his time answering. "Why?"

"Because she's a doctor."

"That all?"

"No, that's not all," Collie said. "Wallace and I, we're reconning the area—the whole province, in fact—knocking off any remaining infected and gathering up anyone still alive. Life carries on, y'know? There's a small community, not many people, but it's there. Protected. They stay where they are and live their lives while we get to do the dangerous stuff on their behalf. Our mission is threefold: kill the leftover undead, gather up the living, and harvest any worthwhile supplies, anything that's still good."

"Like guns?"

Collie smirked. "More like ammunition. We have plenty of guns. Cannons are all over the place. Finding something to load into them—that's a problem. But the real hope is finding people with specific skill sets. Lawyers and politicians we can do without, but doctors, dentists, carpenters, mechanics, and so on—people with functional trades essential to rebuilding what was. There's not a lot of them out there. The virus didn't care who got infected. And if we do find someone, half the time, they've reverted into a dark, dangerous kinda crazy, if you follow me."

"I follow," Gus said quietly. Did he ever.

"I know the little group we serve and protect doesn't have a doctor," Collie revealed. "They'd shit themselves if we had one to bring back."

"Yeah?"

"Oh yeah. A doctor? A qualified, experienced medical *professional* and not just Joe Anybody trying to figure things out from a textbook? Well, let's just say in this world . . . she's worth the weight of a whole town in gold."

Whole town in gold, Gus reflected and fidgeted with that knowledge, studying Collie's harsh mug. He even glanced over at Wallace.

"I . . . I can't speak for her," Gus finally said. "All I know is that whoever has her took her and the kids after they murdered everyone else on the farm. You already helped me out, without asking for anything in return so . . . you help me find them, and we can put the question to her then."

Collie spread her hands. "Sounds fair." Then she regarded Wallace. "You good?"

The frightening soldier nodded once, the rictus of a grin tight around his lips.

"Okay," Collis announced. "We're agreed. Do whatever you have to do then, and let's roll."

Gus wandered away from the pair and went outside of the circle of motor homes. His path took him across the slope of the overpass, and he stopped and studied the not-so-far-off bastion Comeau and his freaks constructed up there. The gradual incline was littered by a few wrecked and not-so-wrecked cars, ending in what appeared to be a collection of vehicles parked at the top. A tarp of some sort fluttered just over a red roof, with a white streak rising and falling as a breeze gave it life.

The thought occurred to Gus that he hadn't seen the bodies, but he suspected they might be up there, just beyond that white flag of rustling tarp. At that particular moment, his vision tunneled, and he centered on that subtle motion. It wasn't that breezy there, at the foot of the overpass, so what could be moving that piece of whatever the hell it was? The more Gus thought about it, the more puzzled he became.

He decided it best to walk up there and check things out.

Wallace's sickly face entered his mind—the soldier's haunting grin and diseased gum lines.

And he hadn't eaten.

At least, the soldier didn't eat when he and Roxanne had sat down to eat. *What was up with that?*

Gus rattled his head. He'd meant Collie, who didn't look a thing like the woman out of his violent past.

Up on the overpass, the tarp rose and fell, waving, beckoning, wanting him to walk on up there and investigate a mystery easily solved. Everything else around the edges blurred. After a short hike, all would be revealed—Comeau and company . . . or their remains.

Their *animated* remains.

He took two steps toward the top.

"Where you going, Gus?"

Wallace's voice smacked him hard upside his senses, and he jerked around as if poked with a live wire. The man stood between two motor homes, head cocked to the side, eyes hidden behind his visor, waiting patiently for an answer. Gus's attention flickered from the top of the overpass to the unwell soldier.

"Ah," he sputtered and stretched his back, spinning his mental wheels through lies. "Just, ah, looking there."

Wallace casually regarded the overpass, untroubled with the world, it seemed. "You wondering what's up there?"

Gus composed himself. "Yeah, I am, actually."

"What do you think might be up there?"

"I think Comeau and his boys might be up there."

"Comeau and his boys."

"Yeah."

"The same men who tortured you and left you for a zombie to feed upon? The same good ol' boys who appeared to rape their victims as well as kill and rob them? Those are the men who you're wondering about?"

Gus had nothing to say to that, so he just screwed up his face and stared, unable to get a read on Wallace.

"Well, they're up there," the soldier reported with laid-back casualness. "Right where Collie shot and left them . . . and searched them. But after being left out for a day and change, they aren't the prettiest to look upon. Fair warning—unless you don't mind looking at decomposing bodies."

Gus had nothing to say to that either. "No, I don't. I mean, uh . . ."

"Don't let me keep you, then. But personally, if I were you, I wouldn't."

With that, Wallace walked away, working legs that might have had cement poured into the joints.

Gus watched him disappear around a corner. A motor started nearby.

He hesitated a few seconds more, pressing a hand over his duct-taped slash wound, before walking off in search of the SUV. Wallace was right about one thing. Comeau and company deserved whatever they had coming to them. All the same, that fluttering piece of white tarp hung in his mind, drawing his attention with sinister implications.

Ten minutes later, Gus located the SUV and inspected its metallic carcass with all the mute reverence an old gunslinger might muster for a reliable horse. They'd shot him off the road, and he'd crashed into the small roadside pond. His hands hung off his hips, staring at the scrunched-in front caked with dried weeds and at the blown-out windshield. Every door lay open, and glass fragments glittered like diamonds on the front seats. Deployed airbags, deflated with a knife perhaps, sagged off the steering wheel and passenger dash. Dirt coated the cookware where it'd been tossed out and kicked.

Shaking his head at the rape of his ride, he peered into the front and back seats before moving to the rear. The toilet paper was all gone, which didn't surprise him, as was the water and food—even the bag of muffin mix. The long-neck lighters he'd gathered were still there, still functional. The duffel bag was in a dusty heap five feet from the rear, which surprised him because it was a duffel bag, so Gus picked it up and shook it out. Frowning, he gathered up everything possible, which wasn't a lot, and tucked it all away in the bag's cloth folds. He found the Nomex gear in a clump of dead grass halfway to the pond.

It all went into the duffel.

But no bat.

Gus scoured the area until he felt time dragging, hoping the weapon might be in one of the RVs. Lugging his gear back, he returned to the encampment. Collie and Wallace hung out in the doorway of a white rig, the one chosen to be a roving pack wagon.

"There he is," she chimed. "Find what you were looking for?"

"Some of it," Gus answered and dropped the duffel. "You see a bat around?"

"A bat?"

"Yeah. Aluminum one."

"Check out the bar."

"Huh?"

"The bar," Collie repeated. "That's the Winny over there. You'll see. Saw a bat in a leather scabbard hung over the back of the driver's seat."

Gus turned in the direction pointed. "That one?"

Collie nodded.

"You guys ready to move?"

"Waiting on you, civvie," Wallace answered drily and with a twinge of impatience.

Gus cocked an eyebrow at the reference.

"What he means," Collie stepped in, "is that we probably have less than three hours of daylight left, and then we're stuck for the night. Not that it's a big problem now."

"What do you mean?"

Collie smiled. "We'd usually camp out in someone's house or even a hotel if we came across one. Never in the open. And there's plenty of comfortable places to stay—if you don't mind the occasional cleanup. Welcome to the apocalypse."

Gus knew what she meant by cleanups.

"How many of these are you taking?" he asked, referring to the motor homes.

"We've stocked up two. Hooked our pickup to the rear of one. You can ride with me or Ollie, your choice."

Gus had already made his choice. "I'll ride with you. No offense, Wallace."

Instead of commenting, the soldier inspected the unzipped duffel bag.

"Is that turnout gear?"

Gus looked at the Nomex. "That's firefighter gear, yeah. Boots and all. What'd you call it?"

"Turnout gear. Bunker gear."

"Never heard it called that before," Gus said.

"You never hung out with firefighters," Wallace remarked pointedly and went on with his inspection. "Good idea, though. Thick-layered material. Fire resistant and puncture proof. The older stuff wasn't, but this can stop most things outside of a nine mil. What's it weigh? Ten kilos?"

Gus shrugged uncertainly. "Yeah, I guess. About that."

Wallace managed a horrid smile. "Adapt and overcome. Very good, civvie."

The mellow approval almost made Gus feel good about himself. "Uh, well, thanks. Give me a few minutes, okay?"

He walked away. Gus pulled himself aboard the motor home Collie had called "the bar." The place had been rudely remodeled, for in the center of the interior was a poker table with accompanying chairs. Gambling chips of various colors littered the surface. In disbelief, Gus spotted the bat, still in the leather sheath Adam had made for him, hanging off the driver's seat. He took it and slung it over his shoulder and looked around further.

His mouth hung open.

"Jeeezus Christ and Mary."

The rear of the motor home, where the bedroom would be, was full of cases of alcohol. Gus stopped on the threshold, stunned cold in his tracks, and simply stared at the cursed oasis. Open and closed boxes of assorted bottles lay about, all full, some stacked tall and some lining shelves. Colored glass gleamed. The *bar*, Gus's inner voice whispered, laying eyes on the unit with three tall stools bolted into the floor. The bed had been ripped out, and in its place . . . spiritual goodness.

"Holy . . . holy," Gus whispered as he inspected the labels. Liqueur, whiskey, rum, vodka, gin . . . and those were just the visible ones. There were boxes stacked behind and underneath each other, to the point that, if someone was sitting at the bar and fell over backward, his head would crash into a glorious bounty.

And, goddamnit, did the ferocious urge to partake ever come over him—just for luck, just for the ceremonious gesture of well wishing. Shot glasses and beer mugs rested on shelves behind the bar, and a small fridge propped on milk crates contained beverages he didn't even recognize right away. It wasn't like the liquor shops in Annap-olis, but it would put a smile on the faces of the desperate and thirsty.

He didn't drink anything, however. Instead, he went behind the bar and stared, shocked once more.

Grinning at him was the Captain, the same Captain stuck on the side of a plastic bottle that had traveled with him up to this point, taken from the SUV wreck and placed among its distilled cousins.

Gus studied the Captain's smiling features and felt his own face lighting up. "How you doin', old buddy?"

The sailor did not respond.

Gus figured that was a good thing. He still had all of his marbles in place. The amber rum sloshed around as he picked it up and tilted the bottle this way and that. Same bottle. Had to be—he *wanted* it to be. With the stash of alcoholic merriment in the bar, Gus could see why this little flask of rum had been tucked away in the fridge instead of being downed right away.

A length of leather twine dangled off the knob of a drawer. Gus pulled it off and ignored the extra poker chips, but a good three feet or so of the material hung there, begging to be used.

So he used it.

24

"Find your friend?" Collie asked when Gus emerged.

The smile on Gus's face answered that. "The bat was where you said it was, which is great."

"Nothing beats a solid bat," Collie agreed. "And one for the road?"

Gus held up the bottle, the Captain's face pointing outward. "This is an old house-and-road buddy of mine. Same bottle. Untouched. Never thought I find that in there. Forgot about him, to tell the truth."

"He a good luck charm or something?" Collie asked.

Gus regarded the naval officer. He'd taken the twine and tied it around the bottle's base and neck, strapping everything in place with gobs of duct tape found in a utility drawer. Only the Captain's head appeared, but now he had a little extra protection with the molded layers of tape. The twine dangled from his hand and, if he wanted, he could slip it over his head as a heavy necklace.

"Big medicine," Gus declared. "It's a good thing."

Wallace looked at Collie and cleared his throat, the sound like a wet phone book being torn in two in front of a bullhorn. Gus hated to imagine what was moving around in the soldier's chest, making that noise.

"You didn't take any of the other stuff?" Collie asked.

"Wha'? The booze, you mean?"

"Yeah, the booze."

Gus shook his head. "Don't need it."

"Well, don't fret any. I loaded up a few boxes. Good trade goods even if we don't get into it."

"Well, I'm set," Gus said.

"Any idea of which direction to go?" she asked.

"None."

That left Wallace and Collie quiet.

"I've just been following my nose," Gus offered. "But that bottled deer meat, that's from our farm. How these guys got it, well, that's obvious. Someone gave it to them while passing through."

"I ask the question because we're at a crossroads here," Collie pointed out, "where the 102 runs into the 104. Now, we came from the east and haven't seen or heard anything. So by default, we could keep rolling west. See if we cross anything. It's a long shot, really, knowing how many side roads and smaller highways there are, spread out over a very, *very* big piece of territory. But seeing what's at stake, it's still a shot. We got a lot of supplies here, but our folks can wait for a bit, so we don't have to head back there right away. Least, not until we see what's what. See if your nose is on. If you're willing."

"I am," Gus said.

"Let's go, then," she said to Wallace. "I'll take the FNG."

"Let's hope they don't turn stateside," the zombie-ish officer rumbled.

"Why's that?" Gus asked while puzzling over what FNG might mean.

"Because that's where the fallout was the worst," Wallace said. "When the machines stopped being monitored, things started falling apart. The containment measures for radioactive cores at every nuclear plant eventually failed, north and south of the border. Just so happens most of our facilities were built along the border. I'd advise against traveling down there. Anyone in, say, Toronto or thereabouts, who weren't turned into something dead and walking, who actually lived, pretty much died from fallout. Don't even drink the groundwater from anything within a hundred klicks of a plant."

"So, what do we do?"

"Realistically," Wallace continued in that trancelike voice of his, "we drive on, drive slow, and keep our eyes open for signs of people. Maybe we'll luck out. Personally, I give us a ten to fifteen percent chance of finding your pecker checker. That's 'doctor' in your tongue. But like Collie's said, she's worth it."

"I don't think she can help you," Gus said after a pause, confronting that dark visor.

The skeletal grin underneath widened.

"Civvie," Wallace said, "no one can save me."

A pair of motor homes—one towing a flatbed trailer with a battered wooden shack built on top, the other dragging a white pickup—moved westward on the 104

TransCanada Highway, gradually curving north. Gus sat in the passenger seat while Collie drove, taking the lead as Wallace followed. The usual detritus of vehicles plagued the highway. Some stopped in a mesh of traffic, while others rested on the shoulders at interesting angles.

Collie slowed the monster motor home and threaded through the worst of the tangles, sometimes scraping the sides. At times, she drove across the dip of a median and rumbled the unit up the other side to bypass knots of stranded vehicles.

"Should've expected this," she muttered, checking her available mirrors.

"The highway?" Gus asked.

"Yeah. We've got a fat ass—made worse by hauling along that generator."

Gus didn't ask why they'd brought it along. A working generator meant power and creature comforts—for a while, anyway.

"Whereabouts you from?" he asked her.

"Originally Odessa. Just outside of Kingston, Ontario. You?"

"Annapolis."

"Never been. Yet."

"I've never been to Odessa."

"Well, you never know. Way the world is now, you can travel as much as you want until the gas runs out. Then it's waiting for someone to figure out how to power up and operate an oil refinery."

"Not me," Gus smiled. "I'll stick to taking the leftovers out of gas tanks."

"How you do that?"

"Drain them with a spike and hammer. I have a pan to catch the gas."

"That's nasty." Collie spared him a quick glance. "Ever have one catch fire on you?"

"Not yet. Usually plastic tanks. Don't worry—I know what I'm doing."

"I suppose so."

"How do you guys get gas out of the tank?" Gus asked.

"Siphon it in the new-fashioned way, with a little rig called a snake. It fools the security locks on the tanks, makes the sensors think the car's about to be refueled, and before you know it, it's draining every drop. All done with a self-charging hand crank, as well."

"That a military thing?" Gus asked, impressed.

"No, that's a little invention of a professional gas thief back at the community." She glanced at him again. "You meet all kinds."

That made Gus chuckle, and he focused on the road for a bit before asking what Collie probably expected.

"What's up with Wallace?"

Collie slowed the motor home down to thread its mass through an alley of transport trucks. "Short answer, he's sick."

"He's not a gimp?"

"A what?"

"A gimp. That's what I call 'em. Or deadheads."

"Huh. That's different. We call them Moe."

"Moe."

"Yeah. Some folks traveling from back East called them that. Name stuck. Shorter than MBs, which we used to use."

"MBs?"

"Meatbags."

"Meatbags." Gus liked that one himself. "Well, how about Wallace, then? Or is that a taboo subject around here?"

"Not taboo," Collie said. "But maybe *classified* is a better word. We think you're okay. Not a crazy, I mean. But we have our secrets, understand—which is why it was better for you to ride with me for now, just to explain this very topic."

"Okay. I'm listening."

"Let us warm up to you a bit. Get to know you. And maybe, in the end, Wallace will tell you himself."

"In the end?"

Collie regarded him with a hint of a secretive smile, her eyes like eerie sapphires.

Gus indicated his newfound pistols. "What about these, then?"

"You can keep those."

Gus whistled softly. "You guys are some cool customers."

"Honey, you don't know half of it."

"All right, all right—I can wait. I'm just glad someone knows what's going on with Wallace."

"Well, I should know." Collie concentrated on her driving. "I married the guy."

The low-hanging clouds darkened, pressing down on spirits as well as daylight, and at the 4:27 mark of the winter evening, the lead motor home rolled to a stop below an east-west overpass. The headlights flared ahead, but they weren't really needed to see what lay on the highway ahead. A serpentine parade of vehicles stretched the length of the road, twisting and gleaming in the fading light. Knots of metal piled up in places, where cars or trucks had seemingly rammed into each other, perhaps wasted attempts to push forward, perhaps frustration or fear finally taking over the drivers. Collie steered the big machine up the ramp, turned left, and slowed to a stop just past the middle of the overpass. Cars blocked the way ahead, preventing any further progress.

"And that's that," Collie whispered, placing the RV in park. She sighed and looked around, appraising the roads and thinking.

"Done for the day?" Gus asked.

"Yeah, I think so. We'll camp out up here. Just like a tree."

Gus stared at the highways, the gloom of the encroaching evening both depressing and hypnotizing. Any moment, he expected to see figures stand up from between the vehicular segments, like sinister prairie dogs lifting their heads to the wind. Nothing did, however, and he had to remind himself gimps didn't walk much these days. They crawled, searching for ankles.

"Well, might as well lock ourselves down and get comfortable," Collie said and got up from her seat, her combat gear rattling. Gus turned around in his seat and stood a few seconds later as the side door clicked open and a gust of cold air came in.

He stepped outside and looked around, spotting Wallace's ride coming to a rest with a soft squeal of brakes. Collie stood at the guardrail of the overpass, studying the terrain. Gus wandered over, adjusting to a temperature much cooler than the interior of the motor home.

"See anything?"

"In this?" Collie asked. "It's almost dark out, bro. Can't see anything right now. But if you listen . . ."

Bro.

Gus thought of Talbert and his death grip, the moment freezing and rewinding in his head.

Collie looked to the north and shook her head at the cars and trucks obstructing the road. She then gestured west, where the highway sloped down the overpass. A collection of houses large and small could barely be seen at the end of a long but congested stretch of highway running underneath them. A zap of lightning would complete the scene.

Wallace opened his door and stepped out with glacial grace. Just hearing him move sounded painful, and Gus had to look to see if the man was doing okay. The soldier was working his strut, taking it slow and easy.

He had his visor lifted.

"Look at that," Collie said, distracting Gus. She nodded toward the distant little town, black and somber looking. "Y'know something? When the world was teeming with people, I used to hate it. Fucking despised it. The attitudes, the fakes, the burnouts, the authority, the crazies, and at the time, the sheep mentality of it all. The nine-to-five insanity. The chase. Now . . . God, I miss it—miss every engine rev, every hello from across the street, every dickhead texting on a smart phone, and every fucking corn flake. I miss it. Talk about not knowing what you got until it's gone, eh?"

Gus didn't have to be a psychic to feel her angst, so he stayed quiet, not knowing Collie well enough to comment. However, despite her physical appearance, her disfigured face and scars, he was beginning to like her.

"See anything?" that Zen voice asked from behind.

Wallace, however, Gus was still undecided about.

"Not much," Collie said and thumbed in the direction of the blocked road to the north. "Not about to go through that. Maybe in the morning, we can back up and get onto another lane. Go around it. One thing's for sure, if we can't get through, Gus's kidnappers didn't either."

"Probably," Wallace said.

Gus turned to see the man's visor lifted, revealing a tightly drawn mask of unsettling flesh and dark veins. The sight robbed him of his voice.

Wallace fixed him with an unfiltered look of annoyed curiosity. "See anything interesting, civvie?"

That dislodged Gus from his gawking, and he turned away, starting to dislike the nickname. He wondered if Wallace had forgotten his real name.

He decided to remind him. "Name's Gus."

Wallace didn't move. "I know."

Gus looked back at the gruesome fright of a face, but Wallace ignored him.

"You guys going to eat now?" the soldier directed to Collie.

"Thinking about it. You?"

Wallace didn't answer right away. "I'm going to head on down there, take a few gas cans and plastic bottles, harvest any fuel for tomorrow because we'll need it. These pigs get thirsty fast."

"Okay. Seeya."

Wallace walked back to his ride. Gus watched him strut that high-noon gunslinger walk of his.

"He can work it, can't he?" Collie asked.

Gus neutrally cleared his throat, embarrassed at having being caught.

"C'mon," she said. "You like pizza?"

"Holy shit, you have pizza?"

"Well, there's a box of pizza IMP in back of the rig. I peeked and saw pepperoni and cheese in there."

"Jesus," Gus blurted. "I mean, *Jesus*."

"Don't get your hopes up. IMPs have come a long way, but even though it says pizza on the box, who the fuck knows what it really is."

"Still . . ."

Collie walked back to the motor home. "Yeah, if you had any beer, we'd be all set. Then again, sooner or later someone will get a still running—or at least some beer carboys. Not too hard to do. All you need is a place with a constant temperature and then some patience."

"We got the whiskey and all that other stuff," Gus heard himself say.

Collie regarded him over a shoulder. "Yeah, we do, don't we?"

"But, pizza doesn't really go well with rye. Or vodka. Or whatever."

Collie reached the door. "In this case, it might very well be needed."

She later extracted the pizza from its silvery packaging and placed it on a cookie pan before popping it into an oven. Gus sat at the table. He split his attention between talking and watching her. When the pizza warmed up and the cheese ran, the interior filled with a glorious aroma Gus had remembered only from dreams.

Then they were eating.

Gus took two wedges, slapped them together like a sandwich, and sliced a section away with a knife and fork. Collie still had her front teeth, so she chomped down into hers. Both chewed for a while, eying the other.

"Well," Gus said quietly after swallowing. "That was terrible."

"Yeah," Collie said, reaching for a glass of water, "that was."

"Smelled great, though."

"True . . . but . . . can't live on smell alone."

She picked up the packaging and mulled over the ingredients. "Y'know, I've heard red meat stays in your colon for up to six months, but in this case, I don't think we'll have a problem."

Gus chuckled and cut away another bite.

"You like that shit?"

"The world ended four years ago. Even the shittiest pizza isn't bad enough to throw away."

"That's true too," Collie said and tried another mouthful. "Shit's dry, though. Should've nuked it instead of baking."

Gus shrugged. "Y'know, I remember this place that served up wicked pizza. I even know the guy who owned the place, and sometimes, he'd even give me free stuff if the crust was just browned a shade too much."

"Yeah?"

"Oh yeah. I mean, he needed it done to just the right color. Too brown, and people wouldn't buy it. A few times, I'd be walking past his place, and he'd come out and ask if I wanted any that were too well done for the customers. Just a little bit dark was all it was too, but it tasted like it slipped out of heaven."

"I like a saucy pizza," Collie said. "The more the better. This isn't saucy at all. I always made a point to ask for extra sauce on my pizza. Extra sauce. Easy enough, right? Nope. I'd get into fights with pizza people over it. 'Where the hell is my extra sauce? There's no extra sauce on that thing.' What part of *extra* do they not understand? Maybe their oven is off kilter by about ten degrees or so, and right in the back is where all the extra sauce slides off and pools up, y'know? Like this bubbling vat of goodness."

"That's a good theory."

"It works for me," Collie said. "You think maybe the other ingredients might be more expensive, but I'm not so sure anymore. At least, you'd never think, the way some assholes guard it. The sauce is where the magic happens. For some people, it's cheese, for others it's the crust, but with me—"

"It's the sauce."

"It's the sauce," Collie finished. "All about the sauce."

"How you think Wallace is doing?" Gus asked.

"Ollie's doing just fine out there. Don't you worry about him."

"He . . ." Gus lowered his voice and leaned over the table. "He creeps me out."

Collie leaned in as well. "He creeps most people out. But he's solid. Trust me on that."

Gus went back to eating. They finished in a few minutes, and Collie got up and pulled out a bottle of Santa Maria whiskey from a cupboard. She placed it on the table just off to the side and produced a pair of shot glasses. Gus eyed that amber bedevilment at his elbow and leaned back, stroking his patchy beard.

"You don't partake?" Collie asked, sitting down.

"Well, yes and no," Gus told her. "I did a couple of years back. Drank a lot . . . but then stopped for one reason or other."

"You sure?" Collie asked, unscrewing the cap.

Gus eyed the bottle. Damn straight, he could use one after the shit he'd seen and been through. Thing was, Maggie, Becky, and Chad were still out there, somewhere. He wasn't an alcoholic, he told himself, and he could have that one drink if he wanted it. He'd *earned* it.

But it would feel celebratory for some reason, and he wasn't in a celebratory kinda mood right then—not while his friends were still in danger.

"No," he decided. "Thanks. I'm good."

"Gus." Collie poured herself a shot. "Augustus. You know your name means 'the exalted one'? The name of the first great Roman emperor."

That set him blinking. "I did not know that."

"Well, it does," she said and smiled, hoisting her glass. It sparkled.

Gus lifted his glass of water and tapped it. She buried her shot with one toss of her head while Gus sipped.

"Goddamn," Collie declared. "That burns."

The bottle gleamed as she refilled her glass. Gus watched morosely.

"You know what this is?" Collie asked as she poured. "Courage. Not quite instant, but it's courage all the same. Or bravery. A remover of fear, even. Not a bad thing in the least. Even needed, I'd argue, relished and savored—but like anything, some people do allow themselves to be carried away with it. That's dangerous. You know what I'm saying?"

Gus nodded. He most certainly did.

Collie smiled comfortably then, and he focused on her scary eyes instead of her face.

"Don't you worry, Augustus," she said firmly, studying his own scarred features, reading him. "One way or another, tomorrow or the next, we'll find your doctor friend and those kids."

With that, she shotgunned her second drink and clapped the thick glass down on the table.

"That's a promise," she said.

Suddenly miserable, Gus finished his water.

Sometime later, Wallace paused outside Collie's motor home. He didn't knock on the door, nor did he make any attempt to enter. He merely stood outside the glow of the lit window, between a pair of cars, and stared at the closed white blinds. Collie and Gus were talking in low tones that he caught snatches of, but he didn't go any closer, as much as he wanted to, as much as the poison of jealousy burned and tortured him.

The minutes went by, every second lethal and demoralizing, like the flirtatious smile of one's mate aimed at another. Chairs squeaked, and he heard them get up from the table and saw a shadow behind the window. For a second, fear gripped him.

Fingers pulled the blind down then allowed them up.

Wallace relaxed.

But he tensed up once more when the lights winked out, dreading the next few moments.

He heard noises then, perking his ears, as either Collie or Gus retired to the end of the motor home, to the king-size bed lying beyond those walls. The other crawled up into the bunk above the driver's seat.

Then . . . nothing.

A tsunami of relief gushed through Wallace. It lasted only a few seconds, however.

He could tell she liked him.

Wallace remained motionless in the dark, becoming one with it, and felt the terrible ache that all souls experienced at one time or another in their lives.

And final days.

25

Collie and Gus got up at seven in the morning from their respective beds and assembled at the kitchen table. They breakfasted quietly on dried cereal without the milk and shared a Mason jar of homemade vegetable soup that Collie had received from the townsfolk she protected. After eating, they lumbered outside to better appreciate the cold weather and the overcast sky. The blocked highway could be better seen, and the knots of unmoving cars and trucks below seemed to thin out in the distance.

"Morning," Wallace greeted them both as he shuffled around the rear of their motor home. Collie and Gus nodded in return, and Gus couldn't help but watch that slow, steady walk of his rescuer.

Wallace's visor was down and stared back. "My fly down or something?"

"Uh, no, no, you're good," Gus sputtered. "You're good. Really. Uh, sorry."

"You get everything last night?" Collie asked, not paying attention to the exchange.

"Filled up what I could," Wallace reported. "Quiet night."

"What time did you turn in?" Gus asked, wanting in on the conversation.

"When I was tired."

"Didn't see the time?"

Wallace regarded him coldly. "No."

"Ollie keeps his own hours," Collie explained as she studied the lumpy padding of cloud covering the sky. "He's the night shift, you could say. Watching our backs while we sleep."

"Oh." Gus thought that was a great thing. "So when do you sleep?"

"When I have to," Wallace stated and wandered to the overpass rail. Collie followed and Gus hesitantly joined.

"Gonna have to back outta here. Won't be too much of an ass pain," Collie observed.

"Not for you."

She regarded Wallace with a questioning eye long enough for Gus to see concern on her ravaged face. She wiped at her nostrils and studied the lay of the land. "The next question, then. Where do we go from here?"

"There are some tire tracks in the grass about a quarter klick back from the overpass ramp behind us," Wallace informed her. "We missed them last night."

"Cars?" Collie faced the soldier.

"Yeah." Wallace led them to the rail on the south side and pointed, revealing a rough trail about a hundred meters or so back. A small line of cars had crushed the cold grass, leaving a trail in the small fields surrounding the overpass—easy to see from their vantage point once revealed. The trail turned off the highway and looped around the knot of the overpass, avoiding the unmoving traffic, and Gus lost sight of it farther up the highway, where tall firs grew nearer the road. He assumed the trail reconnected with the highway just past the worst of the clutter.

"See? They drove off the highway," Wallace explained as he pointed. "Across the field, up over the east lane, then down into that field, before linking up with the road underneath us farther on up, well past all that garbage and continuing onward. About three trucks, I'd say."

"How do you know they're trucks?" Gus asked.

"Tires and wheelbase," Wallace answered in that stoned tone of his. "Two or three days old, so the timeline's right."

Collie glanced at them both. "Then let's roll."

Gus went to the rear of Wallace's RV and guided the soldier backing his motor home and attached pickup down the overpass's slope. Gus did the same for Collie, admiring the way they both handled their rigs and the trailing loads. Both operators aimed the RVs toward the beaten path. Once they were off the ramp, Gus walked back to the side door and met Collie as she stepped out and looked across the field to the northeast, fixing upon the corner of the fir forest. She held up a hand.

"Listen," she said.

"What?"

"Just listen."

Frowning, Gus did and heard nothing other than Wallace's engine idling. Collie stepped away from her RV and gestured for Wallace to kill his engine. He complied, and Collie nodded for Gus to try again.

"Still nothing."

"Follow me." She went to the ladder affixed to the motor home's rear. She climbed to the top, and Gus tried not to look at the camouflage design covering her ass, suspecting Wallace wouldn't be pleased. Still, it was hard *not* to do as she hauled herself up and over the roof, her camos pulling tight.

Gus quickly looked at the ladder and concentrated on climbing.

Once on the roof, he stood next to Collie, who pointed to a section of tall grass. The tire tracks cutting through the overgrown sward made Gus wonder how they missed something so obvious in the first place. The rest of the grassy expanse swayed in the breeze.

Except . . .

Gus squinted. There was no breeze.

Yet in places, the tall grass moved.

"What is that?" he muttered, straining to see.

"You haveta ask?" Collie chided.

Then he saw, and even though he was sick of the dead, they still managed to surprise him at times.

The nearest violent ripple reached the last thin curtain of grass bordering the truck-made trail. The grass collapsed outward as a discolored hand pushed through the yellow stalks. A head oozed out from the wall of grass. The locomotion of the rest of the gimp's body pushed its skull into the dirt to a point where Gus thought its spine might buckle free of its shoulders. The corpse crawled into daylight, one arm flopping along weakly as if the zombie had already taken damage to the head.

Even at that distance, from the top of the motor home, Gus managed to see how the face turned toward him and Collie.

"Jesus," Gus moaned. "Do we have to . . ."

Watch? The word died in his throat upon beholding the breadth of the undead charge. The ripples in the field, each and every one, left broken creases in the unassuming grass, and the deadheads at ground level crawled forward at best possible speed.

"They probably caught a whiff of us last night," Collie said, an eerie ghost of a smile on her face. "Don't worry. We'll get through, but Jesus. You haveta just marvel at what they are at times. What they're capable of."

More dead things pushed through the edges of the grassy trail and seeped into the light with all the grace of pustules bursting under pressure, resembling hunters or soldiers wearing ghillie suits. They shifted, pausing only long enough to sense the aging trail they crept upon, before slinking toward the highway as if escaping a tar pit.

"I'd say," Collie continued, "they were lying dormant out there, somewhere in the grass, with no legs to walk on and nothing to tear into. Just regular old meatbags, lying around and waiting for a whiff of something to come along. Or a noise. Hell, they might've heard those trucks as they passed through here *two or three days ago* and only now are getting here, just in time to say hello to us. An entire mob of them."

She noticed Gus's discomfort for the first time. "You know they can't hurt us now."

"Hm? Huh? What's that now?"

"They can't hurt us. They're fucking *ankle* biters, if anything. I had more than a couple reach out and try and grab my foot, and all it took was a kick to put an end to that—and not a hard kick, either. They can still infect us, of course, but look at them. They're like human-size caterpillars."

Gus didn't appreciate the simile.

"We'll get moving in a second," she assured him. "Just want to see how many are crawling through the grass. You don't see this much anymore. Not on this scale. Or maybe I just haven't come across it in a while."

"Yeah, I think you might've missed a few," Gus said, distracted, pulling on his beard.

"They freak you out?"

"No, oh, no." Then he admitted, "But they do make me nervous at times."

Collie snorted and went back to watching the advance. Some lines deeper in the field slowly curved south toward them with all the speed of tiger slugs, dredging themselves free of their graves. She'd started talking again, but Gus wasn't listening, mesmerized by the number of bodies pulling themselves through the grass.

"—a tidal force about them." Collie finished when a horn blasted, startling Gus and breaking him free from the hypnotic pull of the approaching dead. Collie pursed her lips, not unpleasantly, and scowled at the motor home at their backs.

She's not happy about something.

Then the scowl was gone.

"He's probably right," she said and climbed down from the roof. Gus followed. They got into the RV. Collie deposited herself in the driver's seat and started the machine. Gus jumped into the passenger side, pulled his door closed and locked it.

"Strap yourself down," she said. "Not sure if this rig's rated for off-road or not."

"But you're gonna try, right?"

"Oh, fuck yeah."

She steered the motor home off the pavement and into the tall grass, keeping on the previous path already made by passing tires. The front bumper bit into the edge of the field with a teeth-rattling, gullet-raising bump and jostle. Gus leaned forward in his seat, eyes wide at the decomposing faces flashing in the grass—just before the dead went under the RV. The machine rolled over the zombies as if they were crusty pillows. Bones snapped and clattered off the chassis, and the path became even rockier.

"Like driving over fuckin' beach rocks!" Collie shouted and hollered in pure, adrenaline-fueled pleasure. Beyond the dash and the face of the Winnebago, horrid faces lifted as the machine rattled over and squashed them. A few arms rose, flailing at the monstrosity flattening their ranks, before being squashed themselves.

"Not so bad," Collie yelled.

The start of a disbelieving smile spread across Gus's face. Lord help him, he was *enjoying* the ride.

"Hold on," she shouted.

Just ahead, the cracked, gray lick of pavement loomed, gravel having sprayed to the north where the previous trucks tore off once on asphalt. The motor home hit the soft shoulder, and he was slammed forward. For an instant, Gus thought they weren't going to make it. The vehicle was too much of a boat and the incline too steep, but then he crashed back into his seat, and the world tilted dangerously.

Collie turned the wheel hard to the right, howling like a hillbilly on a year's worth of ecstasy.

Then the ride smoothed out.

"More fun than fuckin'!" She laughed and put her foot down.

The RV responded and jumped forward in a burst of raw power. The trailer behind bucked and *whumped* over the shoulder and followed right along.

It took Gus a second to realize he was laughing as well.

His laugh subsided, and he hurriedly checked his side mirror.

Rising from their wake like a metallic whale came Wallace's RV. The front of the machine hit and rode up and over the shoulder in a spray of crushed stone, clearing it with effort.

"He made it," Gus said, eyeing the vehicle.

"No doubt in my mind," Collie declared as she focused on the empty road ahead. "That boy always makes it."

Gus glanced over and saw a sad sheen of pride touching her warrior's profile.

Then he looked ahead, feeling oddly at peace for the first time in days.

The motor homes rolled north, past wild meadows and trees shedding their exhausted red foliage. The pastures caught Gus's interest in particular, remembering how the deadheads had slipped under the motor home's wheels.

"What?" Collie asked while monitoring her speed.

"Wonder where the hell they all came from."

"The zombies back there?"

"Yeah."

Collie smiled. "The dead travel, my friend. Haven't you realized that yet?"

Gus supposed he had. "Forgot, I guess."

Captain Morgan rested in a cup holder, the leather twine fallen around the shoulders of the bottle. Gus reached down and adjusted him, making the officer a little more comfortable.

"Wallace and I once drove down the Trans-Labrador Highway," Collie stated, glancing over her camouflaged shoulder. "Middle of nowhere. This was about two years after it all went to hell. We'd pull over and camp about half a klick off-road at times. Even more middle of nowhere, right? Not even the odd picnic ground or nothing. I got up to take a leak one night, left my sidearm in the truck—first and last time ever, I might add—and while I was squatting, I hear a splashing coming from the nearby river. Thought it was a bear or a moose or elk or even a fucking crazy-assed monster squirrel. It walked that walk, y'know? Would take a step, stop for a second, and then take another step—like it was strolling—and I tell you, nothing more unsettling than taking a leak in the woods and hearing noises coming closer. Anyway, I finished and just waited—another mistake, but I did have my knife on me. Couple minutes later, I hear the thing coming through the woods, branches all snapping and breaking off. No secrecy there. And this fucking Moe comes waltzing toward me. Five hundred kilometers from . . . nothing, but there it was, and there *I* was, nearly caught with my pants down."

A red SUV appeared on the right, nosefirst into a ditch, bright cherry ass sticking up into the air, side door open and driver missing.

"Couple of dirt roads coming up," Collie noted. "I'll slow down. You look on that side. See if you notice any fresh tracks. Disturbed crushed stone. That sorta thing."

Gus nodded and leaned toward his window, rolling it down.

Most of the roads led to a house or two, scattered along the highway on a whim. Those that could be seen from the road appeared deserted and not deserving of further inspection. What might have been a livestock farm came up on the right.

"Bet it's a chicken farm," Collie smirked.

A green sign appeared, informing them of the turnoffs for Londonderry, Debert, and Belmont. The names didn't mean anything to Gus, and another bolt of despair hooked his guts. So many places to look—so many to get lost in or hide.

But what choice did he have?

A slow minute later, they rolled to a stop at a crossroads.

"One of many," Collie said, scanning left and right as she switched off the motor. "Lots of little towns around here, and I haven't been through a quarter of them yet. Your call on what you want to do."

Gus gazed beyond the windshield. The left road went straight up a small knoll and hung another left, disappearing behind a row of fir trees. The right dipped into a forested gulley before rising, turning left, and vanishing as well. Gus huffed and rubbed his forehead.

"How about we just stop here for a minute? Roll down the windows and listen? Something might come our way."

Collie regarded him, and he had to force himself not to stare at the mess of her nose.

"Army of Christ crazy bit it off," she said.

That jolted him. "What?"

"You were trying hard not to look at my nose."

"I was?"

To that, she only smiled.

"Sorry."

"No need to apologize," Collie remarked. "You didn't do it, and I don't mind telling you the background. Better than having you sneak peeks all the time."

"Sorry."

"You say that a lot."

Then Gus smiled. "Yeah, well, I mean it. Army of Christ, you said?"

"AOC. Operated in Eastern Mali some ten years back, causing hell for the local government. Anyway, the guy actually dropped on me from the ceiling while I was clearing a room—just like a goddamn spider. I pinned him to the ground, but he kicked out one of my feet, and my face dropped into his and . . ." Collie snapped her teeth twice, a disturbing picture. "Needless to say, I lost my mellow."

"Fuck me gently," Gus breathed.

She scratched at an eyebrow. "Yeah, took it off in one bite. Surprised the hell outta me. Right through my balaclava."

Gus shook his head. "What's a bala-clava?"

"That's a ski mask. British troops wore them originally during the Crimean War in 1854. Or '64. One of them years. My military history is getting rusty."

"Never heard of it before."

"What? The war or the balaclava?"

"Both," Gus chuckled.

"You watch action movies?"

"Well, yeah. Used to, anyway."

"You'll see special forces wear them a lot."

Gus knew what special forces wore, but a spark went off behind his eyes, and he regarded her in a disbelieving light. "You're special forces?"

"Was SF," Collie answered. "Now . . . I'm freelance."

"I didn't think women could be, ah, special forces."

Collie smirked. " Not true, though the old guard used to think that way. They used to say women weren't capable enough mentally or physically to carry out covert objectives. Wrong, of course. Hell, I knew some dykes who would throw down in bars with broken bottles if it came to a fight, and they'd use them too. As the world went on, it got clear that female operatives were, in fact, more valuable than a man in certain situations."

"Why is that?" Gus asked.

"Because we're girls." Collie smiled coldly. "No one expects an unarmed woman to rip out a throat with her bare hands or thumbscrew the eyeballs to the back of an attacker's skull."

Speechless, Gus's mouth fell open.

"Well," she clarified. "Not *every*one."

Gus still had nothing to say.

"Don't worry," Collie assured him. "Just remember to drop the toilet seat when you're finished, and we're good."

He'd definitely remember to do that.

"What about you?"

Gus glanced over at her. "What about me?"

"What happened to your face? Since we're disclosing history here. Quid pro quo."

"Parts of my face were burned in a house fire. My nose was busted by an ex-girlfriend. She knocked out my teeth too. Happened about two years ago."

Collie chuckled. "She didn't take kindly to you dumping her?"

"She dumped me."

"And she hit you? Wow. A right vengeful bitch."

A moment's hesitation. "Yeah."

Collie shook her head. "Women, eh?"

"Well . . ." Gus shrugged and stared at the road. "I did shoot her back."

That earned a *what the fuck?* look.

*

Wallace's fingers clenched the steering wheel with growing impatience until he caught himself. *Control,* he told himself. *Control.* What were they yakking about up there? And why had they stopped dead on the road? He turned off the engine and cracked his window, listening. He picked up nothing but soft birdsong. Birds. He wondered how they tasted. *Control* flashed across his mind like a red warning light. Food wasn't an issue then. Not right then anyway, but in a day or two, it might.

Wallace opened his mouth as wide as possible, making his ears pop, and noticed that the aches in his joints had reached his hands—his fingers in particular. He released the steering wheel and shook them out, making and releasing fists. Usually, the pain wasn't so bad after he'd eaten, but that time, his aches sparkled dully, letting him know they were still around.

Perhaps he'd slipped another degree?

That thought rattled through his mind. Yes, he concluded with a pinch of glumness, that might very well be the reason.

Wallace considered getting out and walking over to Collie's window to check on their status, but his fingers made him wary of doing so. His joints continued to ache, but were they worse? He wasn't sure, still too preoccupied with the development of his fingers. Part of him didn't want to find out

Control, he vowed.

26

Hearing nothing but far-off birds, Collie started the RV and drove on down the highway. Wallace dutifully followed, bringing up the rear. A few more houses sprang up along the road, nestled amidst wild-growing lawns and backyard jungles. Most of the structures appeared to be in reasonable shape, considering the apocalypse was into its fourth year. Some homes had boards nailed over their first-floor windows. Others had cars parked haphazardly in paved driveways.

Gus noticed an open door on the third house they drove by and realized darkly that the previous front doors had also been left open.

"You better pull over," Gus said.

"See something?"

"Maybe. The houses on this side. Their doors are all open. How about yours?"

"Only passed a couple, but yeah—why?" She stopped the huge vehicle.

"Well," Gus smiled, "that's what I'm going to find out."

"You okay doing that?"

"Yeah. Yeah, I think so."

"Just holler then if you need any help."

"I'll remember that." Gus thought about all the times he'd cleared a house by himself. He hopped out and unzipped his jacket for easy access to the twin Sigs under his arms. He looped the baseball-bat scabbard over his neck and checked his boot knife. After a second, he checked his jeans. He wished he had something thicker covering his legs.

"You okay?" Collie asked.

"Yeah, just wishing I had something for my legs. Leather pants or something."

"You'll be okay," she assured him. "You didn't make it this far on just leather pants. As weird as that sounds."

Gus supposed that was true. "Be a few minutes." He closed the passenger door.

Dead weeds pushed through gaping cracks, exposing frozen earth and conjuring an image of something massive forcing its way up underneath the paved driveway. Gus walked along the pavement, keeping his eyes on the tall grass. The motor home huffed behind, moved, and stopped again in a squeal of brakes. An empty pool lay to the right, dull green ringing its cement edges. The front door to the house loomed closer, a brass knocker fixed in the center of a glossy wooden design. The home was two stories covered in bright yellow siding. A blue Mustang and a forest-green Jeep were parked before a garage with its door heaved high, the interior gutted.

Gus's boots scuffed to a soft halt, and he studied the garage, knowing full well the difference between sloppy and ransacked. Whoever had gone through the place wasn't being particular. Someone had taken anything there to be had.

That left the house.

Gus crept up to the front door and placed his back against the right side, stepping into what might have been a stomped-out flowerbed. He inhaled and wished he had a helmet. The door itself didn't appear forced.

"Fuck it," he grunted and peered inside the house. "*Hey, anybody home?*"

He shouted perhaps a little too loudly, but what the hell, he'd get back into form eventually. "Anyone?"

No answer. No sound at all.

"All right, listen, I'm coming in. If someone's in there, let's talk first, okay? The door was open, and I'm just checking things out. Just want to make sure all's well, so don't shoot me, okay? No shooting. And don't club me upside the head, either. Already had my bell rung enough this week, and I look like shit because of it. My chest too, for that matter. Don't want to get slashed again or stabbed or strung up by the hands or feet. And since we're on the subject, don't be grabbing for my goddamn balls either, okay? Hear me? Don't. Grab. My balls. Damn things are dangling to my knees now anyway, but I'd like to keep them a little while longer. All right? Got all that? Okay, then."

He took a deep breath. "Here I come."

Fully expecting to hear that dead-lung rasping he'd heard so many times before, Gus stepped into the doorway, hand on his bat, and saw nothing inside the naturally lit mud room or the corridor beyond. A white-carpeted staircase had soaked up a wide gash of blood, some of which splashed spectacularly against the wall. Two plastic twelve-gauge cartridges, blue, lay at the base of the steps, and he nudged one with his boot. Hearing nothing, he sniffed and got only cold, fresh air.

"I have a bat, and I'm taking it out, just in case you're a dead fucker . . ." He scolded himself, suddenly feeling uneasy about the profanity. "*Undead*, I mean. I meant *undead*. Jesus."

Bat in hand, Gus eased into a gutted living room. The guts of sofa and chair cushions had been ripped out and strewn across the floor while a coffee table had been chopped into ugly chunks of fiber. A shotgun blast had killed a flat-screen TV while the corner behind the device had broken beer bottles piled quite high. The fireplace at the far end might have been lit up with a flame thrower, the hearth twinkling with smashed glass.

But no bodies.

It didn't bode well in Gus's mind.

The rest of the house was clear though in disarray, obviously searched for goods. Even the renovated basement, which he descended into without a flashlight, had been trashed. More destruction had been wreaked on the downstairs bedroom and rec room, and the toilet in the washroom was full of dried fecal matter. Gus wasn't an expert on shit—a notion he reckoned some might dispute—but it looked as though he'd missed whoever had used the basement john by days. No more than a week, tops. They'd come into the home, and whatever they couldn't take, they destroyed.

The back deck and yard didn't reveal any wrongdoing and was untouched in comparison to the house. Gus wandered over to the pool and saw that its sea-green depths were filled with dead brush. He lingered at the edge and looked up, seeing Collie walking cautiously along the driveway, her hands on her sidearms. Wallace moseyed far behind her.

Scanning a tree line of elms and the odd fir, Gus stepped back from the pool and meandered along a patio walkway, meeting Collie at the front of the house.

"Thought I'd get out and stretch my legs." She studied the staring dormers of the home. "See anything?"

"No," Gus replied. "Anything happened here happened days ago. The place's been looted. And lived in for a night at least. There's a fireplace in the living room that looks like it might've been lit up with gasoline. No one's in there. No bodies, nothing. Though there's plenty of blood on the walls and dried shit in the cans."

Collie made a face, and Gus immediately regretted his words.

"Ah, sorry, I mean—"

"It's okay," she said, amused. "I'm not a saint, so don't worry."

Wallace's grin, however, even though it hadn't changed at all below the visor, suddenly struck Gus as smugly pleased.

"Something on your mind?" Gus asked him.

Wallace stopped in the driveway, and a person could almost hear the squeals of his joints. The soldier gazed around, his visor taking in the deserted landscape. "Nope."

"You seem pretty happy about something," Gus observed.

"It's just the way my face is these days," Wallace explained with eternal patience. "So fuck off."

That relaxed, delivered-under-the-radar expletive straightened the slouch in Gus's back. "What did you say to me?"

Instead of replying, Wallace shook his head. "Whatever happened here, we missed it."

"I think I just said that," Gus pointed out.

"Now it's official."

"Ah, I see."

"I'm heading back to the machine," Wallace stated. "We should get rolling. See if this pattern continues along the road."

The soldier took his time returning.

"Did I say something?" Gus asked Collie.

"No. Don't worry about him."

"He told me to fuck off."

"Just let that one go."

"Yeah, but . . ." Then Gus dropped it and switched from Collie, to Wallace walking back to his RV, to the house just searched.

Collie scanned the sky. "He's having a hard time these days. For reasons that are obvious. Some days, he's fine; and other days, he can be a little grouchy. I know you don't mean anything by the looks, but he picks up on them, and it puts him off. Just keep that in mind."

"What's wrong with him, then?"

"I think you can see."

"Yeah, well, I don't think I can wait for him to explain things."

Collie faced him, and Gus once again was struck by the twin holes of her face and those startling eyes. "Let's move on. Check some more houses."

She didn't wait for an answer.

By the time the day darkened with evening, they had checked five more residences along the highway. Some places were hidden behind fences of trees while others presided over front lawns that had probably been the envy of the neighbors at one time but were overgrown and yellowed. Sometimes Gus went into the house, sometimes

Wallace. The soldier didn't apologize for his earlier remark, which irritated Gus even though he knew he shouldn't have been staring at the guy. Still, in his mind, Wallace could have been a little more civil.

Or maybe, Gus considered, *maybe the guy had a point.*

Their collective thoughts centered on the growing mystery of the houses. Three of the homes had been forced into, the doors splintered and hanging off the hinges. In two, shotgun cartridges as well as nine-millimeter brass casings lay around desiccated corpses made dead yet again. In the other residences, entry wasn't forced, which suggested someone had actually lived there until whoever was making the rounds had come along. Perhaps the homeowners had welcomed the visitors with open arms before becoming victims. Gus, Collie, and Wallace didn't think they were victims, however, as there were no signs of executions to the degree Gus had witnessed on his farm, nor were there any corpses.

All properties had been scoured clean of clothes, food, water, fuel, and anything else useful.

"Someone's being a pack rat," Collie declared, relaxing in the driver's seat of her RV with a glass of rye whiskey. The interior blinds had been pulled and a single light turned on, drawing from the battery, as Wallace had cautioned them about turning on the generator. Heat was a luxury they'd have to do without that evening, so both sat in the dim interior, bundled up in their day's clothing and outerwear, recapping the day's discoveries. Wallace roamed outside, having volunteered to keep watch through the night.

Gus sat at the small table and swished a glass of water, still holding out on cruising the booze boat until Maggie and the kids had been found. That would be reason enough to drink, although he had twice caught himself wanting to pour himself a shot and down the whiskey like cold tea. He wasn't entirely surprised by the urges, but he didn't give in.

"Yeah," Gus said slowly. "Or something else."

"You got a theory?"

He took a breath, took another pull of his drink, and refilled his glass from the bottle on the table.

"I ever tell you about the time I was almost eaten alive by rats?"

Collie's face furrowed with interest, and Gus gave her a history lesson. The story came out of him easily, minus the details about him attempting suicide by way of alcohol poisoning.

"Holy shit," she breathed when the story had been told. "*Rats?*"

"Rats."

"Never saw anything like that in the last four years."

"Maybe it's just an East Coast thing."

"Sure as fuck hope so," Collie declared. "But there wasn't any evidence of what you just described to me. The dead in the hallways and such were still there, remember?"

"Yeah," Gus conceded. "All right. So it's a living problem, then."

"Possibly. One thing's for sure—this kind of operation takes time, going from door to door and loading up everything of use. If nothing's happened to our raiders, then we'll be coming upon them sooner or later."

"What then?" Gus asked.

"Then we'll see," Collie said and took a shot from her glass. "Some folks have gone over to the dark side, like our little group of independent highwaymen who'd hung you out for dinner. They need to be dealt with case by case."

"Yeah." Gus was not entirely convinced.

"One thing I like about operating solo"—Collie studied her near-empty glass—"without a chain of command. Something both Ollie and I agree upon."

This interested Gus. "What's that?"

"It's the distinct absence of rules."

"Rules?"

Collie smiled coldly.

"Of engagement."

27

Gus stirred, woke up, and stared at the ceiling. He'd turned in early the night before, emotionally and physically drained, leaving Collie to her drinking and removing himself from that particular temptation. He rolled over to the edge of his bunk above the driving area, rubbed his face, and peeked out toward the kitchenette area, seeing slivers of light through closed blinds.

Morning.

The pocket of warmth underneath the blankets made him hesitate to get up, but that wouldn't do in the least—not while Maggie and the kids were still unaccounted for. The night before, he'd dreamed of them being whisked away by, of all things, a large truck with comically oversized wheels.

The bathroom door opened, distracting him from his memories, and he glanced up to see Collie stepping out, wearing her camo pants and a black sports bra. Her skin glistened, wet and sleek. She nimbly padded away into the bedroom area with barely a sound, where she shut the door.

Suddenly wide-eyed and awake, Gus released his breath.

Collie's face had been mauled over the years, and she'd probably be the first to admit it, but that unexpected flash of skin was untouched, muscular, and not just a little tight. The curve of her hips suggested that everything covered by the camos was also unspoiled and perfectly serviceable. *Serviceable.*

He reminded himself that he was having thoughts about another guy's wife.

You sick fuck.

Hot guilt flowed throughout his chest and face.

*

After forty minutes on the road, a house made a break in the blur of yellow-and-red timberland. A long dirt lane linked the highway to a garage. The owners might've been farmers of some kind although the high grass blanketing the surrounding fields gave no hint as to what might've been grown—other than hay. A green tractor stood guard on the first bend in the lane. A Victorian-style, two-story house waited beyond, painted a fading forest green that clashed with the late-autumn fire surrounding the property.

"What do you think?" Gus asked.

"Best check it out," Collie said.

"I'll do it," Gus volunteered.

"You sure about that?"

"Yeah, why not?"

Collie shrugged. "Go on in. I'll keep the engine running. Don't want to take it over that road."

"All right."

"And watch that grass. I don't see anything moving right now, but that could change."

"Yes, Mother."

"Don't you be calling me your mother. I'll slap your ass."

That made Gus snort as he climbed out of the RV.

The fresh, cold air tasted fine, and he paused to take in a deep lungful. Wallace's rig had pulled up behind Collie's and switched off. The soldier was a silhouette behind the wheel. Gus didn't spare any more time looking in that direction. He got walking, hearing nothing except the scrunch of boots on frozen ground. The Victorian's heights consisted of dormers and a lot of awkward angles, which would've taken a lot of fuss and potential acrobatics at the end of a ladder.

Gus didn't miss his old job.

A silver Mustang was parked at the corner, a molded torpedo if there ever was one. The muscle car perked his interest for all of a second before he settled on the Victorian's front door.

It was open.

He stopped a good twenty feet before the threshold. He took his bat in hand, thankful for its reassuring weight, and proceeded.

"Hello?" he asked, slowing as the shade of the front door's overhang engulfed him. "Anyone in there? Anyone home? Just coming in to check the place out, see if all's well. Let's talk, if you're okay with that."

His own voice sounded as though it were lying, and Gus wondered if someone a little less friendly had recently said those same words on that porch. Nothing moved inside, and he held his breath, waiting again for that graveyard wheeze he'd come to know so well.

Time crept on, and the house's main hallway remained empty.

Glancing back at Collie's RV, he waved, scratched his balls for luck, and disappeared inside.

He found eggshell-white walls with elegant baseboards and dirtied hardwood floors. Dried dirt trailed off into the house, ignoring a hall that led to an archway and what appeared to be a staircase. Gus knelt to inspect the granules, glancing back toward the door and the lane he'd walked along.

The tracks spooked him.

Gus stood, softened his step, and followed them cautiously around a corner into a living room. It looked cozy, the furniture in respectable shape.

The tracks disappeared midway through.

The hairs at the base of his neck rose in a chill. Something was setting him off, but he hadn't processed exactly what. Gauze-thin sheers hung over the picture window, whitening the overgrown lawn. Unseen strings of tension filled the room, and with every movement Gus made, he felt those strands tighten on him. He felt for the shaft of his bat, reconsidered, and opened his jacket. His palm slid around the holster of his left Sig Sauer, and he eased it out, keeping it flat against his thigh.

Navigating his way around a sizeable coffee table, he widened his view past the far corner and saw an open dining area . . .

And the remains of what appeared to be a meal—chicken bones.

Gus stood and studied the food, seeing a bit of meat still remaining on a thigh. As soon as he saw the scraps, he realized what was bothering him besides the tracks.

The smell.

The smell had set him off, that cold-chicken odor just starting to stink up the house.

His pulse rate increased, and he fought down the impulse to run through the house just to relieve the swelling ball of suspense in his chest. He stepped softly, carefully, into the dining area and glanced out a window into the backyard. The RVs could barely be seen through those snowy living room sheers. An archway joined the dining area, and Gus kept his gun by his thigh as he leaned around its corner.

Empty kitchen.

Nothing else—at least nothing there.

The sink contained two empty plastic bottles. He took one, saw beads of water on the inside, and carefully placed it on the counter. A second archway completed the circle of the first floor and brought Gus to the white-carpeted stairs leading to the second story as well as a nearby door leading to a basement, presumably.

Straining to hear, Gus moved to the foot of those stairs, his attention divided by the door right there and the upstairs staircase. He wanted to open the door but found himself leaning forward, sticking his head out, and looking upstairs. A hallway and a door to the immediate left were at the top while shadows darkened the upper level, as if someone had closed all the doors and drawn the curtains. Any second, Gus fully expected some ghoulish face to peek out from between the ornate banisters over his head, leering with bug-eyed insanity. He waited, feeling time dragging, licked his lips, and strained to hear anything that might provide a clue, knowing if something *did* appear, he'd probably shit himself.

"Anyone up there?"

He heard no answer but sensed that *someone* had heard. The hardwood stairs might have been steeped in molasses, they were so dark, and he knew just by looking at them the damn things would squeak. Apprehension grew, and Gus knew he was drawing things out, delaying the inevitable, but he'd been caught by surprise before, and he would much rather wait than have his balls grabbed again. Or worse.

"Hey, if you're up there . . ." he said quietly, eyes flickering from the upstairs to the door just across from him, a step and an arm's length away. His nerves thrummed with low-grade anxiety. "Why not come on out, and we'll talk. Hell, I have some bottled deer that might go well with that chicken you were having."

His tongue rested in the empty space of his missing front teeth as he listened for movement, a sign that his words were reaching a set of ears. None came, however.

"Come on, now. You're freaking me out here. Come on down, and we can talk. Maybe even be friends. You . . . you never know, right?"

A sheet of cold slipped over his head and enveloped him, a frightening sensation some had felt upon wandering haunted places. As sure as God was Gus's witness, someone waited for him upstairs, for good or for bad. The Sig patted his thigh, thrumming to be used, and he willed himself to stop. He arched his head to further improve his field of vision but saw nothing. Jesus Christ, why couldn't it have been a gimp? And why couldn't he have a shot of something to calm his nerves? He hadn't been that on edge back in Windsor. *Maybe,* his inner voice suggested, *it's because you know it's a person this time.* Damn gimps were a hell of a lot easier to evict from a house instead of a person. He should just walk around and—*click.*

That soft note froze Gus in place, widened his eyes, and caused him to nearly bolt. His energy level spiked, screaming a flight reflex. He didn't and remained rooted, scanning the upstairs. He leaned forward and *willed* more to happen, but nothing did.

What he heard might have been a hinge moving just a fraction or the weight of a foot making the floor creak.

Get Collie.

Where that thought had come from, he wasn't sure, but as he peered upstairs, it seemed like a pretty solid plan, rather than standing around like a dork hoping to catch a peek. Whoever or whatever was above him wasn't going to come down, and he was becoming far too worried to venture up. Stalemate. He'd reached an impasse.

Well, fuck this. Gus huffed and backed up as quietly as he could toward the front door.

"*Wait.*" A whispery, cancerous voice floated downstairs and yanked his spine like the sensation of mice scurrying over bare feet. Gus stepped back to the landing, pointed his gun at the gloomy upstairs, scanning for a body.

"Wait," the voice whispered again, just beyond the railing, keeping out of sight.

"What?" Gus asked, placing his back to the wall, struggling to contain his fear.

"Wait."

"I'm waiting, so what now?"

Silence. "Wait."

Then a smoker's giggle hung on the air, a deep, soul-frightening rattle that one might hear from a person on a deathbed. That god-awful, sickening sound, chock-full of unseen madness, made Gus weak in the knees. His pulse pounding in his ears, Gus's eyes flickered about the upstairs as a coldness settled in, pricking his scalp and traveling all the way to the root of his ballsack. He reached out and gripped the knob of the closed door next to him.

"Wait." The voice giggled once more, struggling to maintain control. "I want . . . I want you to . . . to *see* something."

Then a ponderous step fell on bare hardwood, accompanied by a rusty cackle that sounded positively dipped in evil. A *scree* of steel on wood followed—then another ominous dragging of a foot.

"Wait there. I want . . . I want *you* . . ."

A shadow thickened through the banisters, the reality of it stabbing through whatever resolve Gus might've had. His breath quickened, and the urge to not want to see what was coming filled him. Whoever was speaking had been touched by the apocalypse, and Gus was certain of the evil taint approaching. The gun in his hand trembled, faltered.

The silhouette dragged itself forward.

A mask of pearly white loomed in a flash of pulse-pounding terror. A mop of bleached hair hung in tatters around the face.

Then Gus saw the machete.

He raised his gun.

But the knob he'd grabbed to steady himself twisted in his palm, making him stumble off balance just as the door burst open and the barrel of a large-caliber sidearm pressed into his left cheek. Gus's breath caught in his chest, as if releasing it would kill him instantly.

Click.

"Don't you move," warned a voice that could've belonged to a human rattlesnake. "Don't you *fuckin'* move."

Gus's arm faltered and dropped. He eyed a face every bit as pale and as crazy looking as the one overhead.

"*Waaaaaaaait,*" the thing at the top of the stairs whispered in sandpapery fashion, ending the word in a wicked giggle. The voice sounded as if it stood at the other end of a very long tunnel.

The Face with the gun on Gus reached around and grabbed his pistol, tossing it onto the stairs.

"Fresh meat, Dwight," the Face grinned, baring a smashed fence of a smile.

"Freeessssssh *meat,*" Dwight repeated, leering. He leaned out over the railing, long hair drooping, machete held against the valley of an elbow. "Cut him up."

Gus's sphincter clenched at the words.

"Can't, y' fuckin' moron," the Face said. "I got the gun on him. You come down here and cut him."

"Wait," Dwight said and leaned over the railing and slashed at Gus's eyes, the wind from the weapon flickering his eyes. Once, twice, and a third time, he waved that blade as quick as the shocked gasp leaving Gus's lungs. He turned his head into the gun, avoiding the last swing of the machete by only a finger width, gouging his cheek on the hard barrel.

Dwight leaned back and cackled. "Bring the little shit closer!"

Oh, Jesus.

Gus's knees must've stiffened, because the Face stood back with his back against the open door, assuming a duelist's pose, and set his jaw.

"Don't you fuckin' move, I told ya. Else I pull the trigger and spray your chin across the stairs. Ruin the carpet."

"Bring him *closer,* I said," Dwight commanded in that smoker's bray.

Gus's eyes darted to the Face.

"You heard him. Go on up."

Gus closed his eyes. "I can't."

"Fuck you mean, you can't?"

"I'll shit myself."

The Face broke into a chuckle, jamming the pistol into Gus's cheek all the harder. "You hear that, Dwight?"

"I heard."

"Boy's gonna squirt out some pipe right here if he comes any closer."

Dwight leaned back like a perturbed Viking and simmered with the information. "Goddamn gross is what that is. It'll fuck up the house."

"Fuck up the house," Gus panted, petrified. "Fuck . . . fuck up the *carpet*."

"Don't fuckin' live here anyway," the Face growled and licked his half-stocked set of teeth.

"That's right," Dwight agreed and swaggered to the stairs, dragging the machete's edge along the railing. "Houses all along this road. I could shit all over this one, and it don't mean a goddamn thing. Just go get a new one. But who else is out there in them Winnebagos?"

That mortified Gus. "Huh?"

"Answer him." The gun gouged deeper, screwing up Gus's lips.

"My friends. My friends, Jesus. *Myfriendsareoutthere*."

"How many?" the Face demanded as Dwight placed his full weight on the first step, forcing a curt squeal to perforate the air.

"Huh?"

The Face tried to insert the barrel of the gun into Gus's cheek. "Fuckin' say *huh* once more, and I'll pull this trigger."

"Two," Gus immediately revealed, his own face as white as the living room sheers, and his will crumbling into nothing. There wasn't any bravado. There weren't any quips. There was only a gun pressing into his face and a machete descending the stairs. Both wielded by two clearly unstable individuals.

"What's that?" the Face asked.

"*Two*."

Dwight stopped three steps away and placed the machete's edge to Gus's bald scalp. "Nothing to chop here."

The blade dropped to Gus's beard. "Could use a shave, though. How about it? How about letting me shave you? That sound like a good idea?"

"No."

The Face dragged the gun barrel up across Gus's cheek and parked it tightly against the corner of his eye.

"No!" Dwight giggled. "We caught a funny one, Ricky!"

"Yeah," Ricky chuckled.

"Or how about . . ." Dwight angled the blade to Gus's chin and leaned in close, all mirth disappearing from his features, replaced by a twisted yearning to perform some medieval science. "How about I just chew that nose of yours off? Just *bite* it off? Bet that would make you dance. Huh? Make you jiggle. Course, you'd be dead anyway 'cause Ricky would put a bullet into your skull. Unless . . . he shoots out both knees. Keep you alive and stationary—to a point, anyway. How's that sound?"

Dwight's frightening mug stopped not two inches from a trembling Gus.

"I asked . . ." Dwight repeated in a hateful whisper, eyeing up his captive's profile from chin to brow, "how's that sound?"

Gus set his jaw, clamping down on the scream boiling toward his throat but failing to stop the pitiful squeal emerging. He looked ahead, through the archway and the distant kitchen . . .

And saw Collie.

She was handling a gun two-fisted and aiming.

Gus screamed.

Ricky's head exploded. The gun at Gus's temple fired over his head. Dwight's threatening leer softened in puzzlement in the split instant of his companion's death, just before his own head spattered against the wall. The machete fell to the floor as both Dwight and Ricky crumpled.

Gus remained standing, bug-eyed and barely breathing.

Then his vision narrowed as darkness rushed in from the edges.

His legs gave out, and he lost consciousness.

Gus came to his senses on the front step of the house and jerked away from the zombie leering down at him.

Wallace.

"You sick bastard," Gus whispered in the shade of the overhang.

"Thank you."

"You're welcome."

"For not shitting or pissing yourself," Wallace pointed out. "Happens sometimes. Especially with folks under moments of extreme duress."

Gus absorbed that and looked away. "Christ. I don't need this right now."

"Take your time, civvie."

That made Gus exhale in exasperation. "Startin' to really dislike that term. Why don't you think about changing it to my name? Just to mix things up."

"I'll consider it."

"Where's Collie?"

"She just finished clearing the house," Wallace informed him, looking toward the open door. "Now she's checking the perimeter out back."

"How'd I get here?"

"She hauled you out."

"She *hauled* me outside?"

"Carried, really," Wallace said with that horrid, permanent smile on his face. "She's strong."

Gus pulled himself into a sitting position against the door frame. Wallace stood back and let him.

"Why aren't you helping her?" Gus asked.

Wallace shook his head. "I'm slowing down in my old age. Just hold her back. She's better without me."

"You're fuckin' slowin' down, all right," Gus muttered.

And for some reason, that one callous comment stuck. Wallace became very quiet for several seconds, his dark visor watching Gus, as if no longer feeling particularly sociable.

"Seriously"—Gus slowly shook his head—"all on the table now. What's happening to you, man?"

"What makes you think anything is happening?" Wallace asked, the visor unmoving.

"That's a joke, right? You just joked just then."

But Wallace didn't answer him.

"Collie said you'd tell me."

"She said that?"

"Yeah."

"She say anything else?"

"She . . . she said you'd tell me when you were ready."

Wallace nodded. "That's my baby girl."

The conversation paused then, but Wallace didn't stop staring as Gus recovered.

"Hey," Wallace whispered at last. "Civvie. You wanna see something?"

"Nah, man. I'm getting my wind back here."

"Let me . . . show you something," Wallace continued, "something that's been making me reevaluate my priorities in life."

With a dignified grace, Wallace reached down and pulled a combat knife from a shin scabbard. It was a straight blade, serrated on one side but deadly sharp on the other, with the barest curve to a tip that might have tapered off into infinity.

Gus didn't like the knife and certainly didn't like Wallace's creepy Zen-master tone.

"You watching?" the soldier asked.

Gus nodded with building unease.

"Keep watching," Wallace stated as he rolled up the sleeve of his left arm, exposing a length of fish-belly flesh. Black veins snaked below the polluted epidermis.

"Jesus," Gus hissed.

"Wait . . . wait," the soldier whispered, bringing back those chills Gus had just experienced inside the house.

"Only found this out this morning, in fact," Wallace went on, holding the knife at guard, "but I think you'll find it just as interesting as I do."

With that, he angled the tip to his forearm, the blade gleaming. Wallace's visor barely moved, if at all, and he held the weapon to his skin for a long, solemn moment before pushing the steel through.

Gus jumped. "Holy *shit*!"

Wallace's skeletal profile remained unchanged as the tip pushed through the other side of his forearm, causing a black fluid as syrupy as snot to drip to the ground, and very little at that. For added effect, the soldier wiggled the blade a little before pulling the smeared steel out and taking his time wiping it off on a camo pant leg.

"Oh, Jesus Christ," Gus panted in horror. "Oh, Jesus Christ."

A heavy clatter rattled from behind the house, followed by two successive thumps and a splintering of wood. In that instant, Gus was completely discombobulated.

"See that?" an unaffected Wallace asked, his voice every bit as smooth as fine chocolate.

"Holy shit, are you . . . ?" But he couldn't finish. *Okay? In pain?* What could a person ask someone like Wallace? Gus studied the soldier and brought his revulsion under control. He'd freaked out twice in one day, and his nerves twanged like out-of-tune piano keys.

"You better tell her," he got out instead.

"Tell her what? About this?" Wallace asked, finishing cleaning off his knife. "No. I think I'll keep this to myself. Ruminate on it. See where it goes."

Gus gawked at the man.

"Don't worry. I'm not turned. For whatever reason. Not gone over yet."

But Gus wasn't so convinced.

"Fuck you," Wallace muttered, as if sensing trepidation.

"Fuck *you*, y' *freak*."

Wallace's grin transformed into a frightening sickle, but then he hesitated.

Gus heard her coming through the house, through a back doorway. She emerged in the hallway and approached her companions.

"All clear," she reported, wiping her forehead with a hand. "Only the two of them."

Wallace straightened, but Gus balked, not sure he wanted to be anywhere near anyone as infected as Wallace. Then a sense of righteousness overtook him, and he got to his feet.

"You okay?" Gus asked.

"I'm okay," Collie said.

"Course she's fucking okay," Wallace said an octave louder than his usual mantra-chanting level of speech. "What did I say, you moron? She'll be around long after you and I are both gone."

Collie regarded the men with a decidedly pensive, unasked question.

"Collie, listen, that guy is . . ." Gus broke into a nervous babble. "Look, I know you've been with him for a while, but there's something wrong with him. More than you know."

At this, Collie's wondering expression deepened, and she regarded Wallace. "What did you do?"

Wallace was no longer smiling.

"What did he do?" she put to Gus.

"He fuckin' stabbed himself through his arm!"

"He *what?*" She glared at Wallace. "You stabbed yourself? The hell you do that for?"

"Yeah, why?" Gus demanded, then ominously. "Black shit squirted out, Collie, like he was leakin' oil or something."

A clearly unimpressed Collie switched from one to the other.

The soldier didn't answer.

"Let me see."

"I would've told you eventually," Wallace finally responded in a low voice, his Zen wavering around the edges. "Only happened last night."

"That right?" Collie asked. "Anything else happen last night?"

"No."

"Show me the arm."

Wallace complied, surprising Gus. He thought the man would've protested more. Wallace straightened out his arm and displayed the wound, which had ceased bleeding. A clearly pissed-off Collie grabbed the offered limb, studying the cut in grim silence.

She shoved the arm away. "You said you were going to tell me."

"There was—"

"Nothing to tell? Are you fucking *kidding* me? The fuck you think *that* is? A paper cut?"

"It's nothing."

"Like hell, it's nothing. I'd say it's progressing faster than you expected. Than I expected."

In the verbal ceasefire that followed, Gus hung back and stayed clear.

"Your color's changed," Collie noted. "You're grayer."

The visor remained still for a moment. "Noticed that this morning," Wallace muttered.

"Ah, shit. *Shit*, Ollie! You're supposed . . . you're supposed to *tell* me these things."

Wallace didn't reply.

Collie rubbed her face and then did a double take of Gus, as if realizing he was there for the first time. "Holy shit. In front of the civvie, no less."

Gus rolled his eyes.

She stood there, visibly battling with the urge to reprimand her husband in front of Gus, when the sound of engines drifted into hearing, drawing everyone's attention to the road.

In seconds, pickups and SUVs screamed into existence along the highway, shooting out from behind a veil of trees and halting in a screech of rubber.

Armed men spilled from the vehicles.

28

"Who—"

But Collie was already pulling Gus through the front door and into the living room. Wallace lumbered in after them, closing the door, the grimace on his face almost painful to see. Collie left Gus at the archway and took position at the edge of the picture window.

"Stay away from the windows," Collie hissed at him, her own Sig Sauer drawn and posed at her shoulder as she peeked around the edge of the sheers.

"Who are they?" Gus asked in an anxious whisper.

"Road savages. Freaks. Killers. Whatever you want to call them."

"What? How do you know that?"

"I don't, but it's best to assume until proven otherwise."

"Jesus," Gus said. He glanced toward the end of the hall, where the stairs began, and his mouth dropped open. There, like a pair of huge cockroaches freshly squashed, lay the leftovers of Dwight and Ricky.

Collie kept her eyes on the road as Wallace shuffled past Gus toward the end of the hall.

"*Hey!*" someone shouted from the highway. Some men had already stormed the RVs while the rest formed a line behind the low beds of their pickups. Gun barrels pointed at the house. "*Hey! You in the house. You got the guys in there?*"

"How many?" Wallace asked from the hall.

"Six shooters facing the house. Three going through the RVs, which pisses me off to no end."

"Nine to two."

"Three," Gus said, slightly insulted.

"Listen! You send Dwight and Ricky out, and we'll let you live. Promise."

Collie cocked her head. A sarcastic smile split her harsh features. "What about the RVs?" she muttered.

"What about the RVs?" Gus asked.

"Talking to myself. They'll take them. Guaranteed. And kill us. They're the same breed as those two sick pups I shot back there—an evil kind of crazy. Who knows how many they've killed up to this point."

On some mystical impulse, Gus glanced over his shoulder to see Wallace standing back from where the dead men had fallen.

The soldier was studying the bodies with brooding interest.

Uncertainty and dread flooded Gus's mental capacities. He'd seen that posture before.

Wallace was considering taking a bite out of Ricky's and Dwight's bleeding hides.

"Ollie?" Collie asked and met Gus's eyes.

"What's it gonna be? Huh?"

Wallace didn't answer. The back of his head moved ever so slightly, studying the meat just lying there.

"You hear me in there?"

"Ollie!" Collie snapped, and Wallace turned his head toward her so slowly Gus thought he heard vertebrae crackle.

"All right, assholes. I fuckin' tried to be peaceful."

Gus's breath caught in his airpipe. In between Collie's whispers and the hollering outside, Wallace was moaning . . . and sizing up the chunks of human steak marinating in their own juices on the floor.

"Ollie," Collie commanded. "You back away from that shit right this instant! You're not like that, mister! You're not like that at *all*! You're JTF for Christ's sake, and you are *not* some walking ghoul."

Perhaps it was her words or the bedrock seriousness in her tone. Probably both. Wallace's shoulders trembled, twitching around the edges like a curtain about to fall to the ground. He stopped making noises and backed up a step.

Gus looked at Collie and was about to give a report when Collie's attention snapped back to the developing scene outside.

"Down!" Collie shrieked and grabbed Gus by the shoulders.

A dragon's whine of smoke and sound ended with the picture window exploding. Scintillating slivers zipped past bodies spinning out of harm's way. The room went white. Time slowed.

Then the house chuffed and blew outward.

It was as if God himself reached down and tore out a chunk of the home. Wooden beams crackled and fell to the living room floor while plaster crashed down in a floury puff. Timbers creaked, and a huge hole appeared in a wall and a good chunk of the ceiling. The second floor revealed itself in a stunning gauze of wreckage. Splintered edges flickered with fire.

Gus was on his back, not knowing how he'd wound up there. His ears were splitting with a pitch that would make dogs cringe. He coughed, wheezed in a lungful of plaster dust, and coughed again. Grainy water polluted his eyes.

Hysterical *whoop*s came from the roadside and echoed in his skull.

A white hand clawed at his shoulder.

"Get up," Wallace's voice warbled with a distorted fishbowl sound effect. Dust clung to his person, making him appear to be smoking. He pulled a dazed Gus upward, and slabs of thick plaster slid from his shoulders. "Collie?"

"Here," she responded, her voice sounding far off, and a ghost pushed itself up from the debris, pulling off a slab of useless-looking body armor.

"Grenade blew through the window," Wallace explained as he helped Gus to his feet. "Chewed up the house."

"We gotta get clear of this." Collie grunted, recovering quickly. "Not out the back."

"Basement," Gus croaked and lurched away. Holding his head, he turned two corners, coughing smoke and dust and stumbling on debris blasted into the hall. Gus ignored the bodies on the stairs and floor and stepped over a set of legs to get to the basement door. He descended, slumping against the wall at one point.

"Down," Collie ordered, pushing him onward.

The door closed behind him, plunging them into blackness.

With another explosion, the house seemed to jump off its foundation. Beams groaned and cracked like arctic ice breaking as another blinding burst of dust blew past the three figures descending into the basement. Gus felt a light switch on a wall and flipped it to no effect before Collie stumbled into him from behind and sent him flying. He crashed over something, clutching at what felt like an easy chair before slamming into a carpeted floor.

"Someone boarded up the windows," Collie gasped.

The house rocked a third time.

A heavy rain of debris pattered the floor over their heads.

"Here," Wallace said and grabbed Gus's collar. The soldier guided him through the blackness of the furnished basement. Gus rapped his lower leg off the corner of something immobile, crippling him and sending him to his knees.

"Move," Collie urged and shoved him forward. They fumbled around a corner while something crashed into the floorboards overhead.

"You can see?" Gus yelled at Wallace.

The soldier didn't respond. Instead, he pulled his two companions through the dusty dark. Gus struck a wall and another chair and hit what might've been a countertop.

"You got a wide ass," Wallace commented when Gus's shoulder careened off a doorway. "Over here."

Feeling his way deeper into the void, Gus touched the cold metal of what might have been a washer and dryer set.

"Where are we, Ollie?" Collie asked from the rear.

Wallace didn't answer. Instead, he stopped and opened a door, its hinges squealing.

Another explosion made the ceiling shiver, and for a brief moment, Gus's attention went heavenward to long lines of fire illuminating the seams of the floorboards.

Then Wallace pushed Gus, sending him tripping and landing on a concrete floor, hands splayed out to cushion the impact. He sputtered, ears still ringing, and glanced back the way he'd come in time to see Collie's shape briefly illuminated by a hellish orange glow.

"Stay inside," Wallace commanded and slammed a heavy door.

"The hell . . . ?" Gus muttered and sat up, feeling shelves against his back.

"We're in a wine cellar," Collie said.

"What?"

The next muted explosion made him cringe. He stared up at the night that was the ceiling, fully expecting to see a fiery sun come crashing down. "The fuck are they using?"

"Grenade launcher," Collie answered. "Don't know the model, but they got their hands on one. Probably from a dead soldier or somewhere. That pause in between means they're reloading."

"My ears are fucked up."

"Are they bleeding?"

Gus dabbed at them. "No."

"Then you're okay. The ringing will pass."

"Where's Wallace?"

"Outside?"

"What's he doing out there?"

"Covering us," Collie said from near the door.

"Covering us?"

"Breathe easy if you can. This place might be airtight. Or if not, the vents might be blocked. Conserve your air in any case. I can't see shit."

Gus shuffled along blindly in the dark, making bottles tinkle in their racks. The shelves ended, and he rested against a wall, taking stock of himself while Collie stood guard at the door. Overhead, the great crackling intensified, as if a swarm of locusts or some other biblical plague had descended upon the house and feasted.

"What's that sound?" Gus wondered aloud, looking up.

"Topside. Things crumbling."

"What about Wallace?"

Collie didn't answer right away. "He doesn't take in air like you or me."

That should have startled Gus, but it didn't, not after he'd witnessed Wallace poke himself without a flinch or a sound.

"Should've gone out the back door," he said ruefully.

"No," Collie said. "With luck, they'll figure we died in the explosions. Only thing we have to worry about is smoke or a fire burning through overhead, but I don't think either will be an issue. The ceiling's concrete. No, we hunker down here until it's safe to dig out."

"And when is that?"

"Jesus, Gus, you're being a pain in the ass here," Collie said. "It happens when it happens. So sit tight. Crack a bottle if it'll relax you."

Something crashed down overhead with all the might of an avalanche, and Gus inhaled a blast of dust. He sneezed an answering salvo.

"Upper floor falling into the first," Collie confirmed. "House is collapsing. They blew the shit out of it."

The rumbling continued, filling the gap in conversation.

"What's going on with him?" Gus finally asked the darkness. He could sense the hesitation in Collie, and for a while, he figured he'd hear another blast from above before she answered.

But to his surprise, she started talking. "We were assigned to protect a government bunker up north. One called Whitecap. Huge installation. Bigger than anything with NORAD. Anyway, the truth is, the virus that turned folks into zombies was the latest in germ warfare, and despite the best precautions, it leaped to a carrier, who exposed it to the general populace. It started in England and jumped the pond. The prime minister was notified by the British PM and advised to make for the hills. There wasn't any cure once the virus was released, but there was an inoculation that was relatively untested as that was the fourth or fifth phase of the project. And it only had an estimated seventy-three percent efficacy rate. Worse, there wasn't enough of it. Anyway, fast forward a year, and the world's population has either eaten itself or had its head blown off. Over fifteen hundred personnel, including silly servants, are sheltered in Whitecap and slowly going stir crazy. The PM starts to get a hankering for information since all satellite communications have expired. He starts wondering about the state of the country, North America even, as he's unable to make contact with the president in Groom Lake."

"Groom Lake?" Gus asked.

"Area 51."

"Oh, I know that place."

"Well, that's where the Americans holed up while they dealt with the apocalypse. And the meltdown of unattended nuclear cores."

Gus didn't like the sound of that.

"We're fortunate in that most of our own nuclear facilities were along the border, so all's not all TARFU. We stay north of the red line."

Gus held up his hand. "TARFU?"

Collie grinned. "Things are royally fucked up. Anyway, the PM decided he wanted recon, so he called on the JTF to sally forth and recon. He had a force of forty stationed at Whitecap. He explained that the research team stationed at the facility had failed to improve upon the serum used to inoculate folks—a little cocktail called TI-48. Regardless, all selected JTF operators got a taste of TI. I did."

"You're immune now?"

"I guess. Haven't been bit to find out for sure."

"But Wallace has."

Collie sighed. "No. That's one we're currently figuring out. Two six-man spec op teams in full battle rattle were dispatched to Ottawa. They never came back. After six months, another six-man team was sent, with the orders to recon and find out what happened to the previous mission. And they never *went* back. Wallace and I were part of that team. We got caught in a running gunfire with a group of crazies calling themselves Norsemen and eventually fought it out in an infested Canada's Wonderland. Well, let's just say Wonderland had the living shit kicked out of it. Only Wallace and I got out of that one alive."

"So what happened?"

"We don't know. As far as we can tell, that untested serum had an above-average probability of successfully immunizing its subject, but there might've been a wee chance of mutation. Wallace noticed the changes in his skin tone. I have to say, when you're out in the middle of the apocalypse, a thousand klicks away from safety . . . well, he handled it well and decided to continue the mission. There weren't any internal adverse effects, according to him. We eventually located the remains of the initial recon teams in a courthouse in Ottawa—all dead or newly undead, in among a mess of terminated zombies. Having done that, we scouted out a good chunk of Ontario, Quebec, and Manitoba, taking stock of survivors from a distance. We helped them fight off roving packs of undead, leftover Norse elements, and other batshit crazies bent on God knows what. During the latter part of the year, Wallace's lips started to retract from his teeth, like you see now. And his eyes became increasingly sensitive to daylight. His sense of taste diminished as well as he experimented with . . . well, raw meat whenever we managed to bag some free-range chickens or rabbits. Needless to say, this was cause for concern, which prompted us to return to base, only to discover the Whitecap's entrance had been blown and reduced to rubble. Something went down there, and neither of us wanted to investigate what, despite Wallace's deteriorating condition. We figured the virus somehow got loose in there and everything went to hell. All the while, Wallace was getting a little slower. And I . . ."

Collie stopped for a moment, gathering her thoughts. At a soft *whump* on the ceiling, Gus looked up, but nothing followed.

"I started watching him for signs of completely going over to the other side," she continued. "Til now, only his joints and strength have been bothering him. The stabbing was new—and the most disturbing instance thus far."

"You know if he's gone over?" Gus whispered.

"He hasn't. Not yet. You saw him."

"I did."

"He's still himself."

Gus didn't add his thoughts on the matter. The guy *had* manhandled him into this improvised bunker. No deadhead would have done that.

"Yeah," he muttered and let his head droop, where it bumped a wine bottle.

Outside the cellar, Wallace kept an eye on the laundry and rec room. His night vision had improved greatly over the past few months. Overhead, things crumpled and fell, hitting the floor. Some smoke had seeped into the basement quarters but not much. Most of it drifted in through the debris that had collapsed and now blocked the staircase to the lower level. Wallace didn't have a gun on him, but he did have his combat knife, not that he figured he'd have to use it on anyone.

Wallace didn't know what had come over him when he pulled that chuggernut stunt in front of Gus. Such a breach of professionalism, in front of a civilian no less, was unforgivable. At the time, however, he'd felt only a morbid curiosity and acted purely on impulse, counterintuitive to his usual self-control. Wallace had long since accepted he was going to die. *How* was the only question, whether it was from a gunshot inflicted by himself or Collie. Lately, Wallace suspected that *any* shot would be to the head.

Standing there in the darkness, he could hear Collie talking on the other side of the wine-cellar door. Her voice was low but comforting in a way.

When he'd been sizing up the dead men in the hall, he completely zoned out and was brought back only by Collie's voice. If she hadn't called out to him, he would have . . .

A wintry freeze stropped the length of Wallace's spine.

Jesus Christ.

He might've tried eating those bodies, downing them like an "old lung in a bag," what soldiers used to call the disgusting-looking IMP ration of omelets in mushroom sauce.

He hefted the blade in his hand. A single beam of light leaked in from the outside, probably through a broken window. Wallace took a breath, discovering he could still do so, and leaned against the cellar door, thinking about what was happening to him and how much his condition had deteriorated.

He lifted the knife. The blade came up like an exclamation point struck by lightning. Wallace regarded his still-working arm, not feeling the wound he'd made before.

Sniffing and catching a whiff of smoke, he sat down and placed his back against the cellar door. The men above might think Wallace and the others had escaped out the back, or they might think they died in the house. Or they just might decide to be certain and search the place after their shelling. That didn't really concern Wallace at the moment. What bothered him was his wife being alone with Gus in a wine cellar at his back—alone with a man he knew she liked. And the knowledge that he'd pushed them in there didn't help. That sandpapered his emotions.

Wallace regarded the knife. Then he looked at his torso.

Slowly, he pushed aside the plate of armor, unbuttoned his combat fatigues, and pulled one tail up out of his pants, revealing skin. He angled the knife past the plate and cloth, the tip touching a bare patch of flesh. Wallace held it there, wondering . . . wondering how badly things had progressed and listening to the evil murmurs of conversation behind the cellar door.

He stabbed himself, feeling a pinch as the knife slipped in, right up to the first serrated tooth. Blackness oozed around the steel—but very little—dribbling down to the waistband. With clinical determination and a little morbid curiosity, Wallace forced the steel knife deeper, taking his time, the serration sawing the edges of the slit like a card in bicycle spokes. The weapon pierced the muscle tissue of his oblique then found the curls of his digestive tract. A dull pang that felt more weird than painful caused him to straighten his back and take a breath, but he kept on pushing, pushing the knife farther into himself, guiding it home. The razor-sharp edge and teeth were gently ruining him without so much as a *flicker* of the agony he searched for.

"Oh, Jesus," Wallace whispered in horror at his half-assed attempt at seppuku. Perhaps, just perhaps, he'd stabbed an area that wasn't sensitive at all, even though that sounded like complete bullshit. He twisted the blade, now half its length deep. The *wrongness* of the probe depressed and panicked him until he regained control of his emotions through a blast of willpower. He sawed deeper, striking toward a kidney, remembering the leak he'd taken two days before and how his urine had dribbled out like watery toothpaste.

The knife was into a kidney now, or so he figured. There should be *pain*. He should be unconscious on the floor.

Instead, he twisted the knife again, screwing it into himself as though he was reaching for a set of keys and his fingertips had nudged them farther out of reach. The steel caressed bone, and that sensation wasn't lost upon Wallace, but it didn't hurt at all, as if his entire abdominal cavity had been pumped full of an anesthetic agent. The blood seepage had ceased. He pushed down on the weapon's hilt, angling the steel upward, feeling the tip clicking off what might have been his backbone, and he stopped with a jolt.

What the fuck am I doing?

Anxiety flared, and he gasped and placed a hand against his side and pulled the blade out between pinched fingers until he freed the weapon. Nothing bled between his fingers. What would have been a killing wound on any battlefield had only brought on a brief panic attack.

He inhaled deeply, feeling his lungs expand—at least he hadn't punctured them— and inspected the slit in his side, which looked like a child's dirty mouth. Wallace prodded the cut, squeezing the edges until tiny beads ran southward. Then, on another morbid impulse, he inserted two fingers.

Nothing. No pain.

Other than the usual arthritic ache in his bones and joints, he didn't feel a thing. He widened his fingers, hooking the edge of the cut back to see, glimpsing dark meat.

That was enough.

Wallace sighed, fighting off his swelling panic, and began taking deep breaths, holding each for several seconds and releasing it in a slow breath. That still worked. And the fact that he recognized it still worked meant something.

He held the knife up to his face, his surprising night vision making out the streaks on the steel.

Overhead, the world smoldered.

29

Every so often, Gus heard Collie lean toward the door of the wine cellar and whisper. She then informed him of Wallace's reply.

"Still quiet topside," she said after the latest report.

"How long we been here, you think?"

"Two hours, give or take a few minutes."

"I don't smell smoke," Gus said.

"Well," a smile accompanied her words, "that's a good thing, isn't it?"

"Maybe they're still outside, waiting for the fire to die down."

"You're a real positive thinker," Collie noted sarcastically.

"I'm just tryin' to think what they might be up to."

"Don't worry. They'll either think we ran out the back or died in the explosions. They'd already be in here if they thought we were still alive."

"You're pretty relaxed about all this," Gus said.

"This is nothing," Collie replied. "Back in the day, we ran operations in Colombia and Nigeria. Along the Ivory Coast. Mali. We assisted SEALs on incursions back in Kabul. So, no, I'm not really concerned with a few idiots with guns or grenade launchers. It's not like what you might read in the books or the movies. The apocalypse wasn't picky about who it turned, and of the people remaining, hardly any know how to really fight. They try, and some do learn hard lessons, but most don't know what they're doing. Even those guys firing the grenade launcher probably didn't have proper training. They did a fine job all the same, though." She ended with a chuckle.

Gus supposed they had.

"Where they got that thing is something I'd like to find out, however," Collie added as an afterthought.

The silence droned on for minutes. Gus rubbed the side of his face and felt the cool glass of a wine bottle on his cheek. It was right there. That made him shake his head. It was a test—had to be.

"Well, if we don't get out of this soon, I'm going to have to take a leak in a corner," he said.

"Just let me know which one," Collie replied. "We could be here for a while. At least until the sun goes down. We'll move then. Back in training, our final mission was a seventy-two-hour evade."

"Special ops training course?"

"Something like that, yeah."

"That include like stealth kills?"

"Yeah," Collie said simply. "It did, actually."

That surprised him, and she paused long enough that Gus started to think he'd asked the wrong question.

"Those guys upstairs got the jump on me. Scared the shit outta me," Gus said, changing the subject. "Especially the machete."

"Well. You're still alive. Fear isn't something to be ashamed of. It's a defense mechanism. I'll give you this advice, especially true if your opponent has a machete or a knife. You ready?"

"Sure."

"Walk away."

That floored him. "That's your fuckin' advice? *Walk away?* What good is that?"

"If you don't have a gun, get out of there. I'm serious. A knife fight is the last thing you want to get into. If your opponent looks like he knows how to use a blade? Run. And I mean *run* like your ass was dipped in gasoline and hell's on your heels."

"Well, that sounds completely dickless to me."

"Hey, if you have a gun, shoot. Or if you know how to use a knife and there's no avoiding a fight, then go in looking to kill. I mean ready to stab for the heart, throat, eyes, or balls—whatever is closest—with whatever you've got. There are a lot of people who don't know how to fight, have no idea of the mechanics involved. They think it's like the movies. Or a game. It isn't. Nothing's choreographed. In a life-or-death situation, forget honor. Mr. Machete upstairs? He was scary—no doubt, crazy—but not stupid. You're talking about a person who decked himself out in a scary-looking outfit and put on a mean face. Great against most civvies, but against professionals? No. Not gonna work."

"Care to teach me some things?" Gus asked, forcing humor into his voice.

Collie chuckled, the sound like bells. "You survived on your own for *years*. That does count for something. Anyone who can hold their own didn't just get by. You're already a badass, son."

"Don't feel like one. Was drunk most of the time."

"Uh-huh. That worked for you?"

"Yeah. To a point. Until I tried to drink myself to death."

She paused. "How do you feel these days?"

"Well . . . better, except for what just happened upstairs. Living on the farm was a good thing. Balanced me. I had people around me then. Some good people. A few assholes." Talbert invaded his mind then. "But even they were okay in their own way. In the end."

"That's why we came back," Collie said. "After finding Whitecap gone, we decided to try and put what was left of humanity back together again—at least try for some semblance of what was lost. And the only way to do that was finding the good folks still out there, trying to survive. I don't think I would've returned to base anyway, knowing there were people out here needing us. In a way, I'm glad the chain of command broke down. Made things less black and white."

"Well," Gus muttered, stretching out his legs. "Thanks for saving me. Again."

She didn't answer, but he thought she might be looking in his direction.

"Sun'll be going down soon," she finally said.

They waited another hour. Wallace eventually tapped on the door before opening it, a wraith sticking its head into the cellar's gloom.

"Time to go."

"All clear?" Collie asked.

"Yeah."

Her shadow passed before Gus's eyes, and he struggled to follow. Remembering the wine, he paused on the threshold and looked back, barely seeing the bottles.

Not a drop. He'd gotten through that without sampling a single drop. The little victory put a smile on his face.

"Happy about something?" Wallace asked, startling Gus.

"Nothin'." Gus moved past the man.

"When did they move out?" Collie asked.

"Maybe an hour ago. Maybe more. Difficult to say. No one bothered looking for us."

"Sloppy."

"But lucky for us."

"Can we get up the stairs?"

"It's pretty hairy. Crawling through a window might be better."

Collie went to the laundry room and located a boarded-up window.

"Well, if the cats are around . . ." She pulled the dryer away from the wall. Once it was out of the way, she produced her knife and stabbed underneath the lowest plank covering the window, working it underneath. Gus cringed at the wooden squeals. If anyone was waiting for them up there, they'd know.

Collie wrenched away three planks and studied the night through a broken window and dead weeds. A wonderful breath of late-fall air flowed into the basement.

"Wait." She picked up a slab of wood and proceeded to clear the frame of shards. Once she was done, Wallace crawled through first and slowly stood up. Gus and Collie waited, seeing only a pair of combat boots.

"Clear," Wallace declared in a whisper.

"You go," Collie said to Gus.

"Okay, but don't be staring at my ass." He was mortified the moment he said it. *Where the hell had that come from?*

Collie only smirked in the shadows.

"Honey, if I wanted your ass, I'd have already taken it."

Gus wasn't sure he liked that response either.

He awkwardly pulled and fed himself through the window. Collie wormed through a few moments later, and all three studied the house, which was blown to hell. The second floor had collapsed into the first, and brick and splintered wood clumped around the still-smoking foundation. Even in the dark, Gus could see pieces of destroyed furniture sticking out here and there like charred limbs begging for rescue. The nearby car parked in the driveway hadn't escaped the destruction, for the fireplace chimney had fallen right across its roof, squashing the vehicle.

Gus understood why no one had checked on them. "Bunch of fuckin' hillbillies," he said.

"They took our rides," Wallace added dourly.

"Well," Collie said, facing the highway, "that pisses me off."

"So what do we do?" Gus asked.

"Find them," Collie said. "We know which direction they came from. We find them and take back our machines."

She turned and looked him in the eye. "And then kill every last one of them bastards."

*

The moon stayed hidden as if ashamed of the past few hours and let the three companions trudge along the highway in darkness. Walking felt good and generated a sweat that armored Gus against the cold. Collie led the way while Wallace brought up the rear, walking as if controlled by remote. They were nearly soundless in their march, which inspired Gus to try to emulate them. A few times, his boots scuffed the pavement, causing him to cringe, but no warning came from the operators.

Abandoned cars dotted the road, pushed off onto shoulders and left to the slow press of years. Collie inspected a few, discovering the fuel tanks long since siphoned dry.

"How far away you think they are?" Gus asked Collie's back.

"Thirty, forty klicks, maybe. Maybe more. Don't worry. We'll probably see or hear them long before they do us."

"Unless something else does," Wallace commented from behind, breaking his silence at Gus's lack of stealth.

"My ninja mode is a little rusty," Gus replied.

"Your ninja mode sucks donkey cocks."

Furrowing his brow, Gus glanced back. "Just asking in case, you know, you feel like stabbing yourself again."

"Hey."

"Yeah?" Gus asked.

"Shut the fuck up."

Gus shook that one off and decided to leave the operator alone. He felt oddly naked walking in the middle of the road yet well protected with the soldiers around, even if one of them was almost a deadhead. But he couldn't quite shake the feeling that this little group had a big problem on its hands.

The kilometers marched by, and the ache in Gus's feet worsened. Sleep called, doing subversive things to the rest of him. The night became an endless void where no sound played other than the shuffle of boots on asphalt. Gus listened, believing they were being watched at times, the sensation strong enough to spread a tracery of chills along the back of his neck, but nothing ever materialized. Nor did Collie or Wallace show any signs of alarm. Still, he could not shake the feeling that something lurked along the road, but he discerned nothing in those deep, tar-like shadows.

After what felt like hours, Collie dropped back to him, her shoulder brushing against his. "You okay?"

"No," Gus answered honestly. "I'm shitbagged here."

"There's a pickup here. Big interior without the suicide doors. We'll stop for a bit."

Gus barely heard her and realized he was dozing on his feet. He'd completely missed the dreamlike bulk of the vehicle on the highway.

"Great," he mumbled and let Collie guide him to an open door. The interior didn't smell of anything, which was a huge bonus—a four-wheel-drive rest stop with unspoiled leather seats. Gus climbed into the back and lay down, throwing an arm over his eyes.

"Just a few minutes." He breathed, relaxing so quickly he felt as if a dial had been flicked from ten to zero. "'Sall I need."

But then he was falling.

He didn't even register the door closing.

30

A hand rustled Gus's boot, and he woke, thrashing, striking out all at once, to a soft clatter of Collie's wind-chime laughter.

"Holy shit," she observed. "You're a human bear trap. Don't think I've ever seen anyone swing everywhere all at once."

Gus collapsed back on the seat and took a breath. "Ain't funny if I shit myself."

"It's *always* funny when someone else shits himself. Good sleep?"

He regarded Collie hunched over in the doorway, dreary daylight beyond her, making him miss true sunshine.

"Yeah." He rubbed his face. "What time is it?"

"I'd say a little after seven. The sky's just lighting up."

"You guys sleep?"

"I catnapped. Wallace, well, I don't think he ever sleeps now."

"Where is he?"

"Not far."

On cue, Wallace walked past her, muttering, "Get that lazy sack of shit up, Collie, before I grab him by the nutsack and haul his ass out."

Collie smiled at the slackening of Gus's face. "He's getting comfortable around you."

"Uncomfortable was better."

Moving his elbows and grunting, Gus worked himself out of the truck. Collie stood back and studied the land. Thick forest lay on either side of the highway. A thick quilt of clouds stopped the sun from showing its face.

"What's for breakfast?" Gus asked, breathing the cold air.

"Not this morning," Collie replied. The dark circles under her eyes spoke of very little sleep the night before. "Today we march. And find those little shits that stole our property."

"They could be anywhere."

"Yeah? We'll see."

As it turned out, *anywhere* was only three kilometers away. Collie pulled Gus off the highway while Wallace followed into the cover of nearby fir trees. They stopped on a hill and looked down upon a sloping plain where a small town rose up on either side of a river. The waterway ran east-west through the middle of the community, while a twenty-meter-or-so arch bridge spanned the slow-moving current. Timberland surrounded the town, the tree line marked by a few huge piles of wrecked debris that might once have been houses. Someone had built a service station with gas pumps on the far side of the river. A small grocery was on the other side of the road. A scattering of smaller buildings encircled the main attention grabber: a two-story motel with the name Cozzzy Inn set on the roof in large red letters.

Two familiar RVs had been parked out front, dwarfing a parking lot full of smaller vehicles.

"Way out in buttfuck nowhere," Gus observed sourly.

"Here's what we're going to do," Collie said, pulling her gun from her hip holster and screwing on a sound suppressor. "We'll move down the hill here, get closer to the town. I'll go in alone. You'd just draw their attention. It's still early, and if we're lucky, I'll catch them sleeping."

"Who, huh, wha'?" Gus blurted. "Why can't Dead Nuts go with you?"

Wallace cast a skeletal grimace in Gus's direction.

"Ollie can't move like he used to," Collie said, pulling her balaclava over her face, covering it ninja style. "I'm up, so stay back and wait for my smoke."

"But—"

But Collie was already moving, hunched over and slipping between trees, toward her objective below. Gus watched until he lost her in the bush.

He regarded Wallace and rolled his eyes. "I'm surprised at you."

"Me?" Wallace asked.

"Yeah, you, y'fuckin' meatsicle. You let her go alone."

"I let her go alone?" Wallace repeated, amusement lacing his tone. "Don't you worry about that one."

Gus's eyes narrowed at the man.

"Back when we were doing black ops," Wallace said, "back when the world was chugging along, that one you're so concerned about was terror incarnate on two legs. Still is. Don't get fooled by the fact she's a woman or by her playing with you. That's a mistake. Old-school military believed women couldn't handle the physical hardships that come with being a top-tier soldier. Believed their bodies just weren't as capable as men's. They even thought—wrongly—that the women couldn't handle the psychological side of a mission, that they weren't mentally tough enough. All horseshit, of course—which is one reason why JTF recruited her. Many old schoolers still don't believe in hard-core female operators. Don't expect them. Certainly not one with her level of training."

Despite mixed feelings on Collie's leaving, Gus was intrigued. "Yeah? What level is that?"

"Most of her opponents didn't know she was a woman," Wallace answered slyly. "And those that found out still died. She was born into martial arts. I'm saying she came out of the womb with black belts in multiple disciplines. A natural sharpshooter, taken beyond Olympic level. If she had only one bullet and three targets, she'd still shoot them all dead. Unmatched with hand weapons and an expert with explosives. Endured torture at the hands of some very dedicated senior operatives for forty-eight hours straight before they passed her into JTF. She outwitted and tagged US Navy Seals in some not-so-friendly exchange exercises. Taught the SAS a thing or two about evade-and-capture hunts. Her face is a historical canvas of pain and survival, of combats won. You only have to roll with her once to realize, thankfully, she's on our side. Then there's the brain powering it all. Masters in psychology, sociology, and biology. She's probably outsmarted and killed more bad guys than you have zombies. Collie's a primal, damn near supernatural, true-to-life tit twister, shit kicker, ball *breaker* if there ever was one. And if you aren't impressed yet, I'd suggest you establish and maintain a healthy sense of *holy fuck* when talking to her. Don't let that lovely exterior fool you. She's a killer."

All that rendered Gus speechless.

The visor of Wallace's helmet did not waver. "Listen good. Only gonna say this once. The grim reaper . . . is a bitch. And whoever it is down there in that motel, they're already dead."

She covered the distance in under three minutes, slowing down to control her breathing as she neared the first houses on the outskirts. The residences appeared savagely sacked, their windows smashed and charred around the sills, as if someone had taken to using them as huge ovens. The smell of shit percolated around the properties. Cars sat in driveways with their tires sliced, their bodies wrecked with sledgehammer blows. A mountain bike lay twisted on its side, both tires warped, the bare bar—where a seat would have been—covered in an unsettling maroon. Gravel pathways had been transformed into dried-mud footpaths tattooed with bootprints. Collie slipped through the little rural jungle, pausing at corners before peeking around, watching for dogs and other, two-legged, strays. She scanned her intended paths for tripwires or sentries before moving. She kept to the shadows when they were available, stayed on pavement, and kept her sidearm lowered in front of her.

In some of their lengthier deployments, the enemy had given the operators of Joint Task Force Two nicknames. The Taliban had called them Death Bringers. Columbian ELN hit squads had cursed them as Green Ghosts. Collie had forgotten how many men and women she'd killed over the years, never stopping to dwell on their faces or their history before they took up arms and made life miserable for ordinary people, private companies, or interests and investments of the Canadian government abroad. On rescue missions or just straight-out "removals" of terrorist elements, she never questioned her orders, only executed. They all did, with a professional pride that they were among the best at what they were trained to do, and supremely confident in their lethal skills.

When the apocalypse came, she had been transferred to Whitecap with the other JTF-2 teams, along with other armed-force segments, to protect the bunker. While the world died on a scale shown only in movies and books, she experienced guilt on a level never before experienced. They were warriors, protectors of the people, yet there she was, posted deep in the earth, waiting for it all to be over.

That inactivity, that inability to serve—along with her leader's detached, aloof belief that all was well since *they* would survive—bothered her. She wondered what would become of those still outside of Whitecap after the world had ceased its death throes. When would they reach out and attempt to establish order? Or make the effort to help the survivors? She had no family to speak of, with the exception of her husband Wallace, whom she'd married while in the depths of Whitecap. The bureaucrats wisely decided to ensure all active JTF-2 staff transported their families to the covert installation. Not all had managed to reach their loved ones, however, and that quietly festered with some operators.

She sympathized but secretly felt as if it were punishment for turning their backs.

That was, as Ollie pointed out, her one weakness.

Collie and Ollie's official honeymoon came when they were deployed to Ottawa to search for the whereabouts of the previous JTF recon teams sent there. Upon determining the fate of those operators and the discovery that Whitecap had fallen, she and Ollie realized they were on their own. Collie believed it had been justice that the underground shelter had been breached. Ollie was more clinical in his assessment.

The virus had simply found a way in.

Some heated discussions had followed between the pair, debating what to do in the absence of a command structure, but they both eventually agreed on one plan: gather whoever was left, whoever was willing to join them, and start over.

It was a proactive mission that Collie found much to her liking. However, the world had changed, gone savage. The undead were the easiest to deal with. Shoot them on sight. The human element was far more cunning, devious, and in some cases, warlike.

Collie figured it was just after nine in the morning, but the town seemed mired in sleep. Nothing stirred as she snaked her way through backyards, closing in on the bridge. A single, forest-green bungalow came into sight, ringed with a smashed fence that reminded her of broken teeth. The house stood on the right, its broken-out picture window giving a shooter ideal coverage of both sides of the river and anyone attempting to cross. There was the chance that no one actually lived on the south side, that they'd relocated to the motel, perhaps even fortified their position.

Collie hugged the corner of one house, looked both ways before proceeding, and walked across the street as if she belonged.

Her senses crackled in the morning silence, eyes flicking side to side, ears on ten. She appeared outwardly calm, as though she belonged to the gang, albeit dressed differently. She suppressed the urge to sprint, forcing herself to take her time to the house. If anyone noticed her and stopped to stare, she'd have only a second or two before her ruse failed.

The house loomed closer, and she walked around the back, found the rear door, tried the knob, and found it locked. As if fumbling for a key, she reached up her sleeve and extracted a small, thin blade, inserted it into the slit between door and doorframe, located the bolt, and knifed her way into the house.

All was quiet inside.

Collie closed the door and walked through a filthy kitchen area, hugging the walls and taking her time peeking into doorways. A smell of alcohol and body odor permeated the house. Her gun came up, left hand steadying the right. The living room was empty, but three hunting rifles lay across a green sofa. An opposing hallway had two of three doors closed.

A toilet flushed.

Collie silently blurred to the side of the bathroom door and waited, gun pointed at the space where a head would appear.

Someone snorted, horked, and spat, followed by a muttering of words.

Fingers fumbled on a doorknob.

Then *two* doors opened—the room that Collie had covered and the other down the hall on the opposite side.

She didn't hesitate.

The man in her sights got his head blown off, decorating the wall and drizzling the air with bloody pulp, before she smoothly adjusted her aim and double-tapped a blond woman in her chest and face. The blast flung the blonde back with a meaty racket, the door sprayed with head jam and other clumps of sagging matter.

Collie did a quick scan of the bathroom, hopped over the T-shirt-wearing man-corpse in the hall, and went to the opened door. She led with her gun, using the wall as cover, and saw that the dead female's bedroom was empty. Having cleared two rooms, she went to the last open doorway and found it vacant. A quick search revealed the closets full of clothes and well-used sports padding. The beds rested directly on the floor, so there was nowhere to hide there.

Collie stalked back into the kitchen, deeming the house clear.

The living room might've been a mosh pit the night before, and parts of the carpet seemed to have either been ripped or chewed through. Empty booze bottles rattled and rolled underfoot, garnished with empty brass shell casings. Collie stopped and took a quick look out of the picture window, seeing how it lined up with the sofa. Lazy. People could sit there and watch the road, rifles in hands, without having to lift their asses. The indentations in the cushion spoke of many long hours for the shooters.

Collie went back to the closet where she'd seen the gear and clothes. She took a light jacket and a pair of cargo pants, both of which she pulled over herself. Having done that, she returned to the living room and picked up the nearest bolt action: a Remington; chestnut stock with a scope, missing its strap; rubber on the grip; hinged floor plate with a full four-shot magazine and one already in the pipe; good for at least three hundred yards. She looked it over and deemed it solid and capable enough, but she didn't like using untested weapons. If she remained lucky, she wouldn't have to worry about that. She jammed the Sig Sauer into her waistband and practiced pulling it free twice. The suppressor hooked both times, but Collie didn't see any alternative. She hefted the rifle and saw an old Red Wings cap hanging from a peg. That went over her masked head.

If she could get across the bridge, then all was peaches and cream.

31

A breeze ushered her across the bridge. Rusty guardrails, crumpled in places, ran along the edges of the construction. The dark water below flowed west, gurgling along, conjuring little whirlpools. Ahead, the remaining houses, service station, and motel seemed to press themselves into a tall fence of fir and spruce trees, all under an ominous carpet of cloud. Collie sauntered across at an outwardly leisurely pace, appearing unconcerned with the world, holding the Remington across her pelvis. Her balaclava kept the chill morning air from her face, the weather reason enough for a person to wear a mask. Her boots clicked off pavement riddled with potholes and long cracks resembling spent lightning bolts, the sound of her passing disturbing the otherwise peaceful morning.

Halfway over the bridge, she kept pace, scanning the houses for lookouts or signs of life and seeing none. Whoever had taken the motor homes had completely relaxed their guard. Collie felt the gun in her waistband slip a finger, forcing her to adjust it while laying the rifle across one shoulder as if in a parade. The breeze slashed at her eyes, making her blink.

No one approached her.

No one called out.

Even better, no shots fired.

She allowed herself a mental sigh of relief upon getting across. Without breaking stride, she sauntered toward the motel and the collage of vehicles parked there, several of which she recognized as belonging to her. She reached the nearest RV, walked along its length and paused, listening for voices or snoring.

Nothing.

The front of the RV beckoned, and she slunk around the front, crouching. The main entrance of the motel wasn't more than twelve meters away, the glass doors smashed out and replaced with stained slabs of wood. A slot had been cut into the surface at eye level, for peeking out at visitors. She looked up and spotted, just underneath the *Cozzzy Inn* sign, a rifle barrel sticking out over the edge of the roof.

I see you. Collie walked to the base of the building. Most of the windows had been boarded up on the outside. She walked around to the back, passing a secondary entrance that had been likewise fortified, as well as a ringed escape ladder going up to the roof.

Collie placed the rifle against the motel wall and climbed, focusing on the top, willing the area above her to be clear. In short time, she reached the top and paused.

She heard the soft buzz of a snore.

Not believing her luck, she scaled the top and saw a fire-escape door leading to the motel's second floor. Across from that was a man dressed as if on a hunting spree and sleeping on his back. His head rested against the lower portion of one of the Zs in *Cozzzy Inn*, with a stocking cap pulled down over his eyes.

Collie crept to the fire-escape door and hid behind the housing unit.

She drew her knife and snuck toward the sleeping man. Once beside him, Collie slapped her hand over his mouth, drove her knee to his chest, and stabbed the entire length of the blade up under his chin, hilt deep, skewering his brain. His arms shivered as she pinned him, relaxing a second later. She rooted the blade back and forth before extracting the weapon and wiping it off on his shirt.

A heartbeat later, she returned to the fire-escape door, surprised to see the guard had jammed a slat of wood against its base to prevent the door from completely closing.

Collie pulled it open with a faint, rusty yawn.

Then she was inside.

"Holy shit, was that her?" Gus demanded, squinting at the distant motel.

"That was her."

"Sweet Christ, did she kill him?"

Wallace turned, his mouth twisting into a *course-she-killed-him* sneer.

"Holy *shit*. Holy shit. I mean, course we couldn't hear anything from here, but that was *her*."

"Let's get moving," Wallace said and started down the hill, keeping inside the tree line.

"We're backup?"

"She doesn't need backup."

*

The air inside the building was fresh, and Collie stealthily descended a flight of stairs to the second floor and paused at another door. She listened at its surface, heard nothing, and decided to proceed. The hinges groaned softly as she pulled it open, making her cringe, but no one responded. Collie eased into an alcove filled with two smashed vending machines—for snacks and soft drinks—and an empty ice freezer. There were no working lights, leaving the hallway in deep shadows. A worn carpet covered the floor, which Collie appreciated. She peeked around the corner, seeing that the corridor ran north and south and she was pretty much in the middle. Another staircase was situated around the corner from the vending machines alcove. Boards covered the windows at either end of the hall, but daylight stabbed through multiple slots, reminding her of murder holes found in medieval castles. A few doors hung partially open, glazing the carpet in a dusty, lazy light.

The hallway was empty.

She wondered how many were in the gang and how many might be sleeping behind each closed door. The knife went back into its sheath, replaced with the silenced pistol. Taking a breath, she placed her back to the wall and moved north, trying each knob in turn with a gentle twist. Most were locked, suggesting that folks weren't so trusting of each other in the little community, and snores ripped through with buzz-saw clarity. Some doors opened to empty rooms, the beds and furniture either trashed or sparkling with dust.

Collie crept toward the end, her balaclava becoming soggy with sweat. She concentrated on maintaining situational awareness, utilizing six senses at once, all cranked up to ten.

The ceiling caught her attention at the same time as a stench, one she'd come to recognize all too well: rotting meat.

Above her head, dangling from the ceiling at varying lengths, were hundreds of cut-out Christmas trees and ornamental glass bulbs. Collie paused and studied this oddity, even reaching up and plucking one of the small trees from its twine for a closer inspection. It was a pine-scented air freshener, its fragrance long depleted. She dropped the thing and tugged free a bulb—another exhausted air freshener.

The farther she crept along the hall, the stronger the smell of decomposing flesh.

The second-to-last door didn't puzzle her as much as it should have. In her time traveling the countryside, she'd seen a few makeshift cells, some holding the pitiful remnants of flesh and bones too weak to bear a name, others holding people who cried upon being freed. That door had two iron bars on the outside acting as dead bolts, one near the top and one at the bottom. They'd been crudely nailed into the door's surface, their ends deep into the doorframe. A wide slot, carved out by chainsaw, was at a tall person's eye level. The opening intimidated her for a moment, dangerous seconds she shouldn't have spent. Memories of horrors from cells past fogged her mind, sounds and images of the depravity people—crazed people—could inflict upon the weak for no other reason than amusement. Or punishment. Or both.

Collie set her jaw, stood on the balls of her feet and looked inside, and when she did, relief coursed through her.

It wasn't as bad as others.

The room was a double—that much she could see from the slot—and filled with about a dozen or more people dressed in winter clothing. Three slept on each bed while the floor seemed to be covered in flesh—the living kind. A big bare toe twitched. Someone coughed.

Collie stepped back and checked the opposite door, with a similar slot and locking bars on its surface. The words PLAY PEN were spray-painted between the bars. A short, extendable aluminum ladder rested against the baseboard. She checked down the hallway and tiptoed once more to see, peering into the room. The smell permeated her mask and wrinkled her nose.

What the hell?

It was a mirror layout of the room behind her, but with a slight difference. A man, battered and incredibly weary looking, had pressed himself into the far corner, as if attempting to meld with the wall. He sat with his head drooping and his legs splayed out. Collie didn't understand what she was looking at, why he seemed to be at the absolute limit of his endurance, or why the interior of the room appeared to be stripped of all furniture.

Then horror set in, prompting her to lift herself a little higher to see, to get a fuller look at the view through the slot.

The floor . . . the floor had been cut away.

The guy was perched on a shred of wood that was a section of the floor, a seat only wide enough for his ass, leaving his legs to dangle into an open pit that seemed to span the entirety of the room.

Collie realized why the ladder was just outside the door.

But what was in the play pen's pit?

Swearing, she looked back up the hallway and made her decision right there. The bars slid across with the barest of squeals, making Collie watch for bandits stepping out of their rooms. No one did, however, and she was able to work the second bar open without incident. She put her shoulder to the door, opened it, and slipped inside. The floor existed a short distance within, allowing access to a dingy bathroom on the right, but where the room opened up was nothing but a chainsawed drop to the first floor. The man's sleep-deprived eyes bulged at her. Collie held up a hand as she leaned forward, cautiously peering into the pit.

Her breath caught in her throat.

This. Was different.

And utterly fucked up.

Whoever these people were, they were twisted. They had sealed off the room directly underneath the play pen—a sick name for its torturous nature—and filled it with the undead, decomposing heads of God-only-knew-how-many zombies.

A writhing, twisting carpet of heads.

Pasty fleshed, even bluish in the pale light, a few had exposed profiles missing ears or entire cheeks. Some heads were attached to shoulders and flagella-like arms but very little else. As she watched, a few of the shaggier heads, the hair strands partially blinding them, opened mouths like dying fish. Eyes with the texture of rotten yogurt reacted to her movement above and widened ever so slightly, some even fixing on her. Some of the heads, the ones on top, opened their mouths, causing them to tumble from their little hills as if freshly chopped from the neck. The smell alone was enough to torture a person, and Collie tore her gaze from the gruesome scene below to the now-desperately awake person clinging to that little perch across from her, his hands splayed out on either side in one last attempt to keep him out of that mulch of insanity.

"Please," he begged. In his exhausted and weakened state, that subtle gesture shifted his weight a fraction off balance and he jerked backward, fighting gravity's pull. Collie reached out in reflex, and both of them froze, afraid that the barest movement would slide him into the pit.

"Help," he whispered.

Collie withdrew to the door and gently opened it. The ladder was there. She hefted it with a soft rattle. Not waiting to see whether anyone heard or not, she maneuvered it back into the room and tried to extend it toward him.

Then it hit her—he had no room to *stand* on that miserable perch, nowhere to butt the end of the ladder while he crawled to safety. And he couldn't hold the ladder in his lap or somehow worm it underneath himself. He simply had no room.

"How'd you get over there?" Collie whispered, pulling the ladder back and laying it on the floor, a portion of its length sticking into the hall. There wasn't any room inside without letting it tip into the pit.

"All right," she told him, hating how the guy's eyes were brimming with fright, terrified she might abandon him. "Listen, here's what we're gonna—"

A door closed down the hall, causing her to freeze.

32

"Hey, they get him yet?" an ordinary voice yelled out, breaking that fragile silence. Footsteps padded toward the play pen.

Collie glanced at the guy in the corner, his legs dangling seven feet above an animated charnel pit.

"God*damn*, I was hoping he'd hold out the night. Must've stuck himself to the wall with some bum butter or some shit. Had a fuckin' quart o' rye bet on his skinny ass clingin' to his shit."

Then the person horked fiercely, drawing up curds of lung butter that turned Collie's guts just hearing it. And the grosser thing was the guy *didn't spit.*

Is he chewing it? She placed the ladder on the floor, the upper end of it well out into the hall. She had no choice.

Another voice shouted from inside another room, too muffled to understand. Collie went to the doorway and readied herself just inside the doorway, bringing her Sig Sauer up to her shoulder. She took a settling breath, relaxing, getting loose, and waited for her target.

"Fuckin' get your lazy, square-holed, bitch asses outta bed, then," the partially filled voice answered with glee. "Y'probably spent the night balls deep in her crack anyway, so why y' wearin' it out?"

A fist crashed against the door of the captives' room, right across from the play pen, loud enough that Collie knew the jig was up. Voices cried out as a man—a *young* man—barely twenty, with an eyebrow of a moustache and dark fuzz coating his chin, turned his cruel *hyuk-hyuk* grin toward Collie.

She grabbed him by the throat.

His grin sagged into astonishment as the sound suppressor shoved into the corner of his mouth. Collie pulled him into the room and slammed him against a wall.

243

If he hadn't been clear on her intent yet, she jammed the barrel of the Sig Sauer deeper into his face, uncovering yellow teeth.

"Now," Collie hissed. "Shit-kicker, you be—"

"Jezuz Chreest! Dere's a wo—"

That unexpected blast blow-dried her face, catching her off guard and causing her to tense up on the trigger just enough to fire, killing the man-boy in a muddy splash of teeth. The back of his head flapped as if an inner clockwork spring had popped free. His legs did a spasmodic two-step, do-si-doing in a terminal square dance before dropping him on his ass. Collie let him fall.

Sonavabitch, she swore.

She flicked a glance at the prisoner stuck in his corner, and his eyes damn near exploding from their sockets was all the message she needed. The corner of the door-frame trembled when Collie butted her shoulder against it, holding her gun two handed and just listening. Across the way, two sets of eyes stared at her from the slot, filled with disbelief. She couldn't do anything for them then.

In the hall, just after the yeller thumped to the floor, there was a moment of silence, an ominous portent of bad things to come.

The muffled shouting and banging came all at once, all from the south end. Then one door slammed open, followed by another and then a clatter of rooms opening. Collie imagined prairie dogs standing at attention at the lips of deep burrows, seeing what was up. But those dogs weren't going to run.

Collie eyed the planks barring the window at the north end of the hall, figuring if she had to, she might be able to summon enough momentum to heave herself wrecking-ball style through the barrier.

But she wasn't ready to go anywhere yet. Collie had never gotten any of her scars or disfigurements from sneaking around—she *earned* them.

"You okay down there?" a man called cautiously.

"That was Ryan," a woman supplied.

"Ryan?"

"Yes, Jesus Christ, yes, Ryan!"

"Everything cool, Ryan?"

A wary silence was fringed with growing whispers.

Collie sighed and waited, adjusting her grip on the Sig Sauer, her fingers flexing.

"Ryan, you still here, bro? Still with us?" The voice was closer, followed by a spidery wall of stillness creeping forward.

Collie could imagine them, maybe a dozen men and women hunched over, hugging the walls, armed and believing themselves ready for one guy seemingly doing the impossible—escaping the play pen.

"Hey, Jimbo," a rough voice called, perhaps no more than twenty feet from Collie's position, "if you've got Ryan with you . . ."

Collie slipped down to the baseboard, edging closer to the corner, back to the wall.

"Let him go."

From his perch in the corner, Jimbo whimpered.

"Let him go, or I swear as Christ is my witness, I'll fuckin' *fork* feed you to the—"

She leaned out from the corner and fired, snapping off a barrage of silenced shots into the people clogging the corridor. A man reeled back after being tagged twice in the chest. A woman gripped her face just below a black headband. Another woman, red haired, shrieked as a round caught her shoulder and spun her around. Another guy grunted and landed flat on his face. Blood spritzed the air. Brass casings jumped across the carpet. Collie continued firing into the mass of torsos, causing the ones in the middle and rear to stampede into each other like squealing piglets as they ducked into now-open doorways.

Six or seven bodies littered the carpet when her Sig Sauer clicked empty and the magazine slipped out the bottom. Collie retreated around her corner, reaching for one of three spare magazines on her belt. Screams of wounded rage reverberated along the walls, but Collie only readied her sidearm, wincing at the stomach-turning stench emanating from the pit. She glanced up at the slot across from her. A set of eyes stared out, utterly shell-shocked at what she'd just done.

Only getting started, honey, she conveyed with a murderous look before directing her attention back to the fight.

A barrage of rifle and shotgun fire ripped past her cover, peppering the boards on the end-of-the-hall window. Shots zinged by, taking impressive bites out of the wood, snapping splinters off the door frame. Glass shattered and blew outward. Bullets punched a path of shredded holes up a strip of wood. Carpeting jumped. A slab of overhead paneling fell to the floor, and Collie lifted a hand to shield her eyes from any debris. The person at the slot across the way had disappeared.

Smart.

"All right, pigfucker, all right," a different voice shouted while the shooters no doubt reloaded. "Don't know who the hell you think you *are*, but I'm here to tell you what you're gonna *be*. You see them heads in the pit? You see 'em? You're gonna be seeing them a lot closer soon enough. There's no way out of that room. No cover except where you are. You come out into the hall, maybe jump through that boarded-up window, and we'll light you up so hard you'll think someone set off two tons of White English in your ass."

Jimbo whimpered again behind her.

A note of finality was in that last sound, and Collie looked around to see Jimbo slowly slouching, succumbing to the pull of the pit.

She wouldn't allow that.

Collie moved away from the door, shoved Ryan's corpse off the ladder before grabbing the end. With a grunt, she heaved the ladder into the fragrant pit, toward Jimbo. It extended with a loud rattle, and the ladder stabbed deep into that morass that yawned and chewed and came to a stop right below his hellish seat. Not happy with seeing the end of the ladder sinking into that fleshy compost, Collie took the chance of pulling Ryan's body to the pit's edge. She propped him over a shoulder with a grunt and dumped him onto the metal rungs. The corpse tumbled and fell heavily onto the heads, but his upper torso covered enough of the undead that when Jimbo finally fell forward, he landed with both bare feet on Ryan's dead ass. Jimbo yelled and slipped, his left foot mashing into the decaying cheek of a zombie before jerking away and stepping onto the ladder.

Unable to spare any more time on him, Collie withdrew to the doorway, gun held at her shoulder. The pit's smell brought water to her eyes, and she took a second to wipe them. *Stink!* She couldn't remember anything smelling so damn foul. Even with her mask on, she felt violated, polluted, just by breathing it in.

A violent hail of gunfire caused her to shy away from the doorframe. Bullets ravaged the wood. Splinters cut through the air.

"We're comin' for ya, shitkicker," an eager voice promised. "And when we get ya, you'll wish you'da saved a bullet for yourself. Best put one in your eye right now."

Collie set her jaw and waited.

The uneven earth was causing Wallace problems.

More to the point, he couldn't lift his legs high enough at times to clear rocks, dips, or clumps of decaying vegetation. Shouts flared up from the direction of the motel, reinforcements being summoned. Wallace didn't like that. Contrary to his earlier comment, there just *might* be more than Collie could handle, and there he was, barely able to walk. He couldn't feel the painful growl of his joints anymore.

A tangle of exposed roots stopped the steel toes of his boot, and he went down hard.

Gus was ten strides ahead and immediately stopped when Wallace fell.

"You okay?" he called out, loud enough to make Wallace cringe.

"Yeah."

Gus ran back through the trees. Wallace did a slow push-up and rolled onto his side, black visor staring up at the bearded man.

"Wait." Wallace put up a hand. "Listen, you're faster, and you're armed. You get your ass downtown and across that bridge. Find Collie. If any wannabe thudfuck points a weapon at you, you blow their goddamn head off their shoulders. You got that?"

Gus nodded. "What about you?"

"The fuck you care? Get outta here and get to Collie. *Now.*"

He hesitated, clearly divided, but only for a fleeting second. Then he was rushing away.

Wallace sat up like a creaky drawbridge, feeling his abs tighten, wondering if anything was about to squirt out of the hole he'd made. He could lift his arms only to his shoulders, and that robbery of movement made him shake in chagrin. He couldn't help Collie in his present state, but maybe sending in a civvie might give her a needed distraction.

Maybe.

His grimace deepening, oozing rage, it was only by sheer force of will he got to his knees.

Bullets zinged down the hallway, perforating the boards at the end of the hall and sending shards of wood and glass spinning into daylight. The daylight returned fire of its own, sending lasers back through the holes being made. Whoever the shooters were, they had no conception of conserving ammunition, pausing only to reload in a ferocious clatter of metal on metal and hillbilly yowling. They cursed at her, screaming vengeance for killing Ryan and the ones gunned down in the corridor, still wrongly thinking she was a dude.

Collie returned fire, squeezing off only a couple of rounds in their direction, letting them know she was still there. They'd taken up defensive positions in the doorways, leaning out only to unload. Only a matter of time before they started to leapfrog up the corridor, one doorway to the next. Jimbo had crawled up from the pit and ducked into the bathroom without even so much as a thank-you.

Ungrateful bastard.

Collie suddenly got tired of waiting and decided to weave some black magic.

When the next salvo stopped, she collapsed on her belly and angled her arm around the corner. Bullets screamed past her head from two different points of fire, the shooters only partially concealed in their doorways. Collie's sights fell on a woman, and she drilled the target through the chest. The woman dropped her rifle and slammed against the frame, falling to a sitting position before toppling over.

"Annie!" a man wailed.

The second shooter rushed his shot and missed, but one shell ripped up a slab of carpet and flung it into Collie's eyes. She scrambled back behind protection, clearing her vision.

"All right, cocksucker, all right," that same voice yelled. "You want to dig in? You ain't gettin' the chance. We *want* you now. We want you *bad*."

Collie didn't like the smug, evil delight in those words. She peeked around the corner and blinked in disbelief.

The gang had moved a wide, SWAT-style tactical shield into the middle of the hall, the kind that would easily protect anyone crouching behind its sheet-metal hide. Bullet-resistant Plexiglas covered the eye slot near the top, revealing gang members already gathering behind the portable barrier, preparing to lift and move it toward her position.

It rested around twenty feet from her position, meant to end the current stalemate.

She glanced around her surroundings, seeing nothing of help. The ceiling was flawless, solid. The windows of the play pen had been boarded too much to escape through. The one at the end of the hallway wasn't damaged enough, and though she'd entertained the notion earlier, busting out that way wasn't something that appealed to her.

Scuffling and angry shouts came from the hall. They were coming, lifting that monstrous shield and moving forward, stepping over bodies as needed.

Creeping closer.

Collie swapped out her magazine for a full one, worked the slide, and hugged the wall. The doorknob captured her attention.

The lock—it was still intact.

The tactical shield's scarred surface came into view as she slammed her door shut and locked it. She jammed the Sig Sauer through the cut slot—which was conveniently higher than the besiegers' portable wall—and unloaded a punishing rate of fire.

The shield crashed down.

Heads jerked back.

A torso got blown backward.

People screamed.

A shotgun blast bit a chunk out of the door, and Collie shied away for a second, but then she continued firing into whoever was behind the shield.

A green, dimpled ball rattled through the slot, pitched almost perfectly. It bounced off her chest before dropping to the stained floor.

Collie's eyes widened.

Grenade.

Rattling about her boots.

She sprang into the bathroom as the weapon detonated, shredding the outer door and scorching the walls in a huff of released fury. Collie rebounded off a tiled countertop and crashed into a pink porcelain toilet, her ears ringing as if a pair of cymbals had been smashed inside them. *The fuck they get one of those?* her dazed mind questioned. A dazed Collie tried to rise but slumped alongside the toilet, legs not quite willing to do her bidding. Her senses tried to equalize, and she met the terrified expression of Jimbo peeking over the lip of the bathtub.

"You okay?" she asked weakly.

Jimbo lifted his face above the rim, squeaked, "I shit the tub," and dropped back down, leaving a pair of bugged-out eyes showing.

Men charged into the room, as big as mountains, amazing Collie that so many could fit into the small motel bathroom. Their voices reached her like angry hunting horns blaring over empty plains. Hands grabbed her and hoisted her up, slammed her into the counter and plied her back over the edge, her pelvis thrusting forward. They pinned her arms against a shattered mirror as faces hot with hate loomed in close. Someone cocked a mallet of a fist and struck her tempered abs. Pain flared from the point of impact, but she kept the air in her lungs. Another punch—and that one hurt—kept her off balance. Voices thundered overhead, like gods swearing at mortals daring to fly. Another fist struck her gut, followed by a granite right to her face.

One of them grabbed her balaclava and pulled it from her sweating face, and the room went quiet.

"It's a fuckin' *woman*," one man wearing a hunter's hat finally whispered in amazement.

"A woman," another echoed, disbelieving she could have gotten so far, done so much damage.

"A fuckin' *butch* of a bitch," deemed the puncher. His voice was the one from the hallway. Puncher grabbed at her breasts. "She's got 'em hidden, but they're there."

Hands pawed over her chest. Collie allowed them, regaining her marbles.

"The fuck you do, huh? Strap them down or something?" Puncher asked as he prodded. Two others held her arms while another eagerly watched over their shoulders.

"You got him?" a female asked from the hall.

"The cocksucker's a *she*!" the one on the right bellowed triumphantly.

"A *she*?" the woman voiced in disbelief. A couple of curious faces appeared between the gathering shoulders before being blotted out.

"Face is all fucked, but everything else seems okay," Puncher muttered. His hand latched onto the fabric around her waist. "Check out what's below the border here. See if this butch shaves."

"She's not that bad," Righty declared with an eager hiss.

"Goddamn *nose* is bit off," Lefty pointed out in disdain, as if their prize had been spoiled somehow.

"Don't have to look at her face anyhow."

The force on her arms diminished just a fraction, and Collie relaxed. She'd already recovered enough to evaluate the situation. Puncher squashed his pelvis against hers, close enough that she could smell morning breath and felt his anger being channeled into lust.

Enough of this *shit.*

She hiked her right leg, and Puncher immediately cupped her ass cheek, misreading the cue as being submissive. He was too preoccupied with pulling at her combat fatigues, pissed by the fact they weren't ripping.

Collie drove her right boot heel into the nearest knee, which belong to Righty. She hit the joint from the side, mashing the bones in a direction they weren't meant to bend. Righty yelped like a kicked dog and released her. He flung her arm away as if it was on fire and limped a step before falling into the open doorway. The scream startled Puncher and Lefty. Collie flashed forward, smashing her freed open palm into Puncher's nose, flattening cartilage with sledgehammer force, driving the man back, his nostrils already gushing. He flipped over the low rim of the tub, ripping down a shower curtain as he went. Lefty's eyes fluttered wide with horror before Collie's hand pistoned into his face. Three short, vicious explosions cracked into his nose with smart-bomb accuracy, softening his grip until he released her and sat down drunkenly on the toilet seat. A man screamed a warning from the hallway, struggling to pull Righty out of the way. Another goon tried to enter. He reached out and latched on to her right shoulder. Collie wrapped her arm around the attacking limb, locking up the man's elbow hard enough to hear and feel bone splinter and bend. He yowled like a man catching his fingers in a car door. She punched him twice, face and balls, and he sagged. Collie released him and crushed his chest with a front kick, sending him pinwheeling backward into the hall, his broken arm waving like a rag, until the wall stopped his momentum.

In the tub, Puncher crawled back into the fight, nose and lower lips coated in blood blacker than crude oil. Collie grabbed the back of his head, simultaneously motoring her knee into his face. The delicate facial bones squished, and Puncher dropped into the tub alongside a squealing Jimbo.

A man stood just outside the doorway, pointing a twelve gauge.

Collie ducked as the gun went off, feeling hot shot shred away a layer of cloth and skin. She bounced over Righty, writhing on the threshold, and zeroed in on shotgun guy outside the bathroom. Shotgun saw her coming and withdrew in fright as if she was the living plague. He swatted her shoulder with the barrel of his weapon, but Collie was on him, grabbing his testicles and twisting as if she'd gotten ahold of fat party snappers. Paralyzed, Shotgun collapsed.

Knife. Flashing. *Left.*

The woman stabbed a hunter's blade toward Collie, aiming for ribs or a kidney. Collie swept her arm outward while moving toward the docile Shotgun, knocking the weapon aside. Collie followed through, her striking arm slowed by coming into contact with the wall. Still, when her punch connected, it was more than enough to almost twist the female's head off her shoulders. The knife attacker went down, and another man roared into the room. Collie hooked an arm under one of his, twisted, and hip-tossed him toward the open pit. He screamed as his ass landed on the edge, not quite enough to tip him over.

A quick boot to the head solved that.

He went over like a drunken freighter being sucked down by the Atlantic, fingers clawing at the carpet, then the edge, before disappearing. Then he began to truly sing.

Collie spun around, crouched over and scanning for others.

One final man stood in the hallway, beneath several smoldering air fresheners, looking as if he'd downed an entire milkshake of "holy fuck" and discovered it not at all to his liking. He held a cheap survival knife and could tell he was overmatched. Wavering between fleeing or fighting, he backed up against the opposite door.

Dirty hands grabbed his face, and fingers hooked into his eyes and mouth, clawing a scream from their victim. Blood burst from an eye socket, dark in the dismal light.

Collie snatched up a fallen shotgun, pumped it, and stepped into the corridor while shrieks and curses erupted from the pit behind her. The tactical shield lay against a wall, pushed aside after the grenade had gone off. Seeing the coast clear, she turned and whipped the wooden stock into the last gang member's unprepared gut. The blow crippled him, and he fell to the floor, slipping free of the hands clawing his face.

A bullet hole magically appeared in the wall in a puff of dust, and Collie whirled around.

Crouching was Lefty, partially recovered, aiming a Sig Sauer he'd picked up from the floor. He fired again, and the bullet passed close enough that the wind made her blink. She fired the shotgun from the hip, ejector spitting a blue casing off to the side. The blast yanked Lefty from his crouch and splattered him across the pink of the porcelain toilet. He oozed into the gap between tub and shitter and stayed there.

Collie whirled toward Righty, still on the floor.

His hands came up to protect his face. "Don't kill—"

But Collie did anyway.

When the sound of the second shot died away, replaced by the screaming from the pit and the retching of Jimbo in the tub, Collie checked on the other fallen gang members.

Then she wrestled with the bars sealing the door across the hall, pulled them back, and freed a wary group of men and women in their twenties or older, who appeared to have been starved, beaten, and broken—all except one tall, balding fellow who looked both menacing and grateful. Collie noted that blood covered his fingernails.

"You folks okay?" she asked him as faces peeked around his frame.

"We are now."

"What's your name?"

That momentarily dispelled the cold wrath from his face, and he looked her in the eye. "Phil."

"Watch these two for me, will ya, Phil?" she gestured toward the one guy still holding his nuts and the woman sitting up and test-flexing her jaw.

"We will," and the wrath returned like thunderheads smothering the sun. Collie wasn't a hundred percent sold on old Phil just yet, so she kept the shotgun handy until she tramped across the red bathroom floor and picked up her sidearm. Holstering the weapon, she shot warning glances at the two surviving members and walked down the hall, checking every open door and clearing every possible nook and cranny while, behind her, the screaming lessened. Bodies of the ones she'd killed earlier lay on the carpet, bled out and staring in some cases.

She reached the stairwell leading to the ground floor in time to hear a door slamming and to smell a breath of fresh air. Collie eased back, taking a low position and aiming at the space where a head and torso would appear below. Footsteps charged the stairs and took them two at a time.

The guy had a bald head and a thick but ratty beard. Gus.

He spun on the landing, saw the pointed shotgun, and immediately ducked.

"Relax, relax," Collie called out, lowering her weapon.

"Christ," a visibly shaken Gus panted and leaned against a wall for support. He glared at her before settling down, struggling to catch his breath. Collie smiled back, feeling a twitch of something she probably shouldn't, and switched her thoughts to Wallace's whereabouts.

"You kill them all?" Gus asked.

"Only the ones who tried to kill me."

"Yeah? How many was that?"

"Almost all, I figure. You see any on your way in?"

"No."

"Where's Wallace?"

"He's comin'. Sent me on ahead. His legs . . ." Gus shook his head doubtfully. "He's havin' trouble. I know he is."

I know he is too. She knew full well her man was hiding much more about his day-to-day self than she could scry. She knew where it was all going, knew there wasn't anything any of them could do, but God as her witness, she couldn't consider a future without Ollie by her side or at her back.

She peered up and down the corridor.

"Stinks," Gus said.

"Yeah. You won't believe what they—"

A blast of shrieks and curses erupted from the direction of the freed prisoners. Figures cluttered the entrance to the play pen. The ends of a ladder lay on the carpeted floor, just between feet and ankles.

An uneasy chord shivered within Collie.

They *wouldn't*.

But they just might . . .

"The fuck's that?" Gus asked, but Collie was already double-timing it toward the collection of people, hopping over carcasses. The women and men fearfully parted for her, all in all, about a dozen. Collie turned the corner in time to see five other men releasing a pair of ankles. No other gang member was in sight.

They'd been fed to the pit.

The men stood back, dirty and hairy, with hollowed cheeks and with hooded eyes watching her reaction. Collie regarded each of them in turn and said nothing, knowing full well whatever they did, they did as a final retribution for whatever physical and mental pain had been inflicted upon them all. The pit thrashed and boiled, and one unlucky gang guy was trying to hoist himself up on the far-off perch Jimbo, peeking out from the bathroom, had once occupied. When Collie met his eyes, he quietly handed over her balaclava, which she took in a fist.

In the pit, three people struggled, up to their knees in biting heads, thrashing against the nightmarish sludge. They pushed, but they might as well have tried to shove back quicksand. One guy, perhaps the first one she had kicked in, bled from a number of bites that revealed cheekbones and scalp.

The woman looked up at Collie with red-rimmed eyes, shaking fingers nipped between a skull's teeth. "Help us!"

Collie considered it and decided to grant her wish.

She shot the woman and one man with the shotgun before the weapon emptied. She used her pistol on the last.

It didn't surprise her that he choked out a *thank-you* before he died.

And sank below the heads.

<h1 style="text-align:center">33</h1>

The survivors descended to the first floor to a large common area designated as the gang's mess hall. A connected room was surprisingly well stocked with foodstuffs. Half of the food appeared to have come from the RVs, but neither Collie nor Gus mentioned that. Collie, still unmasked, told the famished ex-captives to get whatever they wanted from the larder and eat their fill. With that kind of freedom, Gus wasn't sure what he was about to see, but he was surprised that the men and women sat quietly at two rectangular tables, displaying subdued table manners.

"In shock," Collie said out of the corner of her mouth, watching them from a doorway. "Probably don't know what we're going to do either but mostly in shock."

"What *are* we going to do?" Gus asked.

She shrugged. "Feed them. See what's left in the tanks, and head back to Pine Cove. That's our little town. I'll ask them if they want to come along and start over once they're finished eating. Maybe we'll even stay here for the night. If they want."

"Why wouldn't they?"

"Bad memories." Collie eyed the ceiling as if it might collapse. "But anyway, we'll have to go back. Sorry, Gus, but the search for Maggie and the kids will have to be delayed for a bit. Much as I hate to, after this banquet, we'll need to replenish our own supplies before we can head out again."

Gus studied each of their faces. "This all of them?"

"Yep. Don't see your doctor and kids?"

"No . . . How far away is Pine Cove?"

"About a day and a bit. A steady drive if we don't have any distractions. It's on Chaleur Bay. New Brunswick. An hour away from Bathurst."

The one called Jimbo—Jim—eased past, and Collie caught him by the arm. She indicated Gus should speak to him.

"Uh, you guys didn't happen to have an older lady named Maggie here? And a couple of kids named Becky and Chad?"

"No," Jim answered quickly, as if he'd been bad somehow. Collie released him and nodded thanks. Jim went to the table and sat down beside Phil. The older man hunkered over a plate and a portion of cured meat that might have been deer while dipping into a Mason jar filled with purple beets. As he chewed, he stared off into space.

"Come on." Collie pulled away from the mess hall. "Let's check on Ollie. Then the RVs."

Phil stood then, quieting an already reflective crowd of a little over a dozen people. Faces regarded him as he cleared his throat. He eyed Collie, who paused in the doorway, and gave an appreciative dip of his square jaw.

He addressed Collie. "You saved us this day. For months on end, we've lived . . . under the whim of those butchers you executed. Have no remorse for any of them. They tortured, tormented, played with and abused, raped, and killed at leisure. There were over forty people in this town before they came along. Forty. This"—he gestured toward the sitting people—"is all that's left. On their behalf, thank you. For this."

Collie smiled, her scars and ruined nose oddly appealing in the dim light of the hall, and Gus had to tell himself once again she was a married woman.

"You feel like sleeping in here tonight?"

Phil didn't answer right away, and for a moment, a sensation of solemnity descended upon the room.

"If it's all the same to you, miss . . . some of us might very well return to our homes. Unless there's a danger in that?"

"None that I know of," Collie said, "except the chance of another gang coming through here like before. If you do, be careful. Lock your doors. Keep any firearms loaded."

Phil became pensive.

"In the morning," Collie continued softly, "we'll talk about what you folks want to do. We're from a little community in New Brunswick. There's food, water, and homes. Bunch of people living off the land like the old, old days. It's safe and a gathering place for any who want to carry on . . . the best way possible."

The older man listened but showed no indication of approval or disapproval. Gus supposed trust was a rare commodity around there, considering what Phil and the other people had lived through. It might take a while for them to trust folks, even after being saved. He could understand that.

"If it's all the same to you, give us a little time, and we'll consider your offer," Phil finally answered.

Collie and Gus left them.

"You think they'll come along?" he asked as they walked to the lobby.

"Who knows? This is their town, they said. Let's see where Ollie is. And our machines."

They exited the building and approached the RVs. At a glance, the vehicles appeared in fine shape. A few seconds later, Collie broke into a relieved smile and pointed.

There, sauntering up the road like a geriatric gunslinger, was Wallace.

"He doesn't look good," Gus muttered.

"He can read lips."

That mortified him. "What? Shit."

"Don't worry about it," she said and yelled, "You got your swagger back."

Wallace took his time in replying. "You should see me from behind."

Collie smirked.

The afflicted soldier walked toward them, missing the metallic groans and squeaks that sprang to mind. The smell hanging around Wallace preceded him, making Gus screw up his nose and shake his head. Wallace's condition usually just freaked him out, but seeing the soldier walk along as if someone had nailed spikes into every joint made it difficult not to feel sorry for the dying man.

"You made it." Wallace stopped and inspected his companions. "Any trouble?"

"Only bad luck," Collie reported.

"The civvie backed you up?"

Collie's smile broke out again. "About that. Why'd you send a civvie to back me up?"

"Look at me. I wasn't getting there anytime soon. I'm not much good for anything these days, Collie, so I sent the next handiest thing."

"Don't do it again."

"The civvie do something?"

"Hey," Gus interrupted. "I'm getting a little tired of being called a fuckin' *civvie* all the time. If you're going to give me a nickname, call me Uncle Jack."

"That's a shitty nickname," Collie pointed out.

"And you don't get to choose your fuckin' name," Wallace added curtly.

"The civvie didn't do anything," Collie said, drawing a betrayed look from Gus.

"Then what's he bawling about?"

"Hey," Gus stepped in, "both of you, but especially you, meat stick. Let's be clear. I got by perfectly well on my own for *years* before either of you showed up."

"You were lucky we did show up," Wallace said.

"Well, yeah . . . I'm talking about *before* then."

Wallace regarded Collie. "So what happened? Do I get a report?"

She wasn't smiling anymore. "About a dozen bad guys. All taken down. Holding another dozen or so locals here, against their will. Same story as usual. Savages move in, set themselves up as kings and queens, and make life miserable for the rest. Bad guys were the standard dickheads—all bad intentions but no training."

Wallace noticed the back of her singed combat fatigues. "You're going to need a new dress."

"I have spares."

"Good to see you made it."

"You too," Collie said with a barely detectable twinge in her voice that Gus couldn't identify.

"You give these survivors the speech yet?"

"Yeah. They'll think about it."

The visor didn't waver as he absorbed that information, then he regarded the pair of motor homes. "Let's check these puppies out."

Surprisingly, the motor homes remained the same after having been stolen. The interiors, while smelling of spilled alcohol, had hardly been touched. The food stores had been depleted, but Collie and Gus knew where it had all gone. A lot of the alcohol was missing as well, but nothing had been damaged, and nothing was grotesquely out of place. Even the pickup truck and portable motor had been left alone.

"They had plans for these rigs," Collie said when they reconvened in front of one motor home's silver grill.

"I'm surprised, to tell the truth," Wallace added, studying the motel and the boarded-up windows on the first floor. "Not a bad setup."

"You said something about that when you got me out of trouble," Gus said.

"I did."

"Well, you want to elaborate some? Cause right now, you sound like you're admiring them or something."

"He's right," Collie added. "You're sounding like a dick."

Wallace became reflective. "You have to admire these folks. Say what you will about them, they're survivors, doing whatever they can with whatever they got. For us, we've had extreme environment training. We can survive for days in the Arctic Circle. A forest is a banquet compared to what we've experienced. The apocalypse isn't such a great jump for us since all the material is still around, albeit growing older by the day. These people didn't have any training, probably very little preparation, and here they are, doing what they could in the most favorable places and surviving—until they were attacked and subjugated by a superior force. If that hadn't happened, they could've gone right on living, with effort. That river behind us provides fresh water. Barricade the motel's lower level, set up watches on the roof, and be mindful of your supplies until you're able to grow your own. This far north, plenty of game. Good job. Very good job."

"Until the savages came along," Gus said.

"Yeah." Wallace turned the visor on him. "That's the law of the land. I don't condone it. I deal with it . . . with deadly force. Out here, we're judge and jury. Sometimes, the cases are straightforward and easy to pass judgment on. We haven't come across any yet in a gray area, and I hope we don't."

The conversation died then, and Gus thought about what Wallace had just said. He'd heard a similar story from Adam, of all people, back when Gus was the appointed sheriff for the farm.

"We having drinks tonight?" Wallace asked.

"I think so," Collie said.

"Drinks?" Gus asked.

"Drinks." She unleashed the full, frightening power of her blue eyes upon him. "Tonight. You, me, and him."

"I—"

"No *I*'s tonight. Only us. And we drink to celebrate the successful completion of an operation. I think the area's secure enough. Ollie?"

"I'll take first watch, anyway."

"You never did this when you rescued me," Gus pointed out.

"Sure we did. You were passed out, is all. So you're in."

A drink. Or possibly even drinks. He shouldn't. Lord knew what Maggie and the kids were being subjected to. But after the events of the day, hell, the *week*, it was a wonder he wasn't already tits up in a bottle.

Jesus, was he really considering it? After so long?

Then he remembered Ricky and Dwight, and his resistance crumbled. He'd been a good boy up until that one traumatic episode.

One night. A few drinks. Just to take the edge off . . . just a little.

"Yeah. I'm in."

Night closed in around the little community, and the motel became a monstrous black mausoleum keeping its secrets tight to its heart. Gus lugged out a table and three chairs from the motel and plunked them down at the side of Collie's motor home, near the rear so they'd have a good view of the bridge and the highway leading off into the hills. Collie went inside and brought out two bottles of a whiskey blend called Nikka, a brand Gus wasn't familiar with. Coffee mugs got set up on the table, before each drinker. Lit candles stuck into beer bottles gently fended off the dark and were reflected eerily in Wallace's visor, pushed back on his helmet. Gus tried not to stare at the man, thankful for the dimness. Wallace's face appeared as if he'd slept on a block of ice.

The sound of pouring whiskey diverted his attention. Collie allowed three fingers into each mug before setting the Nikka bottle on the table.

Gus took the mug, eyeing the contents as if he could foresee the future. He sniffed it, inhaling the rich scent as if Bacchus himself had brewed the drink.

The last twenty months or so of alcoholic abstinence seemed to hit him all at once. Gus supposed he'd had a good run. He could probably excuse himself, set the whiskey down, and explain how he'd once drunk to armor his senses, to stay sane, and in the end, to kill himself. But, in the end, Gus knew he wasn't an alcoholic—not anymore. He also knew he could use a shot of whiskey right then, even if it meant throwing away all that accumulated sobriety.

Even if it felt like jumping blindfolded into a pit.

Go on, a voice whispered. *You need it. Earned it.*

Wasn't that the truth?

Gus held the mug and noted that the others hadn't drunk theirs yet. They were waiting for him. Nikka whiskey. It wasn't Uncle Jack, but it would do.

"You okay?" Collie asked.

"Yeah."

"Mud in yer eye," she toasted.

"Shit in yer boot," Gus replied without thinking, drawing a look of wrinkled puzzlement from the dead man on his right.

They drank.

The Nikka made Gus gasp. A rye-blended comet shot down his throat and crashlanded in his belly. Heat rippled outward, awakening his body like a bear being poked awake from a midwinter hibernation. Gus didn't wince at the taste, didn't hitch, but laid the drink back down on the table and looked around.

"Good," he whispered. And it was. Too damn good.

He glanced around, fearful of having downed the whiskey too fast, and spotted a few people leaving the motel.

Collie followed his eyes. "Going back home, I guess."

"Should I call them over?" Gus asked.

"No," Collie answered. "Not right now. People don't respond well to Ollie's condition."

Gus could believe it.

"How's the shot?" she asked, changing the subject.

"Good." Gus took a breath to settle his nerves, amazed the whiskey still went down like water. "It's not Uncle Jack or Captain Morgan, but . . . it'll do."

"This is for special occasions," Collie revealed. "It's a Japanese brand. And once they're gone, well, they're gone. Unless I get my ass to Japan, which I doubt will happen."

Wallace held his mug in both hands, studying the drink.

"You okay?" she asked him.

"Yeah," he said as if coming out of a dream. "Just savoring it."

"You looked like you were thinking."

"I was. Thinking that someone will have to set up a still. All the alcohol in the world is now the only stuff left on the planet."

Gus took another drink.

"You like it?" Collie asked him, leaving Wallace to his deep, sobering thoughts. Sobering thoughts weren't scheduled that night. Gus could smell that fact as clearly as the whiskey in his mug.

"I do. It's good."

They finished the first round, not rushing things, and another was poured. Collie then gave a full recounting of what had happened inside the motel and the house on the other side of the river. She described the fight in the play pen and how the gang tossed a grenade through the slot, hoping to kill her.

"Where'd they get the grenade?" Gus's body was laughing at the night's cold as Collie got around to pouring the third round of the evening. He had to slow down, having already guzzled the second shot far too quickly. If the others noticed, they didn't say anything.

"Anywhere," Collie reported. "When the world went to hell, all sorts of illegal weaponry started appearing. The automatic and explosive kind. Maybe souvenirs. Maybe ordered online. Maybe even from a dead soldier. Sometimes trucks carrying munition supplies went missing. Any of them could have gone off the road and been found by scavengers. Same thing might have happened to any of the military bases. It's interesting you haven't come across anyone not having big guns."

"It is," Gus supposed, remembering the gang that had assaulted his mountain abode.

"Scary thing? There are probably caches of missing weapons and ammunition all over the place. Troop emplacements might have been overrun, personnel killed or turned. If the weapons got dropped, well, by now they're useless. The ammunition is another matter. The challenge is finding it."

"Yeah, you said that before." Gus eyed the bottle. The rye was tasting far better than it should. "Play pen."

"Sick, eh?" Collie asked.

"Sick."

"But not the sickest."

The conversation went into horror-story mode as Collie and Wallace took turns—Wallace's turns were more like memory prompts for Collie—recalling the types of individuals who had survived the zombies but had crossed a line somewhere, going from survivalist to killer.

"To warlord," Collie finished, draining her drink before reaching for the bottle. When she did, Gus motioned to be refilled.

"Holy shit, you finished that already?"

"No," Gus said innocently before adding, "Maybe."

For the first time, Wallace seemed to have a genuine smile on his face.

Collie poured Gus another. "Nurse this one, okay? Stop chugging the shit. There isn't much of it left in the world."

"You said. But god*damn,* you got plenty on the table here."

"You did bring out two bottles," Wallace pointed out.

"I didn't know we were in the presence of an Olympic-level boozer," Collie protested, chuckling, the sound pure.

"You don't know half of it," Gus said, debating whether to tell them of how he tried to kill himself with the bottle. He figured that would put too much of a damper on the evening, and he was smiling for the first time in a while. The search for Maggie and the kids would resume tomorrow, but right then, after all he'd seen and lived through, the frights he'd endured, he needed a few good shots of merriment.

"This stuff's smooth."

"The Japanese know how to make whiskey."

They talked on, until the cloud cover split overhead, and the stars made a quiet but brilliant appearance. By then, the cold didn't touch any of them, and they dared gravity by leaning back and taking in the grandeur above their heads. The candle in the beer bottles, already replaced twice during the drinking session, died and wasn't relit. The bottle of Nikka ended, and a shitfaced Collie pleasantly gathered up the empty, saluted it, and grabbed the remaining full one.

"Where you goin' with that?" Gus asked in drunken wonder.

"This one is for next time."

"But you said you had another one for next time."

"*That* one is for the time after next," Collie said. "Yeesh. Slow down there, Gussy. Spare this child. Anyway, you sleepin' with me tonight?"

The question stabbed a bolt of mortification through Gus, and he sat as if whacked with a bat.

"Excuse me?" he finally got out.

"The RV, you perv. You sleeping in my Winny or his?"

"Uh . . ."

"Yours," Wallace said, not nearly as drunk as Gus would have thought, and despite the soldier smiling and such, it dawned on him that perhaps booze didn't affect Wallace as it might, well, an ordinary person.

"I don't want him pukin' in my place. Smells bad enough because of my ass anyway."

"You, then," Gus said meekly.

"Later, buster." Collie winked at him. "And stop scratching at your bird. Jesus Christ, let the little fella breathe."

That slackened Gus's face as if he'd been zapped with a defibrillator. His free hand, the one secretly courting his crotch for most of the evening, went into hiding.

"You heard me," Collie warned and then told Wallace, "Later, bruiser."

"Later, baby girl."

That put a smile on her face, and she did something that saddened Gus even though he knew she was married to Wallace. She got up, leaned over, and kissed her man. Sick though he did appear, she planted the softest kiss on his pallid cheek.

Then she struck her chair as she turned toward her door but caught it before it could fall over. Collie moved like a phantom against the dreamy white hide of the motor home, and as Gus watched, she became two dimensional and slipped through the crack of the side entrance.

"Where'd you meet her?" Gus asked Wallace after she'd retired.

"Training camp."

"Yeah. What kind?"

"The kind where they teach you to kill with your thumbs."

Gus had nothing after that. He pulled his coat a little tighter.

"Thanks for going after her when you did," Wallace finally said.

"I didn't do anything."

"No. But . . . you didn't hesitate," he pointed out. "I said go, and you went. That counts. With me, it counts. And don't worry about the whiskey."

Gus didn't understand what he meant by that, and it showed on his face.

"Hold on." Wallace got up, exceedingly stable for a man who'd just downed a third of a very tall bottle, and walked—amazingly steadily—to his RV.

The night shimmered. Gus sat at the table, listening. A door opened, but he heard little else as he marveled at how beautiful the sky had become. For a while, time ceased being a human measure. The tinkling of another bottle of Nikka being set down canceled the spell. A helmetless Wallace, skull-smiling, sat down with the barest of breezes blowing past his near-apparitional form.

"Jesus," Gus blurted. "You can be goddamn frightening."

Wallace didn't respond.

"Nice night," Gus said cautiously, feeling much more rode upon the wind. He inspected the short black ridge of hair covering the soldier's scalp. It reminded him of an exceptionally thick paint roller.

Wallace sat with that dead smirk on his face, as if he'd just heard an amusing joke. His eyes didn't appear the healthiest either, like the film forming over an opened can of eggshell white.

"Uh, you okay?"

"Don't I look okay?"

"Look, man, this is the drunkest I've been in"—he glanced at his wrist for no particular reason—"in a while. And that's coming from a dried-out drunk. Not that I see myself as a drunk. More like . . . okay, I'm a drunk."

"I don't care. Call yourself whatever you want."

"Cool."

Gus swallowed another shot of whiskey, feeling it light up his insides, but he eyed Wallace over the slender neck of the new bottle, thinking it not entirely wise to take his attention off the spooky special operator. Not that late at night.

Wallace reached for the bottle and poured himself a fresh one four fingers deep. It was a sizeable wallop that brought Gus almost back to the brink of sobriety. When he finished pouring the killer shot, Wallace carefully placed the bottle back on the table, picked the mug up, and saluted.

"*Za tvoyo zdorovie.*"

Gus hesitated with his drink. "What'cha say about my mom?"

The amusement on Wallace's face dulled. "That's a toast."

"Next time, say something I understand then."

"You've never heard *Za tvoyo zdorovie* before?"

"Nope."

"You're something else."

"Might be something else, but I say what I mean. Most the time."

They drank. Gus bared teeth at the gulp. Then he settled in and studied Wallace at length, ignoring the frown on the other's face.

"What?" Wallace finally asked.

"Never seen you before with your helmet off. Or visor up, for that matter."

"The helmet stays on to protect my head. The visor, well, the sun hurts my eyes. Used to hurt it, anyway. Not so sure if I'd feel anything at all now. Not after stabbing myself."

"What was that all about, anyway?"

Wallace shrugged. "When you realize you're not feeling anything, you test yourself. Though I might not have shown it, I was feeling just a pinch of anxiety at the time."

"You fooled me."

"Don't think it would take much to fool you."

Gus thought of long-dead Roxanne and decided to let that one go. "So you don't feel any pain at all now."

Wallace shook his head and listened to the night.

Gus did the same, ears buzzing in the total absence of sound. Collie had already crashed inside her motor home, and no one else in town seemed alive. That left only Gus and Wallace, who leaned forward in a subtle shifting of cloth, fingers tightening about his mug.

"Not a thing," he whispered. "I could . . . I could stab myself right here—right this very instant—and not feel a goddamn thing."

Anyone else might have spoken those words with at least a touch of fear, of desperation, but not Wallace. The admission nearly ruined Gus's growing buzz.

"I'm telling you this because . . . I need to tell someone. Someone not Collie."

Gus felt his stomach flutter at the sound of her name. "And that's me."

"Right now, that's you." Wallace watched him with those darkly luminous eyes. "If I told her, she'd worry. Maybe even freak out. I don't need to see that, but I have to confide in someone. And you owe me."

"I do?"

"For saving your ass. Back when you were hanging out like a slab of meat."

Ah. Wallace had him there. "Collie too, for that matter."

"Just listen," the soldier said to silence him. "I'm not sure how long I have. You understand? I'm not sure how long it'll take before I go full-on zombie, okay? It's going to happen. Almost happened the other day back in that house, just before the grenades came through the window. If Collie hadn't have yelled at me, I think . . . no, I *know* I would've dropped down on my knees and started eating. She yanked me back from doing a very bad thing. And if I started . . . I wouldn't have stopped. Pretty sure of that. She brought me back, and I managed to control that . . . that urge. But it'll happen again. I feel it coming. In the not-too-distant future too. I'll cross over. When I do, and if you're there, save Collie the job of putting me down, okay? You finish me. The moment you hear a moan leave my lips, and I don't respond to questions, you put a bullet in my head. I'd ask you to do it now, but . . ."

Wallace didn't finish the sentence.

Gus prodded. "But what?"

Those dying eyes regarded him, and that cold smile thawed as if touched by warm flesh. "I don't want to leave her just yet."

Though Wallace might not feel any physical pain, *anyone* could detect the emotional hell twisting the soldier round and round inside.

"I can do that," Gus said, not feeling good at all. "If I can, when the time comes. I'll . . . finish it?"

That pleased Wallace, and he nodded. "She's second to none," he continued. "A professional through and through. A woman and . . . and a wife on top of all of that. You know how we were married? At Whitecap? No church service for us—I snuck into her quarters and got into the bed beside her, and you know what she said? 'Would you marry me?' I said, 'Here?' and she . . . she said, 'Yeah, right here, right now.' I said, 'Don't we need an official for that? To make it legal and binding?' And she said every engagement we'd ever fought in, every life we'd ever rescued on a mission, every life we'd ever taken—and we took our goddamn share and then some—was legal and binding. For better or worse. So we made our vows right there. And we didn't need anyone sanctioning it, didn't need any blessing, and sure as hell didn't need a cere-mony. Then she went on about wolves and how they mate. So that was that. We mar-ried each other in her room. In the dark. On just a few simple words that, to this day, are as hard as tempered steel."

The story definitely threatened to ruin Gus's buzz.

And Wallace wasn't finished.

"Listen," he kept on. "I want you to do something else for me. I . . . I don't know how this is going to end, but I'm betting it won't be the way I want it. Never is. The final . . . transition will be a walking corpse, and if past behavior is any indication, I won't realize it's happening at all. My mind will already be gone. So, do me a favor. She'd kill me for saying this, but watch her back, okay? Take . . . take care of her, and she'll . . . she'll take care of you. She's that kind of person. But she's not invincible, so watch her back. Do that for me, okay? When I'm finally gone."

Gus rolled his head on his shoulders in a disbelieving *fuck me* kind of way, not lik-ing the spot he was in or the promise Wallace demanded. Even just speaking of Col-lie in his presence made him feel uncomfortable.

"All right," Gus finally said in a somber tone. "Don't worry about it."

"And one more thing . . ." Wallace began.

"Jesus, how many things do I owe you?" Gus blurted.

"Just one more."

Gus stared at Wallace across the table. "What is it?"

"You sure?"

"Yeah, I'm sure. But no more after this one. That's it. So . . . out with it."

"If you can . . . bury me."

"Bury you?" he asked dubiously.

"Yeah."

"That's probably the easiest one yet."

"I'm serious."

Gus drained his drink, shivered, and reached for the bottle. "Okay. Done. I'll do all that and bury your ass too. Anything else?"

Wallace thought about it. "No. Nothing. Just being buried by people is something. All the missions I ever went on, there was always a risk of not coming back home—dying out there, in secret—of my family never knowing how I went down, you understand. Maybe they'd even bury an empty box with a flag on it. Nowadays, a proper burial is . . . precious. I don't want to be left rotting in the sun. Do it right and return me to the earth. Okay?"

A proper burial is precious. The sentiment echoed in Gus's mind, reminding him of Adam and the others back on the farm.

Wallace noticed his silence. "Believe me, if I could do it myself, I would."

Gus had no response to that.

"You *owe* me," Wallace reminded him with ominous sincerity. "And besides . . ." His expression sagged.

"Besides what?" Gus asked.

"I got no one else to ask."

That frank admission locked Gus into agreement. "All right. Done. If I can, I will."

"Then we're good." Wallace held out his drink.

"One thing," Gus said before tapping mugs. "To make your . . . requests official and all."

"What's that?"

Gus took a breath and stared the dying man in the eye. "Stop callin' me fuckin' *civvie.*"

34

In the morning, the people of the roadside town came forth from their devastated homes. They bore suitcases and long, solemn faces. Gus watched them as he endured a lava flow of guilt of having broken his dry spell. A wicked hangover accompanied his self-reproach, the first in a very long time and an artillery shell right between his ears. He studied the people with a pained grimace. He could tell the ones who'd cried during the night and who'd held it together. He hoped that, wherever Pine Cove was, it was as good as Collie made it sound.

Phil spoke for his people, and the old gentleman from this northern town politely requested that, if it was all the same to them, they'd like to go along to this new place Collie had spoken of.

The rest of the morning passed quickly as they loaded people and possessions into the massive rigs. Jim directed them to a shed behind the service station, containing a treasure trove of red gasoline containers. Collie stood beside Gus and Wallace as they topped off the tanks of the RVs and pickup before loading the remainder into the box.

"There's fourteen of these people," she reported as she placed the last gas container inside the box. "Five men, six women, and three teenagers."

Gus studied the people loading bags into the motor homes. "They're riding with Wallace?"

"No, unfortunately, there'd be too many questions and just a little bit of nervousness. Jim says he can drive the RV."

"You gettin' kicked out of your rig, Ollie?" Gus feigned shock.

"You don't get to call me Ollie," Wallace told him. "And, yeah, I'm getting kicked out of my rig—much as I hate it. No other way to transport all these people."

"He'll drive the pickup," Collie said.

"So we're heading back to Pine Cove?" Gus asked.

"That's right," Collie said, sticking her mask into a deep pants pocket. "Only an overnight detour. We'll drop these civvies off and get back to looking for your people in the morning. Sorry again, Gus."

"'Sokay," he answered and stepped back from the truck. Maggie, Becky, and Chad were still alive out there. One sidetrack wouldn't make a difference in his search, but it would make a difference to Phil and his people.

"We'll take the pickup," Wallace said, nodding at Gus to include him.

"We?"

"We. There a problem?"

"No. No, just surprised, is all." Concern was evident on Gus's face.

"You're become best buddies." Collie smirked. "The therapeutic magic of booze."

"Yeah," Gus said, off kilter.

"What's wrong?" Collie asked.

"Don't worry," Wallace shook his head at the man. "We'll drive with the windows down."

"Nothin's wrong," Gus answered brightly.

The little convoy hit the road just after ten thirty.

Gus nodded in and out of sleep as the moving vehicle rattled through the drabness of the countryside's colors. The residual hangover of the first buzz he'd experienced in a long time still scratched at his skull. The cavernous interior of the truck was comfortable—not quite as roomy as the old beast, but it wasn't a rolling coffin, and for that, Gus thanked the Lord above. Cold air flowed through a cracked open window, keeping Wallace's increasingly bad body odor from becoming too overpowering.

They took the lead in the motorcade, the RVs swelling at times in the side mirrors, shrinking at others. Highways became lineless, bursting asphalt strips where the world gnawed on the edges, leaving white kernels and crumbs. Trees grew up and linked overhead, speckling the ground in early winter light. Decapitated signs made Gus wonder dreamily where the hell they were heading. Ghost towns appeared in the blazing periphery, allowing themselves to be glimpsed only for a few seconds before disappearing. Gus saw all this in timeless, dreamy intervals when he cracked open an eye. He glanced over at Wallace once, but the nightmarish soldier was simply driving on with grim determination, visor lowered, grin in place, both hands gripping the wheel. A name came to Gus's sleepy, pain-wracked mind, but he didn't dare say it, for fear of bad dreams . . . or bad luck.

Sleep pulled him down, and Gus knew no more.

Numbness rushed over the JTF-2 operator's hands and legs as Gus's snoring flipped a switch in Wallace's mind. He glanced over at his passenger, sleeping, mouth slightly opened. Wallace didn't see a tattered beard or balding crown. He didn't see the scarring. All he saw, he realized with dawning horror, was a sleeping man—a defenseless man.

Wallace's attention flicked between the road and his passenger. His stomach clenched, the first time ever, and a pang of hunger so alarming seized him, leaving him dizzy. His jaws ached, and he opened them, stretching them to their fullest like dogs testing their leashes. The road mesmerized Wallace. Colors streaked by at light speed. His heart thumped, softly at first, but then revving up in an irregular tempo like a blown tire. That puzzled him. How could his heart be beating, be *racing,* at a time like that?

A slug of a tongue grazed his lips, and he realized he was salivating.

The road.

Stay on course.

Gus snored, wrenching Wallace's attention back to the sleeping man, whose face turned toward him and rattled along with the truck. A smell came from Gus, subtle yet familiar, tantalizing. The truck coasted to the right, and Wallace corrected the drift with a broken spring-snap of teeth. He had a problem. The cadence of his heart suddenly braked and slowed, which sent alarm signals to his brain. The lingering smell grew stronger. Each muffled drumbeat captivated him. He hadn't realized before, but there was something haunting about that organic rhythm. It unnerved him, and he cringed every time he heard it, hoping each spaced-out beat would be the last.

Wallace corrected his driving again and scowled as the RVs came closer in his side mirrors, urging him onward. It occurred to him he could pull over and let them drive on by.

Long enough for . . .

Wallace set his jaw. *Long enough for what?*

Then fear seeped into his mind. He knew what was happening, as sure as his heart throbbed with mournful purpose. He knew with ravenous clarity.

He was going over.

The trees flashed by, light flickering through the overhead branches, dulled by his visor.

He recognized the smell haunting him.

Flesh.

Living flesh, beside him. His heart kept on pounding, an evil, nauseating sensation in his chest, an unpleasant, tempting drumroll. It boomed in his ears, urging him to *do* something, promising him if he just surrendered to that mounting craving, if he just quit denying himself, the transition wouldn't be that bad—not really.

Wallace stepped on the brake, decreased speed, and pulled over, allowing the others to drive on. He lowered his eyes as if studying the dashboard, in case Collie glanced his way with a question on her face. He waved a hand, and the motor homes rolled on by.

Gus kept on sleeping.

Boom.

His heart had become a primitive, solitary drum, and Wallace regarded his passenger's comfortable face—unconcerned, at peace, unaware.

Boom.

Wallace stretched his jaws to their maximum, yearning to bite, eyeing the sustenance just an arm's length away. Then he drifted, like a boat caught in a riptide, leaning toward the sleeping man on the passenger side until his seatbelt stopped him. Wallace pawed at the release button. A loud click resulted, and the seatbelt slithered away.

Boom.

His heart. His heart wasn't his at all. The organ called him, *insisting* he strike.

Boom.

Wallace winced, his jaws aching. A rumble started at the back of his throat, his *parched* throat. His hand rose, hooked into a claw, and poised to plunge into the sleeping face and rake the eyeballs from its head. The heart continued its gallows gonging in Wallace's ears. Every fiber of his being pushed, *commanded* him to pounce, to feast.

Wallace's hand trembled, his fingers curling in on themselves, creating a vengeful fist that hung in the air like an iron meteorite seized in a magnetic field.

The JTF-2 man closed his mouth, resisting the tractor pull of an easy meal. Wallace leaned back defiantly as every instinct howled at him to chew into that candy shell of a skull, to crack it open and pluck that headcheese free in fluffy clumps and devour it. He straightened, shaking with the massive battle between will and hunger. Gus's heart—Wallace once more recognized the man sitting next to him—still beat its tune, determined to summon the monster lurking within the special operator. Wallace drew back from that calling, tapping into a reserve of self-discipline he still possessed. He pressed back into his seat, defying the malefic craving infecting his person. Wallace reached out and placed one hand on the steering wheel, gripping its knurled curve in a stranglehold and holding on.

But Gus's heart kept calling.

A ferocious, final urge to bite rose within Wallace, surging through the shield of his resolve, demanding he chomp down and let the juices flow. He whined at the strength of the assault. The planetary force that assailed him was the strongest he'd ever experienced, and anyone else would have been instantly swept away.

Wallace was not, however—at least, not right away.

He shivered, trying to think about Collie. He tried thinking about past missions. Each memory stomped a foot down and pulled back, defying that monstrous impulse. He knuckled down and held on to the steering wheel, but the desire stayed, doubling in intensity. Wallace realized he was locked into a losing tug-of-war, where each passing microsecond was a foot sliding in wet sand, dragging him back toward a red line of no return.

Unless . . .

Wallace saw his own arms.

He lifted his left forearm to his mouth and ripped the cloth back from his wrist, exposing graying flesh.

Meat.

His resistance snapped like a steel cable stretched past its limit.

Wallace bit down hard.

Gus woke to the sound of chewing.

He opened his eyes and saw Wallace eating his own arm.

In a moment of sleep-drunken wakefulness, Gus believed he was in the middle of a nightmare until Wallace's visor turned ever so slightly in his direction, caught in the middle of one last round of mastication. Black juice covered his lower jaw, and when Wallace lowered his gnawed arm, shreds of skin and muscle tissue were revealed.

"Jesus Christ," Gus said in horror.

Then his brain crackled and flashed and came totally online, and he jerked away in his seat. The seatbelt restrained him, and for an insane flicker of time, he was divided between clawing at the release button and pulling out a pistol.

"Jesus Christ!"

Wallace spat out whatever occupied his mouth. The gob hit the stick shift with a wet, derisive smack.

"Jesus *Christ*! Oh, *Jesus Christ*!"

Gus heaved against the seatbelt and nearly exploded against the windshield and roof when a finger found the release button. He groped for the truck door. It opened, and Gus tumbled from the interior as if someone had yanked the door from the outside. Crushed stone and chunks of pavement sanded his palms, but he rolled over and crawled away from the truck at best speed, keeping his eyes on the swinging door, looking for that undead cockgobbler to come leaping out after him.

But Wallace didn't.

Gus didn't see a ditch behind him, but his left hand found the empty space. He steamed into it, fell over, tried to roll, and slammed his chin into hard-packed earth, cross-checked by gravity. The impact dazed him. He struggled through the sensation and stood, fumbling at one holster and unintentionally whipping the weapon far away to his right. Squealing, Gus got his hands on his second pistol and successfully pulled it free.

He pointed it at the truck's cab as the swinging door creaked closed.

"Wallace! You there?"

No answer.

"Wallace, you answer, or by fuck, I'll shoot you!"

Again, no answer. Gus stepped to his right and stuck his neck out, widening his field of vision. Wallace sat in the driver's seat, helmeted head resting against the upper curve of the steering wheel.

"Wallace!"

The soldier slowly plopped back against his seat as if recovering from a head-on collision. Black stains covered his mouth.

"You finished lunch in there?" Gus bawled.

Wallace's head and chest heaved, chuckling.

That response made Gus feel a little better. If Wallace had crossed over, the guy would be fighting to get out of the truck.

Gus walked closer and pulled open the passenger door, keeping its bulk before him as a shield. "You okay?"

Wallace didn't answer.

"C'mon man. Say something."

"Shoot me."

That put a frown on Gus's sickened face.

"You heard me." With an executioner's grace, Wallace reached up and pulled his helmet off, revealing black veins webbing his temple. Black worms pulsed underneath the surface of his pallid skin. He flopped back and indicated his head. "Blow it off. Right here."

He tapped his brainpan.

"Do it."

Gus took a calming breath and held it. "You're fine now."

Wallace rolled his head on his shoulders. "Now."

"What happened to you?"

"Came over me all at once. I . . . wanted to chew your face off. While you slept. An urge worse than a jacked-up nicotine craving—if you ever smoked, that is."

"No," Gus admitted. "Never."

"Doesn't matter. I can't do that again. Shoot me, and get it over with."

The command jolted Gus, leaving him hesitant to pull the trigger. He had killed in the past, in self-defense—or so he'd convinced himself—but never as an executioner. The gun wavered, heavy as lead.

Shoot me and get it over with, Wallace had said. He had *pleaded.*

"Do it," the stricken man grunted, opaque eyes narrowed to slits.

Gus shook his head and lifted the weapon, pointing it at the soldier's head and lining up the sights. "I—I can't. You saved my life."

"You'd be saving mine."

That didn't make it any easier.

"Remember what you said you'd do." Wallace made an effort to draw his lips over his teeth. "You remember."

"I can't. I can't."

A sad smile spread over Wallace's face. The sound of an approaching engine broke the tension. Gus and Wallace looked to see a Winnebago coming back up the road in slow, careful reverse. The white ass of the vehicle bobbed this way and that but stayed on the deserted stretch of highway. As jarring as it was to see the RV, it wasn't near the shocker of seeing Collie crouched on the roof and focused on the pair.

The scowl on her face was as mean as Gus had ever seen—and as lovely.

"Shit," Wallace muttered. "Can't catch a break."

Gus lowered the outstretched gun.

When it reached the truck, the Winnebago stopped with a squeal of brakes and exhaust. Collie stood up, her hand on her sidearm.

"What's going on?"

"Going on?" Gus repeated, at a loss before that furious countenance. *What's going on is your man just tried to bite my face off, and now I'm deciding if I should honor his request to put him down.* But he didn't say that. He just stood there like a deadhead with a red dot on its forehead.

"Nothing, Collie." Wallace came to the rescue. "No problem."

"I don't remember asking you a goddamn thing."

The ice in those words flash-froze Gus's balls and guts in one breathtaking instant, and he eyed Wallace nervously.

"Collie—"

"Shut the fuck up, Ollie," she barked. "Gus, answer my fucking question before I forget who you are and who I am."

Gus didn't want her to forget. "Uh, well. Ah, it's like . . ."

"Gus?"

"Yeah?"

"Before you continue, you just remember that was my husband you were pointing a weapon at."

With that, Collie drew her own.

"I told him to shoot me," Wallace said in his Zen tone. "Crazy bitch."

Collie returned her sidearm to its holster and stared off at the trees for a stabilizing moment.

Gus wasn't about to say shit until he was in the clear.

"Gus."

"Yeah?"

"You're good."

Thank Christ. "Thanks, Collie."

"Get aboard the RV."

Wallace and Gus exchanged looks.

"Don't look at that bastard," Collie warned. "Chances are I'll fucking murder him myself in the next few minutes. Get aboard the vehicle. And sorry for the tone of voice."

"'Sokay."

Gus glanced at Wallace again before doing as told. The glum look on Wallace's decomposing face said it all. He was in shit. He *knew* he was in shit, and Gus wondered what Collie would do with her husband. Maybe the special forces had training for situations like this.

"Gus, tell Jim to take you and drive on back to Phil. Then you wait. Wallace and I will be along shortly in the pickup. We'll take the lead from there. Got all that?"

"Yeah."

Collie's boots *pinged* on the rear ladder as she descended. Gus didn't dare look back at the pickup for fear of earning more of her wrath. He climbed aboard the motor home filled with wondering people. They regarded him, faces demanding updates, so he provided one.

"Collie says we drive on back to Phil. She and Wallace have a few things to work out."

"Wallace?" one of the middle-aged women asked. Gus had forgotten her name but noted her missing teeth. "That the one who's sick?"

"Yeah."

"He turn yet?"

"No," Gus said, the need to defend him flaring up. "He didn't turn."

"He will," the woman warned, her eyes looking at the road.

35

The little convoy stopped for the night in a gas-station parking lot, allowing the survivors to stretch their legs for a bit before returning to the relative safety of the motor homes. Collie appeared and gave curt instructions for the following day, and that was the only time Gus saw her. Wallace did not show at all. The operators had maintained a safe distance from them all since the roadside incident when Wallace had almost turned. Gus understood the reason for the separation. With Wallace being a question mark, keeping him away from everyone was wise.

The next morning, the RVs rolled onward.

Gus took a shift at the wheel, following the lead pickup and wondering what waited at Pine Cove. Conversation was low to nonexistent, and Gus didn't engage the survivors traveling with him. He knew as little as they did.

Signs heralded approaching towns like spoilers for a horror movie. If the folks riding with Gus had been quiet before, they were subdued by the sights of gutted homes and buildings, crashed vehicles, and the occasional sprinkling of yellowed bones on the wayside. Terrible battles had scraped these smaller towns off the map, leaving only piles of charred debris and wrecked property, evoking memories of Annapolis's fire-washed streets.

Gus hoped Maggie and the kids were alive.

The sky reddened into evening as the little convoy drove along Highway 17, eventually linking up with the 132, steadily bearing down on the coastal bastion known as Pine Cove. Collie drove along a battered strip of road that might have received extensive shelling at one time. Potholes and pits blotted the pavement while vehicles littered the shoulders. Some cars lay on their roofs, crunched to a third of their size. Others seemed to have been blown apart in spectacular fashion. Gus drove through the mess, spotting a naked and twisted chassis halfway up a tree that might have been napalmed at one time. The forest around that morbid badge had been ravaged by an unchecked blaze, leaving only blackened frames in a thick dew of ash. The entire strip might have been firebombed at one point, intentionally or perhaps accidentally. The chassis suggested someone had a twitchy missile finger.

The rescued folks hunkered down in the RVs, studying the morbid landscape with narrow-eyed sadness, all while the sun blazed a frigid red.

They all wondered where the soldiers were leading them.

Ahead, a single taillight flared to life as the pickup braked, forcing Gus to do the same.

Collie got out of the cab and walked back. He opened the window and stuck his head halfway out. "Yeah?"

"We're almost to Pine Cove," Collie said, all business, which made Gus go cold inside. "We'll lead you to the gate and let Spencer know you're okay."

"Who's Spencer?"

"The gate watch. You'll see. Some real forest up ahead. Not the horror show we went through today. Then it's through a big rock cut, through a hill. At the end will be a wall of piled car wrecks and a bus that serves as a gate. I'll do the talking, and after that, you're on your best behavior."

"Where are you guys going to be?"

"Good question," Collie shrugged, her scarred features showing emotional fatigue. "Wallace is going through a rough time right now. We're going to see it to the end, whichever end that might be. We'll return to Pine Cove when this is finished, one way or the other. Clear?"

"Clear. Yeah."

"All right. You're good, then." She turned to walk away.

"Collie."

That stopped her, and she glanced over her shoulder.

"I'm sorry."

"Yeah, for what?"

"Whatever it is I've done."

"You're fine, Gus. Wallace told me everything. I'm not mad at you. I'm just pissed at him. Just might seem otherwise. We're good. Just gotta get through the next couple of days. If that. Rough times on the horizon, y'know?"

"Okay." Gus felt shitty anyway and didn't understand why clearly, but he figured that when the time came for Wallace to die, Collie had decided if anyone was going to send him off, it would be her.

"And I just wish . . ." Collie started and paused, "we had a little more time together."

"Yeah."

"Later, Gussy."

"Yeah. Later."

Collie continued back to her pickup, and Gus watched her go.

"Tough lady," Phil muttered nearby.

"Toughest I know," Gus admitted.

Twenty minutes later, roller-coaster hills with sharp inclines loomed over both sides of the road. A thick forest covered those undulating peaks, darkened by the oncoming night. Gus hunkered over the steering wheel, minding the highway while sneaking looks at how high those little mountains rose. The road curved to the left and stabbed through the center of one of those tall mounds, through an impressive rock cut illuminated by headlights. Layers of dark stone passed by Gus's window, making him wonder how much explosive was used to split that particular hill and how many working hours it had taken to clear it. The end result, however, was a nearly perfect natural defense for Pine Cove. The undead would struggle with climbing those peaks.

"Been up here once," Phil disclosed. The older man had taken the passenger seat and was staring out at the towering landscape, his posture and profile reminiscent of a weathered sea captain. "Pine Cove's a small fishing town, kept going by a seasonal crab-processing plant. Mostly old folks like myself lived there. Young ones all went off to the cities or whatever. Nice place on the water. Or so I remember it that way."

"They sure as hell blew the shit outta this hill," Gus remarked. "If I didn't know better, I'd say we were in an open pit mine."

The taillights of Collie's pickup flashed red as it slowed and pulled over. Ahead of the truck, a wall of cars piled four deep blocked the road. A walkway bridged the roofs of the cars, shielded with slabs of scrap metal on either side of a main gate barring any further progress. The gate itself, higher than the cars, consisted of a quilt of sheet metal. The dull pattern reminded Gus of a poorly conceived chessboard with uneven squares.

Collie got out of her truck and about-faced, holding up her arms.

Gus lowered himself over the steering wheel once again and tried seeing the tops of the rock cut, wondering who she was trying to hail. He couldn't see anything but sheer cliff walls.

"Can't see shit," he said. "Walls are too close and high."

"It's a bottleneck," Phil said.

Gus cocked a curious eyebrow and regarded the older man.

"We're bringing home some goodies and good people," Collie shouted. "All aboard the motor homes. Wallace and I are heading out again, so be nice to the new folks."

With that, she lowered her arms, saluted at Gus, and climbed back aboard her vehicle. The road was just wide enough to perform a three-point turn, and as she drove by, she held up her hand once more. Wallace was a gloomy cadaver on the passenger side.

Then they were gone, vanishing around the bulk of the second motor home.

"Hey," Phil grunted, pulling Gus back from his side mirror.

Figures pulled themselves into view from atop the wall, revealing themselves from the chest up. Some carried rifles, and others had shotguns. Gus counted eight faces and felt his stomach knotting.

"Hey, you!" A man shouted from the wall, to the right of the gate. "Behind the wheel."

Phil gave Gus a "that's you" nod.

Gus rolled his eyes and lowered his window. He stuck his head out and yelled, "Yeah?"

"Where'd Collie go?"

"Ah," Gus hesitated. "Personal shit that couldn't wait."

"Personal shit?"

"Yeah, personal shit."

"Well, what was it?"

This perplexed Gus. "*Personal* shit, man. That's why it's *personal*. I can't tell you any more than that."

A few of the men and women on top of the wall exchanged worried glances. Gus figured this group was a tight one and no doubt knew about Wallace.

"Hold on, then," the man called back in a disappointed voice. He turned and waved, and a few seconds later, the sheet-metal center of the wall moved to one side. Gus had seen the same deal in *The Road Warrior*, but there wasn't room behind that barrier for a bus.

The people pushing the section came into view.

"Ah." *Mystery revealed.* Gus started up the RV.

"That's a tight fit," Phil observed.

"Looks like one," Gus agreed and put pressure on the accelerator. He drove through the opened slot, guiding the rig through as carefully as possible. The side mirror barely cleared the edge of the cars, but the rest slipped through the opening without problem.

"Not bad," Phil smiled.

"Not this time, anyway," Gus agreed, relieved he'd gotten the bulky vehicle through. A woman protected by a winter coat stood in the middle of the road, bathed in headlights. She beckoned him forward. The motor home stopped before her, and she stepped around to the side door and knocked. They allowed her in, and Gus saw she was around his age, attractive, with rusty-red hair. She studied them all with a critical eye before smiling.

"Welcome to Pine Cove," she said with a mild French accent.

Things happened quickly after that.

Under a full moon, a pair of locals guided the motorized behemoths past a thinning wilderness, where the road eventually opened into an easy slope lined with lanes and houses, all the way down to a shoreline and a seaside bay glittering with ripples. A deserted playground went by, as did a closed Mary Muffin shop. A service station along the road was actually servicing a car inside an open bay. A smattering of houses followed, their windows heavily boarded but with the top foot or so left open. Next were some shops with the fronts barricaded. A small square dominated the center of town with a statue of a sea-green fisherman pulling in full nets.

What surprised Gus most of all, however, were the people.

The townsfolk of Pine Cove slowed in their tracks and stared at the new arrivals. Some opened the front doors of their shops and stepped outside, marveling at the rigs. Children stopped with their parents or guardians and pointed. Gus figured at least a hundred watched the pair of motor homes roll by, as if they were grand floats in an early Christmas parade.

The attention made him smile.

The faces of Becky, Chad, and Maggie appeared in his mind, pleading, and Gus's mood darkened.

"There's so many," Phil commented.

Gus felt someone breathe on his bare head, so he glanced back to see four other survivors hunched around the redheaded Pine Cove woman, sizing up the new town. The lady who'd exhaled on him didn't register his fidgeting. He eventually parked the RV in the lot of a small motel, not fifty meters away from a volunteer fire department.

"This is it," the Redhead announced brightly. "Step on out and stretch your legs. Mind the cold. We have, uhhh, rooms for you all tonight. Who is the leader here?"

"He is," Phil rumbled immediately.

"I'm not the leader," Gus blurted. "I'm just the driver."

"You can talk for the rest of us," Phil said. "I—well, we all trust you."

Trust—a rare commodity, precious but misplaced. Collie had freed those people while Gus had only shown up after the fight and out of breath.

But Phil shut down those awkward thoughts by standing and shooing the others out the side door. An evening breeze laced with the unmistakable hint of salt water caught Gus's attention. That hooked him out of the driver's seat, and he paused only to get a crick out of his back and neck, eyeing the doorway.

"We'll get everyone situated for the night," the Redhead said, studying his face close up for the first time and faltering only for a second.

"Sounds good," Gus answered, letting the startled balk go. "And then?"

"We will see." She smiled, showing uneven teeth and radiating kindness.

Gus smiled back, tight-lipped. He looked at the scabbard with his retrieved bat just behind the driver's seat, even his pistols, but hesitated in picking any of his weapons up. "Ah," he chuckled, "old habits."

"Take them along if you like," the Redhead offered.

That placed Gus's mind at ease. He still had the knife in his boot. "'Sokay. I'll take the chance."

"My name is Marie," she said, holding out a hand.

"Gus," he said, taking it.

"More mouths to feed." Will Duffer scowled from his kitchen window while a burning candle shone through the lower-left corner of the glass.

"Ah, Christ," Jan Pierce lamented, shaking his head. He met the sullen gaze of Sally Fox, sitting on the other side of the table.

Her hand froze in turning the base of the whiskey bottle holding the one candle providing light. "The fuck are they doing, letting them in here?" Sally said in a voice usually sweetened in public. "Winter's here, for God's sake."

"Pisses me off," Will muttered and put his back to the window. He regarded his companions sitting at the bare table. They weren't really friends but rather locals who shared a harsh opinion about Pine Cove and the world beyond its sheltered borders: a cruel but face-slapping fact.

The town could support only so many people.

And every new body lessened the portions of everyone else who had slaved and worked and blistered their hands and feet working the fields or had fished the bay in the summer heat.

It wasn't fair. Or sustainable.

"I'm going to take Minglewood aside tomorrow and have that second talk," Jan said. "In private."

"That chickenshit won't say anything to Collie and Wallace." Sally's words ended with the barest quiver. Some folks thought it endearingly cute, but at night, when she partook in conversations concerning a change in leadership, that little shiver sounded evil. "They're the real mayors of this place," she finished with a pissed-off shake of her head.

"And barely around," Will muttered. "I don't think I've even seen that fucking goofball, Wallace."

"Secretive, hard-core military types," Jan said and nodded warily.

"You believe that?" Will asked in disbelief. "I sure as hell don't. I mean, seriously, *anyone* could go to an army base now and dress up in combat fatigues and pass themselves off as soldiers. Any-fucking-one. Even a cop, for that matter. Wallace. Bugs me. I gotta feeling I'd kick Wallace's ass if it came down to it. That Collie bitch too if she wanted to roll. Turns my stomach they run things here while running around out there."

"Maybe we should step up the day of the vote?"

Will shook his head. The three of them had been making quiet rounds, feeling townspeople out on how they felt about how things were being run in Pine Cove, about new people coming in, and about changing the rules.

"Every day we wait," Jan warned, "is another day them two sheriffs bring in more strays. We'll be taking on *roommates* before too long."

Will glanced toward the window again, thinking about how many people might've ridden in on the motor homes. *Motor homes today—fucking buses tomorrow.* Jan had a point.

"And more people who might turn the vote," Sally finished.

"Yeah," Will said quietly, rubbing his stubbly chin. They figured twenty-five percent of the townsfolk supported the idea of a new election. Will intended to nominate himself, and once in power, he meant to change the town's policy on collecting strays. And that was only the start. Even if he didn't win, that couldn't be allowed to continue. He'd fight Minglewood tooth and nail on that issue.

There was only so much to go around.

And whoever was beyond those walls was on their own.

When the motor homes drove through the gate, Sick dropped his binoculars and stared, his green eyes narrowing into thoughtful slits behind the black ski mask. He lay on his belly, five feet back from the edge of the rock cut and a thirty-foot drop, hidden under the low bows of a fir tree. He didn't fear being detected, not with his ghillie suit rendering him indistinguishable from the landscape and practically invisible in the faltering daylight. Pine Cove, for all of its precautions and defenses, did not have the most observant people guarding its borders, which was just the way Shovel liked it.

Sick had an excellent view of the crude car wall and the makeshift but effective gate. Calloused fingers flexed on the binoculars as thoughts formulated in his brain. The motor homes had been a surprise. Who knew how many bodies they contained, not that they would be a problem for Shovel and his forces. He wondered where the pickup was headed and if it would return. The vehicle might head up one of the many side roads, where his armed companions were waiting for darkness. The pickup couldn't be holding any more than four people. Probably fewer—hardly a problem if they ran into the army parked out of sight.

Sick's fingers continued drumming the binoculars, each digit resembling a meaty leg of a very hairy spider. He wasn't the only person observing the town. Shovel had deployed five of them in three shifts per day, all set up at various points along the sloping tree line beyond the rock cut. The town's natural topography and location defended well against the undead, but against a mobilized and highly motivated unit, sharp inclines and thick trees did nothing, and once you got past that, it was a sleigh ride straight into the main street.

Sick blinked as if emerging from deep sleep.

If the pickup bypassed Shovel's forces, it didn't matter. The town remained the main prize. The driver and passengers were scraps compared to the bounty of potential skills and trades residing by the sea. If the pickup took a right turn and ran into Shovel, the boys would make quick work of whoever drove the vehicle.

The inhabitants of Pine Cove would learn something similar later that very night, in the predawn hours—when a warm bed was all that mattered and dreams ruled.

With all the patience and poise of a spider, Sick slowly replaced the spy glasses to his head and became motionless, channeling all his concentration into studying the guards on the car wall.

After close to a week of hiding, watching and, worst of all, *waiting*, Sick knew Shovel would drop the hammer tonight upon the unsuspecting populace of Pine Cove.

Then the harvesting would begin.

36

Marie escorted Gus to a barricaded RCMP office, led him past the heavy outer door, and knocked for the inner one to be opened. A man in a black sweater, jeans, and work boots appeared and let them into the police building . He nodded at Marie and eyed Gus with amused interest.

"New stray?"

"*Oui.* New one."

The guy grunted thoughtfully, intelligent brown eyes appraising Gus for any obvious defects.

"You were in a fire?" he finally asked, a dab of French accenting his words.

"Yeah."

"Hm. I'm Ray. Minglewood. I'm the elected mayor here."

"Gus. I'm just another asshole."

Ray smirked. "Well, in time, you might think that way about me. Wallace and Collie brought you in?"

"Yeah."

"Come in."

They walked Gus into a spartan office area filled with collapsed cubicles and a few work stations. A gun rack on a wall held five or six hunting rifles at attention, with boxes of shells at the base. Ray didn't seem to carry a weapon, but he appeared in shape, perhaps in his late thirties, and ordinary looking. The only thing Gus really focused on was his shock of brown hair. Ray had a rainforest flowering his scalp, thick enough to shelter wildlife if needed.

The three sat themselves down around a desk, and Ray leaned back, crossing one leg.

"Well, this is the town."

"Looks like fun."

Ray shrugged. "It's the best you'll find out east—though Newfoundland probably has a few places but no chance of getting over there anytime soon. And I expect anyone on the island isn't so keen to get off it. Same deal with PEI since someone over there actually blew up the bridge to the island."

The two men studied each other then, like a pair of weary gunslingers attempting to feel the other out.

"So. Collie and Wallace brought you in," Ray repeated.

"Me and a bunch of other folks."

"Long haul?"

"It was. Comfortable though, in the motor homes. Wish I'd had one before."

"Same here."

"You a cop?" Gus asked.

"Me? No. Just a crab fisherman. But for some reason, they chose to put me in charge of security and the meet-and-greet of newcomers. Not that a little Q&A is a chore, you understand. If Collie and Wallace brought you here, then that says a lot."

Silence fell then, and Gus glanced at Marie sitting at the end of the desk. She stared back, pleasantly neutral.

"They're going through a hard time right now," Gus added, wondering how much he could reveal to these people.

"We know," Ray said. "Hard way to go. We figure Collie still isn't clear. Something could always develop a little later. We're wondering if Collie will be infected just being around him, but I'm guessing nothing will happen unless . . . well, unless *he* does something. As for Wallace, I haven't seen him face-to-face in about two months now, but I've heard from others he isn't looking so good. No one knows what's going to happen there. It's one big shitty question mark."

"They'll figure it out," Gus said.

"They will, don't get me wrong. We greet them with open arms, you understand. They were the ones who isolated themselves from the town. They have a cabin on the shore, about thirty minutes from here. That's where they go on their downtime, when they aren't actively looking for survivors. Wallace said so himself, that it was best for all, until this episode came to its conclusion. It's just taking its goddamn time, is all."

Ray sighed. "How many with you?"

"A little over a dozen," Gus answered. "The RVs are filled with everything. Food, guns, ammunition. A generator too."

Ray's features lightened, and he glanced at Marie. "That's a surprise."

"You know how to set it up?" Gus asked.

"Not personally, but we have a few smart people around—an electrician and a mechanic. Some houses are already powered by solar but not all. Needless to say, hot showers around here are as good as cash."

Gus wondered if that was a hint at his own rank body odor.

"Well, anyway, you look tired there, Gus. It's getting late. Marie will find you a bunk in the community hall along with all the others you brought in and even get you something hot to eat. Hunting and fishing around here is pretty good. And we're fortunate enough that a lot of folks already grow their own vegetables. Wasn't a big leap to convert more land over to farming. We do all right but strive to do better."

"Sounds good," Gus said distantly, remembering his farm in the valley, missing the people.

"Well, welcome to Pine Cove," Ray declared with a flourish of hands. "That's it. We'll have another talk in the morning—see what you and the others can offer the town. This place is only as good as its people, and it's always good to bring in more. Every person is sorta like a little treasure chest. You don't know what's inside. Any doctors among you, by any chance?"

"Sorry, Ray."

"That's okay. We'll find one sooner or later."

Gus hoped they would.

After the meeting with Ray Minglewood, Marie led Gus by flashlight through the deepening night. The community hall could've been mistaken for a church missing its cross, and Gus wondered if Pine Cove still held Monday-night bingo sessions there. Maybe they did. Thick wooded, white painted, and with its windows boarded up, the place looked like a piecemeal bunker in the flashlight's beam. A few of the nearby houses had lights on upstairs, leaving Gus feeling as if all was right with the world for once.

The doors to the hall opened, and the harmonious smells of chicken soup and baked bread smacked him in the face. Phil and Jim and their people sat at three rows of long tables, enjoying their first hot meal in a long while. Three large portable water dispensers, the emergency kind, were set up nearby with stacks of plastic cups. Curtains partitioned an arrangement of cots near the back of the interior. Candles burned in holders and lamps all along the tables, lending an angelic ambience to the scene.

"Whoa," Gus said, a little breathless at the sight of the meal. "You guys got this on quick, didn't you?"

"Not really," Marie said. "They're eating leftovers from this evening. And that bread's fresh baked. We have a few old-fashioned ovens in town that are kept busy."

"Jesus Christ." Gus couldn't remember the last time he'd eaten fresh bread. His stomach tugged on his tongue, looking for attention.

"Eat, relax, and get to bed. Tomorrow, we'll talk again and see who wants to live where."

"Huh?"

"We have plenty of extra houses around, all with wood-burning stoves. There's electrically heated ones as well, but no one lives in any of those, obviously. But there are a couple with solar panels installed that generate good heat in the winter."

"Wow," Gus repeated, caught in another memory.

"So go ahead. See you in the morning."

Marie gestured toward the table before leaving Gus. He sized up the hall once more, smelled the food, eyed the tall pots and ladles, and listened to the sounds of eating and low conversation. It reminded him of an old-fashioned family dinner.

His stomach nagged him once again, and Gus walked over to the seated people, taking a spoon and a bowl from a lady who greeted him with a genuine smile.

After dinner, people settled down for the night.

Not bothering to undress, Gus lay back on a cot near an emergency exit, and if he arched his head back enough on his pillow, he could see the unlit sign designating the door. The bingo hall was warm and redolent with the aftersmells of a late dinner. Some folks whispered beyond the curtains. Someone suppressed a cough. A cot squealed almost musically from a person's weight. Another farted, a long, sonorous note of sleepy contentment, and a chorus of giggles and chuckles answered in agreement.

Gus smiled at being among people again.

Not that Collie and Wallace weren't people, but being part of a community calmed his nerves. He'd lived life as a loner, and he'd lived with a small group of people. He preferred the company of people by far.

Shadows flickered on the dim ceiling, lit by tired candlelight. The cot wasn't as comfortable as the bed in the RV, but the hall's ambience beat the motor home hands down—as long as there weren't any more soup farts.

His smile widened.

The hall's ceiling darkened. Sleep claimed the weariest of the travelers, and Gus closed his eyes.

*

Fathoms deep the night sank, drowning the town in sleep. Fog crept from the smoothed glass of the bay, promising good dreams. The vapor slunk up deserted streets and coiled around mushroom-shaped lamps that lined the road, creating smoky bubbles of light.

Spencer blinked at the scene, perhaps a little longer than he should have. *Dark.* November nights stretched time, making one second feel like thirty. Staying awake during those hours could be a challenge when the only sound heard might be another's whisper or the dirge of the wind. Even though Spencer slept during the day in preparation for the night watches, that wasn't enough. He disliked the graveyard shift. It screwed up his sleep and reminded him too much of a time when a scream carried for miles.

The night shift was damned *lonely.*

Spencer sniffed and dug at an ear, rooting a finger around vigorously before working on the other. As he cleaned, he leaned against the gate's upper barrier and looked out into the rock cut. Pixie lights, little solar-powered units like the ones haunting the town, lit up the road and transformed it into a runway reaching toward infinity. Spencer sniffed again and detected movement on his right. Dalton was doing those ridiculous partial squats on the walkway, forcing blood into his thighs and ass. Below and inside the gate stood Martin and Roy, each with a hunting rifle slung over his shoulder. They'd exhausted the ammunition for the assault weapons almost a year before. Regular hunting rifles did the job just as efficiently, but Spencer liked holding an AR-20 in his hands. He appreciated the military rifle's weight. It relaxed him.

Spencer took his finger out of his ear, wiped it on his jeans, and went to work on a nostril. He mined at an annoying tickle when Dalton's bulked-up form wandered over from the right.

"You know somethin'?" Spencer whispered when Dalton got close enough.

"Wha'?"

"With that winter coat and all on, you look like a goddamn sasquatch."

"Thanks, fuckchops."

"No, really," Spencer insisted, wiping his finger on his jeans again. "That beard of yours, them big fucking saucer eyes, like you've been sniffin' somethin' illegal. And that smell. What is that? Eau d'shit? Bet it's hard to keep that one on the shelves."

Dalton shook his head and studied the empty road of the rock cut. "Keep it up."

"Really?"

"Oh, yeah, you're a fucking snort and a half. Especially at my expense."

"Well, y'shouldn't come over here, then."

"What? And miss all this charming conversation?"

"You are the source of my best material."

"Yeah? Well, glad to make somebody's night. Which reminds me, if you're finished insulting me, that is."

"Yeah," Spencer sighed. "Even that gets old eventually. We good?"

"Fuck no, dickhead." Dalton quietly scoffed, noticing the man still trying to clean his fingers on his clothes but deeming it not worth mentioning. "Y'know, I hope there's no freaks or psychos in those two boatloads that came in today."

"Collie and Wallace have been pretty much on the money so far. With that one exception, and that one took care of himself."

"There's a clinical name for that."

"For blowin' out your headcheese with a .30-30?"

Dalton regarded Spencer in the near darkness. "Spence, put the finger down and listen to what I'm sayin' here, okay?"

With some reluctance, Spencer complied and adjusted the strap of his rifle hanging off his shoulder.

"What I was *sayin'* is, for some people, being isolated and on their own for so long and then coming *back* to . . . well, civilization—or at least integrating with people again—it's sorta like culture shock."

"Yeah, well, just hope there's a few hot-lookin' bitches in that bunch," Spencer said.

Dalton again shook his head in stoic disbelief of his companion's caveman priorities. "We'll see tomorrow. Did see a few women get out of those RVs. Well, I'll get back to patrolling here. Thank you as always for the conversation. Assfudge."

"Dicksquid."

Dicksquid. Dalton mouthed the word in dismay before turning and walking away.

"That's right, bitch—I win," Spencer said to the other's retreating back. "You just walk away. You feel ready come on back, and we'll play again. Prison rules next time. Prison rules, son."

Spencer snapped on an imaginary latex glove and scooped the air with a finger.

A crack of underbrush from the left caught his attention, and he turned and confronted the night. The sound didn't repeat, however, and Spencer stood there, straining to hear. His peripheral vision picked up movement on his left, just below the barricade of cars, and he saw the outline of Roy standing down there. No one else in Pine Cove wore a real bear-fur hat.

"Roy," Spencer whispered.

"Yeah?"

"Hear that?"

"Yeah."

"Think it was?"

"Dunno."

Neither did Spencer. He unslung his rifle. Roy did the same.

"Too dark," Roy whispered.

"Yeah."

"Need to put some of them solar lights on the slope, dude."

"Job for tomorrow," Spencer agreed.

No other sound came forth, but the hairs on Spencer's neck buzzed, and unease filled his guts. He knew the feeling, remembering being pulled over while driving high on a Saturday evening. Spencer leaned forward, straining to hear, and looked at Roy again, who shrugged.

Urgent hisses split the night, ending in grunts from the right side of the wall, distracting both men just as a huge figure of a man wearing a snowsuit and a gleaming hockey mask strode out of the night, materializing from seemingly nowhere and taking huge steps before winding up and swinging an axe. Paralyzed, Roy didn't even have the wind to scream as the blade chopped into his left shoulder, driving him to his knees.

"Jesus!" Spencer shouted in fright and lifted his rifle.

A hand wrapped around his forehead and tipped his head back, an instant before a startling pinch of pain.

The world went white.

Sick withdrew his slick knife from the base of the guard's skull and eased the ragdoll corpse to the floor. He watched the big ex-Norseman called Nolan wrench his axe out of the chest cavity of his victim, wind up, and hack into the head with a clap that resembled fine china shattering on a floor. Nolan's powerful grunts puffed though the punched-hole smile of the funky silver helmet he wore. Although Nolan didn't eat people anymore, unlike his former associates, killing folks and ensuring their deadness remained a much-valued priority. Over Sick's shoulder, four other men emerged from sections of underbrush where they had released their crossbow bolts. Those four confirmed their kills and dragged the bodies off the road.

Sick attempted to hear over the dragging of boots in the dirt, couldn't, and frowned beneath his mask.

Nolan stood up, chest heaving, his work overalls stained darker than dark. He waved, and Sick waved back. Nolan gripped his axe behind its head in one hand while dragging the chopped mess into the dark by the ankle.

Sick regarded the town just a hundred meters away, lost in sleep, and sighed mightily. The first part was easy—boring, even, for one with his skill set.

But the next part thrilled the hell out of him.

Sick hopped from the gate to the wall and waved toward the four henchmen below. They ran to the gate, tossed off the lumber keeping the wheeled barrier in place, and pushed it out of the way. Pebbles crackled under rubber wheels.

Sick waved at the ghostly mouth of the rock cut.

The night exploded in a rock-band stage of lights.

37

Gus dreamed of his mountain lodge. He dreamed of Roxanne by his side, sitting in a deck chair right next to his, overlooking the city. She wasn't the Roxanne who had kicked the living shit out of him, however. She was a more docile Roxanne, prompting Gus to wonder—diverting his attention for a moment—if she was stoned. Not that he minded. On that summer day, Roxanne had elected to go with a thin covering of sunscreen, which Gus heartily approved of. They gazed at the cityscape of Annapolis while lines of clouds scrolled southward at speed, which made him wonder if *he* wasn't stoned. His skin burned in the summertime glare, and he could smell it. Gus scratched at his crotch, covered in beige walking shorts. He shook his mai tai, and the ice in his drink jingled.

"Left the keys in the truck," he said without reason.

Roxanne sat up, her pretty boobs jiggling, not a tan line in sight.

"I'll get them, babe," she said brightly. She stood, placed her own drink on a small glass table, and immediately walked to the edge of the cliff, which no longer had a guardrail.

Gus lurched forward with a warning on his lips just as Roxanne hopped over the edge, her hair fluttering as gravity slurped her down.

"I didn't park *there*," he moaned and climbed to his feet in annoyance. He meandered to the cliff edge, muttering all the way, mai tai in hand, and looked down.

A raging mosh pit of zombies besieged the base of the cliff.

That didn't perturb Gus in the least.

Roxanne had landed right on top of them, her limbs thrown wide as if making an angel in a drift of snow. She smiled up at him even as they tore her apart in a spectacle of blood.

Frowning, Gus downed the last of his drink.

He heard shouts from the pool, sounding urgent.

He stepped into the open air.

Gus woke and sat up straight.

The candles around the hall had expired. People moved about, silhouettes on a dark canvas, shouting warnings. A shadow appeared at the foot of his bed. Gus drew his legs back as a solid block nailed him in the face, flipping him off the warm cot and onto the floor. He landed hard on his belly, stayed put because of the shock, and made the mistake of looking up.

A boot crunched into the side of his head. The darkness exploded into purple and light.

Sleep returned.

Gus struggled in a tar of unconsciousness as the world scratched at his back. He realized then he was *on* his back while voices screamed in anger over him. A gun fired several times, and Gus cracked open an eye.

Not three steps away from him stood a tall man dressed in a snowsuit. The snowsuit Gus could understand. The silver face with the punched-hole grin took him a moment. The axe was an entirely different matter.

"What's happening?" he asked hoarsely.

"Just sit still," an unfamiliar woman whispered, guarded and brimming with fright. "And don't move."

The shiny bastard with the axe regarded him with black-eyed mirth, almost daring Gus to try something.

Gus did not, however, and elected to touch his aching jaw instead.

Armed soldiers roughly handled men, women, and children to their knees and arranged them into rows. Gus slowly sat up, thanking the lady who'd watched over him. The silver-faced lumberjack towered over them, dawn's light playing over the mask's surface while smoke drifted by.

Morning. Gus grimaced and fought through a surge of dizziness. It passed, and he studied the soldiers standing around with fearsome, automatic science-fiction weaponry. Black masks covered their faces, like the one Collie wore, and for a second, Gus wondered if they knew her. Behind a wall of guns rose an awesome three-story dump truck, parked, its headlights blazing. The cab and deck area on the monstrosity had slabs of sheet iron welded or bolted over its more sensitive parts, but the huge tires were at least fifteen feet tall. The indistinct shapes of transport trailers idled beyond the flood of light from this apocalyptic siege tower.

"Jesus Christ," Gus mumbled as he gazed around, earning what appeared to be a moment's chuckle from the silver-faced Axeman. Smoke belched from a pair of houses down near the water. A few more soldiers strutted around them while two others prodded at corpses at their feet. That took Gus a moment to process as the upper curve of the sun broke over a distant ridge of treetops.

"What happened?"

"Pick!" a voice shouted.

"Yeah!" a soldier answered, carrying a rifle with a futuristic optical-sight system.

"How many you got now?"

"After that little episode? Seventy-two."

"Seventy-two."

The speaker came into sight, shaking his head in apparent disgust, another ski-masked soldier, carrying a subcompact machine gun and dressed in an orange survival suit. Something seemed odd about him, and Gus's brow furrowed with activating his memory.

"All right. Enough of this shit," the deep-voiced man yelled and gestured at the captives. "Anyone else tries to run, not only do we shoot the ass off them, but we shoot one of you. Now then, this is how it's going to work. Whatever life you had here is over. You've just been recruited into a much larger body . . ."

Gasps and sobs of disbelief rippled through the citizens of Pine Cove as the masked man delivered a speech about the life after the apocalypse. He told them about a bunker to the north and the unit of special operators having a gunfight for the ages in a stone courthouse. Gus listened in rapt attention, thinking of Collie and Wallace at times but also sensing he knew this masked man who talked with his hands while presiding over them.

"Sooner or later, someone would have found you," the speaker continued in a bass rumble and holstered his hands on his hips, "and would've butchered the whole damn lot of you. You're fortunate we came along when we did. We need you. Preferably, all of you, but I know from experience that isn't going to happen. First things first. Any miners here?"

No one moved, simply too stunned in the dawn's growing light. Someone coughed.

"No miners? Jesus H . . . all right . . . any carpenters or plumbers? Doctors or dentists? Nurses?"

A few hands went up, and heads turned toward them.

"Stand up," the speaker commanded, and three people complied. The soldiers guarding the lot of them hoisted their weapons and took aim at two women and a man.

"Which is it, then?"

"I was a registered nurse," said a woman in her thirties.

"Dental assistant," said the other woman.

"Pharmacist," said the man.

"Well, well," the speaker said, clearly impressed. "Bit of a jackpot here, Pick. Get them folks out of there. You're special to us. We *like* you. You guys get a special deal—a one-time offer, you could say. Anyone else, then?"

No one raised their hands.

"Anyone with any trade skills? Mechanics, for instance?"

Again, no one moved.

"No?"

Gus looked around, remembering Ray saying something about a mechanic. But whoever it was, wasn't budging.

"I'm an electrician," one guy called out.

"You are now?" the man in orange exclaimed. "Get outta there."

Two armed riflemen gestured to the electrician and herded him away.

"All right, that was the easy part." The leader sighed and studied the people in the first row. "What I'm offering you all now is citizenship in a new nation. Anyone can join, provided you can get past the initiation test. Y'see, we're looking for survivors. A *survivor's* survivor, you might say. The kids I see among you, well, they're coming with us, regardless. The parents or guardians, well, that's optional. Allow me to explain."

Gus blinked. Coldness rose and flooded his chest and limbs like a life-threatening allergic reaction. His mouth went dry, and his mind focused on the speaker as the man rambled on with his horrific selection process.

Holy fuck, Gus mouthed and held his jaw as if to steady it. *Holy fuck*. He knew the identity of the man talking. God above, he knew him.

Soldiers moved among the people of Pine Cove, yanking the children away from the parents or relatives. Gus barely registered the activity, even when the kids screamed and kicked. His eyes stayed on the speaker while everyone else watched the kidnappings.

One of the soldiers carrying a toolbox approached the speaker.

But he wasn't just a speaker anymore—not to Gus. He was positive of the man's identity, recognizing the mannerisms, the way of speech, and that unmistakable bedrock voice that could hit the kind of low notes that could shake windows in their frames if he sang. He just couldn't believe the guy was . . . *there*.

Gus stood up on shaky feet, drawing the glowing attention of the Axeman with the silver face. A few nearby guards turned as well, taking aim with their weapons. Then the people of Pine Cove held their breaths, wondering why the newest member was suddenly wigging out and committing suicide. Children's faces looked on in a heart-breaking mixture of fear, desperation, and hope as they saw him stand.

Even the speaker took notice and cocked his head to one side.

"You got something to say, son?"

"Yeah," Gus straightened his back and tried to find the man's eyes. "I know who you are. Christ on a stick, I thought . . . I thought you were dead."

The speaker's head tweaked again in an *oh really?* kind of way, and the henchman with the toolbox regarded his leader.

"Yeah?" the speaker said, his hand tightening about the machine gun hanging from his shoulder. "Well, then introduce yourself. And make it a good one."

Gus's mouth hung open. "Jerry. It's me. Gus. Berry."

The speaker stopped talking as if winded. He released the weapon, his entire posture sagging from one of supreme confidence to heart-attack dismay.

"Gus?" he asked, totally disarmed.

Gus nodded.

"I thought you were dead."

"I thought *you* were dead."

The pair of men quieted then, staring at each other for seconds before Jerry reached up and pulled the mask from his head. Then, remembering where he was, he glanced around to see his followers watching, waiting for the final reveal.

Jerry didn't give it to them, but he waved Gus closer. "Get over here."

As if dreaming, Gus walked toward his brother.

38

In a smoky haze, Jerry clasped both of Gus's arms and held him there, and both men marveled at each other's scars. Amazement swept over the people witnessing the reunion, and the tension of the attack bled away. Figures moved around the two men, allowing them space, but neither noticed.

"Holy shit," Gus said and embraced his once-dead brother. "Holy *shit*. I can't believe it. I can't believe it."

Jerry reluctantly returned the hug, patting Gus on the back, allowing him to hold on. Gus finally released his brother and cleared his constricted throat. "Sid?"

Jerry's face wilted around the eyes. "Sid didn't make it."

"Oh." The word almost became a wail. Jerry shooed away the perplexed soldiers and nodded at the guy with the toolbox.

"Carry on, Pick," Jerry said. "You know the drill. I've got things to attend to. Gus, this way. Follow me."

Gus did as told. To his surprise, the building Jerry was leading him to was the RCMP office. A misshapen lump came into view then, splayed on the ground outside the main entrance, lying on its back. Gus faltered and stepped back, bumping into a wall. He glanced over his shoulder to see the silver-faced Axeman standing right there. Gus switched back to the bloody mess on the ground.

The body was the town mayor, Ray Minglewood. He'd been damn near cut in half by a burst of automatic gunfire. Ray's troll-like mop of hair had sopped up a good amount of the blood pooled around him, but there was so much more.

"Jesus Christ," Gus burst out. "That's Ray!"

Jerry hesitated in his tracks. "You know him?"

"He was like the fuckin' mayor."

The silver-faced goliath chuckled darkly, earning a classic *the fuck's so funny?* glare from Gus.

"When we moved in here, things got a little crazy," Jerry said with a twinge of regret in his voice, diverting Gus's attention back to him.

"Things got a little crazy?" Gus stopped and stared. "What the hell are you doing, Jer? These are good people, and you're fuckin' invading them. And what's with that overlord speech and yanking the children away? What's up with that? You're actually forcing them to join you? You got an insane way of going about things. I mean, Jesus, what happened to just driving up and introducing yourself?"

Jerry regarded his brother stoically for a moment. "You get burned?"

"Huh?"

"Your face is all fucked up."

"Oh. That. Yeah. I . . . I had a hard time back in Annapolis there. Had a place up on South Mountain there—"

"South Mountain?" Jerry blurted and grinned. "That's high country up there. Some rich sonsabitches' balcony. You holed up in one of them mansions?"

"Well," Gus shrugged. "Not a mansion exactly, but it might've been a summer home for someone. Had a wall and solar panels and all that."

"Living off the grid." Jerry approved.

"Yeah, well, yeah, something like that."

"Come on in here," Jerry said soothingly and guided Gus past the dead man at their feet.

"What about—"

"Don't worry about him. Or them," Jerry said, cutting Gus off. "That guy on the ground there shot first anyway. My boys were defending themselves. Ain't that right, Nolan?"

The ogre at his back thought about it for a second before giving a ponderous nod.

"Easy to do at night," Jerry continued, pulling the outer door open. "Shit's going down. Everyone's all short-circuiting on adrenaline like a pack of squirrels jacked up on speed. Unlucky shit like this is bound to happen every once in a while. Wait for us out here, Nolan. We'll be out in a few minutes."

Nolan lurched to a stop right at the door, his silver face watching. Gus glared back, not feeling particularly friendly, and bumped into a corner of the second security door. Inside, the spartan office remained untouched, right down to the rack of firearms and ammunition on the west wall. Jerry circled Ray's desk and pulled out a chair. He gestured for Gus to do the same, and both sat down.

In the morning light, with the smell of smoke on the air, Jerry leaned back and stared at Gus from the chin up, inspecting him, *remembering* him. His mouth became a thin line before puckering into a tight button of amazement.

"Should've known you'd pull through. Goddamn. If there ever was a bastard to kick the apocalypse in the balls and get away with it, it'd be you. Goddamn."

"You too," Gus said, captivated by the last surviving member of his family. "Holy shit."

"Not like you, though," Jerry said with a slow shake of his head. "Not like you. For one, I was up north in deep backcountry, rooting around with pipes and goons and suits, sucking up every last drop of tar-sand oil we could sniff out. Took days to drive onto site and over some pretty shitty roads too. We didn't have to worry about zombies up there. Oh, there were one or two guys that turned, but we isolated them pretty fast. And when we found out that they were fucking undead, well, we put a nail in their head, and that was that. Nothing like what you or anyone else in a city or town had to go through. I'm not saying we had it easy. Far fucking from it. Only different."

Gus smiled. "Good to see you, bro."

"Good to see you too."

"*But*," Gus stressed the words, "the *fuck* are you doing?"

"Feeding the machine." Jerry answered truthfully and stared back, clearly ruminating on how best to deal with the situation.

"Feeding the machine," Gus repeated. "By killing folks? Yeah, that's right—I didn't forget the fuckin' corpse on the doorstep. The same guy who was pretty fuckin' helpful to me a few hours ago. You said *your* boys. You in charge of this outfit?"

"I am."

"So how is it you've gone about corralling everyone in town who ain't dead and giving them this draft speech? *Forcing* them to join you? What kind of fucked-up thought process is that? Jesus Christ, Jer, what would Mom or Dad say?"

Jerry snapped forward and bared his teeth. "*Hey.* You keep them out of this. You keep them *out*. No one had to make the fuckin' choices I had to make. No one crossed the lines like I did. Mom and Dad were lucky they went before the zombies. Quick and painless. One flash of light, and they're gone. They were *lucky*. The rest of us who lived after the shitbagging of everything fine . . . well, we weren't so lucky. Like I said, lines were crossed, moral compasses stepped on and left in the dirt. All just to get by. Now, well, now it's life."

Gus leaned in, blinking in horror quickly changing into anger. "What fuckin' life?"

"*This.*" Jerry swept his hands wide. "Bringing dedicated folks like myself into the fold. Getting them ready for war. You know what's on the other side of Canada?"

"More like you?"

"*Worse* than me. There's guys and gals over there who've banded together and pretty much dance naked in their own shit. Yeah, *that* fuckin' crazy. Armageddon-level insanity. When law and order went down the shitter like two flushed turds headin' out to sea, the anarchists came out to play, and they came out in force. Then the crazies. Then the *cannibals*. Some of them banded together and made small armies. Others made tribes. They got their hands on guns and explosives and either started shootin' people or rounding them up. Why people? Because that's the only resource left in the world that's worth a goddamn. People are *key* to starting over. The more you have, the more power you got. Without them, you're just one shit monkey sittin' in his recliner, wonderin' if he should face the morning or exit with a shotgun blast to the head. And if it's not me waking them up, it'll be someone else—someone a lot less sociable."

Roxanne's voice whispered in Gus's ear then, a soft breath of deadly sweetness, warning him about the west, warning him about what was out there. He couldn't remember her exact words, but her message had been clear enough.

"Like surrounding them with guns and yanking the kids away?" Gus countered, his tone rising. "You could've pulled up and asked for a meeting or something."

"Ask for a *meeting*? How often did someone fuckin' ask for a meeting with you? I mean, when you met someone on the road? Huh? Folks don't ask for *meetings* any-more. They fuckin' blast you first and cattle prod the pieces left over. Maybe they'll wonder about you when they're squatting over a hole and taking a dump. That's all after they've fuckin' *looted* your ass. That's the world today: shoot first and talk about dead assholes later. I've done both, and yeah, this way is far and away more prefera-ble. I've got a system down—pretty reliable. The people I need are behind me: blood brothers who survived up north with me. Seriously, if I had my guys hide out of sight and then approach a group of people all alone, which is a pretty goddamn dangerous proposition to begin with, right? Stupid too, I might add. But, say for argument's sake I do that. What do you think'll happen? Ninety percent of the time? I'm left for dead. That's just all hypothetical, though. Now, say you do listen, and I tell you I'm committed to protecting myself and you—your people. Okay? And I *know* what's out there. What's coming. I tell you everything and make the argument for joining forces. Well, guess what? Sooner or later, there's going to be a disagreement about some shit. There always is. Two clans can't coexist under two leaders, so one will have to assume power. Thing is, a clan is usually pretty loyal to its leader, so the two groups become fragmented once again. Maybe there's debate on how things are done. Then argu-ments. Then fistfights. Then knives and guns. See where I'm heading with this? And even if that new bunch of survivors says, 'No, thank you, it's not our concern,' well, what do you do? Leave those folks alone? Just *leave* that pocket of skills and knowledge for the next, not-so-sociable clan to roll into town? I see you're missing some teeth in front there, Gussy. How'd that happen?"

"Got into a fight."

"Life or death, I take it?"

Gus paused. "Yeah."

"You find a dentist to take them teeth out?"

"No."

"And there you go. Now, maybe you're in need of a mechanic, and the only one you know happens to be part of another group. You'd really leave that behind?"

Gus rattled his head and stared. "Holy shit, skippy. You jumped some big steps in that logic there."

"It doesn't matter," Jerry said. "My point is, you *get* them, whether they want to join up or not. You can't just allow people—skilled labor—to *walk*. You bring them into the fold, show them how the world works now, and if they don't like it . . ." Jerry drew a thumb across his throat and stuck out a tongue. "Because the next group will use them against me. And to that, I say, 'Fuck you.' Better me than somebody else."

Gus sat slack-jawed, his head spinning from the warped logic Jerry was spewing.

"Are you fuckin' insane?" he finally blurted.

This genuinely perplexed Jerry. "Whaddaya mean?"

Gus inhaled and steadied himself. "You can't be killin' people just because they won't fuckin' *join up*."

"I'm the lesser of any evil out there. If I don't do it, someone else *will*. Believe me. And they'll do worse. *Horror* story–type shit."

Gus regarded his brother as if a mutated head was sprouting from his shoulder.

"Don't look at me that way," Jerry said. "There's only one way to make it in this world today, and that's to take it by the nutsack and not to let go. Impose your will, control it, and hammer onward. The only way. Anything else, and you're meat waiting to be fed to a machine."

"What in God's name happened to you? Last time I saw you, you were a shovel operator working with Bolg Oil."

Jerry smirked. "You know the difference between God and a shovel operator?"

Gus once more shook his head, failing to understand what *that* had to do with anything.

"God doesn't think he's a shovel operator," Jerry chuckled.

"The fuck does that mean?"

"Look . . ." Shovel said and stood. He stretched his back and smiled brightly. "Let's get out of here. I have a place up north in Ontario being renovated while I'm over here collecting names."

"*Collecting?*"

"Yeah, so let's head on back, and I guarantee you when you see what I have to show, you'll think differently."

Shovel leaned across, gripped Gus by the back of the neck, and pulled him forward to land a kiss on his forehead. "Good to see you, Gussy. Very good to see you."

He didn't so much release him as shove him away, and he strode back to the inner door.

"Come on." Shovel kissed the air as if calling a loyal dog.

His head damn near swollen and liquid with dark thoughts, Gus reluctantly followed. He replayed the whole crazy lecture he'd just sat through, wondering if his only remaining brother had gone over a precipice of savagery and crash-landed as a wasteland general or had just gone bugnuts *insane. Jesus Christ,* Gus thought pensively, walking through the inner door and ignoring Nolan's silver mask.

Gus stepped outside the office, stomach and mind churning, suddenly believing he should've tried for a rifle from the wall rack.

Sounds of a fight in progress sidetracked his attention.

Just ahead, grunting and fighting within a fragmented ring of armed soldiers, the redheaded woman known as Marie slugged another man across the jaw, laying him out on the ground. In the drifting smoke and brightening day, she jumped onto him and raised a hammer.

She brought it down as if pounding a crooked nail into a knot of wood . . . except it wasn't wood she was hitting.

Marie buried the tool into her opponent's head, and he ceased struggling, limbs flopping as if drilled by a Taser. She ripped the hammer free in a red arc, shrieked, and whacked the skull again, quieting those thrashing arms and legs. She continued hitting the dead man, grunting with every impact.

The killing stopped Gus cold in his tracks. "Holy fuck."

Shovel sighed, half turned, and rolled his eyes with impatience.

"Christ above, I don't want to hear it," he declared and glanced over his brother's shoulder.

Nolan slapped Gus upside the head with the flat of his axe, dropping him like a laundry bag falling off a moving truck.

39

A whirlpool of inky blackness sucked Gus down. Voices crackled in that weightless void, right in his ear at times, far away at others. He came close to consciousness, skimming the underbelly, and floated just beneath, aware enough to know that being so close to the surface wasn't a comfortable experience. Forces tugged and jerked on his limbs, some hard enough for Gus to wonder, *What was that?* just before a warm undercurrent enveloped his sense of self, originating from the crook of his elbow, flooding him in a puff of euphoria, sending him spiraling, hands and fingers outstretched, exploring. The darkness lit up with mute explosions of intoxicating purple, pink, and blue, calming him with their serenity, warping into streaks of light as he flew outward, heading for reaches unknown.

Sand.

He lay upon sand, the earth's heat radiating through his back, shifting and seeping into his weary physical form while luminescent waves soaked the shoreline with a rattle. He glanced right, then left, seeing nothing but beach and heat shimmers. Roxanne stretched out beside him on the left, naked, her skin the color of the sky. This didn't disturb Gus in the least. In fact, seeing the woman delighted him in a subdued kind of way. She smiled twinkling silver teeth at him, and a surreal glow engulfed her head. She pointed, and Gus looked toward an ocean of glittering purple that magically alternated between flat tranquility and gentle ripples, like a plain of velour being smoothed by the invisible hand of God.

"Beautiful," Gus said, feeling the heat at his bare back, the sand working magic into his aching frame, into the very fiber of his spirit.

"I feel fucking amazing," he said, the words formulating in elegant cursive smoke before his eyes, curling into nothing, leaving only a curious taste of vanilla and strawberries. The waves rolled. The sky fled and blotted with fireworks that took eternities to blossom. Roxanne scooted a little closer, snuggling into his arm, her chin becoming part of his upper shoulder. The contact made him blink, the action taking a whole year.

"How much of that shit you give him?" Roxanne asked in a voice that sounded like she was gargling a microphone, but with everything so wonderful, Gus didn't think it weird at all. He went back to watching the sky, his eyes opening to their maximum potential.

"Fuck me," Slick Pick muttered as he studied the opaque shell of Gus's left eyeball. He released it, and the skin slid over the curvature like a slug, easing into a dreamy slit. Slick Pick pulled back the right eyelid with a rough thumb. "You used too much this time."

Sick stood silent next to the trailer's wall and shrugged nonchalantly, inspecting the syringe he'd just emptied into the sedated man's arm. Shovel had okayed the first injection two hours before, a light dose, just to see how his brother would react to the heroin.

Sick didn't do light doses—it was fucking thunderbolts all the way.

To his surprise, Gus had reacted just fine, mellowing out like a sleepy cat.

"This cocksucker's never gonna wake up, Shovel," Slick Pick stated, flashing a dirty look in Sick's direction.

"Hey," Shovel said, offended, "That's my blood you're talking about there. So don't call him a cocksucker."

Slick Pick straightened and frowned. "Sorry, Shovel. Meant no disrespect."

"Well, it fuckin' sounded disrespectful."

"Sorry, bro."

Shovel didn't reply, letting Slick Pick wallow in unease. Sometimes, silence was the best way to keep the grunts in line.

They stood around Gus, who'd crashed, drugged, on a couch in the designated command trailer Shovel had taken for his own. The narrow quarters contained a plush but worn living-room set, bolted down to avoid slippage. A weapon rack for firearms and blades hung beside a desk. The office furniture partitioned off the bedroom section and the double-size mattress in the rear. Thick quilts lay in a snarl upon the bed. Shovel couldn't give a shit about housekeeping.

He stood above his tripping brother and shook his head, pissed at having to drug Gus for the road and aware of the implications.

"So how long you gonna keep him like this?" Slick Pick asked, mindful of Sick and the intimidating Nolan leaning against a wall. The big man still hadn't removed his silver helmet, seemingly enjoying the fear he instilled in Slick Pick.

"What do you mean?" Shovel asked back.

"You can't keep him doped up like that."

"Why not?" Shovel regarded his henchman. "You laying claim to the dust now?"

Slick paled and swallowed. "Course not, Shovel. We got plenty of that. But sooner or later, he's gonna come out if it. Now, I'm no shrink, but I saw his face when you came out of that cop shack, and I can tell you, he's *not* with the program. All due respect."

"He's with it. He's my blood. That alone makes him with it."

"He's gotta fight someone."

Shovel's face darkened into a Halloween mask of displeasure. "I don't like you goin' on about this, Slick."

"Shovel, I'm only *sayin'*. We all follow rules here—rules you set down to make sure whoever came into the fold was reliable. *Dependable*. It's like fuckin' protocol now for all these new bastards. Weed killer for the undesirables, right? And it appears to me, this is one case of true colors you'll want to get to the bottom of ASAP. Christ, how many times have you said we can't have anyone around who don't believe in what we're doing? And brother or not, whoever was in the street there this morning saw that Gussy here might have issues."

Sick's dangerous eyes flicked to gauge Shovel's reaction. At the same time, Nolan straightened, a golem coming to life, pulling his back an inch away from the wall, offering maximum, decisive violence if needed.

Shovel didn't summon them, however, and Slick Pick, perspiring and visibly aware of the two killers, pressed on with his argument like a man threading his way through a minefield using a dinner fork.

"If Giovanni were here, he'd say the same thing."

"You shut the fuck up right there," Shovel warned. "Just fuckin' shut up. The day you speak for Giovanni is the day I fucking take a drill to your skull. You don't talk for him. Got it?"

"Just sayin' if he were here, he'd say—"

Shovel looked toward Sick, which was enough for Slick Pick to raise his hands in surrender and take a quick step back from the three men.

"I got it, I got it," he blurted.

Shovel glared at his mouthy henchman.

"Just *sayin'* . . ." Slick Pick finished in a much lower tone, inspecting the floor of the trailer to avoid Shovel's stare, "was all."

Drool threaded from one corner of Gus's mouth, seeping into his patchy beard before descending to his neck. Gus's feebly smiling face stared at the ceiling, stoned eyes as dreamy as fog on a lake, oblivious to the stormy debate.

Shovel shook his head again, knowing he was fidgeting on this one and hating himself for it. His brother, presumed long dead but not, had appeared during the largest take of living meat yet. What *would* Giovanni say to Gus's appearance? Shovel knew that answer without squeezing his brain for juice. He despised it when Slick Pick could point out the obvious.

"How we doing for time here?" Shovel asked, changing the subject.

"Give us another couple of hours or so," Slick Pick cleared his throat. "The boys are having the new recruits load up the other trailer right now. There's a lot to be loaded. These Pine Holers had prepped for the winter: cured meats, salt fish, bottled jams, root cellars full of veggies, even fucking garlic."

"Weapons?"

Slick scratched his ear. "Nothing special there. Sorry. But there was a portable generator there too. All 'round, this fuckin' shithole turned out to be a plum."

"How many new heads?"

"Forty-two."

That number impressed Shovel. Pine Cove had given shelter to a sizeable number of people. Yet, as time and time again had demonstrated, when faced with life or death, the true survivors had no problem emerging from the captured populace. Some had to be executed straight out, bludgeoned to death just to prove their conquerors were serious. Shovel's men had gunned down two runners who thought they might make the tree line. But after all that, it was down to business. Flaying the fat from the meat took an hour, and the fights were bloody, even by Shovel's standards. In the end however, forty-two new men and women were added to the fold. An additional six kids also joined, all under ten years of age. Shovel loved finding them that young, young enough to fashion into the fighters he needed them to become.

He inhaled sharply. "Where's the next crop?"

"Only one," Slick Pick said. "A back road in Ontario."

Shovel chastised himself. He had forgotten the plan with the arrival of his brother. He needed to get thinking straight again, to get back to the game at hand: strike east and scoop up the residents of Pine Cove first, then pluck the second lot on the way back to base, along with whatever supplies they could find. If they left them, road savages most definitely would not.

Gus.

Who would've known he'd actually survive? Shovel expected he did know, way, way back in that part of his mind where he stored memories of more civilized times. He remembered how, if pushed into a corner, Gus would come out swinging. The apocalypse had been a *huge* corner, and there he was, as glazed and runny as jelly.

Shovel studied the stoned form on his couch.

He knew the same killer instinct flowed through Gus's veins as did through Shovel's. Accessing it correctly, however, was a mystery.

"All right," he finally said. "Sick, you stay here with me. Fix up another shot in case we need it. You other guys get outta here. See that things go smooth. I'll stay here and watch over this one."

A glistening spit bubble appeared on Gus's lips for all of a wet second . . .

Then burst.

"Gus."

"Yeah?"

"About your place."

"Yeah?"

"I'm . . . I'm sorry, okay. It's just that I owed Johnathan first. He'd saved my ass from folks. I owed him. If we'd have met before him, I would have thrown in with you. Really."

"I get it."

"I mean *really.*"

"No, no, I understand. Don't worry about it."

"I'm . . . I'm sorry about knocking your teeth out."

Gus chuckled, and his whole body pulsed in fine humor. "That's okay. It was a damn good shot. No idea you could fight like that."

"I'm so sorry."

"Don't worry about it. Really. I mean, hell, I shot you."

"You did," Roxanne said, not upset in the least. "*Twice.*"

They laughed, at complete ease with each other, glad to put the incident behind them. The surf rolled in over the sands and retreated with a growl, smoothing the grains and leaving a sheen of fine silk. The water slid in again and touched the bottoms of Gus's bare feet, as warm as a bath.

"This place is paradise."

"You understand why it's illegal," Roxanne giggled.

"No. Why?"

"Can't have people doing this all day. They'd die eventually."

"They would?"

"Sure would."

"Oh." Gus found it hard to believe.

The water rolled back, composed itself, and advanced once again, touching Roxanne's feet this time and making her squeal softly. She pulled her feet away from the surf.

"I'm glad we had this talk," she whispered in his ear, as flowering explosions in the sky pirouetted from starry white to pink.

Gus lay back and stared, unblinking, drinking in the pillowy hammering of pyrotechnic glory.

At times, his arm prickled. Tiny tick bites demanded his attention but then were quickly forgotten in a hot—but not uncomfortably so—rush of euphoric bliss that left him gasping. A blast of liquid gold surged along the blue highway of his cardiovascular system, ripping it up at warp speed, cracking the synapses of his nerve endings like fiery whips.

So good.

So *good*.

He wondered how or when these bites came along, if a pattern existed, undetected as of yet. As far as he could tell, no sand flies buzzed around, nor any other aggressive insect life. The bites just seemed to happen.

However . . .

Once, while enchanted by that ever-glowing glitter show above, Gus thought he heard gods speaking—gods who . . . *swore* an awful lot, which made Gus feel better about his overindulgence in expletives. The gods cussed and turned the air blue with flame, and while their amusing and ironic blasphemy thundered throughout the heavens, Gus believed . . . no, he was *positive*, that through the sheer veneer of reality, just beyond those celestial lights far above, shapes *moved*. A tracery moved just behind the sky, like a fingernail popping up and caressing the thinnest of sheets.

They were too indistinct to see clearly what they actually were, but . . . they were there, all the same.

Gus thought and thought about that revelation, wondering if a connection existed between the mysterious beings lurking in the sky and the bites on his arm.

He thought about that for weeks, it seemed, until he came to the conclusion that, yes, an association did exist.

The beach lurched then, one powerful jolt that left Gus staring at the receding surf and then at the balmy tree line some distance behind him. He'd been drifting, cozying up with Roxanne at—in?—his side, watching the scintillating twirls and pops painting the entire sky. The sudden shift ebbed away, and a sunny Gus smacked his lips and smiled, basking in the sand grilling his bare skin.

The smile diminished.

Roxanne was gone.

Brow furrowed, Gus looked around.

The beach stretched into infinity on either side of him. Endless. Empty. Unmoving except for the constant stroking of the surf. He shrugged. Nothing to worry about. She'd probably gone back to the fridge for a few beers. Gus smiled at the thought of cold beers on a hot beach. Jesus, was there anything better? He glanced left and right one last time, hoping maybe the beach had servers so he could put in an order for pizza too. Even chicken fingers . . . if they had them.

Someone slapped him. Hard.

Gus pushed himself back, shocked at the contact, and felt his bowels come close to letting go as the reality he'd been enjoying up to that point split apart with a clap. A storm god's angry face pushed through the bright lights of the sky and stopped inches from Gus's nose.

"*Wake up!*" it roared.

Another slap fell across his cheek, hard enough to bruise, and Gus moaned at the contact.

The lights bled into an off-white flatness draped in dusty webbing.

"*Jesus Christ, he's truly out of it. I swear to fuck, Sick, ease* off *on that shit. I don't want him comatose. Here, you try. Think I threw out my fuckin' arm just then.*"

One of the gods pulled back, replaced by a demonic golem possessing a man's head made of silver. *A man*, Gus realized—tall, mean, with a chin as square as a cinder block. He recognized the features.

Nolan grabbed Gus by the shoulders and shook him, just rattled him as if the big man were trying to extinguish a flaming piece of paper. Gus's lower jaw clacked against the upper until he clenched it, senseless in this violent cement shaker intent on bursting something internal. Nolan released him and threw him back onto the beach—now a sofa.

Jerry stood off to the right while a militarized ninja lurked behind him.

Gus put his hands up and squeaked, "I'm all right. Don't shake me. Don't. I think my balls came off."

That put a satisfied smirk on Nolan's nonmetallic face.

"Morning, sunshine," Jerry greeted in that deep, deep voice of his and moved in past the goon. "Feel all right?"

"Not sure. I think so."

"We had to dope you up a bit. Make you more compliant to travel, but that'll all end soon, I promise."

"Dope me up?"

His brother smiled. "Yeah. Zombie dust 5.0. Or just zed5. Half a dozen other names for the shit. Fuck if I know 'em all. About two years ago, we came across a transport trailer coming up from the states loaded down with every fuckin' illegal drug on the go. Heroin, cocaine, hard and soft o-balls, and plastic two-liter bottles filled with this zombie shit. Makes a person travel without going anywhere."

"You gave me . . . drugs?" Gus asked weakly, grasping the true nature of the bites on his arm.

"Just a little," Jerry admitted with a frown. "Had to. You were just about to open your trap about shit, and I just didn't have the patience or the time to listen. You feel good now, right?"

"What day is it?"

Jerry barked a laugh. "That's the dust talking. Had to bring you out of it, to check on you. A few of my guys became recreational users of zed5. Lost all track of time besides a couple of other effects I won't get into. Can you stand up?"

Gus lay on the couch and stared at Jerry and the rest of the crew present. *Walk?* He considered it, drawing up his legs to stand. Jerry took that as a yes and hauled on Gus's arms until he was on his feet, swaying with a moment's vertigo. Hands steadied him until he didn't need them.

"Not my thing," Shovel said. "But no denying it's useful at times. One time—"

"Jerry, where are we?"

Saying his name silenced Shovel as effectively as a slap. A coolness as sharp as a razor slashed the room, and Gus became very aware of the stillness that one question evoked. He'd said something forbidden, crossed a line, and saw it in the questioning frowns directed at his brother.

Jerry spoke slowly, clearly. "In the presence of the boys here, you call me Shovel. Remember that."

The tone was not to be argued with, which Gus remembered from a long time back, back when they were teenagers.

"Where are we?"

Shovel exhaled and studied Gus with an air of deciding if he could be trusted. "We're just over the Quebec border. Stopped for a day. Had another load to pick up."

"Another load of what?"

"People," Shovel said.

Gus's mouth hung open. A greasy knot of nausea expanded inside of his guts as if a fist had pinched off the southward flow. "People?"

"I don't stutter, man. You heard me."

"You picked up a load of people."

"Well," Shovel scuffed at the floor. "We *had* another load. It didn't go over as planned. Seems like this time, they were waiting for us."

"Why are you doing this?"

"I think we covered this. Me feeding the machine and all. If we *don't* take them, someone else *will*. A better question might be 'Why do they stay?' That's one I've given a lot of thought to. Because, frankly, as bad as we are, as you *perceive* us to be, after a while, a person realizes we're all that's left."

Gus wasn't sure what he was listening to, so he started for the door.

Smiling, Nolan blocked his way, looking down at him with a sympathetic expression.

"I need some air," Gus said.

"Take a breath then," Shovel told him.

"No, I mean I need *fresh* air. If I don't, I'm gonna barf all over this place. And right now, if one pipe opens, I'm pretty sure they'll *all* open."

"Let him out," Shovel said immediately.

Gus stomped toward the door and slap-pushed it open hard enough to make his palms sting. Sunlight blinded him, but the cold air of the afternoon steadied his rolling gullet. A chair was the only step down to the pavement—always pavement, it seemed—and Gus teetered in the doorway.

Faint streamers of black smoke, residual wisps of destruction, rose into the sky over a series of roof tops. The smoke seized his attention. Gus gawked at the billowing trails, took deep breaths, and when he'd seen enough, looked to the right. A second trailer was parked in the lot of a giant strip mall. Intimidating black-masked guards stood in the backs of pickups, automatic weapons held at port arms, eyeing a herd of people sitting on the asphalt.

They were too far to see exactly who they were, but he believed he knew.

"Hafta let them out," Shovel announced from behind, making Gus jump. "Hafta. Let them stretch a bit. We lock them up in the trailer there until transported over. The victors of their individual combats. Whatever. It's not uncomfortable. That trailer has sofas and chairs . . . even bunk beds. Maybe a little cramped, and I sure as hell wouldn't want to be inside if someone cuts the cheese, but hey . . . They made it through part one. Part two is a little easier. A little longer."

"What's part two?" Gus asked, his mouth gone dry.

"Part two is integration. Comes after about six months or so. When all the fight's been bled out. They'll work around camp and such, getting to know folks, seeing that our way is best for all concerned. If they have or had kids, well, they'll see them with our kids, see them getting along. After six months, they'll be evaluated and maybe moved on to something a little more interesting. Maybe be allowed to carry a weapon."

"You'll give them a gun?" Gus asked in disbelief.

"Fuck no. Th'fuck you think I am? Stupid? Maybe a knife or a bat. No guns. But if all goes well and they can be trusted, sure. In time, why not? The more, ah, adventurous ones might even come along on the next roundup of fresh meat."

Gus looked at the motley collection of dejected heads hanging between shoulders. Some hung lower than others, but a few appeared more than ready to . . . *what?*

Prove themselves came to mind.

"You can't do this," Gus whispered, very much aware of the henchmen looming behind Shovel's back.

"Already told you—if I don't, someone else will. Someone who'll use them against me. There's no compromise in this day and age. Only you and the ones against you or who *will* be against you. There's nothing else."

"Jesus . . ."

Shovel pulled Gus out of the doorway and confronted him. Shovel's brown, almost black eyes studied his brother's scarred features, searching for truth.

"Gussy, listen now. You listening? Good. That's good. I need to know you're with me on this. That you're on board here. Some of my guys don't think you are. They don't think your heart's in this in the least. I tell them they're wrong—dead cat wrong. It's in the bloodline, I tell them. But, I gotta ask you now, and you gotta answer and look me in the eye when you do. Are you with me here?"

Gus stared back and involuntarily shivered, staring at Jerry in mute horror, seeing nothing of the big brother he remembered from his youth, nothing of the young man who'd left Annapolis for some Albertan oil field along with their brother Sidney, gone to greener pastures. A few memories shot through his mind of days long gone, but none of them stuck. Jerry wasn't Jerry anymore. Jerry had crossed a line, a very personal line, probably not entirely different from the lines Gus had waltzed across, but where Gus had stopped on the precipice of a very frightening drop, Jerry kept right on going. Maybe he'd been forced to keep on going—Gus could understand that, remembering the faces of people he'd had to kill in order to live.

Maybe Jerry just accepted it faster—learned to live with it—or maybe he'd come to like it.

"What the fuck happened to you?" Gus whispered. "You're like a . . . a *warlord* here. Those are *prisoners* you got sitting on their asses."

Jerry—Shovel—shook his head. "You didn't see them during their initiation. They aren't prisoners. They're *survivors*. They understand."

"Then they're all fucking idiots." Gus firmed up his jaw. The tension ratcheted, and Gus could've sworn that the men behind him would've shot him dead except for the presence of Shovel, who showed no emotion at the insult. Not a trace.

"I'm looking at an idiot," Shovel finally said in a voice that touched bedrock.

"It's in the bloodline," Gus countered.

Shovel's face hardened. "Yeah."

40

Shovel's time for Gus ended then. His men manhandled Gus back into the trailer with barely a struggle. The one called Sick stuck a needle into Gus's arm, and hot ecstasy gushed into that limb, quickly storming his brain. Gus lay back on the sofa, but it had become a cloud, a soft cushiony one, and the roof was the moon.

Fuck me, Gus thought, mouth open. He understood why the shit was illegal.

But that trip turned bad.

The creamy ceiling overhead darkened with images of Shovel doing bad things. A black-and-white movie rolled across the heavens, depicting Shovel killing people without provocation, on the sole premise that if they weren't with him, they weren't with anyone. His henchmen stretched and sprouted into centipedes, swallowing the newly dead whole. Gus told them to stop, but they didn't. He swung at them, but they laughed, red lining their picket-fence teeth.

In the end, a great black sleep sucked Gus down, mercifully dreamless, and when he opened his eyes, his first thought was . . .

Night.

Gus lay on the floor of the trailer, wedged between a plush chair and the sofa. He rubbed a cheek and absorbed the absence of light, sensing it as darker, more ominous than before. He sat up with a groan, his mouth feeling as if his last meal had been sawdust. For long minutes, Gus sat there, breathing, contemplating his situation. His strength returned, to a point, and his stomach tugged on his chain, alerting him that something needed to drop its way and soon.

When was the last time he'd eaten anything? Gus couldn't remember and doubted they'd left anything in the trailer. He stood and fumbled through the furniture. Someone had left a sealed Tupperware dish of cured deer meat and a plastic bottle of water on the desk, and Gus made do with a very late dinner. When he finished, he sat at the desk's edge and just breathed, wondering what he should do. Jerry didn't appear to be listening to reason and, worse, seemed bent on doing things his way. Gus reluctantly concluded that his brother had changed for the worse.

So where did that leave him? Motorboating up shit's creek, that's where.

Gus stood, weathered a rush of wooziness, and studied the blackness of the trailer's interior. He felt around the shadowy desk, stumbling at times, hunting for a lamp or a light switch, anything to help him see. Nothing covered the desk, however, and Gus huffed his impatience. The rear door beckoned, and he lumbered toward it, keeping one hand against a wall. The door had an escape bar, and Gus pushed on it, hearing a click.

The door did not open.

He tried twice more and put his shoulder into the barrier, grunting at the solid contact.

"Christ almighty." Gus rubbed his shoulder. He looked back and swore at his drugged brain. There, at the other end of the trailer, was an opening in the ceiling allowing moonlight inside. He'd missed it completely.

"Still fuckin' stoned here," Gus muttered as he approached the opening, but his bearings were returning quickly. He stopped at the foot of Jerry's bed and looked up, studying a cracked hatchway. Gus stepped onto the bed, noting the springiness in the mattress, and gazed up through a wire mesh. Arms stretched out for balance, Gus craned his neck one way and then the other, watching, listening, and thinking.

What to do, what to do?

"Fuck it," he muttered, hot resentment shooting through his veins instead of that zombie shit or whatever the hell it was called. He certainly didn't like being kept under house arrest. He reached up and discovered the screen could be slid away. It opened with a few testing shoves and a rattle at which Gus cringed, waiting for a reaction. When none came, he found his fingers touched the outer rim of the hatch.

I'm so *not fucking getting out of here* shot through his head as he gently bounced on the mattress. But then he jumped up and hooked his fingers over the edge. His shoulders screamed at him, and he let go, knowing he didn't have the upper-body strength to pull himself up and through. He looked around for something more, noting how that section of the trailer was a little brighter than the rear, but he saw only bolted-down furniture.

The desk.

It was made of hardwood. Gus got down from the bed, pausing while space and time swung him for a loop yet again. When gravity established itself once more, he went to the desk and removed the bottom drawer, long and broad but thin. However, it might do the trick and give him that extra foot necessary for escape.

Gus placed the drawer underneath the hatch and shook his head, knowing he was going to slip off the hardwood bastard and trampoline his dumb ass into a wall where, with his luck, he'd break his goddamn neck. One foot shakily stepped on the box, and Gus panted, tongue steadied between his lips.

He'd have to step and jump, knowing he had only a split second of opportunity before the drawer toppled and took him with it.

Above his head, the open hatchway dared him.

Gus jumped, arms stabbing through the opening and going wide.

Then he fell back.

The edges slammed into his elbows as he dropped. His shoulders shrieked with pain. Gus gasped and scrambled and clawed without coherent thought except to grab for purchase as the hole sucked him back down. His right hand locked onto a metallic knob long enough for his left to grab on to. His feet swung in the air, and for a split second, he looked as though he was driving a car.

A breath of pain and effort squeaked out of him.

With his head and shoulders clear, Gus frantically scanned the roof for something more to grab on to before the trailer pulled him back.

There wasn't a damn thing in sight, however.

Gus slowly pulled himself free of the hatchway, feeling muscles he'd never known existed lighting up in agony. Creating some slack, he reached beyond his handhold and hooked fingers into an unseen groove. He swore, huffed, and steadied himself, glancing around in wide-eyed determination. The moon shone down on the length of the trailer's roof, revealing a metallic runway.

"*You sweet—*" he gasped and in one mighty effort, he wormed his upper chest free of the hatchway, enough to rest his torso on the roof. Gus wheezed and smiled, tucked his arms splayed out and letting his legs dangle, knowing he was a breath away from freedom. He looked around and spotted the shapes of about three other trailers, the motor homes, and the armored beast of a dump truck with the enormous tires. The box of that machine had a medieval battlement ringing the top, which struck the geek in him as incredibly cool.

"All right," he whispered, gathering his second wind.

Someone cleared his throat . . . directly behind him.

Panic surged through Gus, and he glanced over his shoulder as a boot heel cracked into the side of his head. The hatchway angrily sucked him down, arms flailing like party streamers.

The hard wood drawer took him across the lower back before collapsing.

Gus's descent stopped on that springy mattress, skewed at an angle. He moaned and didn't see the head high above, framed in a square.

Sick waited for a few seconds—to make sure the prisoner was breathing—before flicking the lid shut with his boot.

"Tried to get out, eh?"

Gus cracked open an eye and regarded an out-of-focus Jerry, thinking he needed a pair of 3-D glasses. The world behind his brother's head sped by, as if someone had given the globe one mighty spin on its axis, and Gus took a moment to realize that Jerry had a window at his back.

"Yeah," Gus replied in all honesty.

"What then?" Jerry demanded.

"What then?"

"Yeah, moron, what then?"

Gus's wince said, *No need to be* that *way about it.* "Probably would've tried freeing them folks."

"What folks?"

"The ones . . ." Gus tasted his own tongue and grimaced. Then his eyes widened. "I'm back on the shit!"

"You're goddamn right, you're back on the shit. You're fuckin' lucky I didn't have one of the guys just break that fuckin' skull of yours. Now answer the question."

Gus discovered that the zed5 was totally screwing up his ability to lie. He tried to hold on to his words, but they squirted free like a soap bar in a dirty bathtub.

"The folks . . . from Pine Cove."

"Pine Cove," Jerry seethed. "That's the shithole we found you in, right?"

"Yep."

Jerry's face glowed with anger.

"Should try some of those dead sprinkles yourself there, Jerry," Gus suggested, wanting to be helpful.

"Hey, what did I tell you about calling me that name?"

"You said . . . call you Shovel?"

"That's right."

"Aww, c'mon. You still aren't going on with that, are you?"

But then, on the cusp of being completely whacked out of his gourd, Gus realized others loomed around his brother—scary shades all looking right at him.

Shovel backed up and gestured. "Get him up."

The brutish men swarmed Gus, nearly yanking his arms free of their sockets. Gus decided it was a good thing he was practically stoned. They dragged him toward a light at the end of a cave, which was really the trailer, and when daylight sunned his features, he actually smiled as if about to embark upon a leisurely walk.

Then they were on the ground, and Shovel walked on ahead, passing a row of transport trailers stopped in one lane of a highway. An unchecked forest grew on either side of the road. Armed men and women watched Gus being helped along, and he even winked at some of the more attractive ladies.

"You're becoming a pain in the ass, Gussy," Shovel declared. "I should've expected that. You could be a pain in the ass twenty years ago. Listen up. You got one chance at redemption here. One chance."

Shovel stopped under a too-blue sky. Beside him was a beaten and dazed man on his knees, not two feet away from a very gravelly ditch. Confusion short-circuited Gus's increasingly warped sense of reality. The kneeling individual's eyes bloomed an alien shade of purple, transforming them into slits. The guy's lips looked like a fucked-up Botox experiment. Dull red paint covered his face and chest, enough to make Gus wonder if it wasn't paint at all.

The ones called Sick and Nolan stood behind the prisoner. Nolan gripped the guy's shoulder while his other mallet-sized fist swung free.

"Word got out about your little escape attempt," Shovel explained in a sour tone, "inspiring someone to try their own getaway. Can't have that among the new recruits, so I'm going to set an example here, or I should say, *you* are."

Gus blinked in puzzlement at the escapee, recognizing him. "Huh?"

Shovel held out his hand, and Sick slapped a knife into it. Shovel flipped the blade in the air, deftly caught it by the handle, and regarded Gus.

"My boys here have been talking about you, Gussy. They say that you're trouble. That I should probably kill you and leave you on the side of a highway. That the Gus I knew years ago isn't the same person today. But mostly, they're just pissed that you haven't had to pop your cherry like all the other new recruits had to. So I'm gonna change that right now. Right here. You take this knife."

Shovel held the weapon out by the blade, and Gus obediently took it and studied it intently, examining every groove and scratch in the dull steel.

"You show all these people that they're wrong about you," Shovel continued in a softer voice. "You cut this shitstain's throat. Or stab him through the heart. But you kill him. Right now. Kill him, and we'll drive on back home. Get on with business."

Jimbo—the name materialized and faded like smoke in Gus's mind. The prisoner's name was Jimbo. Or just Jim. Poor Jim appeared as if someone had dribbled his head across a basketball court. Collie had freed him from that motel gang. And now, Shovel wanted Gus to kill him.

A chill surged though Gus, dampening his cosmic mellowness.

"Kill him now," Shovel ordered.

Gus regarded Jim's swollen features. Poor brutalized Jim was kneeling in the towering shadows of two demons. A red sky raced overhead, streaming clouds with serrated edges.

Coming to his senses, Jim opened his puffy eyes, revealing blood-filled whites almost spilling over sepia-colored lids. Red water spilled from the corners.

"Stick that knife into him, Gus."

Gus held the knife, clenching and unclenching the handle.

"Stab him through the fucking eyeball, and pop that cherry."

"Jesus, Jerry." That earned Gus a solid clap about the head, stunning him.

"My name's Shovel, you little squirt of shit. Shovel. Now *execute* that fucker!"

Gus hesitantly reached out and held the left shoulder of Jim, whose face drooped in defeat at the contact. Jim grimaced in agony. Sick stepped in, grabbed a handful of hair and yanked Jim's head back, exposing his unshaven throat. His Adam's apple bobbled weakly.

Adam. Where are you, buddy? Gus's thoughts churned.

"Stick him," Shovel commanded.

Gus hesitated, and Jim grimaced again, revealing teeth that had been wrecked by a brick. Or a rock.

"The fuck you waiting for? *Do it.*"

A wind all the way from the arctic face whipped around them all, rustling clothing.

"Might as well," Jim wheezed, releasing a trickle of blood from his mouth. "Beats hangin' out . . . with these dickheads."

Sick tightened his grip on the man's forehead, whisking any more words away in a pained grunt.

Gus exhaled in stoned exasperation. Part of him bobbed on oily currents of despair. He knew he wasn't going to execute *Jim.* The only reasonable idea coursing through his foggy brain was *how* he could perhaps get both of them out of the situation. Nothing came to mind, however, and the knife's point caught a flicker of sunlight, flashing off the tip. Twisting serpentine shadows flashed across the ground, and Gus dared not look up for fear of seeing nightmarish creatures in the sky. His skin prickled right down to his numbed heels. His heart rate accelerated, redlining, threatening to burst.

Jim stared at him, nodding faintly, as if tired of it all.

"*Do it!*" Shovel barked.

Gus shivered from that blast before slowly lowering the knife. Jim's breathing hitched to a stop, his bloody eyes leaking, questioning him with a tortured expression.

Gus rested the knife on his leg. "I'm too fucked up for this," he stated. "Not murdering anyone today."

Those words seemed to hang on the air for years. Whole trees took root and grew heavenward while the sky relaxed and reverted to a healthy blue.

"It's the shit in him," Sick might've said.

"He ain't gonna do it," Slick Pick remarked from kilometers away.

A floating embankment of raw, unchecked frustration swept over Gus then, as distasteful as septic gas, all emanating from his brother.

"You stab that bastard," Shovel warned. "You stab him, or I'll make your life fucking hell."

Gus frowned a *fuck that* and dropped the knife.

"God . . . *damnit*," Shovel exclaimed softly. "Sick."

With bare fingers, Sick gripped Jim's exposed throat and squeezed as if it was an overripe plum. Jim gasped, a horribly wet sound, before blood erupted between Sick's fingers—a spray at first but quickly gushing.

Sick tightened his hold and pulled. All color fled Jim's features. He bled out in a dying gargle.

The sky vacuumed Gus up into its dizzying heights.

41

The motorized convoy arrived at Whitecap five hours later, and Shovel, for one, was glad. The episodes with Gus, from his failed escape to his refusal to kill a prisoner, had exasperated him to the point where he sat and stewed in his command trailer without a word to anyone. He brooded at his desk, gently jiggling with the movement of the rig. After Gus had passed out, a gutless reaction if ever Shovel had witnessed one, he had the unconscious man taken to the refrigeration unit along with the food-stuffs. Sick pumped him full of zed5 once again, enough to sedate the man for the remainder of the day—maybe even the week.

But Gus's refusal to cross over to the other side bothered Shovel.

Anyone else, he'd have killed without a second thought. He knew it. The fact that Gus was family prevented him from pulling the trigger—and in front of his men, no less. That also bothered him. If Shovel wavered in front of them, one or two hotheads might suspect that he was soft somehow, that there was a flaw in that core of steel—that Shovel's command might be challenged.

Perhaps even usurped.

The column of trucks and motor homes rolled through the secretive maze of forest and old dirt roads, past the barbed wire and concrete barriers, onto the white cement surface of Whitecap's outer clearing. The transport drivers eased the rig into a designated parking area and parked it with a huff and squeal of air brakes, not far away from a trio of fuel tankers. The other trucks pulled in around it, taking their place in a chuck-wagon defensive pattern around the base of the mountain. White-cap rose up from the cluster of vehicles, trailers, and buildings like a godlike behemoth ignoring its worshippers.

Shovel opened the trailer's rear door and jumped to the ground. He gazed up at the mountain's tall peak taking aim at the cloudy heavens.

Shovel hoped Giovanni had good news for him. He needed good news right then. He needed a shitload of it.

Shovel walked to the front of his ride and waited for Slick Pick to show up. He didn't wait long.

"Pick! Take care of all this shit. I'll be home if you need me."

"What about your brother?" the man asked.

Shovel cringed at the thought. "Lock him in one of the empty trailers. Put a couple of guards on it."

"An empty trailer, Shovel?"

Shovel glared at his henchman.

"All I'm saying is it gets cold at night in one of those things."

"So give him a mattress and a blanket," Shovel shot back. "And keep him shot up. But nothing else, Pick. Not one goddamn thing more."

Pick waved his understanding and got moving.

Grumbling under his breath and feeling slightly poisoned, Shovel ignored the greetings from the people who had remained at Whitecap and made a line for his trailer. He unlocked the door and went inside. His chair beckoned, and he plopped down behind his desk, yanked open a drawer, and pulled out a bottle filled with some very fine scotch. A mug followed, and Shovel wasted little time filling it and taking a short but greedy pull.

The scotch helped, and he leaned back in the chair and propped up both feet. Whitecap's girth, glowing in evening sunlight, overloaded the picture window at the end of the trailer. Shovel stared at it, pensive, cradling his drink.

A knock at the door distracted him. "Enter," he called out.

Giovanni appeared, crusted with enough dust to make one think of Wild West deserts. He removed a baseball hat and combed his graying mesh of hair and beard with his fingers in a nonchalant effort to make himself respectable.

"Gonna take more than that." Shovel smirked over the ceramic lip of his mug.

Giovanni tossed his head back, shook loose his ponytail, and sat down in the chair before Shovel's desk. "How'd the trip go there, big chief?"

"So-so."

"Only so-so?"

Shovel regarded his number two. "We got a little over forty new bodies to add to the ranks."

"Pretty good draft."

"Lost a few guys on the way back to a group that took offense to us."

Giovanni frowned and let his breath out in a soft whistle.

"Got two trailers' worth of winter provisions: dried meat, fish, bottled veggies, and jam. Plus some of them army meals."

"Good stuff."

"There was livestock, but we'll go back for them in a day or two. Too many bodies and booty to bring back."

By that time, Giovanni's brown eyes had narrowed. His chair squeaked as he settled in for the big reveal. Shovel knew the look. His right-hand man sensed something was coming.

"And . . ." he let it hang for a moment, "we also found my brother."

Giovanni's face scrunched together in disbelief for all of a second before brightening. "But that's great news . . . isn't it?"

"Not if he's a chickenshit."

That left Giovanni speechless.

"Yeah, you heard me." Shovel gave an expletive-rich report to his old friend, who sat and listened in rapt attention, nodding in agreement when prompted. When Shovel finished, Giovanni reached for the scotch and took a swig straight from the bottle.

"Yeah." Shovel chuckled darkly. "Reason to drink, ain't it?"

"Hate to think there's another one of you, but shit, ain't it a shame he's not like you. If he was, we'd get things done at twice the speed."

Shovel had to nod at that assessment and fished out another mug for his lieutenant. They poured fresh drinks, sampled them, and shared a silence.

"Wouldn't kill the guy, huh?" Giovanni finally said.

"Nope."

"Right in front of the girls and boys too, eh?"

"Yep."

"That shit's gotta burn."

Shovel didn't bother commenting and took another clarifying shot of scotch.

"What're you gonna do?" Giovanni finally asked.

"Fuck if I know." Shovel stared out the window. "But I'm gonna have to do it fast."

"You want me to shoot him?"

"Nah."

"You sure?"

Shovel shook that question off with a rattle of his head.

"Want advice, then?"

"Sure."

"You can't keep the guy locked up forever. Can't keep him as a pet. And you're certain he's not gonna come over to the dark side. So, I don't see any choice. You keep him around, and you're only inviting disaster. Sooner or later, he's gonna try and break for it. This life, it changes folks. We've both seen it, both lived through some pretty dark times. I'd say, if it's all the same to you, put this episode behind you and leave your brother, both of your brothers, in the past. As fond memories."

Shovel stared at the man sitting across from him. "And the guy I brought in today?"

"Let Sick take care of him," Giovanni suggested in a low growl. "Let him whip up one of his cocktails of highly addictive substances, something painless but guaranteed to do the job. I don't think overdosing's a cruel way to go. Not in the least."

Overdose.

Shovel stopped drinking and tossed the idea around.

"Yeah, you chew on that," Giovanni said. "No rush. But in the meantime, don't think of him. Now listen. I got some good news for you, concerning the tunnel."

"You broke through?"

"Not that good. But we're close. Other good news. A tease of what's to come."

"Let's hear it."

"Yesterday, we uncovered an armored truck, full with ammunition and a crate full of what appears to be German-made assault rifles—complete with scopes and grenade launchers. Grade-A ball breakers, if I do say so myself."

Shovel sat up, his attention captured. Spirits raised. "How much ammo?"

"A magazine holds fifty rounds. Crate holds about two hundred magazines. We hauled nine crates outta the ass of that truck."

"Jesus, that's—"

"Ninety thousand rounds. Not bad, I'd say. We're dangerous again."

"*Hooah*," Shovel whispered.

"And I reckon we're not that far from the holy land. We're digging around the truck now. Widening it just a little, even hit a bubble in there. Can't be much farther to the finish line. We're in there pretty deep."

"Yeah?"

"If I was to guesstimate, I'd say we'll be inside in another two or three days. By the end of the week at the latest."

Shovel raised his mug in salute.

Fine news, indeed.

The doors opened and bathed the interior of the trailer in light. Gus, reduced to a tight, shivering ball sitting against a wall of stacked coolers, peeked guardedly at his visitors: four figures, a woman and a guy and two more wearing those black masks.

They climbed into the rear, their shadows long and reaching. Behind them, more torsos milled about the lip of the trailer door.

Slick Pick snapped his fingers, making Gus flinch. "You dead yet?" he asked before studying the food stuffed into the trailer.

Gus didn't answer. He trembled instead.

"Looks frozen," the woman observed.

"He should be," Slick Pick said. "Been on ice here for the last five or six hours. Sure as hell would freeze my asshole to the floor. Only hope to God he didn't piss himself while in here."

"You're terrible."

"Yet so cute," Slick Pick said with a greasy smile.

"You are that."

Slick Pick regarded Rachel. She was his height, brunette, and solid looking. Most of the crew were lean and hard, but the women were something else. Nothing like the end of the world to make everyone drop their excess fat, and he imagined Rachel in T-shirts and cutoffs in the summertime. He'd especially taken a shine to her as she'd demonstrated, without a doubt, she belonged to an outfit like Shovel's.

Slick Pick remembered his job and pointed at the doors. "All right. Haul his icy ass over to that empty trailer next to med-house."

The two wearing masks moved in and grabbed Gus by the arms, pulling him to his feet. Gus resisted, feebly at first, but once on his feet, he yanked an arm away and got shoved up against a wall for his efforts. An elbow pressed hard against his throat, settling him down.

"You finished?" Slick Pick asked.

"Yeah."

"Good. Listen. You give these guys any trouble, and they will slap you around. Just so you know."

"Thanks."

Slick Pick stepped out of the way, brushing against Rachel. "That's how you do it."

"I like how you handled that," she said as the pair of guards locked Gus's arms up behind his back and walked him out of the trailer.

"I'm good at handling things," Slick Pick said with a wink.

Daylight made Gus squint in pain. They pushed him past parked transport trucks and groups of people unloading trailers. He took in the compound, awestruck at the size and scope of the valley and the mountain dominating it all. Chain-link fences topped off with twirls of wire ringed the tree lines. A noisy backhoe grumbled up a wide ramp toward a wide tunnel. Work crews carrying picks and shovels followed the machine. At the base of the ramp was a flatbed with an honest-to-God minigun mounted on the back. Ammunition feeds linked crates to the menacing weapon. Gus swore at the sight before being walked past some low housing or office structures as well as the motor homes he recognized as belonging to Collie and Wallace. Where the special operators were now, he had no idea. Alive, he hoped. Preferably planning a rescue. That made him chuckle.

The men twisting his arms behind his back didn't appreciate the sudden merriness from their prisoner. They jacked his joints until the bones and musculature were about to pop.

Gus grunted in pain but smiled it off, basking in the residual effect of the drugs injected into him. People walked with purpose around that mountainside pit stop and paid little attention to him. His eyes wandered to a long trailer parked next to a single-story house. The front door was opened, and—

Gus's eyes widened.

A shocked Maggie stood on the threshold, dropping her hands, which she'd been drying with a towel, and stared back at him.

Holy shit. Here.

That meant Shovel—or a pack of his pyschopaths acting on his word—wiped out the farm. Killed Adam and the others and started this whole goddamn journey of horrors.

Gus's guts curled into icy knots. He slowed, but his guards pushed him on. The guards escorted him to the rear of a forlorn-looking trailer where another masked man appeared like some irradiated ninja.

"Jesus Christ," Gus moaned. "Not you again."

Sick's eyes sparkled with evil intent.

"You're gonna get me addicted to that shit."

Sick pulled on the trailer door, opening it with a metallic groan begging for oil. The guards shoved Gus into the lower lip, catching him unprepared, and he crashed with another grunt. Slick Pick moved and lowered a retractable set of steps from below the doors. Hands dug into Gus's armpits and the back of his jeans, and they pushed him up the stairs into the container. One of the guards tripped him, and he crumpled to his side. Gus rolled over, and the man called Sick was already beside him. He drove his knee into Gus's chest and held him there while guards pinned him down.

"How much you giving him, Sick?" Slick Pick's face appeared over a shoulder.

"Thirty milligrams," the man said in his raspy voice.

"He's getting up there fast."

Sick didn't comment. Instead, he produced a long syringe and rolled Gus's sleeve up.

"No moving around now," Slick Pick's voice instructed. "No moving. Don't want Sick snapping that needle off in your arm. I don't think you're covered under our medical plan."

Gus didn't move. Part of him *wanted* the needle. At least on the beach, things weren't so shitty. And he'd found Maggie after all. Small world indeed.

The needle sank into the vein.

"You're the man," Gus informed the impassive ski mask as Sick held an administering pose.

"Oh, here," Slick Pick pulled out a plastic bottle from a leg pocket of his cargo pants. He slid it across to Gus's hand. "In case you find it cold in there."

It was the bottle of Captain Morgan—the same one with the twine still attached to the neck. No one had chugged the booze yet. Seeing it lifted Gus's spirits like a lucky charm.

Then that liquid heaven rushing through his arm, invading him, finally reached his brain.

Gus's consciousness sped off like a wayward torpedo, spinning into a deep, deep blue.

42

The beach delivered therapeutic heat to his back, seeping through his tired muscles, slowing his pulse, as his detached consciousness sailed over falls of euphoria. Water rolled over the sand, scrubbing it softly, surging and retreating, in tune with his sedated heart and his breathing.

Paradise. Gus exhaled and inspected himself, seeing a ripped body glistening in oil. That he was wearing oil didn't seem strange at all. His memory did point out an oddity, and he took a moment to realize he was missing the scar dear old Alice had given him. He searched for it, probing with fingers, but it was gone, replaced with smooth, sun-browned skin.

Not bad. He wormed his way deeper into the sand, soaking up the rays and listening to the hushed rhythm of the surf.

Too bad Maggie isn't here.

That thought made him crack an eye in drunken puzzlement. He couldn't place the name or a face, yet he sensed it was somehow important. He had a feeling she was close, but for the life of him, he didn't understand why she wasn't on a perfect beach like that on such a day. Not a soul walked the shoreline, and the palm trees waved gently, making him think of the Caribbean, telling him not to worry. All was just *ducky.*

A contented smile stretched over Gus's features, and he idly scratched at his beard, wondering if beach flies might find him. Food entered his mind, but *later . . . later.* The sun dulled the notion away, making it too much effort to leave the beach.

Gus dozed, breathing in the heat and the smell of tropical seawater.

He woke up a while later, maintaining his peaceful vibe, and casually checked out the beach, hoping he'd catch a glimpse of some sand bunnies in thongs—or even topless. Seeing the coast was clear, he settled back and took a deep breath. A brief chill touched him, enough that he wondered where it had come from, then he relaxed and got back to work on his tan.

His eyes opened.

Gus sat up, feeling the surf cream about his lower legs, and glanced left. Nothing. He looked to the right and saw a figure on the beach, too far away for details. Gus squinted, thinking he saw red. The shape continued trekking along, making no attempt to dodge the surf.

"Well, holy shit," Gus muttered.

There, walking a line between the sea and beach, strode the Captain.

The officer waved, his infectious grin leaping to Gus's own suntanned mug, and Gus waved back before staggering to his feet.

They met halfway along the beach and threw their arms around each other.

"My God, it's good to see you again, man," Gus gushed, releasing the Captain for a moment before hugging him again. "Thought I was going to be alone here."

"Never alone, my son," Captain Morgan replied, his tanned crow's feet making him all the more dashing. "Never alone. How's the water?"

"Great."

"And how've you been?"

"Fucking great since I got here!"

That outburst earned a sympathetic smile from the old sailor.

"C'mon, sit down," Gus said. "This place is spectacular. Always wanted to go south, and man, it's everything I figured it would be."

The pair sat, oblivious to the warm seawater rushing around their backsides. The Captain appeared unconcerned by the surf—and the heat, as he'd dressed in his brightest finery. He tipped his hat and swept it from his head with a flourish, uncovering a black cloth wrapping his head. The Captain leaned back with a sigh and studied the horizon, taking it all in with an expert eye.

"Lovely," he whispered and cocked an eyebrow at Gus. "Beautiful spot."

"Ain't it? Only wish there were a few ladies around, eh? Just a little more to look at. And I'm sure there's a place to eat just past the trees there behind us. I haven't gone looking yet, but since you're here, we can check it out. Maybe there's a luau cooking up. If there is, it's on me."

The Captain looked over his shoulder, nodding, and considered the thick curtain of vegetation before returning his attention to the surf.

"Simply lovely," he said. "You've been here long?"

Gus chuckled. "Yeah. Can't tell you how long, though."

"You look good, yeah."

"Thank you, sir," Gus said smartly. "You appear to be in fine health yourself."

"I watch the intake. Mind the grog. Don't mind the ladies too much as that's just as important as food and drink."

"I understand completely."

"This truly is a beautiful place. In all my time on the water, I don't believe I've encountered such waters of clear blue . . . sands so inviting. The very air is a pleasure to breathe. Can you taste that? So fresh it's intoxicating. You've done well for yourself, Gus, my old friend."

Done well for myself? Gus thought, and the corners of his smile drooped just a bit.

"It's almost a shame you can't stay here," the Captain said with a sympathetic sigh.

"I can't?"

A mild frown darkened the officer's face. "I'm afraid not. Things aren't quite done yet, you see. You've traveled far, and you're very, very close. Maggie and the children are very near."

"Maggie . . ." Gus stretched out the word, recognizing the name, a face appearing in his mind. "Oh shit, yeah, she . . . she got taken. Her and the kids."

"But you found them."

"I did?"

"Concentrate, now . . ." The Captain smiled gently, but the glow stopped at his eyes. "Concentrate, my lad. You have to remember. I'm afraid your lives depend on it . . ."

Collie and Wallace returned to their secluded cabin, not thirty minutes from Pine Cove. They'd found the little getaway after exploring one of many side roads along the highway and decided to make it a refuge from the surviving civilian types. As Wallace's condition deteriorated, that choice seemed all the wiser.

They parked the pickup, got out, and unlocked the door to the rustic dream getaway on the bay, smelling gasps of pine and other hardwoods. In truth, the cabin was actually a second home for someone long gone, designed to bestow an open, spacious feel. A modern fireplace and cozy furniture filled the living room. Stacks of paperbacks and magazines lay about. A dartboard hung from a wall.

Collie and Wallace went to the ground-floor bedroom converted into a holding pen. The windows had been boarded from the inside and the door reinforced with a few extra planks and deadbolts. A slot had been cut into the door at eye level. A bed remained in the room but little else. Wallace had long maintained that if he was going over, *really* going over, why the hell should he have any furniture in the room? Collie insisted on the bed.

"Ready?" Collie asked him.

"Yeah."

"Love you, babe."

Wallace hit her with an emotional look that said the same.

Collie closed the door on that face. She locked it from the outside as he did the same from within. Then she sat down on the floor, feeling the gun in her hip holster clatter on the hardwood floor, and leaned her head against the wall.

There she stayed, stationed at the door—waiting, listening, conversing with her husband on the other side. She remained there the whole time. If she got hungry or thirsty, she went to the kitchen. If the stillness made her weary or sleepy, she slept right there with a pillow under her head and a tangle of quilts for everything else.

The first day, Wallace didn't say very much at all. He stayed in the room, lying on the bed and brooding at the ceiling. Just that position alone was almost too much for Collie to handle, reminding her too much of a deathbed. So she refrained from peeking through the slot to check up on him. All the while, he maintained silence. After the episode with Gus, Collie really didn't know what Wallace was experiencing during those long bouts of silence, so she called out to him whenever the quiet started to really get her.

Eventually, Wallace asked her to lay off.

Hours passed, and the sun went down, casting long shadows within the cabin, hiding the bay. Neither bothered with a light. Collie didn't light the fireplace.

Later, deep in the night, Wallace spoke from just inside the door. The sound of his voice so close startled Collie. She hadn't heard him get off the bed.

He started talking about trivial things: people they knew, places they'd been, lives saved and lost, experiences shared.

The hours filled with a litany of *remember when*s and *never forget*s, as they conjured up memory after memory, each one lighting the dark with smiles. Well past midnight they whispered, like children fearful of being overheard by some unseen force lurking just beyond the cabin walls. At times, they chuckled. At others, they paused until the emotion passed. Eventually, Collie could talk no more and drifted off to sleep, barely hearing Wallace's *good night*.

The second day was the same as the first except Wallace's need for conversation disappeared. He paced his room, waiting, at times angry and resentful at having received Whitecap's injection, hating what was happening to him. Curses streamed into a vicious rant, unheard of from the operator. He stomped, slapped walls, and shoved the bed.

She didn't interrupt him, hunkering down until the storm had passed, keeping her sidearm close just in case.

By early afternoon, the poison had worked out of his system, and he returned to lying on his back. Collie scarcely ate, and when she did, she did so quietly, for fear of reminding Wallace he no longer needed real food.

Into the night, Wallace sulked, unresponsive to her questions, unwilling to partake in another evening of sharing memories.

He'd entered a dark tunnel of self-loathing, and Collie wondered if his mood swings were portentous warnings of the final change.

The shadows in the house became pits of palpable tension.

Collie maintained her vigil at the door.

Her weapon ready.

She opened her eyes in the morning, surprised that sleep was even possible. She'd rolled over onto the floor, the pillow mysteriously finding her cheek, hand still on her gun. From where she lay, the kitchen island grew out of the floor and towered over her.

No sound was coming from Wallace's bedroom.

"Ollie?"

No response.

"Ollie, you okay in there?"

She jumped into a crouch and pressed herself against the wall next to the door, her gun at her thigh. She peered through the slot, keeping her face back a safe distance. The corners remained empty, as did the bed, which had been pulled out from the wall and yanked to one side during one of his outbursts.

"Ollie?"

Her mouth felt like a cavern of sun-scorched leather. Her eyes narrowed, and her hearing flicked to its highest setting. The boards on the window were untouched. She stepped softly to the other side of the door, scanning the opposite corners. The closet in the room was a small one, with no door, and offered no place to hide. Wallace couldn't be seen anywhere.

That meant he was at the door.

"Ollie?"

She angled her line of sight to take in the ceiling, as silly as she felt for doing so, then stood on her toes to see the ground.

A boot stretched out, toes up as if he sat and leaned against the door.

"Hey, you . . . still here?"

Collie stepped in closer. The top of a head came into view, the hair shortened to a dark fuzz covering gray skin.

"Ollie?"

The head turned slightly. "Yeah?"

The relief flooding through Collie weakened her knees. "How you doing?"

"Still here."

"You scared me."

Wallace grunted and stood. He unlocked the door. "Let me out of here, Collie."

"What?"

"I'm tired of this FK9 shit. If anything was going to happen, it would've by now. I don't know why it slacked off, but it feels like it has. I'm good to go."

Collie processed all of that before asking, "You sure?"

"Yeah. Muzzle me if you have to. But I'd rather be doing something useful other than this goddamn waiting."

She could understand that.

So she let him out.

When they arrived at Pine Cove's main gate and saw it open, they knew there was a problem.

But neither expected the horrors left in the street.

They got out of their pickup and wandered, stricken, as if forced to explore a nightmare. The bodies left frozen on the pavement stopped them in their tracks. Collie and Wallace *knew* these people, and their violent deaths rendered them speechless. Collie discovered the lifeless form of old man Phil, pale yet noble in death, the front of his shirt punctured in several places as if he'd been stabbed repeatedly through the rib cage with an ice pick or some similar tool. Ray Minglewood lay in a bloody heap near his office, the handicraft of an automatic weapon easy to discern. They inspected a few of the houses and left the rest, knowing no survivors were left in Pine Cove and realizing half the populace was missing.

Including Gus.

Tire tracks had ripped through small fields and left tufts of sod all the way back to the main gate. One set of monster tracks gouged the soil inches deep, drawing their attention. The vehicle's massive weight left six-foot-wide prints in the degrading pavement, crushing the edges into crumbs the size of golf balls. Collie and Wallace stood at the gate, staring, marveling at the machine's mass and wondering who had kidnapped Pine Cove's people. They'd worked so hard to establish the town as a safe haven, bringing people to that little corner of the world and repopulating it, only to discover it *gone* in two days.

They drove off, intent on finding whoever was responsible.

Craving retribution.

They hunted for two days, driving slowly, their windows down, studying the wrecked pavement and sides of the road with a grim appreciation of the force ahead of them. "An army," Wallace stated, still cognizant, still in full control of his mind and deteriorating body.

The search for the missing Pine Cove townspeople focused and motivated him like no other therapy or argument Collie could have mounted. Those missing souls perhaps even aided him in ways not easily measured or identified, holding off the final stages of his condition. At least for a while. Collie hoped it would be long enough. Her man was dying beside her, getting closer with every passing second, and while she mourned for him inside, she reminded herself that he *didn't* mourn, that he pushed on, despite his condition—so like Wallace. He didn't lie down and surrender—certainly not when other lives were at stake.

Instead, Wallace concentrated on the task set before them, and so did she.

Whoever had killed half of Pine Cove and taken the rest, wherever they were heading, Collie and Wallace followed. Unerringly, they retraced a path, happening upon empty bottles and garbage tossed onto the shoulders of the road—the scraps of a massive, landlocked wake.

They discovered more bodies from a shoot-out, a handful of people who had set themselves up roughly four hundred kilometers from Pine Cove, close enough to be neighbors but small enough to escape notice. The army had found them, and the settlers had resisted. Wallace and Collie pieced together the progression of the battle, studied the dead, and picked up spent shotgun cartridges and the brass of military-grade assault weapons.

By evening, they found Jim's body, barely recognizable, for half of his face had been picked away by crows. His throat had been torn out—by fingers, they concluded in dark disbelief. In all of their years and theaters of combat, neither one had ever witnessed such a vicious killing.

The discovery of Jim urged them to search faster.

Four days later, after some cautious driving through the wilds of Quebec toward the northern deep-woods country of Ontario, the feeling came over them that the trail was heading in a familiar direction.

*

A pickup rattled away from the base of Whitecap and soon disappeared into a forest redolent with the midmorning smells of cedar and fir and undercut with a hint of fresh water, running in hidden brooks. The temperature had dipped close to freezing the night before, and a frost coated the underbrush in a sprinkling of white. Three men and two women rode in the vehicle—two in the cab, three in the box. All traveled with newly found hardware locked and loaded, with safeties off. Weapons ready, the three in the box held on to welded side walls of sheet metal and bounced around, hoping to spot a deer or a bear—something *alive*, anyway, to test-fire the big guns in their possession.

Their truck rattled over the road, waddling through an encroaching wilderness, and low-hanging branches tried to slap the closest occupants.

Then they dipped into a gulley and came upon a pickup blocking the road.

"The fuck's *that*?" the driver, whose name was Chris, asked as he braked hard, jolting everyone aboard. The truck lurched to a stop, facing its twin barring the way.

"The fuck *is* that?" Gertrude—called "Gertie"—added as she pulled up her assault rifle and opened the door. "Cover me."

"There's a driver."

"Yeah, but he's slumped over," Gertie said and pulled her balaclava down over her rough features. "No zombie drove all the way up here."

"Be careful then."

Gertie didn't answer because she always practiced caution. She hefted her rifle and nestled its stock against her shoulder, lined up the 1x-magnification sight, and stalked forward as if walking through a minefield. She wasn't formally trained as a soldier— none of them were—so they got by on what they'd remembered seeing in the movies. As she crept closer to the obstructing pickup, with the sounds of the running engine behind her and the hushed murmuring of the surrounding brush, she could make out the person behind the wheel.

The driver's window had been lowered. Inside was a soldier wearing a helmet, a man, head down and resting on the upper curve of the steering wheel. Tactical webbing hung around his shoulders. His mouth hung open as if he'd just finished projectile barfing all over the dash. Gertie smelled him and cringed. She kept her rifle trained on him, however, and glanced back at her companions. The three in the box lined the top of the cab and covered her with readied weapons.

"Well?" a man called out.

"Looks dead." Gertie edged closer. She glanced around, scanning the woods before returning to the body at the wheel. "Guy's a corpse."

"He's dead?"

"Been dead for a couple of days or so, I figure," Gertie estimated.

"How the hell he get up here?" a woman asked.

"Is he a zombie?" questioned another.

"Wait." Gertie reached forward and gripped the door handle. She pulled it open and took two shots to the belly that blasted her backward into the brush.

Collie rolled out from underneath the pickup and grabbed the rifle from the fallen woman, feeling the violent chatter of gunfire answering Wallace's shots. Collie wound up on her chest, leveled the rifle at the truck, and blew out the windshield in a tracery of circles right where the driver would be. The three in the back responded in kind, muzzle fire lighting up the late autumn shadows, blazing into Wallace and their truck. Collie adjusted her aim and fired, making the scalp of a lowered head jump in a bloom of blood and hair. That target sank out of sight, his machine gun popping off a last barrage of shells before falling silent.

The woman in the box wildly returned fire, ripping up dirt and marching a trail of bullets right up to where Collie lay. Collie shifted, aimed, and shot her in the face, jettisoning the woman backward in a chunky halo of gray matter. She shifted targets in the split second it took for the last man to realize he was all alone and killed him with one bullet through the forehead. He flopped onto the roof like a marionette with its strings abruptly cut . . . and eventually slid out of sight.

The firefight ended in less than five seconds.

Collie searched for other targets while the truck continued to idle.

"Ollie?" she called out.

"I'm good."

"Any of them get you?"

"Said I'm good."

Grouch.

Collie got to her feet, training her weapon on the opposing truck and sidestepped over to her husband. He'd shot the first raider through the midsection before flopping down across the cup holders and stick shift, just before the windshield went electric with return fire.

"Check on them," he said as he clawed his way back into a sitting position.

Collie ran up to the opposing truck and quickly confirmed the kills. All had expired by head shots. She studied the road to Whitecap for a few seconds and, once satisfied that no one else was coming, returned to Wallace's kill.

The woman still lived, holding her hands over her messy abs. Collie grabbed a shoulder and flipped her onto her back, eliciting a whimper.

"Are there any more?" Collie demanded. She got a wheezing grimace as a reply. Collie slapped her twice, hard, before gripping her chin and repeating the question.

"No more," the woman squeaked through clamped teeth.

"How many of you are there?"

"Huh?"

Collie whacked her again, vicious palm strikes not quite up to full power, but with enough force to rattle teeth and clear a mind.

"I dunno," her prisoner whined. "A hundred fifty maybe. Maybe two."

"Lots of these?" Collie held up the rifle.

Blood outlined the teeth in the woman's answering smile.

"Thanks," Collie stood up, took aim, and put a single bullet through the wounded woman's head with no more thought than she would give to cracking open a can of beer.

"You hear that?" she asked Wallace as he oozed out from behind the wheel.

"Yeah."

"Recognize this?" Collie held up the rifle, and Wallace's usually wincing face softened just a bit.

"Yeah," he muttered. "German HK H-50Z."

"Remember where you saw one last?"

Wallace didn't answer. He knew. She knew too.

"One thing's for sure," Collie said. "These shitheads sure as fuck aren't soldiers."

"Think there might be some rentals among them?"

Collie fixed him with a *gimme a break* look, and he dropped the matter.

"What do you want to do?" he finally asked.

She glanced up the road. "Let's strip these rat rags, get the rigs off the road, and get on our black Cadillacs."

The dead gave up eight additional magazines, which were stuffed into pockets and webbing. Wallace appropriated a rifle for himself. They then drove the trucks off onto one of the many side roads meant to confuse drivers, left them, and started walking. They stayed close to the main route, ready to dive into the brush if they heard an approaching vehicle. Twice Collie led Wallace into the underbrush. Wary of mines, they approached advance surveillance stations constructed ten meters back from the main road. No one manned the camouflaged, two-person concrete boxes, nor did it appear anyone had in a while. Collie didn't bother searching them. She and Wallace had already scrounged everything of use from the lookouts when they had previously left Whitecap for what they believed to be the last time. Satisfied that no one was monitoring their approach, they returned to the main road.

When Whitecap loomed up through the forest canopy, they entered the woods and stayed low. Collie moved like a two-legged eel through the brush while Wallace struggled. He snapped branches when he should not have, shuffling when he should have floated. Collie glanced back at times, zeroing in on his lumbering shadow five meters behind, cringing yet sympathetic.

Daylight waned as they arrived at the base of a dense hillside, one that Collie intended to climb for the elevated vantage point. She stopped and waited for Wallace to draw up beside her, gasping at his pungent, decaying body odor.

"How you doing, chuggernuts?"

Wallace fixed her with an evil look.

Collie didn't back down. "Think you can do this hill?"

"That's a borderline *fuck you* question."

"At one time, maybe, but I don't think I need to point out the obvious, so just give me a goddamn answer."

The dwindling light reflected off Wallace's lowered visor, and his mouth twisted up like two fat worms. "Yeah. I can make it."

All she needed to know. "Watch your step. Might be some of those mines lying around."

Wallace didn't comment on that, so Collie led the way up the hill, threading her way and passing through the foliage with barely a ripple, blending in and not once looking back. If he wanted to be an unprofessional dick, so be it. The German-made assault rifle felt light in her arms as she climbed, hearing distant engines and the odd shout. When she reached the top of the hill, she planted herself on a copper-colored blanket of leaves and sized up the situation at Whitecap.

"Honey, you got rats," Collie said under her breath, seeing figures milling about in the valley below, black insects against the cement. The collection of office buildings dotting the gray-white concrete plate had been joined by transport trailers, motor homes, and pickups—all arranged in an overlapping semicircle a short ways below the main ramp leading into the bunker. The whole picture resembled a mythological monster about to feed. The Komatsu truck surprised her—no mistaking that tower of industrial might lording over the other pieces of machinery. She lifted the rifle and adjusted her scope to the 3.5x magnification, zooming in and inspecting the truck's curious enhancements. What she saw surprised her even more. Whoever those bastards were, someone knew how to weld, and they had transformed the Kat into a rolling fortress. The only things missing were heavy-gun emplacements.

But the motor homes were theirs. Collie felt a second of satisfaction upon recognizing them. They'd located their property, their people, and their kidnappers.

"Anything?" Wallace asked from behind. He'd taken his time.

"Oh yeah," she whispered back, still sizing up the compound. "All sorts of busy down there. Took you long enough."

Wallace ignored that as he dropped down beside her, one body over, moving like a floundering iceberg. His joints crackled. Collie didn't comment about the noise, but it made her heart just a little heavier. Wallace got his rifle into position, lifted his visor, and placed the sights to his right eye socket.

"They're ours," he said after a moment's study, "and those chicken fuckers are armed. Some of them anyway."

"See the ramp? They're digging into Whitecap. Lord only knows what they might've dug out already."

"They'd have to figure out how to use any of it."

"After the shootout at the truck, I think they're learning."

"You call that spray-and-pray a shootout?" Wallace rumbled, mouth skewed as he panned left and right.

"My point is they know the basics."

"There's beaucoup bad guys down there, with automatic weaponry. Civvies turned road savages or not, them's a lot of assholes and stinky trigger fingers. Lord only knows what else."

"You think we should stay here and just wait?"

Wallace growled then, startling Collie enough that she glanced away from her scope and regarded her husband with an undisguised look of alarm.

"I think," he continued, immediately relieving her, "you should take a walk down to the chicken ranch there and make like a native. Maybe try for the main gate. Or . . . some of those sections where the fence seems to have been taken down."

"You want a daylight insertion?" Collie asked with ready-to-rebuke dismay.

"See what they're wearing?"

Collie returned to the scope.

Balaclavas. Not all but at least twenty walked around with the facemasks, and half of those had pulled them down to ward against the chill in the air.

"Cool, aren't they?" Collie asked.

"As polar bear drool. They almost qualify as a gaggle fuck."

They shared a smile at that.

"See that over by the ramp," Wallace said.

"Where?"

"Lower right."

Collie shifted and spotted the flatbed. "Jesus."

"I think even the Almighty might hang back from that one."

Collie had to agree. The ready-to-roll minigun upped an already high ante. "Where'd they get the war pig? There wasn't one of those topside when we were here last."

"No. There wasn't."

"You think they're inside?"

"Good chance. Firepower's definitely suggesting it. But . . . no. If they were, they wouldn't be running around out front."

Collie thought it over. "Okay. How's this sound? I go down there and find out where Gus is; get him out then try and liberate the rest of our people; make a beeline to that mini and duke it out if necessary; then drive out of there, with you popping some weasels from up here."

"I can do that," Wallace said slowly. "But I think you'd best reconsider our people."

"Why's that?"

"Been thinking. Been tracking them for more than a few days now. Haven't seen many try and make a break for it."

"They left Jimbo on the side of the road."

"One. But not the rest."

"One example's enough to keep the rest in line."

"Just sayin' . . ." Wallace stressed, "I'm not so sure they're all *our* people anymore."

"You think they've gone over?"

"I'm thinking. There were a few disgruntled among Pine Cove, despite our best intentions. Ray knew it. And only the loud ones were heard."

"Yeah, but *half* the town? There's *kids* down there."

"Just sayin'. Be careful. Work that ninja."

"All right, just Gus then. We can talk about the others later."

Wallace grunted. "Understood. Get on the dog. Find him. Get him out if you can manage it. If not, beat it back here."

Collie nodded, crouched, and adjusted her mask over her face. She hefted the rifle to her chest. She checked the weapon's magazine, swapped it out for a fresh one, and placed two others in her tactical webbing.

"You'll need these," she said, handing over the extra magazines.

Wallace grunted.

"Watch over me," she said.

He met her eyes. "Always, baby girl."

That solemn, raspy whisper drew Collie up short, and for a moment, she was deathly afraid she would never see Wallace ever again. But then she firmed up, nodded, and departed, descending and blending into the forest, headed toward the base.

Always, Wallace mouthed as he watched his wife's back disappear from sight.

Then he started preparations of his own.

43

"What's that now?" Gus asked, his mellow forever ruined by the Captain's revelation.

"Concentrate, my lad."

Gus did. He thought hard, burning wood as though it was no one's business, smelling his own pleasantly tanning skin.

Then he remembered. Maggie, surprised at seeing him, was standing tall on a nearby, orbiting asteroid. The kids weren't anywhere in sight, but Maggie was a star, a very good sign—regarding *what*, however, he had no idea.

"They were kidnapped," the Captain supplied.

"Oh, riiiight." Gus nodded as the memory dawned on him. "That's right. Some assholes took them. Slaughtered Adam and the others on the farm. All coming back to me now."

As it did, the sky darkened. The temperature chilled. No longer did he smell tanning skin but dampness and mold, as if the air needed to be refreshed somehow.

Gus sat up with a jolt.

"Where the sweet fuck am I?"

The Captain tugged on one end of his extravagant moustache. "You're still here. In your mind."

Gus blinked at him. "This is in my *mind*?"

The Captain nodded.

"I'm fuckin' high?"

"You are."

"Jesus *Christ*! And here I was wondering when the luau was gonna be," Gus barked in contempt. He looked down at himself and saw his scars returning, his skin aging. "Well, fuck me gently. I'm *stoned* here. No wonder I was feelin' so good." Then he regarded the old sailor with a look of frightened urgency. "Oh shit, you're not real."

"Oh, I'm here," the Captain reassured him. "For a little while."

Water foamed about their knees, higher and a tad cooler than before.

"Thanks, buddy," Gus said after a moment.

"'Sall right." The Captain looked to the water, watching it with longing. "My history lies with the sea, you know—a rich story as vast and deep as Caribbean blue—sailing the waters in huge merchants laden with spirits and gold and women. I'll tell you about it sometime—when you're far and away from here and on another beach."

"That'll have to be some beach to beat this one."

The Captain smiled gently. "Well, as nice as you make it."

"All right, you got me. I'm hallucinating here . . . in a good way, I guess. I'm glad you're here. And I know Maggie's around, so the kids are probably around too. So what's next?"

"You have to wake up."

"All right. Ah . . . how do I do that?"

"Will it."

"Will it."

"Force yourself. As if escaping a dream."

Gus took in the sweeping emptiness of the glorious beach. "Yeah. Okay. That might be hard to do."

"It will be," the Captain agreed.

"Yeah?"

"Yes, because they've thoroughly polluted you with their chemical foulness."

Gus frowned. "Well, it's not all *that* bad. Really. Compared to some of the monster drunks I've been on, this is pretty good. I mean, hell, look at my tan . . ."

The Captain clearly wasn't impressed by this avenue of discussion.

"Okay, maybe there's something off about it, I'll grant you that."

"Wake yourself. Before he comes back."

"Who?"

"The man with the executioner's mask."

Gus remembered, the memory sending another shiver through him just as a fresh wave crashed into his legs. The cold from that surge set his teeth chattering long after the waterline had receded. Sweat suddenly popped out on his forehead, and a twinge of nausea fouled his belly. He nodded, emphatically, and screwed up his features in a mighty attempt to wake himself . . .

And failed.

"Try again," the Captain ordered.

Gus did, forcing his consciousness to surface with all of his newfound willpower, forcing himself to open his eyes—his *real* eyes—and escape to whatever reality waited beyond the beach . . . and fell back with a pained gasp.

"Jesus *Christ*, it's like drowning in cement!"

"Try again."

"I just *did*, you fuckin' imaginary figment! If I try any harder, I'll blow my asshole out. Sweet Jesus, for all I know, I'm stewin' in my own ass sauce right now!"

"Listen to me," the Captain said forcefully, cutting through the protest. "You must surface. You *must*. There are other lives at stake here besides your own. *Younger* lives. So *awake*, Augustus Berry. *Awake*."

Gus shut his eyes and pushed . . .

And the heavens crackled with lighting.

"Morning, princess."

Shovel stopped in the doorway of his bedroom, scowled, and swung a thunderous look at Giovanni, who smiled it off. "How'd you get in here?"

Giovanni shrugged. "Picked the lock."

"You picked my fucking lock."

"Uh-huh."

"You hairy bastard. I deserved that, then. Christ Almighty, I didn't hear a fucking thing."

Giovanni stood next to the door and inspected the aged leather of his cowboy boots.

"Jetlag?" he asked.

"Yeah, fucking jetlag," Shovel grumped and deposited himself behind his desk, where a streaming cup of coffee rested. His face lightened considerably upon seeing and smelling the brew.

"We can't have too much more of this left."

"No, we don't," Giovanni said. "Last of the instant, I do believe."

Shovel saluted him with the mug and slurped noisily. "What's happening this morning?"

"Roused the newbies," Giovanni reported. "Got them fed and outfitted for the morning dig. Around forty or so. Slick Pick's with them, showing them how things are done. Gonna be tight in that tunnel this morning, but once Pick's showed them what to do, he'll send half back out."

"You got people on them?"

"Oh yeah," Giovanni replied. "Course. And the mini's ready, just in case. But I gotta say, looking over them new folks this morning, they looked ready to work."

"Excellent," Shovel said with approval and took another harsh sip of coffee. "You know a few of these Pine Cove people were actually talking it up with our people on the way here? Seems we came along just in time. A revolt was just about to happen in that town."

"Heard about that myself from some of the boys. Slick Pick's already getting friendly with one of the womenfolk. Some folks are quick to see the light."

"Quicker the better. Think they'll punch through today?"

"We'll know if they do."

Giovanni didn't elaborate, and Shovel didn't press. They'd both discussed what would happen if and when their diggers broke through to the bunker. Practice drills had been conducted around that very event. Half the reason armed soldiers accompanied every shift was to protect them from the resulting zombies emerging from the hole. Whitecap was probably full of them—infested, some even suspected. There were two plausible reasons for destroying the entry tunnel: to keep something from escaping and to deter folks like themselves from getting in.

Based on that, they'd taken precautions and remained confident in their countermeasures for dealing with the undead. Once their diggers broke through, everyone would fall back while being covered by armed guards, and they'd exit the tunnel, double-timing it down the ramp. They'd lead any pursing zombies into daylight and the minigun situated on the flatbed just below the ramp.

Allowing any undead to walk out of Whitecap made sense, so Shovel's forces could gun down the lot while they stumbled down the ramp, blasting every last ravenous monster and pushing their carcasses over the side into garbage bins—much better than shooting them inside a pitch-dark tunnel and dragging their asses all the way out for disposal.

"By the way, I've doubled the guards as a precaution," Giovanni said. "Seems some of them newbies been talking. They say Pine Cove had a pair of guardian angels. Real military types."

"Huh. They didn't mention that before."

"They mentioned it now," Giovanni said. "Anyway, I've taken care of things. Countermeasures, just in case."

"They didn't try anything while we were on the road."

Giovanni shrugged. "Probably too many of you."

"All right," Shovel said, filing that mystery away for later. "Good move. See if anything happens."

Silence settled then, a morning quietness wherein Shovel slipped into his usual post-waking stare out the window.

"Still one or two things to resolve . . ." Giovanni began in a somber tone.

"Yeah? What are those?"

Giovanni didn't dignify that with an answer, and Shovel didn't press him on it.

"What kind of person have I become," Shovel asked slowly, steam issuing from his coffee, "to wake up, on a sunny morning—"

"Near afternoon now."

"All right, afternoon—wake up at almost afternoon, and give the okay to put down my own brother. My last living brother. What kind of person would that make me?"

Giovanni looked up from his boots, eyes as cold as a week-dead rattlesnake stuffed into a freezer. "Slick told me about the dust injection. The dust don't let people lie. Just brings out what they're thinking—really thinking—deep, deep down. And I'm thinking he'll be trouble, potentially a fuckin' handful before he'll be a help. With that train of thought, I'm thinking . . . it's best to believe that your brothers—both of them—died a long time ago. In the past. This is the now, and that guy in the meat locker is a problem best solved with a bullet."

Shovel locked gazes with his right-hand man and had another mouthful of coffee, sinister in its silence. The sounds of Whitecap permeated the walls. Motors growled. Someone shouted to another and got an answer. Shovel brooded, sipped again, and leaned back in his chair, making it squeal. He turned his gaze toward the base of the mountain, his eyes dark and contemplative.

"Make it painless, then."

Giovanni waited for a moment before turning and opening the door.

There stood Sick, masked in black.

"Do it," Giovanni ordered.

Sick lurched as he turned away, a golem of skin and bone set into motion. Giovanni closed the door and waited for Shovel to say something.

But Shovel had returned to gazing out his window, drinking his coffee, lost in a morning stare.

The beams of rechargeable flashlights poked and prodded at the wrecked darkness of the tunnel, illuminating debris consisting of rock, jagged slabs of concrete, steel pipes, and beams, all coated with a thick film of dust. The soldiers moved forward first, guns leveled and ready. They crept past makeshift struts and nailed sections of chain-link fence that kept the walls and ceiling from collapsing. Things creaked, disconcerting sounds of straining metal that made people pause and vacillate between running or staying. Dry decay wafted throughout, the smell of composted earth, and the air was warm, warm enough to make Slick Pick perspire underneath his work overalls. He fiddled with the rifle's strap on his shoulder, adjusted the respirator mask on his face, and wished they had full helmets and proper gear for that shit. Who knew what chemicals might be in the air? He wasn't for this work, having been a house DJ in a previous life. But as a team leader, he had to take his turn in the hole with the rest of them, as much as he despised it.

He swished his light about, scanning for movement, revealing a corridor wide enough for the backhoe to fit into. The original tunnel, before it was collapsed, had been much wider, enough for three lanes of traffic once cleared of all the debris. The diggers kept to the wall as they worked forward in a cone, where the tip was no more than the shoulder width of two people. Ten paces behind the lead digger, the tunnel widened into the space of the backhoe's bucket. Pebbly fragments crunched underneath Slick Pick's work boots, and he scuffed them toward a wall, not wanting anyone to slip on the jagged little marbles.

The rear of the armored truck came into view, its violated rear hatchway pried open and plundered. *Thank fuck.* Slick Pick waved the guys behind him to move ahead. Six workers squeezed by, dragging lengths of heavy chains ending in hooks.

"Get in there," Slick Pick ordered.

One man got down on his knees and rolled onto his back. The other fed him the hooks and chains, and his torso disappeared underneath the truck. Slick stood and watched, sweeping his light over the work and the dark ceiling above. Tons of rock and steel and cement hung suspended from . . . what? It could all come down anytime. On cue, a wisp of gravel trickled from an overhead crack, spooking Slick Pick.

"You guys almost done?" he asked nervously.

"Hold on."

"Jesus Christ, how long does it take to hook an axle?"

The feet under the truck wormed about as the nearest worker looked into Slick Pick's light and said, "Takes time to do right, man. Do it right the first time, and we don't have to do it a second."

"This is a fucking waste of time," Slick Pick muttered and sighed heavily, his eyes darting about, looking for signs of an inevitable cave-in. In Slick Pick's mind, what they were attempting was Giovanni's plan, so *he* should have to oversee hooking up the truck and pulling its armored ass out. There would be a minor collapse, but they could clear up that loose debris and be that much closer to the final entrance to the bunker—at least in theory. Slick Pick didn't think a backhoe had the power to pull that squared turnip out of the ground—a bulldozer, maybe, but not a backhoe. The concrete and steel beams overhead had probably harpooned the front of the truck enough to keep it in place, anyway, but Giovanni had Shovel's ear, and he thought using the backhoe would save time. Slick Pick wished they could've found a certified engineer in one of those little towns they'd captured—or even a handful of experienced miners, anyone who knew tunnels and could offer guidance instead of letting the blind follow the blind.

The guy on his back wiggled out from underneath the truck. "All set. Let's get clear."

Slick Pick was all for that. He backed away from the truck, a dark hatch yawning open in a wall of rubble, and signaled his crew to pull out. They regrouped far behind the backhoe, placing a respectable distance between themselves and the truck, far enough to escape any potential danger from a bigger-than-expected collapse.

"Eddie," Slick Pick yelled to the backhoe operator, wearing a yellow toque, "yank on that fucker."

Showing only his back in the reinforced glass cab, Eddie answered with a thumbs-up, and the backhoe's mighty engine roared to life. Chains rattled and snapped taut. The backhoe huffed with power, and Slick Pick watched the spinning yellow and red warning lights atop the cab, waiting for the rumble.

The backhoe's engine growled loudly and pulled. The acrid smell of exhaust filled the tunnel, spewing back toward the opening two hundred meters distant. Giovanni had already assured him there wasn't any risk of carbon monoxide poisoning as the tunnel was big enough for air currents, but Slick Pick firmly believed old Gio often talked out of his asshole.

The backhoe strained and spun its tires, sending up a drizzle of dust and pebbles. The ceiling shuddered and creaked loud enough to make Slick Pick raise his head in trepidation. The armored vehicle lurched a startling inch then stopped as if Whitecap refused to give up its chew toy. Warning lights flashed in a psychedelic rave, swirling within the tunnel confines.

Eddie stepped on the backhoe's pedal, making the beast snarl. Its massive tires spun and squealed. The lengths of chains quivered from the force.

Whitecap protested, shivering with a metallic gasp and a belch of debris, and the backhoe stumbled back, pulling the truck with it. Chunks of ceiling clattered off the truck's hood, falling in flashes through dust clouds swirling in miasmic patterns.

The ground jumped. A gust of bad air flushed the darkness like a whiff of decomposing meat clogged in a throat for far too long. It buffeted the figures standing behind the reversing backhoe, an expulsion of foulness terrible enough to cause even Slick Pick to stagger in retreat. People coughed. Some retched. Slick Pick covered his nose and mouth, feeling as if he'd been forever contaminated. A spinning, tea-saucer-sized slab of concrete with edges as fine as a machete's *swish*ed by Slick Pick's face, close enough for him to damn near fudge his shorts. It crash-landed behind him, shattering like a valuable vase.

Warning lights swirling hypnotically, the backhoe dragged the truck's crumpled shape back, toward the mouth of the tunnel. Slick Pick and his people got out of its way, avoiding any deconstructive mishap.

Once the truck had been cleared, Slick Pick coughed, grimaced, and aimed his flashlight into the resulting hole, reluctant to go anywhere near it. More beams joined his, all failing to penetrate the snaking, swirling embankment of dust.

"Get ready," he called out. "Guns up."

Weapons came up on either side of him, and Slick Pick stepped behind them.

Then they waited.

Seconds passed. The dust clouds settled, and the ceiling whined, but nothing came forth from that whitened gloom. Slabs of concrete fell to the pavement in rude, crackling slaps, startling the men at first, but even that slowed and stopped.

But a whining from above, of fabricated sinews under great strain, grew in eerie pitch.

"I don't think we should be here," the man nearest to Slick Pick muttered, the unease in his voice thick enough to choke him.

His attention focused on the ceiling, Slick Pick agreed with him and drew breath, intent on ordering everyone back to the tunnel mouth, when the squeals of metal culminated in a final, heart-stopping spanking of metal onto pavement. Another gout of dust blasted the people in the passageway, forcing more than a few to cringe away from the unexpected air current.

"The hell was that?" someone choked out.

Slick Pick shook his head. "The ceiling over the truck. Partially caved in when we moved the rig, but the shit that had piled onto *that* ceiling finally pushed it all down. Like the second layer of a flat cake."

"You think?"

"I guess."

"So we're okay now?"

Slick Pick hesitated before answering, "Ask me that again once we get some light in there and see how much garbage fell . . . and how much we'll have to clear."

"Slick." One of the people gestured with his rifle, pointing to the tunnel.

Slick Pick looked, hearing the scuffling of crushed stone, a carpet of pebbles being sifted through. He squinted, gasping at a renewed bubble of noxious air assaulting his person and making his eyes water, his sensibilities involuntarily revolting. *Air!* The mask he wore protected him from the worst of it, and he hated to imagine what he'd be sucking down without it. He composed himself until he could function and then squinted at the darkness.

More crackling. Pieces of debris fell to the floor.

Then—*there*—illuminated in a billowing fog of dust, staggered forth a shadow, and a woman stepped into sight.

A topless woman, her skin a septic gray, she oozed into the light with all the curiosity of a wary deer.

The trouble was the woman was missing both of her arms . . . and her left breast, which in the flashlight beams converging upon her, permitted a glimpse of a kicked-in rib cage. Splintered bones staked a lung—not that it bothered her. She came forward almost daintily, muddy eyes searching, head raised as if catching a pleasing scent.

Behind her, like dogs on their master's heels, other shapes materialized like ghosts in a wafting haze—some hunched over, some tall and imposing, some crawling.

All were moaning.

It had been a year and change since Slick Pick had laid eyes on a zombie, let alone anything resembling the pack filtering out of the dark. His breath and heartbeat skipped from an anxious beat to a fearsome taiko-drum chorus.

Slick Pick gasped and forgot the plan. "Firefirefire*fire*!" he roared.

The guns thundered.

44

With Collie gone, Wallace mentally sighed and took stock of his inventory: one high-powered assault rifle with a scope, a nearly empty magazine, and five remaining full ones. With professional ease, he swapped out the magazine in his rifle and slapped in a full one. He scanned the brush, having a clear field of sight from the main gate all the way along the southern curve of the perimeter, noting the naked kill zone of about thirty meters from the tree line to the heavy coils of wire. He noticed the gaps missing in the chain-link fence about a half a kilometer away from the main gate and checkpoint. He couldn't fathom why they'd removed those fence sections, but he did see makeshift barricades about ten meters back from the gaps and a pickup truck with three armed shitheads in the box. Another shithead sat behind the wheel.

That wasn't the way he'd have done things, but then again, he didn't expect much from a bunch of goddamn civvies with guns.

Knees and other assorted joints had cracked ominously when he dropped to the ground next to Collie. He thought he'd have to get all that checked out when everything was over, which brought on a short but grim chuckle.

All over.

A dire certainty had flooded him when Collie left him and descended the hill, that he was watching her walk away for the final time.

His life was nearly done. Flashbacks blurred through his head, from his childhood dreams of serving his country, to proving himself in basic training and graduating a punishing weeding-out program for the JTF-2, to conducting covert operations in some of the most deplorable and dangerous cesspools of the world, rescuing, combating enemies and genuine evil wearing human disguises. Losing friends and companions, carrying on in their memory. Right through to the end of the world and the zombie threat.

Marrying his wife in the bowels of Whitecap. Gathering up the remnants of humanity for Pine Cove.

To here.

All that was coming to an end.

Wallace thought about the past week, specifically after having dropped Gus and the other survivors off at Pine Cove. He and Collie had retreated to their cabin hideaway and completely missed the invasion force. They'd had other things going on at the time. Collie had gone into intervention mode and locked both of them inside until one of two things happened: he turned for good, or he got out of his self-defeating funk and thoughts of suicide.

Wallace didn't turn.

And he convinced Collie about giving up on his well-thought-out, self-exiting plans. Or at least thought he convinced her (his wife was far more intelligent than he). She also convinced him that she still needed his transforming carcass (his words, not hers) every moment of the day. As long as he still functioned. She needed him.

And as long as she still needed him, he'd *delay* his exit plan . . . for as long as he was mentally able to delay it.

Wallace smiled then, remembering the softer tones she used when conveying her feelings for him, even in his altered state. *Collie*, he mused. Ever the paladin. Always the motivator. She'd worked her sorcerous magic over him, and Wallace had to admit that over the past few days, he hadn't felt any of the cursed urges belonging to the undead. He certainly hadn't gone as far as that one instance with Gus.

Halfway through the previous night, however, things had changed . . . for the worse. He constantly stretched his jaws, popping his eardrums. When Collie asked him what was wrong, he'd reported the stiffening of his joints but seemed fine otherwise. He didn't tell her that the smell of her skin was borderline intoxicating, stimulating a powerful urge to bite. He wanted to perhaps start on her neck—just lean over, chomp down, and rip out great bloody mouthfuls, working his way up that strong curve to the berries of her earlobes and . . .

Wallace shook himself violently, popped his jaws again, and took ten seconds to focus. Once he'd recovered, he took stock of his ammunition and stacked the extra magazines next to the spot where he'd be lying down. The rifle didn't have a bipod, but that wasn't a big problem. He'd manage. The German rifle used a 5.56 cartridge and had a maximum range of around seven hundred meters, or the length of about six football fields and change. All good. The mouth of Whitecap's entry tunnel was easily inside that range, and he didn't think he'd be shooting that far. The trailers, small office building, and vehicles were all within three hundred meters, and there wasn't a breeze in the least.

He located the selector switch just above the grip and thumbed it to single fire with an ominous click. Having done all that, he climbed to his feet and stepped back, to a tree where he'd hidden the pressure mine he'd discovered on the way up the hill. Land mines had been banned well before the turn of the century, but in the defense of Whitecap, against the threat of being overrun by dead things, the base commanders ordered several improvised explosive devices, or IEDs, to be placed in the woods surrounding Whitecap.

The one Wallace had found, affectionately called a *beanbag* and about the size of a small sofa cushion, was a no-brainer to set up. One switch activated the device, then all it took was someone to step on and step off to detonate. Wallace recognized the coded, black-ink lettering of GAZ PLO and knew the weapon contained a sizeable amount of liquid explosive—more than enough to do the job.

There was no way on God's green earth he was going to leave to his wife to do that job. No way was she going to come back and find him staggering about, brainless with an insatiable appetite. No fucking way.

He placed the beanbag on the dead foliage of the hill, on a small rise suspiciously molded to fit his very plan. He leaned over the explosive and activated it, and when a red light chirped, he paused before lowering himself onto the device, centering it under his abdomen. Wallace lay there, aware of the deadly ordnance nestling at his core, eyes darting left and right, and didn't dare move off the device.

He counted to five, shrugged mentally, and pulled his rifle into his arms, resting it on the small rise. His back was arched a bit uncomfortably, but what the hell. He was protected, had a relatively clear field of fire, and discovered he was in a wrath-of-God kinda mood.

The scope fitted his eye, and he peered through, scanning left and right until he arrived at the point in the fence where he expected Collie to make her insertion.

Then he panned a little to the left and spotted four targets.

A mild convulsion overtook him, followed by that familiar, insatiable craving welling up in his gullet and brain like bad gas. He suppressed it with effort. After winning that little battle, he realized that if he'd shaken too much, enough to take pressure off the beanbag, well . . . game over.

Wallace stretched open his jaws, longing to bite into something . . . *anything*. The feeling quivered along his spine and thrummed into his facial muscles like wires dangerously close to overloading.

C'mon, baby girl, he projected mentally.
Daddy doesn't have much time left.

Wild grass and flowers sagged with melting frost as Collie descended the hill and made her way to the tree line. She stayed low, utilizing the ample foliage, scanning ahead and staying aware of the chain fence on her left. Bushes scratched at her camouflaged jacket, but she ignored them. Behind the coils of razor wire, fencing, and gaps in the buildings, vehicles, and containers, people moved with purpose. All seemed well that morning, which suited Collie's purpose.

She approached the gaps in the mesh fence and collapsed onto the frigid earth. She peeked through the underbrush and spied a pickup with three masked, civvie gunmen in the back. They were watching the area where Collie intended to make her insertion. *Nothing is ever easy*, she thought as she looked around. There wasn't anything she could do, not with a band of open territory filled with razor wire.

She blinked and noticed a lump that interested her greatly. A dead black bear lay tangled in the coils of razor wire. The animal had gotten painfully caught and had probably been gunned down. No one had bothered to pull it out of the wire. It lay across the loops, about twenty feet away from the gap in the fence. Collie wasn't complaining.

The unmistakable rattle of gunfire interrupted her thoughts, coming from the direction of the mountain and freezing her. The civvies in the pickup heard it as well. The three in the box turned away, listening to the clatter, before one slapped the roof. The engine started up, and in ten seconds, the gap was left unguarded. The pickup sped off around the corner of an unhooked trailer and disappeared from sight, but Collie sensed the industrial demeanor of the camp had just changed.

She got to her feet and bounded through the brush, emerging and aiming for the dead bear. Being suddenly in the open felt threatening. The animal had been a beast, about nine feet long, and died across the inner and outer coils of razor wire. Collie used its great size as a stepping stone, bounded over the defensive measure, recovered, and chugged onward to the gash in the fence. In seconds, her feet slapped concrete, and she ran toward the nearest trailer. Shouts and the roar of engines ruined the peace.

Once she reached the trailer's door, she yanked it open.

*

The burst of gunfire jerked Shovel out of his morning funk and pulled him to the picture window. Giovanni appeared next to him. Outside, people had dropped what they were doing and looked in wonder toward Whitecap. Figures spilled from the tunnel mouth, running and firing in uncoordinated bursts, and generally pissing Shovel off.

"Goddamn fuckin' idiots," he grumbled and reached for his submachine gun, hanging from a wall peg. "Didn't we fuckin' drill for this?"

"We did," Giovanni said in an equally offended tone.

"And there they are, blasting like a bunch of fuckin' five-year-olds playing cowboys, clogging up that tunnel. They'll sure as shit be the ones clearing that mess up."

Shovel turned away from the window and moved toward the door. "C'mon, then. Let's get to that minigun before one of our retards accidentally mows us all down."

The zombies lumbered into a bullet storm.

Slick Pick's people sprayed instead of aiming. The flashlight beams jumped and jiggled, like spotlights coming unhinged because of an earthquake. Rarely did anyone focus on a head, and any training Slick Pick's crew had was quickly forgotten.

"The *heads*, goddammit . . . Shoot the fuckin' *heads*!" Slick Pick screamed over the sky-splitting jackhammering of the German rifles. Unbreathing chests got stitched up in explosive patterns, flinging corpses back into the surge of bodies pushing forward. Arms exploded off shoulders. Faces burst apart with startled jumps. One zombie, an emaciated kid with upturned eyes, actually *charged* the firing line. A lengthy burst of gunfire destroyed the corpse's legs in an inky spray. The kid fell but continued crawling until someone emptied a magazine into its head, bouncing the figure off the floor as if it had landed on a snare drum. The living were so terrified and focused on the shifting rows of undead that they missed the masses oozing around the backhoe.

Eddie locked his door when a charcoal palm slapped against it hard, scaring him to the brink of shitting himself. He stomped on the pedal and got the backhoe moving, but the armored truck hooked into a protrusion along the wall, twisted, and wouldn't budge another inch. Eddie shrieked and lowered the bucket in a desperate effort to shake the chains loose from the supporting arms, but they'd been fixed too securely. Eddie himself had done the job.

Someone spotted a corpse crawling up the backhoe's ladder and blasted it off with a lengthy burst.

"Out! Out, everyone out!" Slick Pick shouted above frantic reloading.

That sent everyone scurrying for the tunnel mouth, leaving the unleashed horde fumbling about in that cavernous darkness, crawling forth upon machine-gunned limbs, heads resting crookedly on necks half shorn away by bullets.

In the cab of the backhoe, a horrified Eddie saw the retreat and stomped on the gas pedal. The backhoe refused to do his bidding. He slammed the machine into its forward gear and plunged ahead. The bucket collected a writhing gaggle of doll-like limbs and torsos and drove them into the rear of the armored truck. The red and white whirling lights illuminated just enough to show the swell of bodies bursting in places, innards and bones sprouting in a viscous pulp. The zombies' deceased expressions didn't change even as the bucket mangled them. Eddie slapped the machine into reverse and backed up, ignoring how the fleshy clump fell.

But the rig could not free itself from its treacherous anchor.

Eddie's hands trembled on the controls. He jerked his head around, whimpering at the rising flood of heads, shoulders, and reaching arms surrounding the rig. Unchecked fright streaked a light show up and down his spine, nearly paralyzing him. Sweat glazed his skin, soaking his clothing. Eddie knew he was in a bad position and didn't want to become a fucked-up snack for the undead. He put the backhoe into drive and pushed forward again, the bucket heaving the zombies back. Tires squelched over a moist jam of skin and bones. The machine smashed into the truck, and Eddie reversed again, squashing a few zombie seeping into his retreating path. He glanced over his shoulder and saw the way partially clear.

"Fuckohfuckohhh*ohhhhhh*."

Slick Pick and the others had run out on him. Eddie was alone and cooped up in the cab like a slab of beef in a display case. *Totally unacceptable.* He shrugged off the seat buckles and clawed at the straps, bending a couple of fingernails back. He gripped the door handle, eyeing zombies struggling around the bucket.

Now.

Eddie threw open the door, swung himself outside, and hung off two rungs before jumping down. Moaning resonated off the tunnel walls, sounding like an off-key choir warming up. He ran, feeling fingers brush his neck. Eddie bolted for the tunnel entrance, not wanting to be eaten alive.

And in his hurry, he slipped in that chunky stew covering the ground. His face and chest slammed into a mat of crushed bodies. Particles got into his eyes and mouth, and a knob of something invaded an ear. He barked a note of spastic dread and pushed off from the ground in an adrenaline-spiked push-up, feet already moving at full power.

His hands slipped, and he fell again.

Eddie screamed as he struggled to regain his feet, his hands raking the offal of nightmares, close to puking from the smell alone.

A line of zombies piled onto him.

Eddie fell onto his chest, the undead weight pressing him down into that awful decomposing mud under his chin. He screamed and shoved a hand into the neck of a corpse that appeared to wear its dentures on its lips. No, it *had* no lips. Eddie freaked, kicked into what felt like a vat of putrefying fat. His boot came half off, and he struggled even more as more bodies swarmed him, pulling on his workwear, grabbing his face, dripping, smiling, moaning, all while the backhoe's strobe lights whirled overhead like a psychedelic nightmare.

"Don't eat me! Don't, no! NO, NO!"

Rancid skin muffled Eddie's cries then, and the zombies did exactly what he screamed for them not to do.

They ate him alive.

45

Collie double-timed it through three trailers, peering inside each and discovering stores of food and drink until she arrived at a single-story office house. People ran past her, heading for the ramp leading up to the tunnel entrance, weapons jiggling and clutched to their chests. That was fine with her. She went straight to the door and tried the knob.

Locked.

Collie didn't like to be locked out.

She stepped back and kicked the door hard, hitting it just below the knob. The door flew open and bounced off the inside wall. Collie edged around the corner, leading with her rifle, and centered on a single woman dressed in a red sweater and jeans, her graying hair tied in a knot at the back of her head.

"Freeze," Collie said, and the woman did exactly that as the shouting from Whitecap's mouth seemed to level off. "You know anyone called Gus?" Collie asked her.

"What?"

"You fuckin' heard me, sister."

"Yes, yes! Gus! He's here! I know where he is!"

Collie studied her then the room. A doorway and short hall branched off, but with the paper-covered tables, cabinets, and medical charts, there was no mistaking the office's purpose.

"What's your name?"

"Maggie."

Collie smiled behind her mask. She'd just found the pecker checker. "Best news I've heard this morning. Where's Gus?"

"They have him in an empty trailer two units down."

"Yeah?" Collie glanced outside and counted off trailers, spying no guards. They'd probably joined the commotion coming from Whitecap. "You're supposed to have some kids with you?"

Maggie blinked. "Not here. This is only a clinic. But I know where."

"Where?"

"The other office just past Gus's trailer."

"You get them and bring them here?"

"There's a guard."

"Honey, anyone with an asshole is heading to that tunnel right now. We don't have much time, but if we both hustle, I'm pretty sure I can locate some wheels and drive outta here. You with me?"

Maggie's head almost fell off she nodded so hard.

"Let's do it," Collie said.

Maggie hurried to the door only to have Collie stop her with a hand.

She peered left and right then across an open stretch of cement to more trailers, motor homes, and the beast of a dump truck on the other side. "Okay, stay between me and the trailers," Collie ordered. "We go."

Shovel met Slick Pick and most of his gasping crew around the flatbed at the base of the ramp. Pickups with armed men and women gathered behind a thick wall of sandbags. They looked to him for leadership. Shovel didn't disappoint. He got into the thick of it right away.

"All right, calm the fuck down. Calm down and get behind those sandbags. Dig in and aim at whatever comes out of that hole, but don't none of you fire a single fucking shot. You wait until I tell you to shoot. Got that?"

With anxious affirmatives, those wielding guns settled in behind the wall and prepared themselves.

"Giovanni, get up there and fire up the mini—you hold your shit until I say so."

Giovanni nodded, bearded jawline set and grim, and climbed up onto the platform. Two others piled onto the flatbed in support. Shovel whirled upon Slick Pick with an expression demanding explanation.

"We pulled that truck out, and they fuckin' dropped in from the ceiling," Slick Pick babbled. "They fuckin' dropped in and all that stirred-up dust and shit fuckin' creeped me out, and I told the guys to fire, and we did, but that didn't stop them. We shot the living batshit outta them unbreathing bastards, but only a few went down, so I got everyone out like I was supposed to. Eddie couldn't get clear of the backhoe and freaked out—tried to fuckin' rodeo-bang his way out of there, but he couldn't get clear. He couldn't get clear."

Shovel swung a hateful glare to the smoking mouth of Whitecap and waited as the sounds of weapons being locked and loaded filled the air.

"Eddie's dead," Shovel declared. "Get your shit tight and get ready for the slaughter."

He racked the slide on his submachine gun for emphasis and jerked his head in the direction Slick Pick should scamper off to.

Slick Pick bolted.

"Dickless," Shovel hissed, and turned to meet the forbidding countenance of the mountain called Nolan, already suited up as if he might've gone to bed in his gear. The big man carried his axe, and his silver face gleamed in the gauzy daylight.

"You stay around me," Shovel commanded and got a nod. That was all Shovel needed.

"How you doin', Gio?" Shovel shouted and stepped to the side of the flatbed, looking up toward the minigun and the two-person crew ready to swap out ammo boxes.

"Ready to fuck people up," Giovanni replied.

"All right, you sorry-assed sonsabitches," Shovel barked at the people behind the sandbagged wall. Even the new recruits huddled nearby, which was good.

"One more time. You wait until the minigun opens up. You do *not* fire. You prematurely squeeze your trigger finger, and I swear to goddamn, I'll stick my size eleven up your crusty hole and wipe my toes on your ass. Clear?"

They were, and they voiced it.

"All right," Shovel said and set his attention on Whitecap's mouth. "Like the man said. Get ready to fuck some folks up."

As if they'd heard their introduction, figures emerged from the darkness of the tunnel mouth, dribbling forth into daylight. A whole *lot* of people. They were only forty or so meters away, but the morbid glee at seeing all that fresh pulsating meat at the bottom of the ramp was unmistakable. There were soldiers in full but wrecked battle rattle, women in dresses, and kids in summer clothing. Men and women wore lab coats, formal suits, and leisure wear. All looked as if they'd spent a very long time under the earth. All looked famished. They were a veritable blood-and-guts-soaked parade of unholy might, where shriveled streamers of organic matter dragged behind the owners, where portions of faces had been bitten off for decoration.

"Jesus," someone said aloud, saying it for everyone.

"How many we estimate were in there?" Giovanni called down from the minigun, sounding positively rock solid.

"Six or seven hundred," Shovel answered, not quite sharing his confidence but trying to at least fake it.

The trouble was that six or seven hundred seemed like a lot more in reality than in off-the-cuff discussion around the security of a table.

From his concealed perch on the hillside, Wallace watched. He divided his attention between Collie and the forces gathering behind the line of sandbags at the base of the ramp. At a glance, he suspected whoever was trusted with a gun had one. All aimed at the river of corpses that flowed into daylight.

The advancing dead made Wallace smile with cadaverous mirth.

Did he want to deal with shambling meatbags . . . or the thinking living?

He screwed the scope deeper against his eye socket and took careful aim at a head.

Easiest fucking decision he'd made all week.

Shovel and his group watched in horrified awe as the mob lumbered down the ramp toward them. Without any concern for the poised minigun, the undead marched on. Shovel believed every last one of them sonsabitches was smiling. The sound of their relentless approach became frightening, nerve grating. The chilling mesh of famished voices, bare-skin shuffles, and boot stomps was relentless.

He looked toward Giovanni, and his second-in-command's expression froze somewhere between collected and grossed-out. Giovanni caught Shovel's eye, straightened his back, and cocked his head just as it exploded as if under pressure. Blood and brain matter drizzled the two accompanying men as Giovanni's headless body crumpled back onto the flatbed.

Speckles dotted Shovel, who stood shaking in shocked disbelief.

Then he heard the shot.

But by then, the whole of his militia opened up on the zombies, lighting up the line in a barrage of angry fireworks.

46

The barrage of gunfire made Sick stop packing a loaded syringe into a carrying case and listen with interest. He glanced at the door of his new motor home—only just inhabited—and went to the living area, where a window faced the inner ring of gathered trailers and offices. Spying nothing, he tried to angle himself to see farther north, past the general quarters and the towering Kat truck. There he glimpsed the flash and smoke of a gun battle.

Sick straightened and considered the engagement. Then he considered his orders.

The orders stood.

Besides, Shovel had the mini up at that end. Any fight would be finished by that lead-spewing beast. Sick put the syringe in a carrying pack and zipped it up, depositing it in a leg pocket. He turned away from the window but froze, catching movement between the gaps of trailers across the way. That flutter made him stop and squint, willing whatever it might be to reveal itself.

And it did.

Sick's eyes widened at the sight.

Collie and Maggie rounded a corner of a trailer and moved quickly between units, sprinting through the gaps. The automatic fire freaked Maggie out a bit, and Collie had to hold onto her arm for a grounding effect.

"Don't worry," she said close to the doctor's ears. "We pick up Gus and then the kids. Okay?"

That seemed to do the trick. Maggie took a deep breath and pointed to the next trailer over.

"You sure?" Collie asked.

She nodded she was.

No guards, but Collie figured everyone might be at the ramp with the bullets zinging overhead. That didn't concern her. Phase two was extracting Gus, and she was nearing completion. They jogged to the trailer, and Collie took a moment to undo the chains wrapped around the door handles.

"You stay out here and keep watch, okay?" Collie instructed her. "Anyone asks, you just say you're being careful and heading over to see how the kids are doing. Got it?"

Fearfully, Maggie pressed herself up against the trailer and nodded.

"We're outta here in a minute," Collie assured her and yanked on the chain, letting it puddle on the cement in a noisy rattle. She pulled down the folded steps underneath the bumper, opened one door, and charged inside.

The gunfire didn't sound so bad inside the empty trailer.

"Gus," Collie asked the gloom, waiting for her eyes to adjust. She lifted her rifle, ready if needed, and slowly proceeded.

"Gus? You in here?"

The sky roiled and thundered, and Gus thought a tsunami might charge into sight, a tidal wave from which nobody could escape, and the only thing left to do would be to stand and wait for the water to hit. The Captain laughed at his unease, which didn't sit well with him.

"That's not very fucking nice," Gus scolded him. "I'm freaking out here."

"Don't be worried," the Captain said. "Help is on the . . ." His face paled, his moustache drooping.

Gus noticed the change. "What?" He lurched forward, wondering if the old guy was having a heart attack.

The Captain regarded Gus, alarm flaring in his eyes. "You *must* wake up now."

No sooner had he finished the sentence than Gus thought he heard the voice of a woman, coming from down the beach.

The voice was Collie's.

"Collie?"

Hearing her name through the shadows of the trailer put a smile on her face. She hurried ahead, toward the far end, scanning the shadows from behind her upraised rifle. "That you, babe?"

But Gus didn't answer.

The shape of a white frame rested on the floor, and on that, Collie realized, was a body, one that stirred and flopped over onto its back.

"Gus?"

He answered with a grunt.

Smiling under her mask, Collie dropped to a knee at the mattress's edge and gripped a shoulder. Gus groaned again. She rattled him before pulling on an arm, noticing how he was nursing a bottle of what might've been booze.

"You okay, Gussy? Huh? How you doing?"

"Collie?"

"It's me," she pulled him to a sitting position. His head rolled stupidly on his shoulders, mouth open wide enough to gulp down flies. She placed her rifle against the wall and gripped his face, pulling it in close and studying the tiny flecks of light residing therein.

"Are you fucking *high*?" Collie blurted in amazed contempt.

"Uh-huh."

"Jesus Christ! How the hell did you . . . All right. We're leaving this place. Can you move?"

Gus's head lolled on his shoulders. "Sick."

"You think you're gonna puke?"

"No."

"Don't shit yourself. Please don't shit yourself."

"Sick."

"Got that part. Just hold it, okay? Clench. Tighten up every sphincter you got."

Then, in a display of physical and mental might, forcing his rubbery limbs to obey his will, Gus lifted a finger . . . and dropped it, still utterly shitfaced.

Collie shifted into a crouch and took a deep breath, knowing she'd have to toss Gus over her shoulders to get him out of there—not something she wanted to do—but she could drop him in the office when they reached the kids.

Then she heard something.

A whimper.

Collie snatched up her rifle and whirled, seeing the rectangular doorway at the back of the trailer and identifying Maggie's outline from the shoulders up.

A shadow peeked out from behind her.

Not a shadow, Collie corrected herself. *Some bastard wearing a ski mask.*

"Let her go, and I'll let you live," Collie commanded and walked toward the frame of daylight.

"Stop," Maggie blurted, barely heard above the continuous gunfire. "He says stop or he'll—"

Her voice failed her for two seconds. Then, "He'll blow my head off."

Collie stopped but didn't lower her weapon.

"He says . . . he says drop the rifle."

The bastard stood directly behind Maggie, a sliver if that, not presenting a clear shot in the least. Collie could shoot anyway, quickly killing the doctor and the man behind her, but she didn't want to do that either. The doctor was the most important person on base.

The doctor was gold.

Would he shoot her? She was worth too, too much to them all.

Then again, Collie knew firsthand plenty of crazies were about. Grinding her teeth, she sniffed and slowly placed the rifle at her feet. She wouldn't take that chance. Not with Maggie's life.

"He says to kick it forward."

Collie complied, and the weapon slid forward.

"He says further."

Screwing up her lips, Collie walked to the rifle and reluctantly did just that, sending the firearm skidding past the halfway point of the trailer.

"Now the side piece. Pinch and toss it."

Collie complied.

"He says to step back. To the back wall."

Lifting her hands, she prepared to duck the hail of bullets soon to come and did as told.

"Sick," Gus repeated weakly, turning his head in the direction of the doorway.

Jesus, Collie fumed. *Give it a fucking break.*

Then it hit her. Gus wasn't sick at all.

47

Wallace's bullet struck home with spectacular results, and after plugging the first target on the minigun, he trained his sights on the next dingbat with balls enough to try to use the weapon. People scurried along the line, and he recognized a few of the faces crouched and fidgeting as the ones with guns opened up on the closing front. The trouble with handing a civvie a military-grade weapon is that they could be trained—even trained well—but until they were in a combat situation in which the enemy was returning fire and their friends were dying around them, you couldn't depend on their morale holding up.

It was Wallace's intention to break them.

He lined up the second target, a guy with a shaven scalp marveling over the dead man at his feet with no head. Wallace placed the red dot of his scope over the chest of the man, relaxed, realizing he didn't have to exhale, and squeezed the trigger.

Boom.

Brass ejected to Wallace's right as the bullet tore a hole through the road savage's chest, jerking the man off the flatbed as if he'd been hooked from behind.

Two. Wallace took aim at one along the sandbag line. *There.* One hairy putz was waving his rifle back and forth, emptying his magazine into the horde. Wallace let that one live. A woman, her hair in a ponytail reaching her waist, remained steady under pressure. Wallace smoothly lined her up and fired, punching a bullet through her shoulder blades and lifting her up and over the sandbags.

Three.

That shot caused a ripple effect. The minions next to the woman started freaking out, screaming, and other heads along the defensive measure took stock of the kill. Wallace drew a bead on one guy near the end of the sandbags, still unaware of anything amiss in all the noise . . . and squeezed.

The impact smashed the shooter away from the wall and into the legs of a nearby companion.

That shot *really* stirred them up—like kicking an anthill. The cutthroats started looking around, not paying attention to the zombies crawling over the recently, more permanently dead. A furry fuck of a man started bawling orders, even stepping up to the wall while directing the last guy on the flatbed to grab the mini.

Wallace aimed at the leader, intending to pop that noise-making cherry and truly invoke chaos.

A surge of mind-shattering hunger lanced through Wallace then, causing him to look away from the scope and claw the earth, raking up fallen leaves. *Hunger.* It erupted from his core and drove hooks of craving into his brain, demanding sustenance. It practically commanded his limbs into abandoning his position to wade down into that scrimmage and dig into whatever was breathing. Daylight became a stinging white-out, a buzzing field of static, and he shied away from it. In the darkness, he summoned Collie, seeking shelter in her laugh, strength in her smile, but a rising hiss like leaves skittering across asphalt flooded his ears, shredding all memories, all sound.

Wallace placed his forehead to the ground and popped his jaws. He chewed into the earth and spat out foliage and dirt. The urge to feed receded, but only for a moment . . . then a second wave of hunger hammered into his core, splintering and almost breaking his resolve. Wallace gasped, realizing his heart wasn't beating any-more, and in its place, a black hole was revolving voraciously, sucking on his mind. Wallace dug in, refusing to leave, actually whimpering under the mental pressure, feel-ing the steel plates of his conscience and his resolve buckling, warping.

Tentacles, slick and black, wormed out of the whirling cavity where his heart once resided, and Wallace knew if they reached his mind, he would cease to be. He needed a distraction.

So he gnashed into the nearest thing to him, biting off the index finger of his left hand, and when that went down, he chewed off his middle finger.

"Aim your fuckin' shots!" Shovel roared at his panicked forces, dividing his attention between the zombies and the sniper picking them off one at a time. "Shoot the head! If you can't get the head, shoot the legs *then* the head."

"There's a sniper!" someone shouted back, and as one, every head turned toward Shovel. Some of the new folks staying close to the ground bolted, and Shovel whirled and gunned them down. After dispensing that punishment, he aimed at the recruits, promising a similar fate for anyone else who broke away.

"Get on that mini!" Shovel barked at the third man on the flatbed, who cowered on the other side. A silver-headed Nolan moved on him, grabbing the guy by the back of his uniform and throwing his unwilling ass onto the platform.

"Who's shooting at us?" a woman screamed.

"Never you mind that!" Shovel yelled back. "I'll take care of that. You take care of *them*!"

Shovel stepped up to his people crouching behind the sandbags, ignoring the bleeding dead littering the cement.

"Stop spraying your fuckin' shots! Aim and shoot! Aim and *shoot*! Do it, you god-damn dummies!"

To show what he meant, Shovel shouldered his machine gun and blew the heads off three zombies not twenty feet away. One of them wore a combat helmet, and the metallic *twang* of the ricochet sizzled heavenward. That caught his minions' attention. Shovel lined up the face of the undead soldier and put a decisive bullet through it, dropping the undead in a heap.

"*Like that*!" Shovel waved his weapon as he retreated. "Do it like *that*!"

Lesson learned, they took to it in earnest, and a cutting hail of lead slashed into the advancing front, decimating the corpses. Chests and heads exploded violently, sending bodies earthward. Some skulls backed up on their shoulders while others had their midsections shredded to grisly ribbons.

"That's it! Do it! *Do it*!" Shovel encouraged them, shifting his attention to the land and hills beyond the trailers, searching for that sniper . . .

And very much hoping he'd get his hands on him.

Wallace came to with a deep-throated humming in his ears. The second thing he noticed were the oozing stumps on his left hand. *Jesus.* The thought buzzed through his head along with that incessant mechanical whine filling the air. Wallace swallowed, feeling a lump sink into his gullet. He forced that ugly sensation from his mind and regarded Whitecap as hot recognition flashed through him.

Dragon fire was flashing from the minigun's rotating barrels, shredding White-cap's zombies in a dazzling display of destruction, its one-note song blaring through the valley and mountains.

Appalled at the swath of devastation, Wallace fumbled for his rifle.

48

The wall stopped Collie from backing up farther, and she readied herself to dive and flip the mattress Gus had been sleeping on once Sick started firing.

However, the masked man standing behind Maggie surprised Collie. He slammed Maggie's head into the closed door, and the doctor crumpled from sight. Then, holding a pistol on Collie, he nimbly pulled himself into the trailer, daylight framing him.

Then he advanced without so much as a creak.

"Sick," Gus muttered repeatedly, introducing the newcomer. "Sick."

"I know, babe," Collie whispered.

That quieted Gus.

Sick approached them, and when he reached Collie's rifle, he kicked it back toward the open door as if clearing the dirt from a batter's box. He did the same for her sidearm. That completed, he walked toward them and stopped within ten feet of Gus. While gunfire crackled outside the trailer, the masked man sized Collie up. She studied him in turn, noting the dark combat fatigues. He wore a black mask, like herself, but in this pack of apocalyptic wasteland hellpups, a balaclava meant nothing.

Sick, however, carried himself a little differently.

He's had training.

All thoughts sped from her mind then as Sick struck a duelist's pose and aimed his pistol at Gus.

Collie licked her lips, willing the man to come a little closer, thinking of the combat knife in her shin sheath. A little less space was all she needed to end him.

But Sick surprised her again.

With machine-gun fire intensifying beyond the metal walls, he relinquished his aimed pistol and tossed it far away, back toward the daylight filling the open doorway.

Amazed, Collie relaxed just a fraction more. "The hell you up to?" she asked in wary puzzlement.

Sick didn't reply. Instead, he reached down and slipped out his Bowie knife, revealing it inch by gleaming inch, the sparse light transforming the blade into something sorcerous, frightening. He turned it one way and then the other, making sure Collie saw it, before dropping back into a fighter's stance, flipping the weapon to an underhand grip.

Collie met Gus's drugged gaze for a second.

A knife fight is the last thing you want to get into.

He remembered the conversation, evident in his fearful expression. And that was true, Collie knew from experience, but as God above was her witness, evil radiated off this masked freak like heat from a furnace. Little bastard drew his knife as though he was in a porno. Lord only knew how many people he'd killed with that blade, and no doubt Sick got off on it. He was a certified crazy, Collie realized, one of the few who had probably rejoiced when civilization collapsed.

With dramatic grace, she reached down and unsheathed her knife, pointed it at her foe, and extended her left hand as a guard.

Gus moaned at her intentions, drawing her attention.

Collie winked at him.

And went forth to kill one nimble psycho.

As she walked toward him, Sick dropped back, smoothly switching up his stance while practice-punching the air. Collie performed no such theatrics. She'd been born loose and ready to fuck the enemy up.

From behind her extended hand and raised knife, Collie slipped into her own combative groove, aware of the walls.

"Let's see what you got . . . boy," she whispered.

Sick attacked, flashing forward with an adder's speed. He flicked his Bowie out in an expert weave, slicing the space Collie had occupied only a microsecond earlier. She countered just as quickly, thrusting her hand toward his face while her knife stabbed for a backbone. Sick darted to the side and brought his knife hand down across Collie's arm, slapping it away in a bruising connection. She responded in an instant, reading his intentions perfectly, and cracked an elbow across Sick's jaw, driving him back. She pursued, stabbing for his gut once again and meaning to drive her steel into his heart, but Sick kicked out her knee in a crippling flash of pain, forcing the joint to buckle. Collie collapsed onto her back and caught her enemy's descending knife in a knot of forearms, stopping the weapon not an inch below her throat.

There, they gazed into each other's narrowed eyes, grunting and pressing.

She gripped a wrist and twisted it hard to snap it, but he rolled with the attack and tumbled away, toward Gus.

Collie scrambled to her feet, wincing at her knee, just as Sick sprang up like a twisted jack-in-the-box.

They circled each other for a moment, composing themselves, analyzing each other like doctors of a different, more sinister science. Their knives gleamed. Both breathed hard, chests heaving from the short but meaningful clash, but neither backed away.

Collie lunged, stabbing, turning it into a backhand slash, cutting cloth and air, punching with her free hand before initiating her own combination of thrusts, open-hand strikes, and slashes, jacking up the combat's tempo. Sick evaded the knife, blocked or slapped away the more uncomfortable punches, and circled away from her before unexpectedly charging back in.

Collie didn't retreat, and for mesmerizing seconds, they stood toe-to-toe, blades tinkling, hands and elbows blurring forward, blocking and striking with the rapid fury of a muffled snare drum. They ducked and weaved, probed and feinted before stabbing, all powered by quick intakes of air and short puffs of breath.

With an uncharacteristic bark, Sick retreated from two scything sweeps of Collie's combat knife before stabbing for a heart. Collie swung out of the way like a door caught in a windstorm and smashed her palm into his cheek, snapping his head back. She slashed for his throat, but Sick blocked her arm in an evil display of speed.

They broke away from each other.

Machine guns continued to blaze outside.

Collie realized she was near the doorway. Somewhere behind her, at her feet, was a collection of firearms.

"Wishin' you kept that Glock now, right?" Collie huffed, eyes fixed on her opponent.

Sick didn't reply, his shoulders heaving. He stalked her, loose as a boxer, poised to strike if given the opportunity, whirling his knife in a defensive figure eight meant to frighten and hypnotize.

Collie didn't go for that—didn't go for the guns either.

She went for his throat.

He blocked the attack, but her forward momentum backed him up into a wall. They mashed together like similar pieces in different machines, grunting now, ferocious in their exchanges. He cut her above the eye. She slashed the outside of a thigh. He uppercut, zipping a deep kiss through mask and skin, licking her chin to the bone. She elbowed him hard to the head, three close-quarter strikes that squished his nose to one side. He got a free hand around the back of her neck and attempted to pull her down onto his knife tip, but she stopped the ascending Bowie with her forearm, the point deflecting off bone and parting cloth around her shoulder. He pushed off the wall, arms enveloping her, slashing her lower back as he went, lifting her off her feet and charging forward. Collie rained down a pair of punishing pommel strikes to his neck before slamming against the trailer wall. Her feet touched floor, and she stabbed for his throat again.

This time she got his shoulder.

Sick squealed at the impalement, frenzied, and unleashed everything he had left, all surging through the torpedo of his right arm—his knife arm.

Three blurring shots pistoned into Collie. She deflected the first, slapped the second down—a mistake as the blade unzipped her thigh to her knee—and magically parried the third aimed for her face, lifting it enough that the blade's edge parted her mask straight up the middle, the pain electric. The connection stunned her.

Sick stabbed for her heart.

Collie darted away, slipping gracefully through the opening left by his lifeless left arm. Sick slapped the wall face first, absorbing the impact before whirling into Collie's hand. She slammed his head against the wall like a fleshy mallet before he spun around, clapping her skull with a forearm.

Collie collapsed against him, and their hands knotted, tired now, pushing each other away like children not wanting to eat their vegetables, seeking control while forcing openings . . .

Until Sick missed a thrust.

Collie's knife sank into his kidney, producing an unmistakable sharp hiss of breath.

For an instant, she stared him straight in the eye.

Sick's face dipped until he rested his forehead against hers in a solemn meeting of minds. There they stood for seconds until she twisted the knife, hard enough that his legs gave out, and he sat down as if very, very tired.

Gasping for breath and feeling blood flow, Collie bent over. She almost passed out, seeing blood coating her hands. She located and picked up the fallen Bowie.

Sick sat with chest heaving, dark eyes twinkling with all the smoky hate and malice of a spider only partially crushed.

Taking deep breaths, Collie pushed his head to the side. He did not resist.

There were no witty one-liners.

No speeches.

Only immediacy.

Collie inserted the knife deep into the hollow of his neck. She twisted the blade as if coring an apple and ignored the resulting, bubbling fountain. Sick twitched, grunting softly before exhaling in a gush.

He toppled over, painting the wall in an oily smear.

After confirming the kill, Collie gave the dead man no further thought. She staggered back, holding herself together.

She glanced at the doorway, the guns, and finally Gus.

Collie took two unsteady steps toward him before sinking to her knees with a groan. She bent over, palms flat and sticky against the floor, until her forehead rested against the boards in a deep meditative bow.

Then she rolled onto her back and did not move.

Feeling as if he'd downed a two-four in twenty-four minutes, Gus watched her creak to a stop and blinked with blood-rimmed eyes. He dragged a hand over his face and struggled to sit up, fell over onto a shoulder, and made a second attempt, meeting with some success.

"Collie."

No answer.

"Collie." He crawled toward her, wondering why she was moving away, then realized he was actually moving backward. He changed gear, feeling internal cogs rumble and finding "forward."

"Collie."

Nothing. Then . . . "Yeah?" as if she was waking from a dream.

Eyes widening, Gus stopped an arm's length from her with his mouth open. "You're alive."

"Mm," she answered neutrally. "Just gimme a minute."

"Sure, sure," he managed and dropped to an elbow, staring fearfully at her profile. "You need me to do anything? Collie?"

She turned her head and frowned, not impressed with the interruption.

"Sorry, sorry."

Seconds dragged by, then Collie took a painful breath. "Gunfire's . . . not as . . . heavy."

That prompted Gus to listen, and he listened very hard. Shots still rang out, but not as heavy as earlier.

She indicated her mask, trying to lift it. Gus reached over and pinched it, making a face at the gruesome pair of cuts from her chin to her cheek. He sat up, swooned, and then got both hands on the mask and hauled it off her entirely.

The face beneath it momentarily stunned him.

Doused in shadows, the left side of her face resembled an oozing slab of ham. Collie hissed as he pulled the fabric away from her head, the blood smeared on her skin.

"Should've . . . left that in place," she slurred.

"Yeah," Gus replied, balling the mask up and pressing it to the parallel slits, seeing another cut above her left eye dribbling into her ear. "Thought you were supposed to run," he said.

A smile brightened the train wreck of Collie's face. "I'm not . . . dickless."

"No, you're not." Gus chuckled nervously, wringing the mask out and alarmed at the amount of blood. More blood seeped from Collie's form, and he felt his heartbeat quicken in panic.

"Might . . . have a problem," Collie whispered.

"Is she alive?" a woman's voice asked.

Gus looked up to see Maggie at the doorway, a hand to her head.

"Yeah, but she's bleeding bad."

"Bring her here."

"She's *bleeding.*"

In a surprising display of strength and willpower, Collie crunched her stomach and slowly sat up, silencing the man at her side. "Let's get out . . . of this shithole."

She placed a hand on Gus's shoulder, and together, they stood.

Collie winced at placing weight on her legs but got walking. They shuffled toward the door, stopping near the rifle. She bent over with a soft groan and picked the weapon up, her blood pattering the floor all the while. Gus slid over to her left side as she looped the rifle's strap over her right shoulder.

Gunfire popped and crackled beyond the trailer walls.

"It's still war out there," he said.

"I know who started it," Collie replied.

49

For whatever reason, the sniper stopped shooting.

Relief flooded through Shovel. He aimed and fired short, blazing burps from his weapon, exploding heads and dropping zombies as they struggled to close the distance to the sandbag wall. His followers got more consistent with their shots, punishing the undead, even picking off the ones who stepped off the ramp and skidded to the sides.

Then the main act opened, and the minigun screamed, sounding like an industrial-strength vacuum cleaner. The sole gunner of Giovanni's gun crew bit down and bared his teeth as fifty rounds a second thundered from the six rotating cannons, straight into the mass of zombies spewing down the ramp. A killer mixture of lead and tracers shredded heads and upper torsos in spectacular fashion, misting the air with flying chips and tissue. It seemed as if God himself had lowered a monstrous weed whacker directly upon the advancing dead and swept them away. The gunner panned left and right, mowing down whatever shambled forth, ripping the evil spark of life from those unsightly husks in an unrelenting hail.

Some of Shovel's people grabbed their ears and stared at the destructive maelstrom before them. Shovel himself crouched in cringing awe at how the dead's upper trunks blew apart, the minigun's wrath blitzing entire rows in a blink.

The gunner strafed the right side of the ramp, cutting a messy line across the zombies collecting there. In ten seconds, nothing stood, and a silence fell over the scene only as long as it took to turn the minigun's wrath onto the left side. The weapon rattled to life once more, and gleaming brass tumbled from underneath the cannon's barrels. The gunner howled at the power under his command, directing the murderous stream at the leftovers farther up the ramp. Tracer fire leaped up the incline, blowing apart everything it touched in great puffs of chalky gray.

The few zombies remaining withered and did not rise again.

"Jesus H. Christ," Slick Pick muttered nearby, the curse ringing in Shovel's ears. People stood from behind the sandbags, forgotten rifles dangling at the ends of their arms.

Then a defender buckled over, and a single report rang out.

Shovel flinched and looked about as his raiders yelled warnings. A ski-masked man flew backward as if yanked by his collar, a hole in his chest.

"Find that cocksucker!" Shovel yelled. *"And kill that sonavabitch!"*

Wallace sank his head into the leaves and mewled in conflict, fighting, struggling, subduing that mindless craving that attempted to wrench away from him all control, all sense of *self.* Never had he experienced such an overwhelming urge to forget everything and just feed. He slammed his head into the ground, but that did nothing. He shook. He swore. He gripped his rifle and pulled it to his cheek. The craving pushed, *willed* him to push, to transition over to zombie unlife. A black cloud of needles seemed to engulf him, evil stimuli seeking a reaction.

Collie. He mentally projected her name inside himself, once more summoning memories. Every image darkened around the edges as if blistered by extreme heat before they winked into nothing.

Wallace growled and moaned, and his hands attempted to push himself off the beanbag. Unchecked fright burst through his person, and he felt that dreadful tide lessen its grip. He grabbed his rifle, not remembering having let it go.

Anchoring himself, Wallace focused and mentally pushed back.

The urge relented, subsided, and slunk back to that pit in his core.

Wallace held on to his weapon like a man clinging to a cliff's edge, waiting for another attack.

None came.

The virus was there, however, circling the rim of his consciousness, gathering strength for the next assault. The thought made Wallace ache with weariness.

A harsh mechanical *whhrrrrr* stole his attention, a sound like a hair dryer set to its maximum power.

He recognized it at once.

Wallace fitted the rifle's stock to his shoulder, screwed his eye into the scope, and zoomed in on a mass of unmoving corpses littering Whitecap's doorstep. The dead resembled a raked graveyard of coleslaw, chopped, diced, and served. The living down there rose from their positions as if finishing prayers.

Living.

Hatred coursed through him. He swung back to the last place he'd spotted Collie, panned around, and froze, rooted to the spot.

Collie.

She was bleeding and being helped along by Gus and another civvie. They headed toward one of the single-story office buildings.

Wallace's scope shifted, a little awkwardly because of his missing fingers, and saw the pack of road savages turning, looking for other targets. They would find Collie and Gus and the other woman.

They would, unless he did something about it.

Wallace aimed at a torso and blew a hole out of it.

He took his time, sighted another, and killed that one too.

He panned right, sighted another target, a woman, and saw bodies flutter around the edges of the scope. She moved, looked his way, crouching and running forward.

"Shit."

He couldn't rightly draw a bead on her.

She stopped to fire, and suddenly bullets whined and hissed around Wallace's position. Splinters flew off a tree. The ground around him coughed violently. Wallace remained calm, placed the scope's aiming dot on the shooter's chest.

Bang.

The impact smashed her backward, skidding perhaps three feet across the cement.

Wallace hunted for another target.

50

The three of them reached the office, ignored the little faces pressed up against the glass, and crashed through the front door. Fourteen kids, aged maybe six to twelve, drew back with screams as Gus shrugged Collie off in a high-backed chair.

"Gus!" Little Becky cried and ran to him. He hugged her, embraced the moment, and then repeated with little Chad until he drew back from both, still feeling the final residual effects of whatever Sick had pumped into him.

"You guys stay here with Maggie, okay?"

The kids had questions on their anxious faces, but he didn't have time to answer.

"Where are you going?" Maggie asked.

"Where *are* you going?" Collie said weakly.

Hearing her speak got Gus moving around the office area turned play pen. "We don't have much time. We gotta leave before they know we're here."

"Motor home?" Collie asked.

"No keys—unless you have them?" he put to Maggie, returning from a cabinet with a roll of duct tape.

"No, I don't."

Gus peered out the window and saw the towering bulk of the Kat truck.

"I'll take that."

"You can drive it?" Maggie asked skeptically.

"Yeah. Well, maybe. It's an automatic. Probably outfitted with a push-button start. My . . ." Gus's throat constricted at a memory. "My younger brother used to drive one. He told me all about those rigs."

"That's all the way across the lot!" Maggie blurted. "Open ground."

"Go," Collie told him, hefting the battle rifle to her chest. "I'll cover you here."

Gus went to the door and figured it was a hundred meters to the Kat—almost twice that if he took the scenic route, following the chuck-wagon ring of parked vehicles and trailers. Maggie was already bawling at Becky and Chad and the rest of the youngsters to lie down on the floor.

Cracks and pops of gunfire rang out across the cemented field. Shovel's people fired over the roofs of the trailers, toward the hills.

Gus met Collie's eyes.

And ran out the door.

He sprinted, feeling giddy, taking the long way around and ready to roll under a trailer or whatever was next to him if bullets flew in his direction. Part of him couldn't believe his brother would fire upon him, but another part wasn't so certain. Gus's feet pounded across the cement-covered ground as he glanced north toward the mountain, seeing figures crouching and firing into the hills. Some spilled backward violently, shot dead.

Wallace, Gus realized, already gasping. *Keeping them busy.*

Gus focused on the truck.

Wallace swore as he missed yet again. The little ridge he'd taken cover behind popped and sprayed dirt in the constant hail of return fire. One bullet had hit half a foot from his right elbow, surprising even him. But he stayed focused, kept the hunger at bay, and returned fire, allowing Collie and Gus to formulate a plan of escape.

Dirt peppered him to his left, but Wallace ignored it, sighting a big man with a silver face and axe crouched near the flatbed.

He aimed . . . fired.

The shot blasted a hole through the silver-faced guy's chest and out his back. He fell over like an ancient tree.

A shot pinged off Wallace's helmet then, jerking back his head and upper torso. Wallace dropped down, blinking, waiting for the explosion . . .

Nothing happened. He was still on the beanbag, still in one piece.

But the impact distracted him enough for the virus to make its final assault.

It attacked his mind in a tidal wave, slamming up against his refusal to give in. The craving didn't stop this time, flooding his mental defenses, hitting him full on. The urge to bite caused sludge-choked cords in his neck to bulge. Wallace no longer felt pain, but he became aware of the flagella-like movement around the thin membranes of flesh surrounding his mouth. He groaned, set his jaw, and attempted to impose his will once more, but another bullet rang off the bell of his helmet, distracting him at the worst possible moment. Anger ignited, fueled by an untapped reservoir of hate, which whipped along a thin cord toward a flash point.

The hunger . . . the all-powerful, all-consuming *hunger* . . . a druggie's addiction times infinity.

Black-headed knobs sprouted around Wallace's mouth, pushing out from his skin like overripe pustules.

Collie, he tried to say, but the hunger swallowed the word, just as it downed Wallace's remaining resistance.

The last fleeting, smoldering thought that fired through his overwhelmed mind . . .

Was the face of his wife.

Then it was over.

For long moments, Wallace simply lay there, twitching and grunting. He released his rifle, having no further need for the weapon. The fight for Whitecap continued without him. He mumbled and squirmed, sensing gunfire but making no effort to go anywhere, as if his infected brain was momentarily confused at finally seizing control. He remained that way for a few indecisive seconds, moaning in the decaying foliage, clawing and releasing the earth.

The need to feed grabbed him, insisting that he rise and seek out sustenance. Wallace glanced up, eyes dark and cloudy, and detected people scrambling for their lives in the valley below . . .

People he could eat.

The once-special operator got to his knees and pushed himself up from the ground.

When he opened his mouth to moan, to curse at the living, the beanbag explosive on the ground before him detonated with all the force of an artillery shell.

The blast shocked Shovel and his people in the valley, and they stopped firing to stare at the dust cloud shrouding the hillside and hear the patter of debris bouncing off the land. Part of what looked like a tree crashed down, enough to earn a few cries of surprise. Then all was still. The sniper had shot seven of his people dead, the most recent being Nolan, who'd hung off Shovel's ass like a protective mastiff. The bullet had blown a hole through the enforcer's chest and dropped him not five feet away from where Shovel stood firing off short bursts. He didn't spare time to grieve.

"Holy shit," Shovel said, confused by the unexpected explosion and sensing change in the air. "Hold up. Everybody, hold up."

The resulting silence thrummed in his ears, and he wondered if the violence had truly finished. Shovel waited . . . waited for someone to die. Someone would definitely die if the sniper was still up there, as they were all standing around and gawking—easy pickings for whoever had been gunning them down.

But no further shots rang out. No one else died.

Shovel considered sending a handful of people up to check out that area, maybe find out who had been firing on them, at least inspect the crater left behind. Shovel drew breath to give the order.

Then one of the women, the new one called Marie, shouted, "Hey!"

She stood with an automatic rifle in her hands, pointing toward the trailers.

Shovel looked, as did most others, and felt his bearded jaw drop in shock.

A second later, fear yanked on his spine.

51

Sweating torrents and struggling for air, Gus pulled himself up the short ladder hanging off the front bumper of the Komatsu truck, his boots clanging against the metalwork. He groaned upon seeing the long set of stairs, perhaps a story-and-a-half tall, going up the front of the machine. Slabs of metal welded to the staircase's railing provided substantial protection for anyone heading up to the driver's cab.

Jesus. Gus gasped for breath as he climbed.

They'd turned the Kat into a tank.

He got halfway up before gunfire started ricocheting off the armored hide. Gus flattened himself, covered his head, and continued at a hurried crawl. He pressed himself up against what might have been the grill of the monster, cringing from the starbursts exploding over and around his head. Bullets shrieked in his ears, and Gus understood one of those bounces could very well—

A scorching spike of pain hammered into the upturned heel of his left boot, shredding the material and flesh there. Gus howled, fell near the top of the steps, and twisted onto his back in the narrow slot. Crying in pain, Gus lifted the stricken leg and blinked at the blood streaming from the torn padding of his foot. Whimpering, he clawed his way onto the top deck and turned a corner. Railing surrounded the upper deck of the truck, and that too had been armored with sheet metal, with gun ports cut into the iron.

Tears in his eyes, Gus huffed, lay on his side, and located the cab for the truck operator.

Jesus H. Christ.

The cab had been encased with slabs of iron, and Gus had to search for the door handle for a moment. He found it and crawled toward the door on his three good limbs, his ass stuck into the air. A bright, broken ribbon of blood trailed him. Bullets crashed into the upper deck, some even whining through gun ports and bouncing inside with all the energy of blinded comets. A ricochet *twanged* off the metal plate next to the door handle just as Gus reached for it. He jerked his hand back in fright before grasping and hauling the door open, pulling himself into the seat.

"Jesus H. Christ," Gus moaned in pain and awe, still fighting for breath. He sat in the worn chair and studied the instrument panel ahead of him. Light came from the narrow cut in the sheet metal covering the removed windshield. Dials, gauges, and dead displays regarded him stoically, waiting to be powered up. He grimaced, despair creeping into his head and chest like mild poison. He hoisted his ruined foot to a rest on the far right of what appeared to be a brake, screwing his face up at the blood dribbling to the floor.

Gus huffed in frustration. Piloting a *jet* might've been a better idea.

But then, just as the bullets seemed to target the cab, he saw a push-button start.

"Lord"—Gus aimed a thumb at the large button—"hope you gassed this fucker up."

He depressed the button and held it.

The dashboard exploded with light.

Air vents in the dash and underneath all exhaled in a cold rush.

Folksy rock music blared out from loudspeakers overhead.

And the Komatsu truck, a sleeping armored behemoth the size of a respectable bungalow, coughed, grumbled, and shook like an awakening, monstrous ogre left for dead on a battlefield. The machine rumbled underneath Gus, and he squinted at the steering column, remembering the detail his brother Sidney had given him.

Just like an automatic, his ghost said.

Gus grabbed the wheel and the gearstick, eyed the glowing red lettering above the steering column, and shifted. A red bar moved across the lettering familiar in all vehicles and stopped on the one representing DRIVE.

"Jesus H. Christ," Shovel exclaimed as the machine roared to life. Air brakes screamed, the sound rolling across the valley floor, the very cement crackling under the brunt of the six tires, which weighed fifteen tons each. He stood and stared until Marie, God bless her, took the initiative and resumed firing at the awakened monster. And a monster the Kat was. Shovel had no illusions about what the thing could do, having driven it himself over the years.

It was a six-wheeled kraken, a three-story giant unleashed . . .

And he had no control over it.

"Pick your shots! Shoot the cab!" Shovel yelled and remembered the minigun on the flatbed. He whirled about and saw Slick Pick up there, struggling with the bands of ammunition as he sought to reload the boxes.

The minigun.

Shovel took one last look at the mechanical titan rumbling across the open space, toward the office building where the kids were.

He bolted for the flatbed.

A slit ran across the left side of the cab, allowing Gus to peek out if he wished. He didn't, however, as a barrage of bullets tinkled off the sheet metal, making him jump enough to step hard on the accelerator. The Kat jumped up to thirty klicks an hour of a possible eighty, and Gus wasn't averse to seeing what the leviathan could do.

He hunkered over the wheel, forgetting about the pain in his foot, and watched as the office building came into view. The electric brakes screamed as he applied them, their sensitivity surprising him as he eased the eighteen-meter-high machine to a stop. Two feet remained between the armored staircase and the building's wall.

Gus laid on the air horn, and a torpedo of sound exploded above him, surprising the hell out of him.

He recovered, opened the operator's door, and screamed, "Get in!"

Children cried in fear, almost drowned out by the impact of bullets against the sidewalls of the fifteen-foot-high tires.

"Gus!" Collie shouted.

Hearing her voice spiked his spirits. "Collie, get them in!"

Footfalls rang out on the metal steps.

It seemed like years before he saw the first pale face appear—little Becky. Gus glanced around the cab. There was precious little room for a kid, and he didn't like the way the cab seemed to be attracting bullets. He stuck his head out and took in the upper deck, seeing steel crossbeams above, extending into the dump body. A long metal box extended from the cab to the far side with cushions attached to the top.

"Fuckin' *sofa?*" Gus blurted.

Chad appeared, not too big to be bawling his eyes out in fright.

"Get down," Gus shouted at them. "Get on the floor!"

Sitting on the sofa just wouldn't do.

Children filed up into the deck, screaming as the bullets continued blasting off the truck. Gus swiveled and grimaced as he peeked out a side slot, wishing he had something to shoot back with.

"Gus?"

"Collie," Gus said, seeing her coming up the stairs behind Maggie. "Get on the floor. All of you."

"Fuck that," Collie said and crouched in an open gun port, jamming her rifle out.

A youngster Gus didn't know went to the sofa and, to his surprise, flipped a section of it up. One after the other, six children loaded themselves into that wide coffin of a couch, which had to be at least a dozen feet long, two feet wide, and equally deep. Only then did he notice air holes in the base.

"Get in there," he shouted at Chad and Becky. They did.

Maggie urged one more inside. She then lowered the lid and pressed herself into the far corner. The other children clung to her as if she were a rock.

"We all in?" Gus shouted, grimacing over the steering wheel, hand on the door.

"All in," Collie answered.

He slammed the cab's door, jacked the gearshift into reverse, and backed the monster up.

"You can drive this thing?" Collie shouted.

Gus hunkered down and peered through a slot, seeing her wounds had been plugged by taping down her combat fatigues with rolls of duct tape. Several strips even held her slashed cheek together.

"Oh, fuck, yeah," Gus answered.

Just as the shit hit.

An unrelenting salvo suddenly replaced the rifle fire pinging away at the tires and cab of the Kat, sounding like a storm of angry hail. It slammed into the truck's side, hard enough that Gus believed the contact had spun the gigantic machine around. He glanced out his view port and looked to the north, and his bowels turned to liquid.

"Minigun," Collie shouted. "Get moving!"

Tracer fire streaked across the open field, ripping into the Kat's steely side, creating a pyrotechnic show to slacken jaws. The minigun hosed the machine from ass to nose, raking the steel-laced sidewalls, pelting tires coated in foot-deep rubber, and creeping up toward the driver's cab. The tires held, but a frightening crash of metal erupted from the exposed underbody, making Gus wonder if he would be able to get moving.

He shoved the gear into drive and hit the gas.

The Kat jumped ahead and took out the corner of the office building, hip-checking a pile of rubble as he turned away from the deadly hail. Gus turned the wheel hard to the right, peering out the forward slit as light speckled the front in a dazzling display. The truck slammed into a parked pickup, crushing the box in a terrifying crunch of metal and a moment of lift that leaned Gus to the left. Children screamed in fright. The pickup's cab and engine buckled like a dying insect.

The Kat slammed down.

And rolled on.

When Shovel reached the flatbed, he pulled himself up and took over from Slick Pick. He manned the minigun and immediately sent a killer storm after the chuffing Kat, suspecting the doctor might be aboard the machine and hating the chance of losing her.

The kids, well, they could be replaced—not so the doctor.

The buzz of the rotating cannons deafened Shovel, but he continued spewing bullets at the Kat, lighting up its steel ass.

Gus wasn't anywhere in his mind.

Shovel winced at the job the Kat did on the pickup, but it wasn't unexpected. He knew what that machine was capable of.

He also knew the defenses at the main gate didn't stand a chance.

Gus concentrated on steering, very much aware of the hammering on the Kat's rear. Light streaked by his right side, chewing into parked vehicles and trailers.

"Pull it left!" Collie yelled from her gun port.

Gus nodded and bobbed. Trailers streaked by, seemingly missing by fingers.

Then he spotted the main gate, closed, along with a pickup of armed men, parked behind lines of teeth.

Gus felt his balls draw up.

They weren't teeth. They were spike strips, steel fangs attached to lengths of extendable and collapsible metal, designed to shred tires.

Gus slowed down.

"Fuck you doing?" Collie shouted.

Three of the gunmen in the box opened fired at the slowing Kat, and Gus cringed away from the onslaught and jerked on the steering wheel, pulling the machine away to the right. Collie returned fire, blasting one then a second shooter from the back of the pickup.

"Roll through it!" she yelled before the turn forced her to hold on.

"The spikes'll fuck up the tires!"

"*Nothing*'s gonna fuck up these tires!"

But the dump truck was already committed to the turn. A trailer loomed up.

Gus didn't have time to avoid it.

The Kat smashed through the rear of the long unit in a slap and clap of twisting, collapsing metal. Paneling flattened against the stairway like a flimsy sail. A section tore free and flashed before the driver's view port like a tablecloth caught in a tempest. Gus bared his gums, controlling the big truck as it rolled over another pickup, and felt his molars clamp together as the children sang out in unholy terror.

The Kat crushed a pair of cars.

It bashed aside a low trailer with a generator affixed to it.

The heavy-duty beast bounced, came down, and slammed through an office building. Wooden planks flipped up and clattered past the machine in a flurry. One slapped the front viewport Gus used to see through, scaring the piss out of him.

The kids screamed.

Maggie screamed.

Collie *howled*, her bloodied features ghoulish and delighted all at once.

And the Kat kept turning.

"Crazy fucker's turning around!" Slick Pick yelled, but Shovel ignored him. The leader of this pack of top-tier predators swung the minigun around, struggling to keep it on the rampaging Kat, pissed off and exultant as he unleashed the full uninterrupted might of the land cannon at the oncoming vehicle.

Gunfire strafed the flatbed, distracting Shovel.

A knot of new recruits, maybe the shitheads from Pine Cove, had gathered up assault weapons from the fallen and taken up position on the other side of the sandbags.

Treacherous little pricks.

Slick Pick took a full burst in the chest, flinging him from the flatbed in a mist of blood and bone.

The raiders loyal to Shovel started running and firing back at the armed newbies.

Shovel brought the minigun to bear and hosed down the sandbags with lead. Bags exploded. Geysers of grit and gravel burst into the air. And through it all, men and women screamed as the minigun tore them apart.

That diversion took only ten seconds, then Shovel swung the cannon back toward the Komatsu rampaging across his driveway.

*

One, two, the Kat punched its way through the ends of two trailers, upending the rigs in explosions of glass, fiberglass, and aluminum. Crystal pelted the front sheet metal, some raining through the narrow port and making Gus cringe. A motor home appeared, and he reacted slowly, stomping his bleeding foot down as the Kat's jawline smashed and heaved the vehicle out of its way. A gleaming length of plastic snapped forward with all the power of a yew bow and lanced the Kat's armored stairway. A storage compartment flew free of the motor home and crashed against the view port, all while a refocused squall of tracers and bullets made Gus's existence miserable.

He flinched, yanking the wheel, and felt the left side rise by a foot before slamming back down, diverting the truck toward Whitecap, to face the source of bullets head-on.

Straight into the remainder of Shovel's pack.

And the hateful breath of the minigun.

The Kat steamed straight at the flatbed.

Shovel didn't know who was driving that industrial pile of shit, but he unquestionably liked the odds of the minigun over the dump truck any day of the week.

"Come on!" Shovel shrieked, mirroring the mounting fury of the minigun as he aimed at the machine's armored face. His surviving soldiers fired upon the charging rig.

The chatter of impacts intensified as the space between the flatbed and the monster truck shortened.

Gus winced when the edges of the view port cracked from multiple impacts.

But he did not relent. Instead, he *stomped* on the gas.

Collie raged and unloaded short bursts at multiple shooters on that gray plain. A series of meaty explosions ripped across one bandit's chest, marching him back three steps before he realized he was dead. A woman screamed when her shoulder disintegrated in a red cloud. Collie shifted and mowed down a guy crouched into a tight tuck, tearing him apart like an overstuffed pillow.

The two dozen or so left returned fire.

The minigun strafed the Kat from right to left, striking the face of the monster in a ferocious ripple of sparks, bearing down on the cab.

Collie ducked down behind the armored wall, and bullets exploded off the sill of the gun port, bouncing around inside the upper deck like a hundred super-springy balls of light, terrifying the children and Maggie. One streak took the last two toes of Collie's left foot off in an eruption of blood. Another zinged through her left bicep, spattering her against the bulkhead before she rolled over onto her side. Gus glimpsed her head dropping out of sight before he cringed under the punishing onslaught. A deluge of bullets streaked forth from the minigun and etched a line across the face of the Kat, scarring it, making it snarl as Gus charged the flatbed. Rage flooded him, erasing all coherent thought as he stole pain-wracked peeks through his view port.

"Gonna ram that fucker!" he cried out over the popcorn impacts of *ping*s and *pang*s.

The Kat thundered toward the flatbed.

The minigun strafed the giant machine with a banshee's death cry, concentrating everything on the driver's cab. Light sheared through the view port, exploding and rebounding around Gus's head. One bit hard into his shoulder, making him jump in the driver's seat. Meteorites lasered across his back, rattling him, before blasting his side door open in a startling crash of metal. The last two fingers on his right hand disappeared at the knuckle in a painless burp of blood. The unconcerned bullets nailed bandits outside the truck as well, flipping them back from the oncoming truck.

The flatbed loomed closer.

Gus screamed at the barrage of tracer fire spattering the cab.

The minigun roared light.

And the Kat powered straight into it.

The last thing Shovel saw—before the Komatsu truck plowed through the flatbed—was the angry glare in his brother's eyes.

And his last thought . . .

Gus had the killer instinct after all.

The Kat mashed into the flatbed dead center, like a cement block being shoved into a high-powered band saw. Rubber screeched on cement. The monster truck took the minigun's wrath straight on the chin before the momentum behind tons of charging industrial steel silenced it. The Komatsu flipped the weapon's stage in a scream of stars and a clap of mountains. A section of the flatbed rose and slapped the Kat's driver's side as if insulted, crunching the cab. The impact ripped the wheel from Gus's pained grasp. The bright, blazing world filled his viewport and slanted for gravity-defying seconds. Steel shrieked a death-metal chorus, almost making eardrums bleed.

Then the Kat slammed down.

The noise subsided to dull groans and a disturbing patter.

The world darkened.

Stilled.

Gus opened his eyes, sucking in ragged breaths, and smelled blood, smoke, and burnt rubber. The last thing he remembered, besides the supernova of a minigun unloading itself straight into his face, was being slammed into the steering wheel . . . and the sight of the flatbed's end flipping up and swatting the side of the Kat like a plank.

Crossbeams of painted steel lay above him, and he realized he was on his back, gasping. Each breath hurt, and he suspected broken ribs. Probably a lot of broken ribs.

Sounds. Kicks. Coughs and crying children.

Alive.

That put a smile on his face.

Gus turned his head and saw an unmoving Collie stretched out on the floor, pale face splashed with blood. His smile faltered.

Warm hands clutched his head, righting it.

"Gus," a voice echoed softly.

He tried to speak but couldn't.

A shadow hovered over his eyes, blotting out the day.

And oblivion sucked him down.

52

The surf rolled onto the beach and dragged itself back. Gus sat on the sands and watched it, thinking thoughts as clean and sparkling as the receding water. Clouds speckled the sky, perhaps southward bound, and while he couldn't see a sun, that didn't bother him. It was summertime, and all seemed very well with the world.

"Gus."

He turned around and saw the Captain, swishing a red hat at his knees, resplendent in his foppish attire. The black scarf covering his head made him appear dashing, with a pinch of rapscallion thrown in for taste.

"Didn't hear you."

The Captain smiled and squinted at the sky. "Fair skies. Trade winds. Good traveling weather."

Gus regarded the heavens and nodded slowly. "You'll be heading off, then?"

"I think so."

"Caribbean bound?"

This time the Captain smiled and nodded. "Do you miss him?"

"Jerry?"

"Yes."

Gus thought about that. No. He didn't miss him. The man who was his brother had died a long time before. The man called Shovel would not be a part of that memory.

"No."

The Captain absorbed this for a moment, allowing the silence to mellow before slapping his hat and turning to leave.

"Leaving me alone?" Gus asked, smiling.

That gave the old sailor pause. "Never alone, my son." He smiled then, and Gus joined him.

When the moment passed, the Captain left him.

Gus watched his friend walk away, down the beach, until his outline faded into the shimmers of heat.

Gus opened his eyes and saw a window and forest beyond.

He took a shallow breath and made a face at the twinge of discomfort around his ribs.

A battered man sat in a chair at the foot of his bed. His name was Marty. Marty had been one of Shovel's group who didn't share the warlord's worldview but went along with the pack for fear of his life. At the battle of Whitecap, Marty and a few others had seen an opportunity, and they'd seized it, turning their guns on the few remaining followers bent on killing everyone in the Komatsu truck. When the dust cleared, only Marty and a woman called Melissa lived to help the survivors from the Kat.

"Gus."

"Marty," Gus greeted. "How you doing?"

"Could be better."

"Hear that. Where's Mel?"

"She's out making rounds. Not too far, I guarantee that."

Gus lay on the gurney, his bed ever since a week before, since the battle at the base of Whitecap.

"You sure you want to do this?" Marty asked.

"Yeah."

"I could finish it and leave it at that."

"Just help me up."

Marty did as told.

He could walk, slowly, careful not to get his blood flowing too much as the pain could be dizzying. According to Maggie, he'd fractured four of his lower ribs, and she'd done all she could with the resources available to her. His lungs were fine, but he wouldn't be doing anything heavy for quite a while. That suited Gus. He could use a little R and R.

The little convoy, consisting of a motor home and the last remaining pickup, had pushed east under Maggie's direction until they stopped for the night in the parking lot of a deserted motel and gas station. Gus had asked Marty to do something for him, and he'd done it.

One last request had to be honored.

The two men stood at the edge of the parking lot, their breaths vapor in the air. The season's first snow glittered in their flashlight beams. A pick and shovel had been thrown down in the weeds next to a cone of cold dirt. When Gus came upon it, he stopped and stared down at the nearby hole and the ice cooler it contained.

"This okay?" Marty asked, carrying one of several assault rifles they'd picked up after Whitecap.

"Yeah," Gus said.

"Who was he, anyway?"

"He was . . ." Gus started, staring down at the cooler containing the last few remains found of Clay "Ollie" Wallace. *Who was he?* He was a soldier, a condescending bastard—at least in the beginning—and a husband who loved his wife. He was determined, focused, Gus decided, and he'd sacrificed himself in the fight against Shovel's pack of killers.

"He was the man who saved my life," Gus admitted quietly, "and a friend."

Marty nodded, satisfied with the answer, and asked no more questions.

Gus appreciated that. "Guess I should say something," he muttered, feeling the onset of the cold. "Give me a few minutes, willya? I'll call you over when I'm ready."

Marty didn't object. He walked off into the night.

"Wallace. Ollie," Gus began after a few moments. "At least, I hope I can call you that now. Listen. Ah, sorry for the cooler. There weren't any coffins around, and, well, Marty didn't really find much of you to fill one even if we did."

Gus thought that sounded lame and tried again.

"It snowed yesterday. I slept through the whole thing, but it's covering the ground now. And, from what I can see, you're going to rest next to a motel and a gas station. Looks nice. Good location. Bet they did steady business here in this part of New Brunswick."

He stopped then, reflective, holding the flashlight and seeing a few flakes just starting to fall.

"Spoke too soon. Snow's falling now. Anyway, I'll keep this short. I'm not one for this kinda thing. Never had to do it before. Certainly never had to bury anyone before. We're all here, safe. At least those of us still living, because of you. We got the kids, and we got Maggie back. She's leading the group. Seems like she got word of a place back east, a safe place Shovel was planning to take after he got into Whitecap. No one went in there, in case you were wondering. I was out for it, but Maggie had Marty and Melissa and the kids gather up whatever was useful over two days and pack it away. Food. Guns. Ammo. Y'know. Regular camping shit."

Gus became somber. "During that time, I also asked Marty, with Maggie's blessing, to head up into the hills and find you . . . gather up what was left. Like I said, there wasn't much, but Marty got it. You . . . you didn't bite anyone. So rest easy, knowing that. And we're heading, hopefully, back east. To a safe place. So don't you worry about anything."

Gus felt his throat constrict for a moment. He cleared it, flashing his red eyes over to check on Marty. Seeing the coast was clear, Gus exhaled and softly, ever so softly, whispered, "Amazing Grace . . . how sweet the sound. That saved. A wretch. Like me . . ."

When he'd finished, he signaled Marty to return, who threw dirt in, covering the little coffin.

They placed a battered helmet on the grave, one that had seen better days, and ringed it with rocks.

On the side, scratched into the surface with a nail, was the name of the man laid to rest.

When Gus returned to the motor home, he walked past the sleeping children camping out on the floor and made his way to the bedroom. He smiled weakly at Maggie, and she gave him a dirty look, knowing he was pushing himself.

Pushing is the name of the game.

He entered the bedroom at the back and closed the door behind himself. Careful not to upset anything, he felt his way to the bed and sat down stiffly. The mattress felt firm and smelled clean, odd since the rig had belonged to Wallace. There wasn't much of an odor at all.

Gus waited.

"That you?" Collie asked sleepily from where she lay, trussed up in stitches and bandages like a fresh mummy.

"Yeah."

She didn't speak then for a while, but that was fine by Gus. Maggie had warned him Collie would be too weak to do much of anything for a few days, until her body replaced the blood it had lost. She would've died in the Kat if it hadn't been for the ER doctor working her magic.

"All done?"

"All done. He's buried."

Collie breathed deeply underneath the comforter, and Gus felt her gaze upon him.

"Nowadays, not many . . . get that . . . you know."

Gus knew it.

Her hand slipped out from underneath the covers and touched his fingers, curling around them.

"Thank you," she whispered, fading.

Gus squeezed her hand back.

And held on perhaps a little longer than he should have.

53

The motorcade rumbled into a little collection of houses and shop fronts that materialized out of the falling snow like pieces of a dream. They drove past a half-destroyed sign that read "ndford." *Blandford. Country town.* Modern and old-fashioned homes and oceanside cabins, all well spaced along the road, faced a rocky beach slapped by the sea. The motor home slowed down to stay on the slick, crumbling roads the winter was attempting to hide for a few months.

Gus sighed in relief upon reaching the town. They'd come perilously close to running out of gas. He imagined that, with the way octane levels in the leftover fuel were finally petering out, not too many people would be traveling to this part of Nova Scotia.

Maggie knew the way, knew that town and their destination: Big Tancook. Gus had never been to the island, but that was apparently going to change.

"Almost like nothing ever happened out here." Melissa was driving the motor home, her eyes just as wide as the children's looking out at the water. She and most of the kids, even Becky and Chad, had never seen the Atlantic.

"Where do we go?" Gus asked, hunkered over and standing next to Maggie sitting in the passenger seat.

"Look for an old government wharf," she answered.

Ten minutes later, they found it, a mighty pier jutting out into the sea, built of strong timbers upon white beach rock. A beaten motel, two stories high with an impressive deck, lorded over a deserted parking lot not twenty meters back from the water's edge. The pier itself looked like a forlorn gangplank, stretching toward a hazy screen of white where reality seemed to end.

Melissa brought the vehicle to a stop in the parking lot.

"Marty, you come with me," Maggie said.

"I'll come along too," Gus said.

Maggie didn't argue. Nor did she say anything when Marty lifted an assault rifle and hung it off his shoulder. They got out of the motor home and walked a few feet away, looking everywhere at once as a tourist might, unsure of exactly where to turn, where to go.

"This it?" Marty asked.

"I don't know. But"—Maggie shrugged and nodded at the motel—"we might be able to stay there for a little bit."

"You think that's a good idea?" Gus asked.

Maggie regarded him. "Well, it's the best one I have right now. Giovanni said that Pick saw people gathered along the shore here, so he assumed there was a community."

"Slick Pick," Marty scoffed. "A real piece of work. Glad he's dead."

"So"—Gus turned back to Maggie—"there might not be anyone around here?"

"Well,"—Maggie looked unsure—"he said they were going to come here, and it was my impression it would happen after they finally got inside Whitecap."

Water lapped against the shoreline. Fog hugged the coastline on either side of the pier. They waited and watched for a short time before Gus finally turned toward the motel.

The dark figure of a man stood on the building's upper deck, his arms hanging over the railing. The snow and fog darkened his features.

"Hey, where you guys from?" he called out.

His appearance surprised all three weary travelers. Marty's hands tightened on his rifle, but Gus cautioned him with a hand.

"The valley, originally," Maggie said. "But we just came in from Ontario."

"Valley's a nice place. Meaning to travel down there sometime. Ontario . . . not so much. Too 'Wild West' out that way. What'cha doing out this way?"

Maggie paused. "Looking for people, to be honest."

"That so?"

Something familiar about that individual made Gus take a few extra steps, bringing the stranger's features into focus. A black knee-length winter duster hung off the man's frame while an impressive stocking cap topped off his head and ended somewhere wrapped around his neck. The beard wasn't as trimmed as last time Gus had seen it, but it was enough to rattle his memory.

"Hey," Stocking Cap said, his brow crinkling. "I know you. Met you a few weeks back, right?"

"You did. Noodles and Kraft Dinner."

Stocking Cap chuckled. "Ha, that's right. Appreciated that. You were, let's see now . . . you were looking for some kids or something."

"Yeah, I was. You didn't get down to the valley?"

Stocking Cap shook his head. "No, plans changed. Won't get down there now. Not until spring. Decided to just take it easy for the winter. Dig in and do some thinking."

"Just yourself?"

"Well"—Stocking Cap shrugged—"there are others. But I gotta get away from them sometimes. I'm more of a loner, y'know?"

Gus knew. He knew both worlds and preferred the one with people.

"Can we come in?" Gus finally asked.

"Oh, sure! How many are you?"

"Nineteen." Maggie stepped up beside Gus. "Including fourteen children."

"Kids? Jesus! Yes, come on in. I'll get a fire going. We can talk more."

He straightened and sized up the vehicles and people below. "Bet you got a few things to trade . . ."

They went into the motel, where a huge fireplace dominated the lobby. Comfortable chairs and sofas had been arranged in a horseshoe around a country hearth, and a coffee table was piled high with a stack of paperbacks. Stocking Cap, whose name was Bruno, got a fire going and welcomed the kids with all the affection of a long-lost uncle. Bruno didn't seem too concerned about Marty and his automatic rifle, which Gus found strange and oddly comforting.

"You live out this way?" Gus asked him.

"Ah, not here exactly, but around," Bruno answered, feeding long pieces of split wood into the growing fire. "Me and the other folks. So what's this about you coming out here to look for people?"

Maggie sat and told him the story of Shovel and his pack of raiders. Bruno listened while the fire took hold and slowly warmed the lobby. The kids wandered off to explore the halls and the opened rooms. Bruno didn't seem to mind. Gus remained quiet, as talking too much put stress on his mending ribs.

"So," Bruno asked when Maggie finished her story, "that lady—Collie—is out in the motor home right now?"

"She is."

"You guys had quite the run."

"Almost at an end now if we can find a place."

"And you're a doctor?" Bruno asked. Gus sensed eagerness there.

"Yes."

"Whoa," Bruno let out. "You are a rarity in these days."

Movement outside the picture window of the lobby caught Gus's eye, and he saw three figures walk to the main doors. "Friends of yours?"

Bruno leaned over. "They are. A few others of the crew. Good timing."

The doors opened, and the men entered warily, led by a tall individual taking stock of Marty and little Becky, who had hung back with Maggie. The lead man nodded at them but balked noticeably when he spotted one unexpected face.

Gus stared back in return, recognizing the tall height and the fat face dusted with thinning blond hair. His beard had thickened, but there was no mistaking the blue eyes.

"Jesus Christ," Scott Harris breathed. "I thought you were dead."

Gus took his time replying. "Couple of times, I thought I was."

"What're you doing here?" the big man asked, face collapsing into a smile.

"Looking for you guys."

"Jesus," Scott repeated. "You found us."

Then, completely unexpectedly, he stepped up to the person who had saved his life so very long ago and made to throw his arms around him.

"Ah, wait," Gus cautioned. "Not a great idea. I've got some broken ribs on me."

So Scott gripped Gus's shoulders instead and beamed at him.

"Few extra scars, eh?" Gus asked.

"You too."

"You find that guy you were looking for?"

"Yeah. Where's whatserface?"

Gus sighed and rolled his eyes. "That's a story for when the youngsters aren't around."

Scott chuckled. "You're staying, of course."

Gus hesitated and glanced at Maggie. "That's what we're hoping to do."

"Wouldn't have it any other way. Good to see you, man."

Scott chuckled then and embraced Gus in a soft hug anyway.

"Welcome home, brother," the big man said through his smile.

54

Four Months Later

Bundled in winter clothing and an exceptionally warm thermal coat, Gus stood on the beach of a frosty cove just down from the old dock where the ferry would tie up. He gazed out at the rough waters. Fogbanks misted the horizon, but neither that nor the cold bothered Gus. He remembered something his father, long departed, had once said about winter having a memory as short as its days. Gus hadn't understood what his father meant by that at the time, and he still wasn't certain, but he suspected it had something to do with time and letting some recollections go.

Over the past few month, while his hurts healed, Gus had taken the time to let some memories go—not all, as he remembered Wallace warmly. He even remembered Talbert and how they'd seen eye-to-eye in the end. There was also the farm, and his need to return to put Adam and the others into the ground properly. It would be unpleasant after all that time, but as Wallace had said, *a proper burial is precious.* And Gus meant to see his friends buried by the earliest of spring.

Returned to the earth.

Scott entered his head then. And Amy. And *little* Scottie, who kicked enough to be a soccer player. Gus was happy to find this brother in one piece, unchanged, and doing quite well for himself.

The people of Big Tancook . . . a collection of folks drawn from various parts of the mainland, all with their own familiar personalities and idiosyncrasies. Scott had come into a good group of people here, and every day, Gus was thankful for finding them. In that daily, challenging puzzle of survival, each person brought a skill set or a charm that fit and made life a little easier for the little community.

And, finally, there was the Captain.

Gus held up the bottle, discovered in his pants pocket a while back and kept in a drawer until Collie questioned him about the rum's future.

My history lies with the sea, the officer had once said.

Gus looked about the shore's rocky edge, cold wind sawing at his face—so unlike the beach paradise in his mind—but Big Tancook had its share of nice beaches too, and Gus meant to explore them in warmer weather. He'd chosen that one purely for the sake of convenience.

He ran a thumb over the plastic surface of the bottle before popping the seal and untwisting the cap. For all the good old sailor had done for him, staying and seeing him through some rough times and some very dark places, Gus meant to return his guardian angel back to the sea.

He smelled the rum and took the barest nip, treasuring the burn.

"Thanks, buddy." He poured the alcohol into the water. "You take care now."

The icy surf lapped up the drink, and Gus lingered for a second, perhaps expecting something special to happen. Nothing did, however, so he sniffed, ribs feeling mended, and made his way back up the snowy incline behind him . . .

Back to where she waited.

Collie leaned on a walking cane. She was dressed in similar winter gear and watched him all the way back until he stood next to her, and together they watched the rolling of the open waters. She wore a new stocking cap, which some folks on the island insisted on calling a toque, and though her face had a few new scars, Gus thought they did her no harm. She glowed all the same.

"All done?" She smiled, hiding her dislike for the cold.

"All done."

"Can we head back inside now?"

"Thought you were tougher 'n this."

"It's fuckin' *cold* here, man."

"You head on in. I'll be along shortly."

But she didn't leave him.

In Gus's mind, she'd let him know when the time was right. Wallace was still only recently deceased in his mind, and while Gus knew his feelings for Collie grew stronger with every passing day, he had to respect a period of mourning, for both her and Wallace. There was no rush. Neither of them was going anywhere. And the houses made available to them were practically side by side, as if the whole town knew something he didn't.

Well, when she was ready . . . assuming she would be ready for anything at all. That was how Gus saw things.

So they stood, side by side. On safe land. Facing the late morning of a March day seized by a winter reluctant to leave.

Collie's hand, protected by a red mitten, reached out and took Gus's own. She sidled up to him and placed her head on his shoulder.

That simple contact left him speechless. Gus didn't move, stunned with happiness, refusing to even breathe for fear of ruining whatever magic swirled about them.

But after a short time, he squeezed her hand back.

And together, they walked away from the shore.

About the Author

Keith C. Blackmore is the author of the Mountain Man, 131 Days, and Breeds series, among other horror, heroic fantasy, and crime novels. He lives on the island of Newfoundland in Canada. Visit his website at www.keithcblackmore.com.

DISCOVER
STORIES UNBOUND

PodiumAudio.com